Paupers' Paris

Miles Turner is an impoverished American, living in Oregon. He spent his fourteenth birthday in Paris and never recovered from the experience. Over the years he has spent vacations there whenever possible, living cheaply, exploring the city, and researching this book. He has made numerous Parisian friends and contacts, whom he has persuaded to divulge up-to-the-minute hints, and some well-kept secrets, for the penniless traveller.

Miles Turner

Paupers' Paris

Pan Original
Pan Books London, Sydney and Auckland

First published 1982 by Pan Books Ltd,
Cavaye Place, London SW10 9PG

Revised 1983, 1984, 1986, 1988 and 1990
This new edition published 1992

9 8 7 6 5 4

ISBN 0 330 32421 7

Phototypeset by Parker Typesetting Service, Leicester

Printed and bound in Great Britain by
Cox & Wyman Ltd, Reading, Berkshire

Contents

Introduction 1

Allons-y (Preliminaries) 4

En route (Getting there) 15

Entrée/sortie (Arrivals and departures) 23

Aux alentours (Getting around) 32

Au lit (Sleeping cheap) 56

La nourriture (Eating well) 98

Les spectacles (Sights and sounds) 171

À bon marché (The shops) 212

Paris pratique (Staying afloat) 243

Au secours (Emergencies) 283

Maps 297

Index 302

PARIS

Introduction

This book is for paupers – or if not paupers, cheapskates – who would love to spend some time in Paris, but would prefer not to spend much money. It sets out to prove that, while Paris has justly earned its reputation as one of the world's more outrageously expensive places, there are hundreds of ways to avoid the city's grasping hands and still share in its pleasures.

Now that 1789–1989 has faded into history, Paris is coming back to itself, Parisians who flocked out of the city to avoid the hype and hysteria of the bicentenary are all home again, and once more it's one of the great affordable pleasures of this world.

If we have a single motto, it's 'Sleep cheap and eat well'. It turns out that you can sleep *and* eat for next to nothing, and do both rather well if you set your mind to it. There are cheap routes to Paris; there is limitless cheap transportation all over the city; there are hundreds of low-budget hotels that are clean and friendly and charming; there are incredible meals to be had in the humblest restaurants; there are more – free – spectacles, sights and attractions per square block than anywhere else we can think of. We've tried to fill this book with specifics – a mere scratching of the surface – of all these subjects, and with some pointers on how to use the information.

To make maximum use of our information, you'll need at least some of the following:

A sense of adventure. If tripe is half the price of steak on a menu, and you've never had tripe before but have a queasy idea of what it is, still you're *driven* to order tripe.

A low entertainment threshold. That quality which makes a person a cheap date. In Paris it means that the clientele of the nearest brasserie are as interesting and amusing and exciting to you as the entire cast of Covent Garden.

Unqualified adoration for the city. Everyone loves Paris in theory.

To relish that slightly gorgonzola-like aroma in the lower depths of the Métro is a measure of true love.

A sense of self-mockery. If you can't enjoy the spectacle of yourself as a total imbecile when it comes to haggling (or saying 'good morning', for that matter) then you should go to Denmark where they speak English.

A tourist's loathing of other tourists. The best thing that can happen to you is when a Parisian asks *you* for directions.

More taste than money. While you can't actually bring back a Cézanne or two, or the contents of Lanvin's windows, at least you will have paid them a visit.

A good deal of low cunning. The ability to wash (and dry) your entire wardrobe in a hotel basin without leaving a trail of evidence for the chambermaid.

We suggest that you take with you at least a few words of French – even if they're all in a pocket phrase book. Parisians are rather proud of their language, and on their own turf would rather converse in French than try their English out on you. If you need help, or just crave human contact, remember that the French help those who help themselves. The ice begins to break when you make the effort to communicate, but it's up to you.

It's this lack of linguistic hospitality – and also some misunderstandings about customs and manners – that has given the French a reputation for rudeness among travellers. *La politesse* is central to all transactions in France. The French are formal: they'll preface every question with 'Pardon, Monsieur . . .' or 'S'il vous plaît, Madame . . .' They'll consider *you* rude if you don't do the same.

Remember also that Parisians who habitually deal with tourists, with apparently ill-mannered Americans, Germans and English, who may in fact be less callous than tongue-tied, develop their own callousness for dealing with foreigners. If you stay off the beaten track (and with the help of this book you can), you'll avoid these unfortunates and come into contact with a friendly, garrulous, buoyant race of Parisians you've never met or heard of before.

You will note that certain *arrondissements* – the 5e, 7e, 8e, 11e, parts of the 19e and 20e – have been given fairly lengthy descriptions in the Footwork section (pages 46–55), while others better-known apparently have been slighted. This is highly personal; the ones that are in are there just because they are places we have enjoyed which may have been missed out in other publications. The 6e, especially around St-Germain-des-Prés, has been written about everywhere; visited by everyone. As a consequence, waiters can be rude, hotels over-crowded and over-priced, meals in the main to be avoided. You'll go there anyway, and find your own pleasures without help from us, so there's no general talk about it here. But it would be a pity to miss, for example, the less-known areas such as the Batignolles (pages 46–7), the hidden and charming parts of the haughty 7e *arrondissement,* and the pleasant, rather domestic bits of the forbiddingly elegant 8e. Two neighbourhoods which are changing so fast that it's impossible to include them with complete accuracy in this edition are the 11e around the Bastille, and the 13e near the rue de Tolbiac – Asia in Paris – you'll have the delight of discovering them yourselves.

Paupers' Paris is the result of the labour and support of all my friends and relatives: many contributions from people I've never met but am most grateful to. Bawn O'Beirne-Ranelagh took over the task of editing, co-ordinating information, and putting it all on disc for this new edition. A crew of young Paris residents ate their way through restaurants, and in the process turned up many new ones: we thank Gloria Girton, Adam Steinhouse, Tim Allan, Emmanuelle Pingault, Jonathan Browne, Joshua Kobb, Jonathan Gilbert, and all their friends. I still owe thanks to my mother Martha Lomask, who researched and rewrote entire sections of the original editions, and my father, Milton, who covered art galleries, museums, and music as well as verifying dozens of addresses. Leonard Yoon helped me plot the book over countless bottles of wine, and Charlie White closed his eyes to my long absences from work. M. Patrick Goyet of the French Government Tourist Office in London has helped with letters of introduction, and Marc Humphries answered our last minute questions. The Office de Tourisme in Paris has been generous with advice and information. And to the kind readers who have contributed useful tips and corrected egregious errors in previous editions of *Paupers' Paris*, many, many thanks. I hope the city will always treat them as well as they have treated me.

It should be noted that prices in this book were correct in autumn 1991. We hope they'll still be as accurate as possible when you read these pages, but costs do have a habit of creeping upward when your back is turned. Still, Paris continues to offer, at very good value, hundreds of good hotels, charming restaurants, and its own distinctive attractions for those who know where, and how, to look.

M.T.

Allons-y *(Preliminaries)*

Who?

Before anything else you must decide – who's going? Just you, your nearest and dearest, your bridge club? A few pros and cons:

Travelling alone is the best way to see and do exactly what you want. If you get lost or bungle seriously in a restaurant, feel like sleeping till noon, or decide to spend the rest of your life in Paris, the decisions (and the responsibility) are all yours. If you make mistakes, nobody else gets blamed. You don't have to adjust to anyone else's diet, or standards of hygiene, or attention span. If you can handle being on your own, it's the best way to go.

But if your gregariousness and your French aren't up to it, you can die of loneliness. You'll have to survive on a few encounters a day – in cafés, restaurants and shops. You'll always be treated well, if you make the effort to make yourself understood, but it's unlikely that anyone will adopt you.

Travelling in company guarantees that you'll have someone with whom to share the experience, and a helping hand if things get dicey. The drawback is that your tastes will differ. *You* will want to spend eight hours in one room of the Louvre; *she* will choose to spend the day playing pinball machines in a café behind the Bastille.

Our solution for days when your energy and interests don't coincide is to split up: plan to meet for lunch, and plan to meet again for dinner. (Agree in advance on the restaurants. No last-minute searches on an empty stomach.) If one person doesn't show up within 15 minutes, the other forges ahead with the meal. We've found this to be a good way to avoid getting bored with each other. Travelling in company can have an odd, isolating effect. You can get on each other's nerves. And it's bad for your French.

Small groups can be worked the same way: you can pack the kids off to the Bois, send Granny to the flea market, and you're on your own. The one thing you must not do is travel in packs. Even a benign dictatorship can end up in communal misery.

When to go?

Of course it's best to go when the spirit moves you. When you can't stand the grind a minute more. When your boss *lets* you go. But if it's not purely a matter of impulse, desperation, budget, or tight scheduling, there are a few matters about timing to consider.

High season, normal season, low season

Naturally, this affects airline fares: get a good travel agent, or do a real study yourself of what the flying people are up to at any given moment. Equally important: there are certain times of the year when it is all but impossible to find a room in central Paris or anywhere near it at short notice. The Office de Tourisme in Paris has this advice:

Most heavily booked periods:
10–15 January
1–5 February
3–10, 15–19, 29–31 March
1, 22–27 April
8–12, 18–20, 24–31 May
3–23 June
5–10, 20–25 September
3–9, 14–31 October
11–19 November
28–31 December

Do not arrive on any of these dates without a firm booking.

Normal periods:
The second half of January, a week or so in March, most of April, some of May and September, the first two weeks of November and December.

Low season:
Surprisingly, July, August, late December, and early January, and most of February are times when you can almost always find a room somewhere, even on short notice. However, it may be a good precaution to have a firm booking for the first few days if arriving in July or August. For real Paris-lovers, December and the first week in January (when the wonderful sales are on) – when Paris is at its silvery best, the light shining through the bare trees and the life of the city vibrating all around – can be the choicest time to be there.

We once found ourselves, through ridiculously bad timing, in Paris in the first week of March during two major trade fairs and the opening of an important art show. We managed to get a room in a very good, low-priced hotel, in a great neighbourhood we'd never stayed in before, which immediately became our second home. This was done by exerting ourselves somewhat, visiting a number of hotels until we found one that would have us for one night, which stretched to six. We wouldn't care to do this if arriving at midnight after a long flight, tired, drunk, or travelling with small children or an elderly companion.

Climate

The weather can influence your plans, and will certainly influence your wardrobe. To give you a rough idea – the mean temperature in February is 36.5°F (3°C), in July 65.5°F (18°C). East and north-west winds keep Paris cool and fairly dry in winter and spring; there can be stretches in December and January when bitter winds come shrieking across North Europe from, apparently, Siberia, and you'll be glad of woollies and a warm coat. Prevailing south-west winds bring the heaviest rains in summer and autumn, so pack a folding umbrella and a light waterproof coat then.

What to take

Your wardrobe naturally depends on what you have, and how much you are willing to lug around. 'Travelling light' is a phrase that has an adventurous ring to it – people who drag along only one steamer trunk rather than three, probably consider themselves light travellers – it's a relative term, but a worthwhile goal. We figure you can live comfortably, and indefinitely, on about 14 kilos of luggage; more if you are strong of arm or not averse to porters; less if you're a wimp, anti-porter, or have read the next paragraph and know how to pack intelligently. In either case, here are a few suggestions:

1 Dress in layers – for all climates and most seasons. Everything easily washable or dry-cleanable. Everything easily folded, or preferably rolled, which cuts down on creasing. Think twice about heavy items. If your overcoat is going to be a millstone, don't take it. In all but the dead of winter, rely on piling one sweater on top of another under that light waterproof coat.

2 Take nothing you haven't worn before, and nothing that you don't love. Take nothing you can't walk or climb in.

3 Take a couple of pairs of durable, comfortable, well-broken-in shoes; for women, they should be of different heel heights. Armies may travel on their stomachs – *you* travel on your feet.

4 *Indispensables*
A cotton kimono
A pair of rubber flip-flops (thongs, *zoris*, or whatever these Taiwanese sandals are called)
For cold weather, a really warm, soft scarf – lambswool for preference. And two identical pairs of gloves, because you're going to lose one glove the day you arrive
A telescopic umbrella – one that fits easily into the suitcase
A good plush hand-towel – not too small – which will help pad breakables and will supplement the sometimes meagre one common to Paris hotels
Soap in a plastic box
Blow-dryer, heated rollers, electric razor (see Electricity, pages 251–2)
A plastic carrier bag for unwashed clothes. A few plastic bags and twist-ties. A featherweight bag that folds into your luggage, and can double as an overnight case or to carry home all the extras you will buy
Nail scissors and, even more important, toe-nail clippers – real agony-savers
If you wear glasses or contacts, take an extra pair and/or a recent prescription
If you can't sleep with the French bolster, your own inflatable pillow
Medicines: an adequate supply, and a refillable prescription
Indispensable for picnics, hotel and otherwise: a cup and an immersion heater if you *must* have tea (see Electricity, pages 251–2)

A saucer-sized plate, a small sharp knife, a fork, a spoon. Be as ingenious as you want about this
Clip-on reading light (220 volts) if you can't live without it and don't trust hotel lighting
Three or four lightweight plastic hangers for drip-drying. A few clip-type clothes pegs. A little detergent in a plastic squeeze bottle (see Hotels, page 60)
A corkscrew
And, not to belabour the obvious, don't forget your toothbrush.

All of this, excluding what you wear on your back, should fit into a fairly small suitcase that could be carry-on luggage, bypassing that awful wait at airport or hoverlanding. Take along a thin, strong, nylon soft-sac for *en route* essentials such as book, flask, camera, tissues, maps, whatever.

Money questions

(For denominations, mechanics and equivalents, see Money, pages 262–3.)
How much to take? Some advance decisions are going to be necessary here. You'll have to decide after considerable thought what's important to *you*, not to us or your next-door neighbour. Budget for your extravagance, and save somewhere else. Do you feel best in a room big enough to spread out wet coats, luggage, bottles, flowers, newspapers? That's what you should budget for. Can't live without *petit déjeuner* served in your room, or your own shower, a private loo, a lift? A hotel within an arm's length of the Louvre, or a quieter, cheaper, possibly more spacious place 10 minutes away on the Métro? Budget for it. Save on museum entrance fees by going on Sundays (free or half-price), or have a week of picnic lunches instead of eating in restaurants, and spend your money how you will.

Transport to and from Paris

Maximum: will buy you airfare,
London–Paris and back, open-dated   £168
ticket and ultimate convenience.

Minimum: provides the
cheapest bus/boat/bus service,
and a modicum of discomfort.   £43
See pages 15–22 for details.

Hotel per night

Maximum: a nice, bourgeois
hotel in a 'good', close-in
district, all facilities including   270F
shower and loo.

Minimum: cheap, clean, away
from it all, no frills.   90F
See pages 63–93 for details.

Food per day

Maximum: breakfast in bed; a
lunch that will take up half the
afternoon, and dinner half the   250F
night.

Minimum: coffee at the *zinc* of
the local café, a picnic lunch
indoors or out, a modest but   125F
satisfying dinner.
See pages 98–170 for details.

Getting around

Maximum: includes a few taxis
for quick getaways to station or   150F
airport.   (20F per day)

Minimum: unlimited Métro/
bus/RER travel for seven days.   54F
See pages 37–50 for details.

The sights

Maximum: full-price museum
admissions; a movie;
innumerable cups of coffee,
seated.   120F

Minimum: everything gratis, or
very, very cheap.   35F

The shops

Maximum: a matter of taste and
income.   ?F

Minimum: don't buy *anything*.   0F

Necessities

Maximum: enough to get your
laundry done, your hair cut,
your baby sat, your post sent,   250F
and your pockets full of change.

Minimum: an afternoon in the
laundrette, one cup of coffee, a
visit to the lavatory and one   30F
postcard and stamp.

Emergencies

Maximum and minimum depend entirely on you. If you're
accident-prone, provide extra money for crises. If you have an
invisible plastic shield, or a lot of sensible insurance, take less. But
always keep some money in reserve.

See pages 283–297 for details.

How to carry money

Cash

You'll need some within five minutes of your arrival in Paris: enough to get your *Carte Paris Visite* or *Carte Orange* (see pages 37–8); enough to get a bite to eat and transport you to your hotel; a few more francs for a left-luggage locker; possibly a phone call home, or to pay the *Hôtesses de Paris* for locating a room for you (see pages 27–8). Arm yourself before you leave with at least 150F in cash to get you into town. Change pounds or dollars before you leave home, at a bank or *bureau de change* where you know you'll get a good rate.

Traveller's cheques

Your own bank or building society may offer them as a free service (but avoid the lesser known brands which can be difficult to cash in some Paris banks or bureaux). Size of denominations depends on how often you want to sign your name, and how careless you get when you've cashed a big one.

Personal cheques

Fortified with a cheque-cashing card from your bank, you can get up to £100 a day – Barclays let you cash one cheque in that amount and charge 7F50; other banks insist on two £50 cheques and two fees.

Eurocheques: see pages 267–8.

Visa, Access, Mastercard, Eurocard and such

Credit cards used abroad may not protect you against fraud, unde- livered merchandise, or defective goods, as they do in this country (for purchases over £100). This was reported in the *Sunday Times* 'Questions of Cash' column, 14 July 1991: the case involved an English traveller who bought jewellery in Mexico City for over £500 on his Visa card, then found the jewellery was worthless when he got it home. NatWest, which issued the card, contacted the Mexican bank handling Visa cards, who refused to co-operate or even investigate. Visa itself cannot investigate or negotiate in a case like this.

THEREFORE: Only use credit cards for smallish purchases, for meals, petrol, etc., in other words, something you can eat, wear, use up, take home or discard. Even in France, it's dicey to buy something on a credit card (or with cash, for that matter) to be shipped to you later, unless you know the merchant is long-established and reputable. Big buys which go bad can leave you exposed to fraud, and nothing the UK bank which issued your card does will alter this.

In France, some shops will accept credit cards only for purchases over a certain amount (usually 100F), but must display a notice to that effect either in the window or at the cash desk. This is true in Gibert Jeune bookshops in Paris; some restaurants will refuse to accept credit cards for inexpensive meals (such as a 50F set lunch menu), and must make this plain on the menu card.

Many small hotels, shops and restaurants cannot afford to pay the credit card companies a commission, so may not accept your plastic: however, a surprising number of them now will take major credit cards, and it's certainly a great convenience to keep your cash in your pocket and let the card do the work. You can use your plastic to buy the *Coupon Orange*, *Coupon Jaune*, a *carnet*, three- or five-day travel pass, and so forth, at ticket windows in the Métro, and many times, from automatic machines in the Métro station, with your PIN number. Of course, you can use your credit card to get cash advances from banks showing the appropriate sign, or from an automatic cash dispenser out of hours. The ACD is nicknamed the Harvey Wallbanger by certain West Coast Americans.

Elaine Bate of Great Barrow warns of the high-roller stakes demanded by certain cash-card dispensers in France. Chancing her BarclayCard/Visa at the local bank, she was informed that the minimum withdrawal possible was for 18,000F (about £180 at the time). Fearing her card might disappear forever, she withdrew the full amount. Back home, she exchanged the 1120F she had left over for sterling, which cost her £6. She was still awaiting BarclayCard's own handling charge for the withdrawal which she didn't want to make. It might be a good idea, if you are a forethoughtful kind of person, to check with the local bank in person to find out what the minimum withdrawal amount is; or contact the BNP, the Crédit Lyonnais or other major French banks which have branches in this country, before you come up against the problem.

Booking hotels in advance

If you know more or less what you want, where you want to be and how much you want to pay (see 'Au lit', pages 56–97), it's a good idea to reserve in advance. It's not in the least difficult if you have a little time to work it out. It can save you energy and anxiety at the moment of your lowest ebb – your arrival in the chaos and confusion of the Paris airport, terminal, or railway station.

Once you've picked a hotel, write a letter to the management. In French. Use, if you like, the form letter – a service of the Office de Tourisme – reproduced below. Specify the dates of arrival and (if you can), the date of departure, number of people, and your requirements – with or without a loo or *salle de bain*, single or double room, and so on.

Form letter to hotels (freely adapted from that used by the Paris Office de Tourisme)

Le Directeur
Hotel _____
Address _____

Monsieur le Directeur,

Je vous serais obligé de me communiquer vos conditions
(I would be grateful if you would let me know your terms)
et tarifs pour un séjour de _____ nuits, commençant le _____
(and prices for a stay of _____ nights, beginning _____)
à _____ heures, et se terminant le _____ à _____ heures.*
(at _____ o'clock, and ending _____ at _____ o'clock.)

Nous souhaiterions réserver _____ (chambres à un lit)
(We would like to reserve) _____ (single rooms)
(chambres à grand lit) (chambres à deux lits) (avec WC/bain/douche).
(double rooms) (twin-bedded rooms) (with WC/bath/shower).

Avec mes remerciements,

*Use the 24-hour clock.

Use an International Reply Coupon

Whether you're reserving a room or just asking for information from any French source (other than a government tourist agency). The hotel, shop, or agency, or whatever, can exchange the coupon for return postage. Many of these operations are running on a tight margin, and cannot afford to send free information to rich tourists. The courtesy will be appreciated. A self-addressed airmail envelope is another form of good manners, and can help ensure that you do get a reply.

IRCs cost 60p in Britain and are available at post offices.

Postscripts to preliminaries

Life-saving tips from the most experienced travelling paupers we know:

1 Never travel without a good supply of soft toilet paper (not just for obvious purposes, but for blowing noses, mopping brows, even as napkins for picnics).
2 Never travel with more luggage than you yourself can carry in comfort, without porter or taxi.
3 For dire emergencies, never travel without a little bit of cognac in a flask.

En route (*Getting there*)

Your choice of routes to Paris will depend on your finances and need for comfort; how much you want to spend *en route*, how long you want to stay, what time of year (or time of day) gives you the best deal.

London to Paris and back

Myriad possibilities, listed from the cheapest to the dearest.

Eurolines

National Express, the giant spiderweb that links all of the UK to London, can take you to Paris – and beyond, with its Euroline coaches. They leave from Victoria Coach Station, and run two daytime and one overnight trip in summer, one daytime and one overnight in winter. Return trip to Paris can cost as little as £51, and you can buy one-way tickets for about £30. Prices vary with the seasons, so check with your travel agent or any National Express office in the UK. It's a flat fare, no reductions for students or the elderly, though children between 4 and 12 pay £21 for a single and £39 for a double fare. Children under 4 travel free, if they sit on their parent's lap. Here's how you travel:

Coach/Boat/Coach: Day trips are about eight-and-a-half hours, depending on road conditions, night trips as comfortable as can be expected – and you do save a night's hotel bill. But you'll roll into Paris with the dawn, and the first day can seem endless, as most hotels won't book you in until noon. The buses are equipped with reclining seats and all the usual facilities, and ventilation is reasonably good. Departure: Victoria Coach Station. Arrival: Porte de la Villette, Eurolines Coach Station, 19e *arrondissement*; tel: 40 38 93 93.

Book through any National Express office in the UK. In Paris, at the Porte de la Villette and 55 rue St-Jacques, 5e *arrondissement*, or at SNCF (French Railways) offices.

Other coach services: Have a look at *Time Out* or the free-sheets distributed on the street, mainly for young Aussies and New Zealanders, for details of other cheapos . . . we have varying reports which range from 'not too bad considering the rock-bottom fares', to 'beer-drinking all night long, smoke you could cut with a knife, and a coach driver who hadn't had his licence long'. You make up your own mind.

Paris–London–Paris, and sometimes one-way fares are offered by City Express, Tel: 42 28 52 80.

Hoverspeed

City Sprint: Faster but more expensive than the above. Clean, comfortable coaches which take you from Victoria Coach Station in London to Dover and across on Hovercraft, then on the Autoroute into Paris. About eight hours travelling time.

Departures vary with the seasons. In spring, there are three departures a day, then four departures; from mid-July, five departures a day, dropping back to three a day in September. The first bus leaves London at 8:30 a.m., the last at 11:30 p.m. or 12:30 a.m. according to the season. Returning, you leave Paris on the first bus at 8:30 a.m., last bus at midnight or 1:00 a.m. A useful way to travel if you plan to return from Paris by another route, or are going on to other European stops, as you can buy one-way or round-trip tickets and it's pretty cheap.

Adult	one way	£30
	return	£51

There are no reductions for youth, student, or senior citizen, though children under 4 go free.

Round-trip tickets are good for one year, but book your return journey four days before you plan to travel. Between the two countries, the Hovercraft trip is fast, noisy, with a smooth-as-satin ride or a lot of bounce as the weather dictates. People who order drinks are apt to get their come-uppance: what goes down, may come up.

Train/Seacat/Train: Two trips a day, but again it depends on the season. It's clean, not too expensive, and free from the restrictive conditions which hedge in cheapish airline flights. And it's surprisingly fast – can be as little as five-and-a-half hours from the centre of London to the Gare du Nord in Paris.

Trains depart from Victoria and the outward journeys are in quite new and comfortable carriages with few stops. Coming back, trains from Dover to Victoria can be fairly fast or all-stops-between, depending on how prompt or delayed the Channel crossing was.

There's usually plenty of time at each end (Dover and Calais) to collect some duty-frees and have a snack or a beer.

The one big catch in this mode of travel is that at the English end, trains to and from Dover begin and end at Dover Priory, *not* at the port. In between it's pretty good hell, with too few double-decker coaches crammed with back-packers, duty-free plastic bags, and some incredibly huge suitcases, all of which have to be lugged and jammed up the coach steps and into the narrow aisles. Although it's a short ride, it is incredibly uncomfortable. You may travel with hand luggage only, others don't.

At the French end, trains are direct from the Calais terminal to the Gare du Nord and vice versa. You can have an on-board meal of croissants, wine, coffee, or soft drinks, served from rolling carts to the airline-type seats.

	2nd class single	2nd class return	5-day return
Adult	£54.50	£87.00	£69.00
Young persons (16–25)	£45.00	£76.00	£69.00
Child (12–15 inclusive)	£37.00	£58.00	£48.00
Child (4–11 inclusive)	£28.00	£44.00	£35.00
Senior Citizen*	£33.00	£65.00	£69.00

Children under 4 travel free.
Return fares are valid for two months.

*To get all the reductions possible, Senior Citizens should have UK Senior Citizens Railcard (£16) *and* the Rail-Europ Card (£7.50). You can't get the Rail-Europ card alone.

Hovercraft and Seacat tickets are available from Hoverspeed (Reservations, Tel: 081-554 7061) and British Rail centres and most travel agents. In Paris, at 135 rue Lafayette, 10e *arrondissement*.

Beware: some travel agents will try to apply a surcharge on any fare which includes continental rail travel. Others won't handle Senior Citizen rail tickets. If this happens to you, make your displeasure known on the spot and go to a more amenable travel agent.

Sealink

Train/Boat/Train: Can be slower than the Hovercraft or Seacat, and conditions can vary from reasonably clean to unreasonably squalid. The boats sail in fog or dicey weather, when Hovercraft or planes may be grounded or delayed. You can jog around the decks. *Take your own picnic*, unless you *want* to eat in the restaurants or snack bars. For obvious reasons, you won't choose this way of travel at football-match time. Up to five sailings a day, about eight hours Victoria–Gare du Nord.

	2nd class single	2nd class return	5-day return
Adult	£51.00	£82.00	£65.00
Young persons (16–25)	£44.00	£72.00	£65.00
Senior Citizens	£30.00	£60.00	£65.00

There are varying reductions for children between 4 and 11, and between 12 and 15. Children under 4 travel free.

For under-26s and students

Many travel agents specialize in inexpensive rail and coach and air fares for travellers in these special categories: they advertise in school and college magazines, and in *Time Out*, *City Limits*, and free-sheets such as *LAM* and *TNT*. STA Travel, 86 Old Brompton Road, London SW7, and 117 Euston Road, London NW1, Tel: 071-937 9921: and London Student Travel, of the Campus Travel Group, 52 Grosvenor Gardens, London SW1, Tel: 071-730 3402, are both long established in this field.

Cheap flights

Magazines like *Time Out* and *City Limits*, *LAM*, *TNT* and *Girl about Town*, are crammed with ads for cheap airfares. These days you don't have to depend on bucket shops for such good deals, most major travel agents will probably do you just as well and save you some footwork.

The Air Travel Advisory Bureau (in London, tel: 071-636 5000; and Manchester, tel: 061-832 2000) is a clearing-house for information about agents who offer cheap flights world-wide. We have found them quick, helpful and accurate, and one phone call to them could provide you with the names of the five or six agents who might give you a good deal on the day of your inquiry, for flights – one-way or return – to Paris, saving you dozens of fruitless calls.

In Paris, it's possible to book cheap charter flights, one-way or round-trip, to London/Dublin/Edinburgh, etc., through various agencies; in July 1991, USIT, 12 rue Vivienne, 2e (Tel: 42 96 15 88), and 6 rue de Vaugirard, 6e (Tel: 43 29 85 00) were offering one-way flights to London for 290F, round-trip for 490F. Cash and Go, 54 rue Taitbout, 9e (Tel: 42 82 93 90); Métro Chaussée-d'Antin; has good prices for long-haul flights to Los Angeles or New York, for instance, and often has charter flights to England, one-way, low cost; and they speak English. Wasteels, a chain of travel agencies all over Paris, often has remarkable last-minute bargains on both major airlines and charter flights – check the branch nearest where you are staying.

Major airlines insist that you book your return journey when you sign on for the outward leg, and you can't alter dates or flight times without a bitter penalty (be sure to take out adequate travel insurance to cover costs of cancellation for illness or whatever). At peak holiday times all fares go up. But there are ways around these fixed-price deals. Read on.

Among the best fares during the summer and autumn of 1991:

£49–£65: for students under 29 and anyone under 26. Gatwick–Beauvais, then on by coach to Paris. Offered by, among others, London Student Travel, 52 Grosvenor Gardens, London SW1 (Tel: 071-730 3402); and STA, 86 Old Brompton Road, London SW7 and 117 Euston Road, London NW1 (Tel: 071-937 9921).

£69.00: Cathay Pacific from Gatwick, out departing 10:00 a.m. and back departing 7:45 a.m. from Charles de Gaulle, on Mondays,

Thursdays, Sundays. Flights both ways must be booked, but the ticket is open for three months and you can change the return flight date, with a small penalty charge. Few travel agents handle this, but it's a 'must check' for any penny-wise traveller. Flyair, 17 Heddon Street, London W1R 7LF. Tel: 071-287 1954; and Travel Arcade, Triumph House, 189 Regent Street, London W1. Tel: 071-734 5873.

Cathay is also offered by American Express, Haymarket, London SW1. Tel: 071-323 9003/4, whose documentation, insurance, and general level of service were impressive. And by Dodo Travel, Suite 2000, 16 Woodford Road, London E7 08A. Tel: 081-471 7117.

£79.00: Dan-Air, Gatwick–Charles de Gaulle, nine flights a day, but there's a £12.50 surcharge on Fridays or Sundays. Holidayfax, 48 Sheen Lane, Sheen, London SW14 8LP. Tel: 081-876 1118. (Non-cancellable, and outward and return flights must be booked.)

£98.00: British Airways, Air France, British Midland; APEX fare, direct from airlines or through agents. Flights must be booked both ways and cannot be changed, and you have to book 14 days in advance.

£116.00: Special deal from Travel Arcade, Triumph House, 189 Regent Street, London W1. Tel: 071-734 5873. Same restrictions as the 'Superpex' fare below.

£130.00: British Airways or Air France, Superpex fare, direct from both airlines or through agents. Your Paris stay must include a Saturday night, but you can book the day before you travel.

£188.00: British Airways or Air France, Eurobudget fare, direct from both airlines or through agents. Valid for a year, but there's a large penalty for changing your booking.

One-way fares: While the major airlines tie you up with all the restrictions they can devise, others are more flexible. Many airlines flying to the Middle and Far East pass on to you the benefit of something called the Sixth Freedom of the Skies, meaning that they can offer you a one-way-only seat to Paris at a moderate fare. Someone is waiting there to sit in that seat on the longer leg of the flight. In Paris, check the travel agents mentioned above for one-way flights to London. For tickets from London, try these:

£29–£37: for students under 29 and anyone under 26. Gatwick–Beauvais, then on by coach to Paris. Offered by, among others,

London Student Travel, 52 Grosvenor Gardens, London SW1. Tel: 071-730 3402; and STA, 86 Old Brompton Road, London SW7 and 117 Euston Road, London NW1. Tel: 071-937 9921.

£60: Air India, Travel Arcade, Triumph House, 189 Regent Street, London W1. Tel: 071-734 5873.

The agents we mention above are those whose information we have found accurate. Some others will advertise alluring prices which have mysteriously disappeared when you call. The practice is known as 'bait-and-switch', and originated in the used-car lots of Los Angeles, where it belongs.

Package tours

These come in all shapes and sizes, and, naturally, all prices. They range from the antiseptic (everything through a coach window, with English commentary) to the spartan (transportation, bed and breakfast, no frills), to more luxurious but still affordable packages.

The advantage of the no-frills package is that it takes the guesswork out of the basic amenities, and leaves you free to explore the city on your own. The means of transportation (air, hover, coach, and the rest) and the types of accommodation (1-star to 4-star) are varied, and you'll want to sort through the possibilities very carefully.

We have had good reports on UK package tour agencies which specialize in Paris (French Leave and Time Off) – there are a number of others which are undoubtedly equally good, but as we never give you information that hasn't come directly from someone who has been there, we can't comment on them.

Colour brochures featuring Paris have almost impenetrable charts – prices, number of nights, type of accommodation, supplements for holidays, and so forth. The chart we give you here is a simplified version from a major tour agency's brochure to give you an idea of the possibilities.

We've given the cost for *two nights only*, to make things easier; for longer stays, just add on the extra cost per night.

The tour operator whose brochure we've used offers much glossier stays in 3-star and 4-star hotels, even in luxury-class Hôtel Louvre – but if you travel in such circles, stop reading now and give this book to some deserving pauper.

The prices here are for good, centrally located, well-run 1- and 2-star hotels only. One-star places have basins and sometimes bidets in each room, 2-star will give you a private bath or shower and possibly a private WC. One-star hotels do *not* have lifts, 2-stars often do.

You can often save £££ travelling by night by Euroline coach on the Dover–Calais service, at the lowest package tour prices, if you don't mind sitting up, drowsing in fairly comfortable surroundings. Most costly, of course, is travel by scheduled services from Heathrow to Charles de Gaulle, and coach direct from the airport to the city centre.

	City Sprint	Rail/Ship/Rail	Gatwick Paris	Heathrow Paris
Low season (15 November–19 March)				
1-star	£91	£93	£126	£134
2-star	£95	£97	£130	£138
High season (1 April–14 November)				
1-star	£102	£107	£140	£145
2-star	£124	£129	£162	£167

Prices are based on *two people* sharing *for two nights*. Continental breakfast included. For single rooms, low season, add £13 per night for a 1-star hotel, £16 for a 2-star hotel; high season, £15 for a 1-star, £25 for a 2-star. Extra nights, of course, are available at additional cost. Check the tour operator's brochure carefully for the small-print footnotes that add all sorts of supplements.

Many package tour operators offer special terms for Winter Bargain Breaks, Weekends and Long Weekends, and some good cheapies like a three- or five-night holiday by coach, ship and coach.

Several of our well-travelled friends warn: Think carefully before you sign up for package tour Paris excursions – the Bateau Mouche cruises, trips to Chartres or Fontainebleau, the Moulin Rouge and Lido Cabaret shows – they can be much more expensive than using this book and doing it on your own. Others are happy to have everything organized for them, and consider the extra money well spent.

Entreé/sortie
(Arrivals and departures)

Passports, visas, customs

You ought to have a valid passport to enter France (although strictly speaking it isn't necessary for EC residents).

In Britain, standard passports are good for 10 years, and cost £15 (for 30 pages) or £30 (for 94 pages). Get forms from your local post office. Two photographs needed. Return the application, with fee and photos, countersigned by someone impressive who knows you – vicar, solicitor, doctor, or JP – either to the passport office or to the nearest main post office in your city. Expect to wait about 10 days for the passport in winter, or up to a month in heavy periods. Don't leave it until the last minute.

A British Visitor's Passport is good for one year only. The fee is £7.50. Apply for forms at the post office. Two photos. No countersignature needed. Valid only for Europe. This seems an expensive way to travel, but the waiting time for issue is less than for the standard one.

A British Excursion Document, for travel to France only – and for a duration of only 60 hours! – is available from post offices at £2.50: good for one month from date of issue only.

Length of stay

Up to three months, a resident of the EC countries needs no visa. For longer stays, apply at the Préfecture de Police nearest to where you are living. Take along your passport and a good reason why you want to remain in Paris. They will issue a *Permis de Séjour*. Keep this with your passport and produce it when necessary (in time of trouble or when leaving France). If you are going to study in France, take to the Préfecture some kind of proof of enrolment in a school or college.

On leaving Britain, you must for some reason show your passport to an immigration official. On entering France (airport, or at boat or Hoverlanding) a French official looks at it but probably won't bother to stamp it. Likewise on the return. As a foreigner entering either country, you *could* be asked the reason for your stay (business, tourism, family matters), how long you'll be around. With the advent of the EC, this has become – in France, at least – the merest formality.

Douane/Customs

Again, these days, it's mostly a matter of waving you on. If they're looking for you for some good reason, they'll stop you. Or they may hold you up briefly, by pure chance, rifle your luggage, and leave you to repack. Contraband is illegal drugs, firearms (except hunting guns with permits), explosives, pornography. A respectful demeanour and a blank face will probably keep you from getting hung up in Customs at either end. Do not attempt to charm or chat up a customs officer anywhere. They are not susceptible to charm.

Health

English travellers in France get a pretty good deal. Almost free medical care is available through the reciprocal scheme of the EC, and it applies to the self-employed and the unemployed as well as to full-time employees. If you're going abroad as a family, a single form covers all of you.

Before your departure get Form E-111 from the Post Office and fill both parts out. There's a very useful leaflet with it that tells you everything you might need to know about how to get medical treatment in Europe, and what to do to claim most of the cost back. It also warns you that it is NOT, repeat NOT, a substitute for adequate health insurance (see page 89). Then take the forms back to the Post Office with your passport, and they'll process it.

If you're well organised, take your National Insurance number or your NHS number, and your passport to the Post Office, fill out the form, and the Post Office should be able to validate your E-111 on the spot. Guard it with your life, as it can't be replaced by post if lost, nor can it be reissued. Our advice is to take a couple of photocopies.

Arriving

First impressions can make or break your trip. If you step off the train or plane confused and disoriented, you can expect to stay that way for days. It helps to know what to expect: instead of floundering around in the chaos of the Gare du Nord you can begin immediately to develop a Paris expertise which will see you through your visit.

The airports are smoothly organized, well signposted and furnished with *bureaux de change*, information services and so forth. But like airports everywhere, Charles de Gaulle/Roissy and Orly are sterile, unamusing places, pervaded by a kind of travel *angst*, and you'll want to be on your way at once.

To reach central Paris from Charles de Gaulle or Orly, you have several choices:

Charles de Gaulle/Roissy

Bus: cheapest and reasonably fast: take the free bus from your arrival point to the SNCF station, buy a *carnet* of 10 tickets, walk about 15 yards and find the service bus stop to Paris – No. 350 takes you to the Gare du Nord, No. 351 to Gare de l'Est. If you have bought a *Carte Paris Visite* in London, the ride costs you nothing – but don't put the little ticket into the ticket-stamping machine as this will invalidate it. Otherwise, it's six tickets from your *carnet*, or 33F in cash. The advantage of these buses is that you climb directly on and off, without having to cope with the railway turnstiles, escalators, stairs and platforms. The buses are blessedly uncrowded, and when you arrive in Paris you're at ground-level ready to take another bus or the Métro. About 45 minutes travelling time, depending on traffic.

Roissy/Rail: very fast direct train service to the Gare du Nord. Take that free bus to the SNCF station, where trains leave every 15 minutes from 5:05 a.m. to 11:50 p.m. Ticket to Gare du Nord is 27F50, or 32F if you are changing there for an onward journey on the ordinary Métro. Our only problem with this superb service has been manoeuvring luggage through turnstiles, and picking our way out at the Gare du Nord end. 25 minutes travelling time.

Air France bus: swift and luxurious, to the Étoile and Porte Maillot in the 17e *arrondissement*. (For an explanation of the *arrondissement* system, see pages 33–4 and the map on pages 298–9.) Buses run every 12–15 minutes, and your luggage is taken off your hands. 38F; or 80F for 3 people, 112F for 4. About 25–45 minutes.

Orly

Orly/Rail: fast train to nine stations on the Left Bank, every 15 minutes from 5:00 a.m. to 9:00 p.m., then every 30 minutes to 11:00 p.m. 29F.

Orlybus: high-speed, low-fare bus directly to Denfert-Rochereau Métro station, 14e *arrondissement*. A smartly designed coach with plenty of luggage space leaves every 15 minutes from 6:00 a.m. to 11:30 p.m. 31F per person (or 6 Métro tickets, *Formule 1* pass or *Carte Paris Visite* for four zones). Group discounts are 80F for 3 people, 100F for 4. About 30 minutes.

Air France bus: to the Gare des Invalides, Left Bank, 7e *arrondissement*. Runs about every 12 minutes, your luggage is dealt with for you, and it's around 30 minutes' travelling time. 38F; or 80F for 3 people, 112F for 4.

Railway Stations

Boat and Hovercraft are linked to the Gare du Nord by fast train – about two-and-a-half hours from Calais or Boulogne, and included in the cost of your ticket.

Railway stations are large, chaotic, and always crowded, even early in the morning. It takes five minutes and three wrong answers to find anything, but there are centrally located information booths, usually with English-speaking personnel, who can provide authoritative answers.

If you're burdened with luggage, look for free, energy-saving luggage carts. Avoid porters: the fixed charge per bag is 10F.

If you haven't provided yourself with some francs in cash before arrival, seek out the *bureau de change* and pick up some survival money. Not much: you'll probably get a better rate of exchange at one of the large commercial banks in Paris itself.

Help

If you haven't already reserved a room, and need help . . .
If you need a simple but comprehensible map of Paris, the Métro, buses . . .
If you need to know how to use the telephone, figure out the transportation system . . .
Or if you are merely tired and totally disoriented . . .

Look for the Hôtesses de Paris: These run a service provided by the Office de Tourisme de Paris, they speak all useful languages and they know almost everything. For the first-time traveller arriving in Paris without a place to lay the head, for someone arriving after dark, the Hôtesses can be invaluable. They have a list of hotels in each price range where they know there are vacancies at that moment. They will not call a specific hotel of your choice (they reckon that if you know that much, you can fend for yourself), but they will find you a room no matter how many phone calls it takes. The charge is 17F for a 1-star hotel, 23F for a 2-star, 38F for a 3-star, and when you're on your last legs, worth it. And they also make Youth Hostel reservations, 10F.

It has been our experience that they will not necessarily find the cheapest room in the best-value hotel. A sign displayed gives minimum prices for the kinds of hotels they use: 175F for a single, 275F for a double in a 1-star hotel, 200F for a single, 375F for a double in a 2-star, and so forth. This may be broadly true, but in practice you can do better for yourself (see 'Au lit', pages 56–97). The Hôtesses can only book for you on the day you want a hotel, not in advance. They can be invaluable – if you don't speak much French, can't face the telephone system, and haven't the energy to start the search on the Métro with your luggage. Let the Hôtesses book you a room for your first night, and strike out on your own the next day.

Try to get to them, either at the railway stations or at the main office, as early as possible, as from late morning until closing time, in summer, the queues build up to bursting point.

If the Hôtesses de Paris at the railway station where you arrive look slightly weary and sceptical, especially at the end of a long hot day, don't be too surprised. Considering the number of idiot travellers who fall into their offices at all hours, often armed with nothing more than touching faith and a copy of an out-of-date or fanciful guidebook, expecting to find a double room in a good hotel, in a quiet neighbourhood, within walking distance of St-Germain-des-Prés, for 100F, their slightly disillusioned air may be justified. And they will indeed make umpteen phone calls, until they place you in a room.

Gare d'Austerlitz (arrival hall)	Mon–Sat 9:00 a.m.–8:00 p.m.
	(10:00 p.m. in summer*)
Gare de l'Est (departure hall)	Mon–Sat 8:00 a.m.–1:00 p.m.
5:00 p.m.–8:00 p.m. (10:00 p.m. in summer*)	
Gare de Lyon (arrival hall)	Mon–Sat 8:00a.m.–1:00 p.m.
5:00 p.m.–8:00 p.m. (10:00 p.m. in summer*)	
Gare du Nord (mainline hall)	Mon–Sat 8:00 a.m.–8:00 p.m.
	(10:00 p.m. in summer*)
Main tourist office (Bureau de	Mon–Sat 9:00 a.m.–8:00 p.m.
Tourisme de Paris)	(10:00 p.m. in summer*)
127 avenue des Champs-Élysées, 8e	Sundays and holidays
Métro: George-V	9:00 a.m.–6:00 p.m.
	(8:00 p.m. in summer*)

Also: tel: 47 20 88 98 for announcements in English of almost everything you need to know, 24 hours a day.

The tourist offices are a mine of information and a great source for free maps and other handouts. Most useful of these are several varieties of Métro and bus folders: individual pamphlets on certain sight-seeing bus routes; a comprehensive list of hotels and restaurants listed by *arrondissement* (see map, pages 300–1), alphabetically, and classified by price and amenities. In addition, the main tourist office in the Champs-Élysées has posters displaying current cultural events; they give information about other parts of France; and there is a travel bureau in the basement run by SNCF.

If you're just a little knocked out, but don't need the immediate assistance of the Hôtesses for hotel booking or map help, take time to get your breath. We strongly advise you to spend the next half

*Summer indicates Easter to 1 November.

hour getting acclimatized to Paris (what could be more pleasant?) before jumping on a bus or Métro.

First: find somewhere to leave your luggage. In all the railway stations there is a left-luggage place, the *consigne*. Cart your bags there in your trolley, and check them in. Cost 11F per bag. If you are travelling light, a storage locker (5F for a small one, up to 11F for a big one) will do nicely, if you can find one that's empty when you need it.

Then: get a bite to eat, a glass of wine, or a cup of coffee. A brasserie is perfect, but don't head for one in the terminal (too hectic), or directly opposite (double the cost, as they know how to soak the tourist). Walk one street away, in any direction, find a bar-tabac or a brasserie. Here you can sit down, catch your breath, relax for a bit before you go on. Try out your first five words of French. Begin to figure out how the money system really works. Don't be shy about laying the coins on the table, getting used to the colour and feel. Plan the route to your hotel, with the aid of the *Plan de Paris* (see page 32).

For a little basic brasserie vocabulary, see under 'La nourriture', pages 98–102. Smile. And finish with 'Merci, au revoir, monsieur (or mademoiselle)', which will surprise them so much they'll smile back.

If you haven't already booked a hotel, and have (as you should have) absolute confidence in this book, consult the chapter 'Au lit', pages 56–97, for information, and pages 277–9 to find out how to use the phone.

Getting to your hotel

If you are really weighed down, take a taxi. If necessary, write down the address and show it to the driver. There are taxi ranks outside all the stations and terminals. See the information on page 280 for tipping.

If you are ready to brave the Métro or the bus, see pages 34–46, in 'Getting around'. At railway stations, airports, and major Métro stations you can pick up a *Carte Paris Visite* or *Carte Orange* (see pages 37–9 for how to do it), and start using it to travel for almost nothing right away. The process for *Carte Orange*, including getting a picture taken in a photomatic booth, takes about five minutes; for *Carte Paris Visite*, a fast 30 seconds.

Leaving Paris

By the time you're ready to wrench yourself away from Paris, you should be able to do this part walking on your hands. But just in case:

In railway stations: Departure times, train numbers, destinations and track number (*voies*) are marked in huge letters, on an immense blue board in mid-station. Trains leave very strictly on time, and with almost no warning whistles or horns. Anyone coming to see you off will need a platform ticket, although as there are few officials actually at the gate this can sometimes be dispensed with.

Airport buses: Air France takes you to Charles de Gaulle from Porte Maillot (16e *arrondissement*) and the Étoile (avenue Carnot, 16e *arrondissement*). They claim half an hour travelling time; knowing traffic, you should double that. Buses leave every 15 minutes between 5:50 a.m. and 11:00 p.m. Fare 38F. (Unless you are actually staying near Porte Maillot or the Étoile, the Roissy-Rail service from Gare du Nord is faster, easier, and cheaper.)

The Air France bus to Orly leaves the Aérogare des Invalides (rue de Constantine, just north of the Invalides Métro, 7e *arrondissement*), and also from the Gare Montparnasse (15e *arrondissement*), every 12 minutes, and takes at least half an hour – allow plenty of leeway for traffic. Buses run between 5:50 a.m. and 11:00 p.m. Fare 38F.

Trains: *Roissy-Rail*: Gare du Nord to Charles de Gaulle. Tickets from automatic dispensers in the hall leading to the train, marked Roissy-Rail, or from a ticket window – but be wary of this last, as the booking clerk also issues the *Carte Orange* and *Coupon Jaune*, student passes, etc., and you can get blocked for ever while he does the paperwork. If you are well organized and don't lose things easily, get your return ticket to Charles de Gaulle when you *arrive* from the airport and are not pressed for time, and put it with your airline ticket. Trains run every 15 minutes from 5:30 a.m. to 11:30 p.m., fare 27F50.

Orly-Rail runs between the Gare d'Austerlitz and Orly every 15 minutes, and takes about 35 minutes to reach Orly Sud and Ouest. Departures from 5:50 a.m. to 10:50 p.m., fare 29F.

Service buses to airports: DON'T, unless you're a masochist with plenty of time to waste, take the bus to Charles de Gaulle, even if you have the *Carte Paris Visite* and the ride is free – the nervous strain is just too much. However, the new fast direct service to Orly, from Denfert-Rochereau in the 14e *arrondissement*, is great – about 30 minutes travelling time to Orly-Ouest, 35 minutes to Orly-Sud. Every 15 minutes, 6:05 a.m. to 11:00 p.m., fare 31F.

Buses and Métros to railway termini: Consult your maps. If you're on a direct route, with no changes, there should be no problems. But if you must change anywhere on the Métro, forget it: negotiating stairs and intersections with luggage is out of the question. Take a taxi. In hot weather, and in rush hours, Paris buses are intolerably hot; the windows are made to keep out draughts, not to let in fresh air. Doors are closed when the bus is in motion – and sweaty human bodies can be really unpleasant.

Aux alentours
(Getting around)

You'll probably spend much of your time in Paris getting from place to place, just wandering around with eyes open. Nowhere in the world will you have such beauty to absorb as you go! But getting muddled can take the shine off anything, even Paris. To make the most of your wandering, we suggest arming yourself with a really first-class 'atlas' of Paris.

The best we know is a thick little book called *Plan de Paris*, published by Éditions A. Leconte and available in bookshops and *papeteries*. The hardcover edition is dark red, and costs 69F, which seems like a lot, but it's packed cover to cover with everything you need to know. There are cheaper, paperback editions of the *Plan*, but with hard use they tend to lose the covers, the maps drop out, and you end up frustrated. Other atlas-type books exist, some with larger and more legible maps, but none we have found includes so much and such accurate information.

The *Plan* of M. Leconte lists all streets, alleys, *quais* and squares alphabetically, with their beginning and ending points, *arrondissements*, nearest Métro stops, and a keyed map reference which takes you to the individual, coloured *arrondissement* map.

Each *arrondissement*, from 1er to 20e, has its own page. Métro lines and stops are printed in red. The maps themselves are laid out with alpha-numerical grids. Some plans (not, to be sure, the estimable M. Leconte's) are smallish and blurry, and therefore useless no matter how cheap. A good copy is child's play to use, and a treasure to keep long after your visit to Paris. Don't lend it to anyone.

The suburbs (*banlieues*) are also mapped in this book with the same format of street listings, map reference, etc., but probably won't be of much interest to you at this point.

A highly useful section lists addresses and map references for anything you want to know, and quite a lot you might never need: embassies, theatres, hospitals, schools, churches, monuments, police

stations, city halls, race tracks, museums, post offices, state minis-
tries, stadiums, tennis courts, swimming pools, shops, radio and TV
stations, principal cinemas, cabarets, concert halls.

All the Paris bus routes are listed in numerical order, and what is
even more important, shown in chart form, each with its starting and
ending point and the principal stops in between. For that alone, the
Paris Office de Tourisme should give M. Leconte a gold medal, as it is
the only thing lacking in their own otherwise excellent bus folder.

If you are in Paris for more than a day or two, and intend to move
more than a quarter mile from your hotel in any direction, the *Plan*
is indispensable. The good news is that you can get a copy before
you leave London, from the French Bookshop, 28 Bute Street SW7.
Cost £5.90 for the paperback edition. Tel: 071-584 2840.

Less detailed but very useful maps of Paris, with pictured locations of principal tourist attractions – museums, monuments, and
so forth – are available free from the Bureau de Tourisme. And the
big department stores (Au Printemps, Galéries Lafayette, among
others) have prepared very much the same sort of thing, showing of
course where *they* are located.

The streets of Paris

The *arrondissement* system

In the mid-19th century, Paris was thoroughly overhauled by
Napoleon III's urban planner, Baron Haussmann. Slums were
cleared (fortunately, he didn't get around to the Marais), sewers
and aqueducts installed where the Romans had left off, and a web
of wide thoroughfares, the Grands Boulevards, was laid. The city
was thereupon divided into 20 *arrondissements* (there had previously
been 12, based on the old traditional *quartiers*, some dating back
2000 years). Numbers 1–7 cover the three historic parts of Paris:
the *cité* (official and religious, located on the central islands), the *ville*
(the Right Bank, commercial and industrial), and the *université* (Left
Bank, commercial and scholastic). To a great extent these medieval
distinctions hold true today.

The *arrondissements* spiral clockwise from the centre of Paris (1er,
part of the Île de la Cité and the area around the Louvre). The
numbers which you will see on street signs and in newspapers and
magazines (and in this book) are expressed thus: 1er, which means

Premier; 2e, which stands for *Deuxième*, and so forth. Each *arrondisse-ment* has quite distinct identifying features or landmarks which can serve to give you your bearings. The Eleventh (you might as well get used to seeing it written as 11e) is roughly the area which stretches outwards from the Bastille; the 8e is Gare St-Lazare and the Madeleine; the 7e is the Invalides and the Tour Eiffel. Street signs in Paris are large, legible, and almost always include the *arrondissement* number (thus: avenue de l'Opéra, 1er).

With map, *arrondissement*, landmarks, street signs, and clearly written house or shop numbers, you shouldn't ever get *totally* lost, but it can happen, and for some reason even people with a good sense of direction find it hard to work out which way is north in Paris.

When you do feel really lost, the simplest thing to do is seek out the nearest Métro station: ask anyone, with the simple formula, 'Pardon, monsieur (or madame) – le Métro?'

Le Métro

It's impossible to lose your way in the Métro. You can't walk 10 paces without a clear, explicit sign informing you of your destination. How to use all this information:

1 In the *Plan de Paris*, look up the name of the street you want to go to, and you will find the nearest Métro stop.

2 Find the station on the Métro map in the front of the *Plan*, or in one of the small free maps dealt out by the municipal transport system at every chance. Or look on the big map outside the entrance to the nearest Métro station, or near the ticket office, or on the platform from which the trains run.

3 Trace your route. Each Métro line is known by its beginning and ending points. Between any two stations in the system, you will be coming from and going towards one of the terminals of the line. For example, line 12 runs from Mairie d'Issy to Porte de la Chapelle. If you were at Gare St-Lazare and wanted to go to Pigalle, you would take a train in the direction of Porte de la Chapelle. From St-Lazare to Sèvres-Babylone, your direction is Mairie d'Issy. You then follow the appropriate signs to the platform where your train comes in. On Métro maps, each line is numbered and colour-coded. The terminals are marked in good big capital letters on the map, at the outskirts of the city.

4 If you need to change trains to get to the stop you want, it's equally easy. Paris Métro lines are linked together in a remarkable system of *correspondences* (intersections) of two, three, sometimes five or six lines. You may have to walk underground for what seems like miles before you find your train, and it's hard on the feet. But keep calm, and you will never be lost. The signs simply don't allow that to happen.

The Métro runs every day, but with reduced services on Sundays, holidays, and after about 8:00 p.m., when intervals between trains become longer. Most trains begin running at 5:30 a.m., and stop at 1:15 a.m. But take care: if you have to change trains you can easily find yourself stranded at the connecting station, after 12:45 a.m.

L'autobus

Trickier, and takes longer to get you from A to B, but infinitely more fun than the Métro. Like the train system, each bus is marked large and clear with its point of origin and destination. The buses are designated primarily by number. On the sides of the bus, the major stops are displayed so that even when it moves past you, you can read the route in a flash. An overall bus map, available at Métro stations, bus termini, and the Office de Tourisme at 127 avenue des Champs-Élysées, gives a fairly clear, colour-coded overview of the routes. But it's intricate, and you could miss your bus while you're trying to work it out. Best of all is the chart-form bus information in the *Plan de Paris*.

If you read French and plan to use buses often and for a long period, try to find the *Le Guide Paris-Bus*, now being reprinted after a lapse of several years by the publishers Prat/Europa in conjunction with the RATP (the municipal transport system). It shows you every bus route, the street address opposite each bus stop, and best of all, what other buses connect at every bus stop on every route. Using it, you quickly learn which combination of buses will serve you best, thus saving a lot of walking. In addition, the index tells you which bus, or buses, take you to every point of interest in the city.

Bus stops are clearly recognizable, often as a kerbside shelter, with a good visible display above of which buses stop there. Otherwise, look for a pole at the kerb with a numbered disc on top, and a panel that tells you everything you need to know about each bus.

Inside the shelters, you are shown a clear chart of the bus route, all its stops, a helpful marker that shows exactly where you are on the route, the nearest place to buy tickets. On the bus you will only be able to buy single tickets, not *carnets*, and this costs real money (page 38 for price). If you have a *Carte Orange* with a monthly or weekly pass, a *Formule 1* ticket, or a *Carte Paris Visite*, just hold it up for the driver to see. Single tickets are 'composted', date-stamped in the machine near the bus door.

Inside, just in case you've missed the other information, there are two or three route maps, overhead. So you can know instantly where you are, what the next stop will be, and even, if the worst comes to the worst and you are really mixed up, which direction you are going in. The bus stops along the street display names clearly and legibly, so you know whether you need to hop off and change direction.

Times: In general, buses leave their starting points at 7:00 a.m., and run to about 8:30 or 9:00 p.m. Others have a night service (these all begin at the place du Châtelet, avenue Victoria, 3e). Sundays and holidays: buses Nos. 20, 21, 26, 27, 31, 38, 43, 44, 46, 52, 62, 80, 91, 92, 95, 96, and the Petite Ceinture bus which runs around the outskirts of Paris.

All Paris buses run on the request-stop system. If you are standing at a stop marked for only one bus, the driver will stop (if he sees you). But it may be safer to wave your arm or an umbrella. If more than one bus serves your stop, you *must* signal the one you want.

The same system applies when you want to get off. No automatic stops. You must push a small, well-concealed button on one of the upright stanchions near entrance and exit doors. This activates a sign in the front of the bus: *Arrêt demandé*. This system lets Paris buses move fairly fast, considering the narrow, often crowded streets in which they run.

Noctambus

There are 10 night-service buses which run from 1:30 a.m. to 5:30 a.m., all beginning at Châtelet and fanning outward to the outskirts of Paris:

A:	Châtelet to	Porte de Neuilly, via Étoile
B:		Mairie de Levallois, via Opéra
C:		Mairie de Clichy, via Pigalle
D:		Mairie de St-Ouen, via Gare du Nord
E:		Église de Pantin, via Gare de L'Est
F:		Mairie de Lilas, via Belleville
G:		Mairie de Montreuil, via Gambetta
H:		Château de Vincennes, via Nation
I:		Rungis, via Place d'Italie
J:		Porte d'Orléans, via Luxembourg

As the RATP says, 'Pas de voiture? Pas de taxi? Pas de vélo? Pas de panique!' – Just signal the bus. Night buses will stop anywhere you hail them, not just at bus stops. They run only one an hour. With *Formule 1*, or *Carte Orange*, or *Coupon Jaune*, or *Carte Paris Visite*, you travel free; otherwise it's three or four tickets, depending on distance.

Métro and bus travel

Paris transport is heavily subsidized, a great break for the travelling poor as well as for hard-working Parisians. Tickets can be used on Métro and buses interchangeably, which saves a lot of time and trouble. Prices have risen only fractionally since the last edition of this book, and although in 1992 they may go up slightly, the increases will in all probability be gentle. Beginning with the least expensive – and why we prefer these – here we go.

Carte Orange: this is a catch-all heading for cards that give you all-inclusive travel by the week or by the month (you can even get a yearly ticket). The *Carte* itself is a small orange card in a shiny grey plastic folder with a pocket for your weekly or monthly *coupon*. It's free. Take a passport-size photograph to any Métro station. You then buy a *Coupon Jaune* (valid from 1:00 a.m. Monday to 11:59 p.m. Sunday) or a *Coupon Orange* (good for one calendar month). The *Coupon Jaune* is on sale from the Sunday before it becomes valid, through Wednesday of the following week. The *Coupon Orange* goes on sale on the 20th of the previous month.

Now that the Paris region has been zoned, you will have to say at the pay window which zones you want to travel in – zones 1 and 2 cover the whole of the city, so that's the most useful one. Outer zones extend to the limits of the region. In our experience, these *Coupons* are the greatest travel buy ever invented. If you're in Paris even for four or five days, the *Coupon Jaune* will give you your money's worth in hassle-free travel.

On the Métro, push your ticket through the turnstile and immediately slip it back into the plastic pocket of your *Carte*. On the bus, flash your *Carte* at the driver. On no account feed the ticket into the ticket-punch machine. This will invalidate it. There are no refunds for idiocy.

What you get for your money: unlimited travel on Métro, buses, certain segments of the high-speed RER, the Montmartrobus, and the Montmartre funicular.

Coupon Jaune, zones 1 and 2, 1 week	54F
Coupon Orange, zones 1 and 2, 1 calendar month	190F

Formule 1: This one-day pass gives you unlimited travel as above. You get an identity card (no photograph needed) which you can keep for ever. Buy a ticket (*coupon*) for each day you need it. 23F.

If for some mysterious reason your ticket won't open the gate, go back to the ticket window and show it to them; they'll press a magic button and buzz you through. This is no great help if you've entered through one of those entrances without ticket booths (marked 'reservé aux passagers munis de billets'), because then you'll have to trudge along to a manned entrance.

Tickets and *carnets*: You can buy them singly (extravagantly) at a Métro station or on the bus, or in *carnets* of 10 from Métros or in many tobacconists' shops. On the Métro, push your ticket through the turnstile but don't discard it until you leave the train – there are occasional spot-checks of travellers, and the *contrôleurs* can be fierce, even taking you and your passport to the nearest police station to be fined. On the bus, tell the driver where you are going and he'll tell you whether to punch one or two tickets. Suburban buses – those with numbers higher than 100 – will cost two to six tickets. Bus drivers do not sell *carnets*, only single tickets. And you can be *contrôléed* on the bus too, so keep your ticket handy.

Single tickets	5F50
Carnet of 10	34F50

Carte Paris Visite: It does open every desirable door in Paris, but strikes us as somewhat expensive. Decide for yourself. You can buy it in London from Continental Travel at the French Railways office, 179 Piccadilly, W1 (Mondays through Fridays). In Paris, get it at the SNCF stations at Charles de Gaulle and Orly airports, at most Métro stations, and from some banks and travel agencies. It allows you the same unlimited travel on buses and Métro as do all other forms of tickets. The 'Zones 1–3' pass gives you the city of Paris and its immediate suburbs. 'Zones 1–4' adds the surrounding region (e.g. Versailles) and Roissy and Orly airports.

Zones 1–3	3 consecutive days	80F
	5 consecutive days	150F

As you see, a three-day *Visite* costs more than a weekly *Coupon Jaune*, and even more than three *Formule 1* day passes. A five-day *Visite* is nearly triple the cost of a *Coupon Jaune* . . . but you *can* buy it any day of the week.

If you're a really dedicated money-saver, arrive in Paris on a Monday morning, pick up your *Coupon Jaune* and be on your way. Use it 15 times and you're travelling free the rest of the week.

Now that you know how to get around – where to?

You might just want to set off at random – head in any direction on foot; hop on the first bus that comes along; take the Métro to the end of the line and try to find your way back as a pedestrian – no matter what, something will come of it.

Or perhaps you could use some pointers on the *quartiers* before you set out – a few landmarks – some guaranteed bus routes. Possibly some areas to avoid, as well.

Major monuments (the Tour Eiffel, the Arc de Triomphe, the Louvre, and such) you should be able to find with one hand tied behind your back. If you're really in doubt, ask a tourist. What follows is a sampler: general reflections on a few *quartiers* (central and out of the way) and some routes you might like to try, on foot and otherwise. It's anything but exhaustive. You'll discover far more than we have space for on your own.

Paris by bus

Commercial sightseeing buses in Paris cost an arm and a leg, as the saying goes. Why pay from 125F for a trip when the glorious RATP offers you an incomparable set of bus trips for practically nothing?

If you are armed, as you should be, with the indispensable *Carte Orange* (see page 37), or your *Carte Paris Visite* (page 38), your sightseeing is on the house, so to speak. The RATP has even started a special Sunday service, called the Parisbus, which does the highlights in a 50-minute run. Full details below.

RATP have also laid out, in a well-designed folder called *Billet de Tourisme*, available at all major Métro stations, a list of 17 'sightseeing' bus routes that can show you the most beautiful, historic, curious, and provocative parts of Paris. These 17 could take up your entire time in the city, of course, so we've narrowed down the choices to a magic seven – some of which will show you parts of Paris most tourists haven't even heard about.

If you have time for only one leisurely, luxurious bus ride, choose No. 24. If Sunday afternoon is what you've set aside for an excursion, try the Parisbus.

Note: in 1990 and 1991, the new 'Axe Rouge' traffic scheme came into being, to help clear up the awful *bouchons*, gridlocks which often left buses, vans, cars and bikes immovably locked together at crossings and in narrow streets.

Some bus routes have, necessarily, been altered, much for the better. The information that follows is as accurate as we can make it, but more traffic-speeding plans are in the making, so you may find some of these buses unexpectedly running on another street. Don't panic and climb off the bus: stay on, you may find something you like even better. If you do, write to us so we can include new facts in new editions.

Parisbus

For a quick, enjoyable trip that will give you your bearings in Paris, take a ride on the Parisbus. It runs only on Sundays from noon to 9:00 p.m., and you get on anywhere along the route at the stops marked 'Parisbus' (though the old name 'Balabus' might still be on the signs). It starts at La Défense, and comes past Neuilly and Porte Maillot to Charles de Gaulle and Étoile before running down the Champs-Élysées to Concorde, the Tuileries and the Louvre. On the outward journey, it crosses the Pont St-Michel and the Île de la Cité to the University sector and on to the Gare d'Austerlitz and the Gare de Lyon. The return journey takes a slightly different route which passes Notre-Dame, Pont Royal, and the Musée d'Orsay before crossing back to Concorde.

Bus 24

From Gare St-Lazare, it takes you round the place de la Madeleine (luxurious shops) into the place de la Concorde, then sweeps along the quai des Tuileries beside the Seine, past the Louvre. As you go, you have a most enticing view of the silvery buildings lining the opposite side of the river (the Left Bank – Rive Gauche). Glancing to your left, you can see the exquisite church St-Germain-l'Auxerrois, where all the kings of France worshipped privately. At the pont des Arts, look across the river at the Hôtel des Monnaies (the Mint) and the Institut de France which houses the 'Immortals' of the Académie Française. Crossing the river on the pont Neuf to the Île de la Cité, the bus passes the Palais de Justice, then crosses the Petit Pont to the Rive Gauche. From the boulevard St-Germain, the route follows the quai St-Bernard, skirting the edge of the four-centuries-old Jardin des Plantes. If you stay on the bus all the way to its destination at Alfort, you will catch sight of the monumental new Palais Omnisport built on the site of the razed wine warehouses along the quai de Bercy – passing a real working-class area on the way. On the return journey, the bus goes along the left bank of the Seine, with a good look at Notre-Dame; then past the Mint and along the quai Voltaire (where Ingres, Delacroix, and Wagner lived at various times), before recrossing the river by the pont Royal and returning to St-Lazare by way of the place de la Concorde and the magnificent rue Royale. Mondays through Saturdays, 7:00 a.m. to 8:30 p.m.

Bus 29

Also from Gare St-Lazare, the No. 29 takes you around the Opéra, down the rue du 4 Septembre, passing the Bourse (the stock market headquarters), and the place des Victoires with its statue of Louis XIV on horseback. You suddenly come to the great ultra-modern dazzler, Beaubourg (Centre Georges Pompidou), towering over the small crooked streets of the Marais, almost the oldest part of Paris. The bus goes past the elegant place des Vosges, built for the king in 1612, then into the wide boulevard leading to the place de la Bastille. The Bastille prison itself is gone; but the new Bastille Opéra House now dominates the area, and the immense circle itself is very impressive. If you like, get off here and catch the No. 87 bus for another fabulous sightseeing trip to the Champ-de-Mars (for the Tour Eiffel and Napoleon's tomb), or stay with the No. 29 and go on, past the Cimetière de Picpus where many of the victims of *la guillotine* lie buried. Mondays through Saturdays, 7:00 a.m. to 8:30 p.m.

Bus 32

It begins at the Gare de l'Est, but you may want to catch it at one of its more interesting stopping places, such as place de la Trinité, going in the direction of Porte de Passy. The route takes you through the 'Quartier d'Europe', so called because almost every street is named after a capital city: Amsterdam, Budapest, London, Stockholm. Past the Gare St-Lazare, you are in the faded elegance of the boulevard Haussmann, named after the man who reshaped the city in the 1860s. Along the rue de la Boëtie, look for the wildly expensive and beautiful boutiques and galleries. Then up the Champs-Élysées, and to the Trocadéro, the palace built for the Paris World's Fair in 1937 and now the home of three museums. You may want to stop off here and see the Museum of Mankind – fascinating. The bus goes on to the smart, but not entrancing, Passy neighbourhood with its mansions and streets overhung with huge old trees. On the return trip, the route is slightly different, and you'll pass along the avenue Matignon and through Faubourg St-Honoré, wall-to-wall with the great couture houses. The bus will give you an overview, but this is really for people who like to walk. File it for future window-shopping. No. 32 runs Mondays through Saturdays, first bus from Gare de l'Est at 7:00 a.m., last one at 8:30 p.m.

Bus 52

Begins at the Opéra, takes you around the lovely shopping area of the boulevard des Capucines, past the Musée Cognacq-Jay (again, file for future reference), and through the place de la Madeleine with its entrancing food shops: Fauchon, Hédiard and Michel Guérard. Around the place de la Concorde (a circus of killer traffic has taken the place of the guillotine that stood here for years), and a wonderful view up the vista of the Champs-Élysées. The big avenue de Friedland takes you to the Étoile/place Charles de Gaulle, where there is always a silent crowd at the Eternal Flame that burns over the tomb of France's Unknown Soldier. Beyond that, you are in the streets of the 16e *arrondissement*, a smart, conservative residential area. The avenue Mozart on the return journey is charming; the local café is called The Magic Flute. This is a pleasant place to step off the bus and have coffee, and walk around a neighbourhood that is real Paris, far off the tourist beat. The bus continues to the place de la Porte d'Auteuil and takes you to pont de St-Cloud, a fairly sterile area, so you might want to end your trip at the place de la Porte d'Auteuil and either walk west into the Bois de Boulogne – NOT at night – or head back into central Paris on the Métro. No. 52 runs seven days a week, including holidays, first bus at 7:00 a.m. weekdays and 8:00 a.m. Sundays, last bus about 10:15 p.m.

Bus 63

Begins at the Gare de Lyon, takes you along the quai St-Bérnard, and almost at once you are in the *Quartier Latin*, the home of Paris students from the time of the monks in the Middle Ages to the motorbikes and demonstrations of the 1960s. It traverses the rue des Écoles, crosses the boulevard St-Michel, and passes the church of St-Sulpice before threading its way through the stately streets of the 7e. The 63 touches the fringe of the boulevard St-Germain, then takes you along the quai d'Orsay (political and diplomatic Paris). If you stay with it to the end of the route at Porte de la Muette, you see 'untourist' Paris – but it's more interesting to get off at the Trocadéro stop for an unparalleled view of the city from high on the hill. Take the bus back in the direction of the Gare de Lyon, and this time step off at St-Germain des Prés: yes, it's a cliché, but not to be missed because of its bookshops, its galleries, its cafés. There are still those who swear that a costly coffee at the Deux Magots is worth the price, just to see and be seen by *le tout Paris*. And it costs nothing to browse in the side streets, to see Picasso drawings or primitive paintings. Bus No. 63 runs seven days a week, from 7:00 a.m. to midnight (leaving times from the Gare de Lyon).

Bus 72

Runs from the pont de St-Cloud to the Hôtel de Ville, and back again, and on the way gives you sight of both modern and historic Paris. In between you will see some of the glitter and splendour, and some of the less savoury and picturesque parts too. To get the most from this 'tour', catch the bus at the Hôtel de Ville end: you travel first along the lower and less chic end of the rue de Rivoli, past the great sweep of the Louvre, along the Tuileries Gardens, and past the lovely and newly renovated Jeu de Paume gallery. Turning around the end of the place de la Concorde, it enters the cours de la Reine – high above you are the bright, shining, gilded Horses of Marly. It runs along to the wide streets named for City of New York and for President Kennedy – if you want to get off here, you can climb a steep set of steps to visit the Modern Museum of Paris (see page 44). From here, it takes you to the avenue de Versailles, most interesting for its buildings such as no. 142 by the architect Hector Guimard, in Art Nouveau style. Beyond this point, the ride isn't particularly exciting, except as all Paris's untouristy neighbourhoods are; you may want to get off in the avenue de Versailles, wander a bit and absorb its feeling, then return by No. 22 to the Opéra. Mondays through Saturdays, first bus from pont de St-Cloud at 7:00 a.m., last one at 8:50 p.m. On Sundays, there is a partial service, from pont de St-Cloud to Concorde only.

Bus 83

Begins at place d'Italie, in the 13e *arrondissement*, a seldom-visited but quite interesting part of Paris (some very good hotels and restaurants there, see pages 88–9 and 149–51 for more about them). Running down the avenue des Gobelins, it traverses the boulevard du Port-Royal. On Saturdays, there's a street market worth stopping for in this street, near the rue St-Jacques. Here it skirts the 5e *arrondissement*, the Latin Quarter. The rue d'Assas on this route is absolutely littered with good little bistros and cafés. The bus passes the Jardin du Luxembourg, where you might want to stop to inhale some fresh air and watch the Paris kids at play; then it runs along the river by the quai d'Orsay, past Invalides. Along the way, you glimpse the Tour Eiffel, and the dome of the Invalides with Napoleon's tomb. The bus crosses on to the Right Bank into fashionable *haute couture* Paris, around the Rond-Point des Champs-Élysées and the Métro station of St-Philippe-du-Roule. You could go as far as Levallois, but you have really had the most interesting part of its route by now, unless you want to see working-class Paris as it really lives. If you prefer, finish your trip at the Rond-Point, and sit for a while on a bench in the pretty little park while all Paris goes by, or walk up the Champs-Élysées towards the Étoile. This is a wonderful bus ride to take late in the afternoon (but be prepared for crowds during rush hour), as you may be lucky enough to see the lights along the Seine and the Champs-Élysées coming on as dusk approaches. Mondays through Saturdays, first bus from place d'Italie at 7:00 a.m., last one at 8:30 p.m.

Montmartrobus

A minibus service for the inhabitants of the steep streets that snake around the Hill of the Martyrs. It's a few years old, enchanting, hardly publicized, and as yet sussed out by only a handful of tourists. For one ticket, or free with *Carte Orange, Carte Jaune*, or *Carte Paris Visite*, you get a breathless, bumpy, roller-coaster ride from Pigalle to the end of the line at Métro Jules Joffrin. On the way you are treated to the Moulin de Galette, the place des Tertres, the lovely place des Abbesses, the pure-Utrillo rue Tholoze, the centuries-old Montmartre vineyards, and more views up and down each winding street than you can take in. If the scenery goes by too fast, you can hop off, take pictures or merely wander and gasp, and catch the next bus in 10 minutes or so. The return trip takes a slightly different route, if anything even more *pittoresque et historique*. The drivers are nerveless and daunted by nothing: not even a beer *camion* stuck in a hairpin turn will blow their cool. The marvellous thing about Montmartre is that the moment you're out of the sleaze of Pigalle, the landscape reverts to quotidian serenity: an area in which real people live and work as they have for centuries. If you jump off the bus at the northern end (Mairie du XVIIIe) you can pick up a snack lunch in one of the unbelievable places in the rue Poteau, and sit in the exquisite square de Clignancourt among flowers, trees, and children. If you have any luck at all you'll get there when the band is playing in the toy-town bandstand. The Montmartrobus runs every 10 minutes northbound from Pigalle from 7:30 a.m. to 8:00 p.m., returning from the Mairie du XVIIIe with the last southbound bus leaving at 7:50 p.m. promptly.

RATP tours

In addition to these free or almost free bus routes through Paris, the RATP has some extraordinary tours of its own from the place de la

Madeleine (8e) to – among other places – the châteaux of Chambord, Chenonceaux, Poitiers, to Bayeux for the Tapestry, to Colombey-des-Deux-Églises to see de Gaulle's house, to Beaune for the wine country, to Cabourg for Proustiana, to Mont-St-Michel, to Domrémy for the route of Jeanne d'Arc – and even a day trip to Luxembourg if that's a thrill for you.

For information: Services Touristiques de la RATP, place de la Madeleine, near the flower market. Pick up the folder called 'Excursions (plus de 100 circuits)' from major Métro stations and all railway stations. Prices are low, compared to commercial bus tours, but you will need at least a minimal command of French to make sure you understand their instructions about leaving times and boarding places. They also have guided tour buses to Versailles, Malmaison, Paris by night, and so on, but only in French.

Footwork

The Batignolles

Just north of the Gare St-Lazare, 8e, in the web of streets named after European capitals, begins a pleasantly varied, fairly gentle cluster of neighbourhoods. Heading north up the rue de Rome, you begin to run into music stores: *luthiers*, guitar-makers, violin shops, sellers of sheet-music. This was, until 1991, the *quartier* of the Paris Conservatoire, now moved to La Villette. But the bar-tabacs, cafés and restaurants that cater to music students are still here; the prices are accordingly low and the whole neighbourhood is a find for the pauper astray in Paris. And it leads you, very quickly, into an oasis of calm. Take a left on the boulevard des Batignolles, past the Théâtre Hébertot, and you are in the beginning of the rue de Lévis – a street market, jammed on Saturday mornings, which most tourists miss because they've never heard of it. This leads to an airy little square, and you are in the rue Legendre, heading towards Montmartre. In three blocks, you've arrived at the Église Ste-Marie. Behind it is the square des Batignolles – placid, delightful, a good place to sit for a while. It's a small park rather than a 'square', and contains a series of artificial duckponds, a carousel, and raked gravel paths. If you're still energetic, continue eastward and gradually uphill into Montmartre. The Batignolles is a backwater of calm in Paris – quiet, unimposing houses, a *petit-bourgeois* population. At one edge is the place de Clichy, the epitome of sleaze; at the other, the tracks that lead back to the Gare St-Lazare. In between, absolute peace.

The rue Mouffetard and the Fifth

Since medieval days, the precincts of the 5e *arrondissement* have been the student quarter of Paris. The rue Mouffetard itself has somewhat more diverse origins. It began as a Roman road from Lyons, developed into a rich residential area in the 12th to 14th centuries, then fell into the hands of skinners, tanners and dyers (the Gobelins factory nearby is the only remnant of this period). The resulting stench gave the street its name: *mouffette* is French for skunk.

The Mouffetard today consists of a street market at its southern end, and a string of small shops and restaurants running north: *boulangeries, triperies, boucheries chevalines* (for horsemeat), *fromageries*. The restaurants run mostly to Greek, Arab, and Vietnamese/Chinese food. Everything here is startlingly good value: it's impossible to pinpoint a restaurant that offers a better meal than its neighbour, for about 45–60F, usually with reasonably drinkable wine and service thrown in.

At its north end, the rue Mouffetard becomes the rue Descartes. At no. 39, now a restaurant, the poet Verlaine lived and died – it has always been a *quartier* for the artist, the writer, the poet, the student, the poor scholar, and although it has been thoroughly discovered by generations of tourists, the Mouffetard and its neighbouring streets remain triumphantly what they are.

The surrounding streets include the rue Geoffroy-St-Hilaire with the only fully fledged mosque in Paris; the Arènes de Lutèce (remains of a Roman arena), the place Monge (outdoor market), the Panthéon, and the Bibliothèque Ste-Geneviève, probably the first use of structural steel supports and lots of glass, worth having a look at. The 5e is loaded with schools, technical colleges, branches of the sprawling University of Paris, and at odd times of the day bands of students flood the streets. It's wonderful walking country. The most you'll spend, perhaps, will be the price of a good, cheap lunch or a sandwich eaten sitting on a college wall, or, extravagantly, a coffee, sitting at a café table resting your feet and watching the world of student Paris wander by.

Rue St-Dominique and the Seventh

The 7e is rich but sterile. You'll see that the hotels and restaurants we have picked in this area are rather few and far between. Lots of trees, wide streets, and most of the *arrondissement* seems to be made up of the Tour Eiffel and its gravelly park, and the Invalides – haunted grandeur, with Napoleon's tomb as the major *frisson*. In general, we find the neighbourhood parched and almost devoid of interest, certainly very low on anything that counts for strolling, listening, enjoying the free delights of Paris.

But turn the corner off the boring boulevard de la Tour Mauborg into the rue St-Dominique, and it's like opening the top of a magic trunk. Bustle, shops, sales, ebullient cross-bred dogs instead of blanketed Yorkshire terriers, girls in tight skirts and men in faded jeans, a most typical and joyous neighbourhood restaurant or two (see pages 135–7), even a few hotels that are worthy of note (pages 75–8). The little side-streets that run off from St-Dominique are equally beautiful, and it's almost impossible to believe that a 100 yards away are the flat-faced, dull apartment buildings and pompous antique shops. Spend half a day in this neighbourhood: you'll spend almost no money unless you decide to splurge on a down-filled ski jacket for a big 150F, or a slightly used Christian Dior scarf from a street barrow.

Another startling street that redeems the whole 7e from its sterility is the little rue Cler, a pedestrian precinct that is like a microcosm of a French provincial town set down whole in one of the richer areas of Paris. The shopping is entrancing, and there is an hotel (see page 76) which has a faithful year-after-year clientele, French, English, American, Japanese. Perhaps there are other rue Clers and rue St-Dominiques which we haven't found; if so, we apologize to the 7e and next year perhaps we will have the time to discover its 'villages'.

The astonishing Eighth

One of the least homogeneous *arrondissements* of Paris that we've encountered is the 8e, which ranges from the quiet music-student life beyond Gare St-Lazare, to the bustling commercial area around Au Printemps department store, the boulevard Haussmann, and the rue Caumartin; and takes in the supreme elegance of the rue Royale and the place de la Madeleine. Imagine a neighbourhood that encompasses both a public bath-house where a hot shower costs 5F50, and the super-luxury atmosphere of Fauchon, the most expensive food shop in the world! Hermès, with its silk scarves and perfectly made saddlery-stitched handbags – 4000F is nothing here – is in the rue Boissy d'Anglas. So is Lanvin, which seems to exhale Arpège from its windows.

Look into the lovely Jeu de Paume on the edge of the place de la Concorde to see if there's an exhibition there. If you think of having a meal within 1,000 yards of its doors, be prepared to blow the week's budget – Maxim's is a few steps away. Yet in the same street that houses the creations of the couturiers is a pleasant little café which feeds the mannequins and the *vendeuses* (not the customers, of course) for about 60F a lunch. The Hôtel Crillon is only a few feet away from the American Embassy, and it costs nothing to smell the expensive hyacinths in its window-boxes, or to sit for a few minutes in the downy chairs in the lobby (looking as though you are waiting for a rich friend). Yet in the immediate neighbourhood, just off the place de la Madeleine, is a very good, moderately priced hotel (see page 78), such remarkable value that it is only sheer generosity that makes us put it in this book, instead of keeping the name for a few favoured friends.

The bit of the 8e that surrounds the Gare St-Lazare is too little known to those who merely take trains or buses from the station. Real people live here, work here, send their children to school, look for jobs, buy flowers and pastry, newspapers, electric toasters, shoes, get their hair done and their cars repaired. Walk along the rue Rocher, or the rue de Vienne, have a very good meal at a price that would not even buy you a pub lunch in London; go into a sheet-music shop in the rue de Rome, and you might find a flat, a cello, a baby-sitter, a ride to Marseilles, a tandem bicycle or a chance to play chamber music. Towards the river, it is mink jacket country; but even paupers can drop in for a free spray of the new Hermès scent.

The 8e is not as beautiful or as historic as the Marais, not as bubbling as the student quarter, the 5e, not as snobbish as St-Germain-des-Prés, not as pretentious as Passy and the 16e – it's dead at night, except for the rich sweeping out of Maxim's – but for daytime walking its mix of characteristics makes it very special indeed.

The unknown Eleventh

This *arrondissement* seems to go on for ever – a huge sprawling collection of neighbourhoods which have grown together without having much in common. At one end, it begins at the place de la Bastille – almost unrecognizable now that it is dominated by the monstrous new Opéra looming like a beached ocean liner at the eastern edge. Streets radiating out from the place, once shabby, characterful, and crowded with family-run shops and humble restaurants, have been blasted out of existence, and rebuilt in new shapes since this 'artistic' complex has gone up.

The *Onzième*, however, is so big and so varied that it will survive everything, even the yuppification of the Bastille area. The rue St-Antoine is still the street of furniture-makers. The place d'Aligre (page 240) remains a real flea market, surrounding the fruit and vegetable stalls, tiny shops and the big covered market.

To get the flavour of the Eleventh, take the No. 46 bus from the Gare du Nord, which goes past the Bastille, to the rue de Charonne, the Faidherbe-Chaligny Métro stop – there are some wonderful restaurants around here – or all the way out to the Porte Dorée for the African Museum and the Château de Vincennes. If you get off the bus at Faidherbe-Chaligny, walk slowly down the rue de Reuilly. Have a look in the window of Christ et Rudel for the most extraordinary collection of knobs and knockers. Look into the *junqueries* along the rue de Chanzy. In the rue de Charonne, there's the extraordinary Palais de la Femme, a women's hostel, with a really fine restaurant open to everyone (see pages 146–7).

One of the most interesting streets is the rue Godefroi Cavagnac: at no. 16 catch the chef's shop flashing with copper pots. At Lumière Diffusion, great hi-tech lamps like science-fiction creatures, from 250F up. Graphics at no. 12, Kie Kai for Chinese furniture at no. 4, and at the Centre Esthetic, the really vain can have a perm for their *eyelashes*. At the passage de la Folie Regnault, look into Mikado for *faux-bois*, *faux-marbre*, *trompe-l'oeil* finishes. In rue de Charonne, Chéri Bibi for fantasy hats, la Vieille Lanterne for exquisite old books, framing, small precious objects.

A long and lovely street in the Eleventh is the rue Jean-Pierre Timbaud, named for a hero of the Resistance of World War II: it runs from the boulevard du Temple to the boulevard Belleville in the north. Here you will find little shops crammed with semi-antique and real, low-priced junk. One of our favourite restaurants, Au Trou Normand (page 144), is at no. 9. There's a triangular mini-park with a drinking-water fountain. At the Vietnamese Hoa Binh, no. 82, you could lunch for 42F. Foto 2 sells prints showing the neighbourhood as it was a century ago. At Fondation Animaux, no. 90, you can adopt a stray kitten or just buy a postcard to benefit abandoned animals of Paris. No. 2 is a smart re-sale shop with some very classy clothes, and near it, a place sells unbelievably cheap T-shirts from bins. At the other end, as you approach the Chinese/Vietnamese/Arab/Jewish *quartier* of Belleville, you could eat different food every day of the week.

Down near the Gare de Lyon is what is known to the *Brigade des Stups* (the drug squad) as the Golden Triangle. Up near the avenue de la République, around the Métro stops Parmentier, St-Maur, Père Lachaise, the *quartier* is staid bourgeois. At the place de la République, you can buy T-shirts at Tati for 15F, or spend £75 a night in a big posh hotel. Just off the boulevard Ménilmontant, you could visit the Edith Piaf museum; not far away, see where Maurice Chevalier once lived; and at Père Lachaise, see where Colette, Gertrude Stein, and Jim Morrison now lie. All and much, much more, in the Eleventh – still unknown to most visitors to Paris.

The other Paris

Jewish, Tunisian, Algerian. If you have a fancy for seeing what foreign parts of Paris are like, take the Métro to Pyrénées or Belleville, in the 19e/20e, on a Saturday night after sundown, or from about 9 o'clock on Sunday morning. Walk the length of rue Belleville, and here you will find that the old traditional Jewish working-class quarter is gradually meeting and mingling with the new wave of Arab, Chinese, Vietnamese Paris, without political thought or collision. Belleville dies at sundown on Friday, comes alive again on Saturday nights and Sundays. Whatever the weather, all Belleville is out on the street, talking, eating, embracing, arguing, smoking, shopping. Here you gradually begin to realize that almost every face you see is male. Arab women, if they have been brought to Paris, keep steadfastly to their houses and families. The Arab man in Paris lives to work, and works very often in the low-end job no one else wants to do. On weekends, they are all out drinking coffee in crowded cafés and socializing on street corners. The women, if any, are buying fruit, vegetables, dripping-sweet pastries, fresh-killed chickens.

Here in the rue Belleville and the rue Ramponeau, you have the feeling of being surrounded by a world infinitely more exotic than anywhere else in Paris. Half a dozen varieties of Arabic, plus Yiddish or a strange French heavily injected with words from both languages, are all around you.

It is true that the civilization of North Africa has affected Parisian life in all its aspects. Hardly a quarter of Paris (except perhaps the stuffy 7e and the formal 15e and 16e *arrondissements*) is without its restaurant serving couscous, *mloukhia*, *merguez*, *bric à l'oeuf*, sugary Oriental pastries. But none is like Belleville.

In the last few years, the racial mix of Belleville has been further enriched by a new wave of South-East Asian residents, with their restaurants, shops, and mini-supermarkets. The Belleville area, historically, is the preserve of not very well-to-do Jews, many who survived concentration camps, many strictly orthodox. Then came the influx of Arabs, many North African Jews, and now the people from the Far East. It is intensely alive, with a cosmopolitan mixture of cinemas, posters, news-stands, food stalls. If you want to get your hair cut on a Sunday, make for Belleville.

If you are there on a Sunday morning, and of an adventurous turn of mind, go into one of the numerous places that sell take-away food. A *sandwich tunisien* is a North African/French sandwich: a crusty loaf split open and crammed with tuna, black olives, tomatoes, lettuce, hot green peppers, capers, bathed in an orange sauce that could start a fire. Drink only beer or mineral water, not wine (too sweet and too expensive). Finish with ruinously sweet Arab pastries, and you will have made a very adequate meal, about 18F all told.

Tourists are not exactly fawned upon in Belleville, any more than in Brixton, but nor is the casual stranger sent packing. We suggest you keep a low profile: flashy clothes and expensive cameras will do nothing for your image; at best you'll feel uncomfortable and out of place. But if you can manage not to look or behave like a gawker, there's no reason to avoid the area.

If you decide that you want to see this *quartier*, so rich in life and colour, don't wait, as many of the old, crumbling buildings are going or gone. Bulldozers have done for the worst slums, modern proletariat housing is going up. The boutiques are already moving in, but this richly varied multi-cultural part of Paris can never become banal, its many roots go too deep in the history of the city.

Street scenes

Much of the beauty of Paris, ranging from the small and exquisite to surprising grotesques, is alive and thrilling to the eye and the – possibly furtive – touch of the fingers. Not just the endless turning vistas of streets, trees, mansions and monuments, but the decoration in the form of carvings, capitals and statues which reveal themselves often in unnoticed places, and always free.

Paris churches are part of this 'living museum', and although there is never an admission charge, it's a civilized gesture to leave a few francs in the unobtrusive offering boxes near the doors.

In the oldest surviving church of Paris, St-Julien-le-Pauvre (in the street that bears his name), look for a marvellous group of flying harpies among its 12th-century stone capitals. Otherwise it's a dull little place crowded with columns, which comes to life only when its occupants, an Eastern Catholic sect called the Melchites, sing on Sunday morning.

The oldest bell in Paris is in the tower of the Church of St-Merri, 78 rue St-Martin, 4e – it was cast in 1331. The bell-tower porch of the church of St-Germain-des-Prés was begun in 1040, and two of the windows in the church itself date from the middle of the 11th century; while just outside in the little garden is an astonishing head of a woman by Picasso.

The last period of Gothic architecture, known as the Flamboyant, blazed out as though in reaction to the stark horror of the 15th century (plague, civil war and occupation by the English were all visited on Paris in a space of about 30 years). Perhaps the most fascinating survival is in the vaulted interior of the church of St-Séverin, at 1 rue des Prêtres-St-Séverin, 5e: an extraordinary spiralling central column seems to move and vibrate as it flings upwards and outwards a series of interlocked ribs.

This might be an appropriate place to mention that Paris churches *are* churches, and are primarily for worshippers. It would be wisest and nicest not to talk loudly, walk heavily, or jostle the chairs and benches: and as for the groups of tourists who chatter and flash their way around Notre-Dame, we would cheerfully see them suspended by their cameras from the mouths of gargoyles.

It is almost impossible to write dispassionately about the Sainte-Chapelle, the most queenly example of Gothic architecture of Paris, built to hold relics of the Passion and consecrated in 1248. It is no longer a church, but an historical monument, and in changing identities it has been very nearly vandalized. Its lower chapel now sells guidebooks and cassettes, its frescoed walls are scratched with graffiti. An unforgettable sight of recent years was a bare-footed tourist peacefully eating a sandwich under the great Rose Window.

For uncompromising medieval grimness, have a look at the tower of Jean the Fearless, built about 1374, and tacked on to the Hôtel de Bourgogne, at 20 rue Étienne-Marcel, 2e. At the other extreme is the Hôtel de Sens, aristocratic and elegant, standing at the corner of the rue de l'Hôtel de Ville and rue Figuier, 4e. Its conical tower and superb doorway are among the gems of the Marais. All through this district are scattered beautiful examples of noble buildings of the 16th and 17th centuries, which survived wars, plagues, riots and revolutions but nearly went down in the heedless 20th century. Mercifully, they have been saved, restored, cleaned. See the Hôtel de Lamoignon at 24 rue des Francs-Bourgeois, 3e, dating from 1580, and another beauty, the doorway with pepperpot turrets of the Hôtel de Clisson, even earlier, and now tucked into the National Archives at 58 rue des Archives, 3e.

Centuries later, Paris produced a most tremendous variety of 'pompous' architecture – a riot of academic taste, from about 1850 to 1900, so bad as to be utterly endearing. A classic is the Hôtel de Ville, 4e. Don't miss the main staircase, whose decorations mix up cowboys, Indians, and French merchants wearing solar topis in what seems to be Ceylon or Equatorial Africa.

The Universal Exposition of 1900 produced Art Nouveau and 'Le Style 1900', which has been loved, hated, collected and argued about ever since its birth. Many of Hector Guimard's sinuous, serpent-green Métro entrances still survive, and are now especially prized since the Museum of Modern Art in New York bought a discarded one and re-erected it in its garden.

At 10 rue Pavée, 4e, there's a synagogue designed by Guimard in 1913. A less famous architect, Jules Lavirotte, did a block of flats at 19 avenue Rapp, 7e, that has *everything*: peacocks, butterflies, enamel, entwined flowers, and – peering out of the maze of design – a bust of Ophelia with streaming hair that turns into tendrils of vines. At 33 rue du Champs-de-Mars, not far away, Art Nouveau lilies crawl all over the front.

At the corner of the rue Victor Massé and rue Frochot, 9e, where whores patrol the street from about 4 o'clock in the afternoon, there's a most delightful piece of art deco stained glass set into the walls. And don't fail to see a perfect Paris townscape: the avenue Frochot, a locked private road with sedate houses, small front gardens, and an academy of painting, a prim little island in the midst of squalid Pigalle.

A series of Utrillo paintings unrolls when you walk into the rue Germain-Pilon, 18e, just off the place de Clichy. At no. 13 is a delightful courtyard and house, and nearby is the Grande Boulangerie Viennoise with beautiful painted glass art deco panels bordering its doors. Oddly enough, many Paris bakeries of the early 1900s have these little works of art.

At the top of the street you emerge into the rue des Abbesses – another Utrillo – and nearby is the tranquil place des Abbesses, with a famous, perfectly preserved Guimard Métro entrance.

Paris abounds in statues and carvings on its buildings, balustrades and pedestals – it's impossible to describe or even to list the main ones, and anyway they've been photographed and written about almost to the point of boredom. Our personal picks: the brackets that support the flying buttresses of the church of St-Germain-l'Auxerrois in the place du Louvre, 1er – a delightful nightmare of hippopotamuses, monkeys, madmen, and a rat busily destroying the globe of the world; the heart-stopping 'St Francis in Ecstasy' of the 16th-century master Germain Pilon, in the church of St Jean-St François, at 6-bis, rue Charlot, 3e; the rearing Horses of Marly at the bottom of the Champs-Élysées; and the Seated Lion, by the 19th-century sculptor Barye, on the quay side of the Tuileries.

Scheduling

Prime time for Paris-watching varies for various events.

Early morning (really early) from about 7:00 a.m., is the time to see what Parisians are really made of. For the most part, they actively enjoy work. Sidewalks are sluiced and swept, shopfronts washed down (with soap and polishing cloths), market stalls are arranged like jewellery shops. The cafés are full of banter.

From noon on, life becomes more leisurely. Lunch may be drawn out over a couple of hours; by 4:00 p.m. the population strolls rather than bustles. At dusk, the fountains and monuments are illuminated: at least once, try to be standing in the place de la Concorde, ideally inhaling the scent of money from the Hôtel Crillon, at the magical moment when the lights in the square, along the river, and all up the Champs-Élysées, go on.

Au lit *(Sleeping cheap)*

The hotels that follow have been personally and recently vetted by our experienced Paris people. We emphasize *recently*, because it has been our experience that hotels can change, renovate, redecorate, re-price, go to rack and ruin, even disappear, with extraordinary speed in Paris. Because of the uncertainties of the European economy in 1991–2, we're certain that many hotel prices will have gone up after this book has gone to press. We have done our best, but be warned, and try not to be affronted if what we tell you today is different the day you arrive.

Many of our choices are those officially classed as 1-star in the *Guide des Hôtels* produced by the Office de Tourisme in Paris. They collect their information from three professional bodies (the Syndicat Général de l'Industrie Hôtelière, the Chambre Syndicale des Hôteliers, Cafétiers, Restaurateurs de Paris, and the Syndicat National des Chaînes d'Hôtels et de Restaurants). With all that expertise, you aren't taking much of a chance. This professionalism means that hotels have been inspected for adherence to certain standards, their prices registered, their amenities and number of rooms verified.

On the whole, the *Guide des Hôtels* is accurate, but between the time the data comes in and publication date, many things – including prices – can alter, especially if the hotel has upgraded its services or accommodation.

Every hotel we have included here is clean, well run, and well above what we would consider minimum standard of comfort. A certain number we have found are actually classed as 2-star, but with prices that bring them within our budget. Most of them are, as you would expect, walk-ups, but a surprising number even of 1-star hotels have lifts, which makes life easier for those with luggage, with small children, or for older people. Many of the hotels now have a telephone in each room, and a switchboard service night and day.

In most cases, someone on the hotel staff speaks English, and where no English is spoken we have noted the fact. You will then have to get by with smiles, goodwill, and a little French remembered from school.

The price of every room in any hotel vetted by the Tourist Office must be displayed at the registration desk and again in the room. Most hotels display their range of prices and accommodation on an official printed form on the door or an outside window, so you know even before entering what you are getting into. Others may put it up on an inside door. If you go in and don't see it, a polite request will bring it forth.

These days, few hotels include *petit déjeuner* (the Continental breakfast of croissants, bread, jam, coffee, tea or chocolate) in their prices. If it *is* included, and you don't want to eat it or to pay for it without eating it, say so politely but firmly *when you register*, and ask how much the room *alone* costs. Breakfast in an hotel can range from a fairly moderate 15F to a shocking 30F. Even at its cheapest it will be double the price of coffee and croissants taken standing at the *zinc*, the counter of the nearest bar-tabac or brasserie – and there you have the fun of tuning in on the conversation of Parisians going to work.

The 1-star classification of hotels is rather a loose mesh, taking in anything from a very clean, well-run hotel with a fax machine, and only 10 minutes from Beaubourg – efficient but not the friendliest in the world – to a strange hostelry where the hot water runs out early, the towels are child-size, the proprietor never visible – but where you can have *charcuterie* lunches in your room, or hang dripping laundry from the radiators, without anyone taking the least bit of notice. A sweet, rather shabby, friendly place located near the rue St-Honoré is 1-star, and so are some others which we think will soon climb into the 2-star category.

One or two of the hotels we have found have no stars at all, although they are comfortable and spotless – many of them hope to be reclassified for the next *Guide des Hôtels*, but the inspectors haven't got around to them yet.

On the whole, we have found that even in the time of inflation you can get a single room with a *cabinet de toilette* (that is, basin, bidet, and constant supply of really hot water) in a pleasant hotel for as little as 90F. A double room with a big bed is even more of a bargain, as it costs as little as 155F even in a very remarkable hotel in the Marais. If you want a shower, expect to pay from 130F for a single, and up to 250F for a double room with a large bed. Twin beds, and a bath instead of a shower, can push prices up to 300F, a few go as high as 450F – a considerable climb over prices a few years ago, but in every case well worth the money.

In terms of other capital city prices, even the most expensive hotels in our list are not exorbitantly priced. Often the price of a room with a complete bathroom – shower or bath and WC and basin – will be the same whether it's occupied by one or two people. Less expensive rooms, those with basin only, or with basin and bidet, may charge a lower price for one person, and put it up slightly for double occupancy. For a small supplemental charge, a third bed can usually be put in a double room so that it sleeps three or even four, bringing the price per person down sharply.

Rooms that have no lavatory are always within 10 feet or so of such a facility, and every hotel we have listed is careful to keep a shower or a bath on almost every floor, for which you can expect to pay about at least 15F, and up to 22F for each use. You'd be surprised at how clean you can keep without a daily bath, in a room with that luxurious and versatile necessity, the bidet.

Expect to pay the highest rates for location: near the Opéra, around the Louvre, almost anywhere in the 1er, 6e, 7e, 8e, or 16e. St-Germain des Prés, which was for decades the refuge of the poor traveller, is now one of the costliest areas of Paris. A few old faithful hotels in the much loved Latin Quarter, 5e, try to keep their prices down, but they seem to be closing for good or else renovating and upgrading. The Grand Hôtel des Balcons, near the universities, was home from home for generations of American, English and German students. It finally tottered under the weight of breadcrumbs, empty wine bottles and dripping laundry, and was renovated, now wearing well-deserved extra stars.

If you are willing to spend an extra 10 minutes on the Métro, away from the tourist heart of Paris, you can save from 30F to 50F a day. Some of our hotels are in what may seem unlikely neighbourhoods often brushed off by travel writers as 'uninteresting, working-class, too far from the action' – beyond the Bastille, around the place de la République, up near the place d'Italie, in quiet Passy, and so forth.

Actually, every one of these *quartiers* has an indigenous life of its own, and many have changed and are changing with great rapidity. We know all these areas ourselves, on foot, and consider every one well worth getting to know. They are often far more truly Parisian than the more obvious areas known as *'historiques et pittoresques'*. In these well-known neighbourhoods, they've seen tourists for generations, and you sometimes have the feeling that they couldn't care less if they never see *you* again. In more out-of-the-way places, you need only to take breakfast two days running, at the counter of a bar-tabac, and the third day it will be 'Bonjour, Monsieur – comme d'habitude?' – the usual? The news-stand person will probably hand you *Le Figaro* before you ask.

Some hotels which have been mentioned repeatedly in guide books begin to lean back and take it easy. In a well-known 1-star hotel in the Quartier d'Europe, our researcher found the shower head had fallen off, the windows didn't quite close, and the blankets were like Kleenex. We dropped it. Now it's being renovated, and we're waiting until the new plumbing is in and the new prices set, to go back to see it again.

One of the hotels we have listed in previous years as 'simple, fairly comfortable, being renovated', etc., was nearly thrown out of this book this year. Two of our readers wrote to us in a high state of indignation about it, citing terrible towels, dirty loos, invisible management, even a black beetle (cockroach). We had already sent someone round to see it after a year's time, and he had reported that it was clean, simply but well renovated, with a good new manager. After hearing from our enraged readers, however, we asked another French friend to see it – a cool-eyed girl whose report we have used in this new edition.

This year many simple hotels are renovating, upgrading, rising from 1-star to a higher status, with prices going up to match. The sensible Paris administration seems to give financial help to small enterprises where needed, but this of course can result in some of our hotels going up in grade and price after we've vetted them. 'NN' against the hotel name means redecorating is imminent.

Most hotels listed here have shaver points with 220-volt current, so you can use your electric razor, blow-dryer, mini-boiler for a cup of tea, and so on. For Americans used to 110 volts, all appliances must be dual voltage, or need a converter (see Electricity, page 251). Many hotels have reading lights above or near the bed, which is a necessity for a lot of us.

If you use the telephone from your hotel, expect it to cost more than a phone box would. It does give you the convenience of having someone deal with getting the number for you, in French. If the *concierge* has done anything extra for you – getting a taxi, theatre tickets, or whatnot – it's polite to leave about 15F in an envelope at the end of your stay. Service charges and TVA (VAT, in English) are included in your final bill, and the chambermaid needn't be tipped, unless of course she has done some washing or ironing chores for you. In this case, leave some money in the ashtray in your room – or in an envelope at the desk.

If you can dust off your school French and smile a lot, you will find that in almost every case the atmosphere in these hotels will be astonishingly warm, personal and friendly. A few phrases of hotel French are on the opposite page, and more general conversation about *la politesse*, which oils the wheels of Paris, on page 274.

Eating and laundry in your room

Many Paris hotels have had their hospitality abused by travellers lured to the city by budget airfares and charters, in the last 15 or 20 years. So they now post polite notices in their lobbies or in their rooms: Please, no eating and no washing. We can well understand this, having seen some hotels almost vandalized by inconsiderate guests. We can only advise that if you *do* want to picnic – and it's a great temptation with all those succulent *pâtés* and jewel-like *pâtisseries* – do it with neatness and discretion. Tidy up after yourself. Don't carry an obvious, warmly smelling roast chicken in a plastic bag right past the desk. Put down newspapers on the floor, pick up your crumbs, don't stain the table with wine-glasses, don't get grease stains and lipstick on the towels. We have eaten in hotel rooms for much of our adult life, from the elegant Montalembert long ago, to several of our favourite small hotels in the 1990s, without anyone ever saying boo.

When it comes to laundry, it's obvious that it isn't the washing, it's the *dripping* that drives Paris hoteliers up the wall. Hangers with wet shirts, draped over radiators, can make a soggy mess of a carpet. In the old Grand Hôtel des Balcons, (now fully renovated and upgraded), students draped wet tights, bras, jeans and jerseys on curtain rails, until even the walls ran with damp.

You'll be washing out your smalls in the basin or bidet, so have the courtesy to blot them reasonably dry in a towel, then hang them over the basin or a tiled floor. That way, no drips will damage the carpet or curtains. If you feel self-conscious about this, wring them as dry as you can, and put them on hangers in the cupboard before the chambermaid comes to clean. While she's not a management spy, it is part of her job to let the front desk know what condition each room is in, each day.

We have found a few things indispensable for staying in modest-priced hotels: some light-weight plastic-coated wire hangers – buy them if you have to from a French supermarket – four or five clothes-peg clips to hang up socks and tights, or to pull together curtains over an open window. An over-sized metal clip from a stationers' shop comes in handy for all sorts of things.

Hôtel French

The notice-board dealing with prices of rooms is often couched in an esoteric shorthand, but once you've cracked the code it's quite easy.

Chambre avec e.c. – room with hot and cold running water, basin, no bidet

Chambre avec cabinet de toilette – room with basin and bidet in their own compartment

Chambre avec douche – room with basin, bidet and shower

Chambre avec bain – basin, bidet and bath (often with a hand shower)

Chambre avec douche/bain et WC – basin, bidet, shower or bath, and lavatory

Petit déjeuner – Continental breakfast (see page 57)

En sus means 'extra charge', e.g. *petit déjeuner en sus, 20F*.

Baths, showers

As noted, if you are staying in a room without these amenities, you can command one by ringing down to the office. The charge will appear on your bill at the end of your stay. Really skinflint travelling couples can manage to work in two showers for the price of one if they are quick and wily, but don't say you read it here.

Part of a poor traveller's experience in Paris can be the public baths. Don't shudder and turn the page. They are clean, supervised by the city, offering showers with plenty of really hot water in private cubicles, and catering to the 700,000 or so Parisians who have no baths in their homes. They are open, usually, Thursdays, Fridays, Saturdays and Sunday mornings, although some of them have other opening days. A fairly fastidious friend agreed to try one for us, and was surprised to find out what an agreeable experience it was. Great value, clean as can be, well-run and efficient. For the current price of 5F50, you get a shower stall and a dressing cubicle with mirror, tiled floor, hooks and shelf, and hot water for 20 minutes. This is plenty of time to get really clean, and to wash your hair. Everything is mopped up between clients. It's a good way to avoid spending 15–20F for a shower at your hotel. See pages 244–5 for addresses and more information.

Finding an hotel on your own

If all the hotels listed here are full, wander around the neighbour-hood you like best, after stashing your luggage at the station. Even have a look at hotels that have no stars at all. They are often clean, respectable, cheap, run by a couple who may not speak much English but want you to be satisfied. If you are staying more than three days, you could try asking if they have a weekly or monthly rate. They save on laundry, you save on hotel costs.

Note: the hotel day begins and ends at noon, sharp, and if you overstay you will be charged for an extra day. Most of the hotels in this book are very good about letting travellers leave a small amount of luggage, coats, and so on (at their own risk, of course) in lobby or office until time for the train or plane. Some, however, have been so thoroughly imposed upon by those who dump rucksacks, skis, car-rier bags and raincoats for days on end, that they are no longer so willing. Others may have little space and really don't want their lobbies cluttered up with the increasingly hideous magenta and bright orange nylon luggage that travelling paupers lug around – don't be offended if they politely refuse to keep them for you. Take the stuff to the nearest *consigne* at a railway station, making careful note of their opening and closing times.

Never book without looking

Go hotel shopping in the middle of the day, or not later than teatime, not at night or when you're dropping with fatigue. If they won't let you look at the room, say a polite 'merci' and be on your way.

For some cheap alternatives to hotels

See Other options, pages 94–7.

Recommended Hotels

1er arrondissement

Hôtel du Lion d'Or 1-star
5 rue de la Sourdière, 1er
Tel: 42 60 79 04
Métro: Tuileries

Room with *cabinet de toilette*	1 person	175F
	2 persons	220
with shower	1 person	220
	2 persons	280
	3 persons	340
with bath	2 persons	320
Petit déjeuner		25
Shower		20

This small hotel on a quiet street is a long-established favourite of *Paupers' Paris* readers. Over the past two years it has added some rooms with bath or shower and WC, and rates have risen somewhat, but not steeply. The location is superb, close to the Louvre, the Palais Royal, the Tuileries, the Seine, and a fair number of good restaurants. It has many regular clients, situated as it is, so book early. VISA, American Express, Access/Mastercard and Euro-cheques with Eurocard accepted. The *patron*, M. Dahmane, speaks excellent English.

Hôtel du Palais 1-star NN
2 quai de la Mégisserie, 1er
Tel: 42 36 98 25
Métro: Pont Neuf, Châtelet

Room with *cabinet de toilette*	1 person	180F
	2 persons	230
with shower	1 person	280
	2 persons	320
with bath and WC	1 person	350
	2 persons	380
Extra bed		70
Petit déjeuner		25
Shower		no charge

Really basic accommodation, this, but the welcome is warm and the
rooms clean – and just at its feet is the delightful plant and flower
market along the Seine. Rooms facing the *quai* have a view of the
river, but will get the noise of traffic continuously – ask for one at
the back of the hotel. The *patrons*, M. and Mme Benoit, say theirs is
the last inexpensive hotel on the *quai*. You might ask if there are
special rates for a week's stay, or off-season. Redecorating is
imminent, and the Palais will probably convert its rooms to higher
categories. A bit of English is spoken, but correspondence should be
in French. All credit cards, and Eurocheques with a Eurocard are
accepted.

Hôtel Richelieu-Nazarin 1-star
51 rue de Richelieu, 1er
Tel: 42 97 46 20
Métro: Palais-Royal, Pyramides

Room with *eau courante*	1 person	160F
	2 persons	180
with shower and WC	1 or 2 persons	250–270
with bath and WC	1 or 2 persons	290
Petit déjeuner		22
Shower		10

A minute hotel – only 14 rooms, and these usually snapped up by
regulars – so to be booked well in advance. It's clean and tidy,
recently redone, panelled in wood, decorated with posters (the
earth seen from the moon), and very pleasantly staffed. Somewhat
noisy on the street side, but location is all: you can hardly stay in a
more central spot – a stone's throw from the gardens of the Palais
Royal. No lift, no credit cards, but the rooms are fine and the *patron*,
M. Daniel, is very efficient. He now speaks some English – but write
for reservations in French.

Résidence Vauvilliers
6 rue Vauvilliers, 1er
Tel: 42 36 89 08
Métro: Les Halles, Louvre

Room with *cabinet de toilette*	1 person	110F
with shower	1 person	145
	2 persons	200

| with bath and WC | 1 or 2 persons | 300 |
| *Petit déjeuner* | | 24 |

Really small, really basic, but very, very central, and to find a hotel so well located at these prices is quite unusual. For two people, a double room with complete bath for about £30 is rare in this part of the city. The Vauvilliers is within walking distance of the Louvre, two Métro stops, the rue de Rivoli, and some of our favourite restaurants. As you can imagine, it is heavily booked the year around, so telephone a couple of weeks in advance if you want to stay here. English is spoken, and things run efficiently. No credit cards, no Eurocheques, cash only. The *patronne* is Mme Religue.

3e arrondissement

Grand Hôtel des Arts-et-Métiers 1-star
4 rue Borda, 3e
Tel: 48 87 73 89
Métro: Arts-et-Métiers

Room with *cabinet de toilette*	1 or 2 persons	160F
with shower or bath	1 or 2 persons	200
with shower and WC	1 or 2 persons	350
Petit déjeuner		18

This hotel has a welcoming and 'sympa' air, according to a Paris correspondent. However, as it is in the process of being renovated, you may fall over painters and plasterers at work. Some rooms have recently had WCs added, and more are being installed in bathrooms. There are telephones in each room, and it is quite prettily decorated considering its low rates. What's more, in the Conservatoire National des Arts et Métiers, just around the corner in the rue St-Martin, you'll find Foucault's Pendulum! The rest of this great jackdaw's nest of a museum is being explored for our next edition. The hotel has applied for an upgrading in status, so rates may go up in late 1992–93, but at the time of writing it is still a 1-star, and a great value.

Hôtel du Chancelier Boucherat 1-star
110 rue de Turenne, 3e
Tel: 42 72 86 83
Métro: Filles du Calvaire

Room with *eau courante*	1 person	150F
	2 persons	170
with *cabinet de toilette*	1 or 2 persons	190
	3 persons	250
with shower	2 persons	250
with shower and WC	2 persons	280
with bath and WC	3 persons	390
	4 persons	420
Petit déjeuner		20
Coffee or tea alone		5
Shower or bath		12

This pleasant, quiet hotel may not be at its best in the height of the
tourist season, but it is trying to improve: tatty carpets replaced, and
a washer and dryer installed. The prices given are not necessarily
those of the cheapest rooms – so you might be lucky and pay less.
And if you arrive between November and May, ask for the winter
prices – they are cheaper. The street is noiseless at night, and
breakfast in the countrified green and white room is inexpensive. If
all you can face in the morning is a cup of tea or coffee, you'll only
pay what a local café would charge. The big room with two double
beds for two couples or a family of three or four, is a very good deal.
English is spoken, and major credit cards and Eurocheques accepted. The *patronne* is Mme Martin.

4e arrondissement

Hôtel Andréa 2-star
3 rue St-Bon, 4e
Tel: 42 78 43 93
Métro: Hôtel de Ville

Room with *eau courante* or	1 person	160F
cabinet de toilette	2 persons	170
with shower	1 person	220–250
	2 persons	280–300

with bathroom and WC	1 person	250
	2 persons	300
Petit déjeuner		20
Shower		15

We liked the good feeling in this hotel, where everything seems solid and the prices are reasonable. The air of *politesse* here is most agreeable, and the people who run it seem to take pride in the comfort of the Hôtel Andréa. The rooms are well decorated, clean, tidy, everything well kept and comfortable. The double room with bath was delightful, with a TV and a terrace from which you could see the dome of the Panthéon across the river. Altogether, a find, since it is very near Beaubourg, walking distance to the river and to Les Halles, and with great transport. The big Samaritaine department store is just around the corner; and the Marais, with its great restaurants, museums, shops of every kind, is a short bus ride or one Métro stop away. English spoken. The *patron* is M. Valls.

Grand Hôtel Jeanne d'Arc 2-star
3 rue Jarente, 4e
Tel: 48 87 62 11
Métro: St-Paul

Room with bath and WC	1 person	300F
	2 persons	350
	3 persons	400
	4 persons	450
Petit déjeuner		27

Now resplendent in its 2-star status, this charming little hotel is very clean, perfectly neat, and decorated in white-lace bourgeois style. It has a lift, the rooms are large and well arranged. As the prices make obvious, it's a better buy for two, three, or four people than for the solitary visitor. The street is peaceful and pretty, in the very heart of the Marais, close to the superb place des Vosges and to many of our best-liked restaurants. English is spoken, and VISA, Access, and Eurocheques with Eurocard accepted. The *patrons* are M. André and Mme Hélène Aymard.

Grand Hôtel Malher 1-star
5 rue Malher, 4e
Tel: 42 72 60 92
Métro: St-Paul

Room with *eau courante*	1 person	120F
with *cabinet de toilette*	1 or 2 persons	150
	3 persons	200
with shower or bath	1 or 2 persons	200
with bath and WC	1 or 2 persons	275
	3 persons	320
Petit déjeuner		20
Shower		15

Just across the street from the Hôtel Sévigné, this hotel is rather a
mystery. Spotless, good carpeting and wallpaper, old-fashioned
wardrobes and bed-frames, marble-floored lobby, perfect location
in the Marais, great restaurants all around, and astounding prices.
On the busy rue Malher, rooms can be noisy, but the rest of the
hotel is almost eerily quiet. No credit cards or traveller's cheques,
but Eurocheques with Eurocards are accepted. The *patronne*, Mme
Fossiez, is calm, soft-spoken and speaks some English.

Hôtel Castex 2-star
5 rue Castex, 4e
Tel: 42 72 31 52 (Fax: 42 72 57 91)
Métro: Bastille, Sully-Morland

Room with shower or bath	1 person	165F
	2 persons	235
with shower and WC	1 person	180
	2 persons	250
	with two wide twin beds	260
with bath and WC	2 persons	290
Petit déjeuner		25

This little family hotel has been overhauled, and raised to a 2-star
rating, and it deserves it. The prices are remarkably low for the
location in the Marais, and for the amenities offered. A room with
single beds and a bathroom is a bargain for three people. All the
rooms now have either a shower or a bath, and a telephone. The

hotel has a fax machine, so you can speed them your request for a room in French or English. The rue Castex isn't one of the really picturesque streets of the Marais, but only two minutes away, across the rue St-Antoine, is the historic place des Vosges. To feel wealthy for a day, on a pauper's money, take a picnic lunch to the well-groomed gardens. The Castex accepts VISA and Access cards. The *patrons* are M. and Mme Bouchand.

Hôtel de Nice 1-star
42 bis, rue de Rivoli, 4e
Tel: 42 78 55 29 (Fax: 42 78 36 07)
Métro: Hôtel de Ville, St-Paul

Room with *cabinet de toilette*	1 or 2 persons	220F
	3 persons	270
with shower and WC	2 persons	300
with bath and WC	2 persons	330
Petit déjeuner		25
Shower		no charge

We have always liked this hotel, which has a lift, and is well painted and wallpapered, clean, and run by helpful English-speaking people. However, traffic on the rue de Rivoli is continuous, night and early morning, and you are advised to take ear-plugs. The site is superb, only minutes from Beaubourg and on the edge of the Marais. Very popular, so book at least a month in advance for peak periods; reservations should be accompanied by a deposit for the first night's lodging – traveller's cheques in francs only, or Eurocheques. VISA, Access and Eurocheques with a Eurocard are accepted. In the larger double rooms, an extra bed can be added for a reasonable supplement of 80F. The *patrons* are M. and Mme Vaudoux.

Hôtel Pratic
9 rue d'Ormesson, 4e
Tel: 48 87 80 47
Métro: St-Paul

Room with *eau courante*	1 person	120F
with *cabinet de toilette*	1 person	170
	2 persons	175–180
with shower	2 persons	210

with shower or bath and WC	2 persons	280

No *petit déjeuner*
Shower   15

Clean, and with evidence of extensive renovation: hall and staircase, showers and bathrooms, and almost all the rooms have been redone. The Pratic closes at 2:00 a.m., which is not unreasonable. The staff are a trifle cool, though always correct. But the prices are *rock bottom*. No credit cards, but traveller's cheques (in francs only) and Euro-cheques (with a 37F surcharge) accepted. The *gerant* is M. Zaidi.

Hôtel Sévigné 2-star
2 rue Malher, 4e
Tel: 42 72 76 17
Métro: St-Paul

Room with shower	1 person	240F
	2 persons	282
	3 persons	370
with shower and WC	1 person	291
	2 persons	320
with bath and WC	1 person	324
	2 persons	340
	3 persons	440
Petit déjeuner		included

Long ago this good hotel was known as the Grand Hôtel du Sud et du Pôle du Nord, and we can't help feeling that the new, more aristocratic name doesn't have the same flavour. The old easy-going atmosphere is gone, but it's still well run, and extremely clean and tidy. Unusually for a hotel so well renovated, they will accept three people to a room, which brings down the price per occupant; and if you and your companion share a double bed, that's cheaper too. Every room has a bath or shower, and there's a minute padded lift. To reach it, however, you must walk up half a flight from the lobby. The receptionists usually speak good English. Drawback: one side of the hotel is actually on the rue de Rivoli, with its continuous traffic. On Friday nights when the motorbikes seem to rally at the Bastille down the street it is NOISY. Ask for a room on the rue de Sévigné side, and pack ear-plugs. Traveller's cheques and Euro-cheques with Eurocards accepted, but no credit cards at the moment. The *patron* is M. Claude Rantier.

Hôtel Stella 1-star
14 rue Neuve-St-Pierre, 4e
Tel: 42 72 23 66
Métro: St-Paul

Room with *eau courante*	1 person	195F
	2 persons	220
with shower	1 person	225
with shower and WC	2 persons (double bed)	285
with bath and WC	2 persons (twin beds)	300
Petit déjeuner		20
Shower		20

One of the several unrelated Hôtels Stella in Paris, this small one is wonderfully located in a quiet street in the Marais, near the rue St-Antoine. For several years, it was considered one of the more basic, simple hotels of this increasingly fashionable neighbourhood. But it seems to have been through a bad patch a year or two ago, and clients complained, quite rightly, about the state of affairs. Now, however, it has a new *patron*, M. Nicholas Vivant, and is part of Les Jardins de Paris hotel chain. So, cautiously, we are suggesting it for its new look, and for its surroundings – many fine and inexpensive restaurants, five minutes' walk to the Bastille, two minutes to the Métro St-Paul or to the river. Traveller's cheques accepted, and Eurocheques (with a 10 per cent surcharge).

5e arrondissement

Hôtel le Central
6 rue Descartes, 5e
Tel: 46 33 57 93
Métro: Cardinal Lemoine, Monge

Room with shower or bath	1 person	130–150F
	2 persons	190
with shower, basin and bidet	3 persons	220

Basic is the word that springs to mind for this useful hotel, in the centre of the student quarter, next to the Polytechnic of Paris. You wouldn't want to spend long dreamy hours here, it's really a place to sleep and to get ready for a busy day in this historic and endlessly interesting area. Nearby: the Cluny Museum, the Luxembourg Gardens, boulevard St-Germain, bookshops everywhere, plenty of places to eat, sit, gaze. But we have to pass on the comment of an English college student, well versed in cheap Paris hotels, 'The communal toilet I saw is so small that the advantage of being a man is not applicable!' But as he says, it's simple, clean, and the location is one of the best on the Left Bank. Book well in advance, this hotel is very well known on the student grapevine. Eurocheques are accepted as a deposit for a booking, but not in payment for the actual stay. As you would expect, no credit cards. No English is spoken, but somehow the residents get along. The *patron* is M. Julio Neiva.

Grand Hôtel d'Harcourt 2-star NN
3 boulevard St-Michel, 5e
Tel: 43 26 52 35
Métro: St-Michel

Room with *cabinet de toilette*	1 person	205F
	2 persons	270
with shower	1 person	240
	2 persons	300
with bath and WC	1 person	260
	2 persons	340
Petit déjeuner		25

A redone 2-star *with a lift* in an area where prices are usually over the top. It faces the St-Michel fountain, and is a short walk from Notre-Dame, the Cluny Museum, Luxembourg Gardens, and the liveliness of the streets around St-Michel and St-Germain. Rooms are freshly painted and papered, and each has a TV. There's a spacious breakfast room, and even in summer a bed is sometimes available on very short notice. The street can be noisy, early and late into the night, so take ear-plugs. VISA, American Express, Eurocheques with Eurocards accepted. The *patron*, M. Abed, speaks good English, and the reception is genuinely friendly.

Hôtel des Grandes Écoles 2-star
75 rue du Cardinal Lemoine, 5e
Tel: 43 26 79 23
Métro: Cardinal Lemoine

Room with *eau courante*	1 person	260–320F
with *cabinet de toilette* (with use of shower free)	1 or 2 persons	400
with shower or bath and WC	2 persons	470
Extra bed		100
Petit déjeuner		30

'Unquestionably my favourite hotel, quite expensive but not as high as other places on the Left Bank which are much less beautiful and friendly,' says our Paris friend. To reach this unbelievably pretty hotel, you walk through a rustic-looking courtyard off the rue Cardinal Lemoine. Turn the corner, and you see a miniature country mansion in its own gardens. The rooms are delightful, each decorated differently – and the elegance and charm of the furniture and decorations are worthy of at least two more stars. There's a lift, but the hotel's not very accessible for anyone with a wheelchair, as there are steps up to the entrance door. English is spoken; telephone reservations are taken between 2:00 p.m. and 6:00 p.m. VISA, Access cards accepted. The very agreeable *patronne* is Mme Le Floch. It is wise to book at least two weeks ahead in high seasons, and a week before even in quieter months.

6e arrondissement

Delhy's Hôtel 2-star NN
22 rue de l'Hirondelle, (6 place St-Michel) 6e
Tel: 43 26 58 25
Métro: St-Michel

Room with *eau courante*	1 person	150F
	2 persons	200
with *cabinet de toilette*	1 or 2 persons	200–250
with shower	1 or 2 persons	300
Petit déjeuner		20
Bath or shower		20

Delhy's is in a pretty little narrow street leading off the busy boulevard St-Michel, and if you like the Left Bank you couldn't want a better place to stay. It's basic, clean, and very quiet – that alone makes it a find in this fairly noisy neighbourhood. There are no rooms with private bathrooms, but some do have showers.

Obviously, the rooms with *cabinet de toilette* (basin and bidet) are more comfortable than the very slightly less expensive ones with basin only. Surprisingly, VISA and Access/Mastercharge cards are accepted, and Eurocheques with Eurocard. Everyone here is pleasant, and English is spoken. M. Ali Kenniche and his wife Mme Françoise Kenniche are the helpful *patrons*. Book a month in advance in high season, 10 days ahead in spring or autumn.

Hôtel Nesle
7 rue de Nesle, 6e
Tel: 43 54 62 41
Métro: Odéon

Room with shower	1 person	180F
	2 persons	240
Petit déjeuner		included

The Hôtel Nesle is a riot. Full of students and back-packers, it has the atmosphere of the laid-back, what the hell 1960s. It may seem chaotic, but the *patronne*, Renée, runs the place with benign autocracy and a nice sense of fantasy. Each room is decorated in a different style – one is 'Grandma's room', with lace, old furniture, sepia photographs; another has medieval murals. If you're travelling alone, and are willing to share your twin-bedded room, you'll only be charged 120F. There's a Turkish bath, the 'Hammam', with deep blue tiling and lion's head basin, and a washer and dryer for the use of clients. Breakfast is served on brass trays to the sound of Arab music – and staff and guests join forces to keep the everything going. One day when we were there, an American motorcyclist was helping plant shrubs in the terrace-level garden behind the hotel. Drawbacks? Some of the rooms are small, and the partitions thin, so it might be noisy. Booking weeks in advance is imperative, especially if there's a big jazz or rock event scheduled, when fans congregate at the Nesle. Cash only, and paid in advance when you arrive.

Regent's Hôtel 2-star
44 rue Madame, 6e
Tel: 45 48 02 81 (Fax: 45 44 85 73)
Métro: St-Sulpice

Room with shower and WC	1 or 2 persons	370F
with bath and WC	2 persons	420

Extra person	100
Petit déjeuner	32

Almost too expensive, we said a few years ago – and prices have gone up a bit since then. But if you want to spend your money on a relaxing, comfort-filled stay rather than on opera, music or films, this is the place. The little garden is beautiful, full of flowers, and breakfast is served there in good weather. The hotel itself is quiet, clean, neat, respectable, and gives you space, ease, a feeling of being lapped in comfort without the cost of a 3- or 4-star luxury hotel. It has a lift. We advise booking well ahead in high seasons, as the Regent's is known to French travellers who like easy charm at affordable prices. VISA, Access cards accepted, Eurocheques with a Eurocard, and American Express traveller's cheques. English is spoken, but it is best to write for a reservation in French if you can, using the Tourist Office form letter as a guide (see page 13). The *patron* is M. Crétey.

7e arrondissement

Hôtel du Champ de Mars 2-star NN
7 rue du Champ-de-Mars, 7e
Tel: 45 51 52 30
Métro: École-Militaire

Room with shower and WC	1 or 2 persons	300F
with bath and WC	1 or 2 persons	330
	2 persons (twin beds)	360
	3 persons	430
Petit déjeuner		30

Rates here have hardly gone up in the two years since we last wrote about the Champ-de-Mars. It's not the cheapest hotel in Paris, but given the superb location, and the fact that it's a 2-star, it's a good buy for two people visiting Paris. The solo traveller may find the rates rather high. Our French researcher this year remarked that it was 'clean, nice, cosy – some rooms not as bright as others, but as it has a lift and is on a delightful street, I'd recommend it.' The street is 'neighbourhood' Paris, and endlessly fascinating. At night it's very quiet. Have your morning coffee in a neighbouring café or *tabac*. It will be much more interesting, and considerably cheaper than *petit déjeuner* at the hotel. Little or no English is spoken, so this is a good place to polish up your French. VISA and Access cards accepted, and Eurocheques on all banks except those of the UK. The *patron* is M. Guillochon.

Grand Hôtel Leveque 1-star NN
29 rue Cler, 7e
Tel: 47 05 49 15
Métro: École-Militaire

Room with *eau courante*	1 or 2 persons	180–195F
	3 persons	260
with shower	1 or 2 persons	260–275
with bath and WC	1 or 2 persons	285–300
	3 persons	370
Extra bed		80
Petit déjeuner		20
Shower		no charge

Most of the 7e *arrondissement* is so correct, so sterile, that it's a happy shock when you turn a corner and stumble into anything as full of life as the rue Cler. It's a pedestrian street busy in the daytime with a street market and many shops. At night, it quietens down to a pleasant hush. The Hôtel Leveque is a walk-up, and we like the rooms on the top two floors best – so this is a hotel meant for the fit. The rooms are well furnished, and the upper ones light and airy. Some of the rooms are big enough for three people to share, so a room with a complete bath and three beds must be one of the best value-for-money offers in this neighbourhood. English is spoken, and despite the lack of a lift, those who stay here seem to settle in and stay for ever. Reserve well ahead, especially in high season. VISA, Access and Eurocheques with a Eurocard accepted. The *patronne* is Mme Fouchet.

Hôtel Malar 1-star
29 rue Malar, 7e
Tel: 45 51 38 46
Métro: Latour-Maubourg

Room with shower	1 person	230F
	2 persons	260

with shower and WC	1 person	280
	2 persons	320
with bath and WC	1 or 2 persons	310
Petit déjeuner		22

The Malar is well known to savvy travellers – we can't claim it as our discovery. All the rooms have showers or baths, many have WCs, and an *appartement* for four people at 550F is spectacular value. Several of the double rooms can accommodate a third bed at a supplement of only 110F, useful for a travelling family or three really good friends. Perhaps the atmosphere is somewhat more formal and 'correct' than it was when we first saw it years ago – due, no doubt, to the pressure of those tourists who have discovered the 7e *arrondissement*. The Malar is still a pleasant place to stay, and you will love the *quartier*. English is spoken. The Hôtel Malar accepts AMEX, VISA, Access, Diners' Club cards, and Eurocheques with a Eurocard. The *patron* is M. Attoun.

Hôtel Prince 2-star
66 avenue Bosquet, 7e
Tel: 47 05 40 90 (Fax: 47 53 06 62)
Métro: École-Militaire

Room with shower and WC	1 person	300F
	2 persons	400–430
with bath and WC	2 persons	450
	3 persons	490
Petit déjeuner		30

This hotel, a favourite of ours for nearly 10 years, was in the throes of complete redecoration and renovation in the summer of 1991. The new plans seem to justify the jump in room rates. There's to be a garden for its clients, and a new room for handicapped travellers. All rooms are being refurnished, all have bathrooms, with baths or showers, and all will have TVs. A pretty new reception room on the ground floor is in the making. There is a lift, and the Prince is located in one of the more interesting parts of the 7e *arrondissement*. The avenue Bosquet is the epitome of *haut-bourgeois* Paris. Although it has a lot of traffic, rooms facing on the street are double-glazed for quiet. Reserve several weeks in advance, as it is very popular with French families and business people from all over the country. English and German are spoken, and the *patron*, M. Roussel, and his son, are endlessly helpful. American Express, VISA, Access cards accepted, Eurocheques with a Eurocard.

Le Royal Phare 2-star
40 avenue de la Motte-Picquet, 7e
Tel: 47 05 57 30 (Fax: 45 51 64 41)
Métro: École-Militaire

Room with shower and WC	1 or 2 persons	260–300F
with bath and WC	1 or 2 persons	320
Petit déjeuner		25

M. Le Rousic, the *patron*, speaks little English but understands it well and is always busy but helpful. The hotel has been redone over the years, and his personal involvement really shows. The Royal Phare has a lift, TVs in the rooms, and there are reading lights at the beds, something many Paris hotels do not have. A happy atmosphere and very good value, and close to excellent shopping (a good Prisunic and Fran-Prix), and to the charm of the rue Cler for more shopping, strolling and gazing. The avenue de la Motte-Picquet traffic begins early, about 7:00 a.m., if that matters to you, but it's quiet at night. AMEX, VISA, Access cards accepted, also traveller's cheques, Eurocheques with a Eurocard, possibly a surcharge for these last.

8e arrondissement

Hôtel de Marigny 2-star
11 rue de l'Arcade, 8e
Tel: 42 66 42 71
Métro: St-Lazare

Room with *cabinet de toilette*	1 or 2 persons	170F
with shower	1 or 2 persons	205
with shower or bath and WC	1 or 2 persons	300
Petit déjeuner		27

A truly remarkable bargain, if you can manage to get one of the six 170F rooms in this charming 2-star establishment. It's about a 100 yards from the Madeleine and five minutes' walk to the Gare St-

Lazare and the place de la Concorde. The Marigny actually provides pillows in addition to the usual Paris hotel bolster, and is one of the few that provides an individual piece of soap for the traveller. Sparkling clean and prettily furnished, too. But watch out for the self-service lift as the doors can give you a rap on the elbow if not firmly controlled. Reading lights. VISA, Access cards, traveller's cheques in francs, and Eurocheques accepted. The *patron* is M. Maugars.

9e arrondissement

Hôtel Confort 2-star NN
5 rue de Trévise, 9e
Tel: 42 46 12 06
Métro: Rue Montmartre

Room with *cabinet de toilette*	1 person	160F
with shower	1 person	230
	2 or 3 persons	255
with bath and WC	1 person	255
	2 persons	295
Extra bed		100
Petit déjeuner		24
Shower		15

This is a pleasant hotel with not much to distinguish it from hundreds of others, except that it is 2-star with the NN classification, which means they have done a lot of painting and sprucing up. It has a lift, and facilities for people in wheelchairs, and you can bring your dog with you. And there's a TV in every room. It's cheap, considering all these amenities, and although impersonal and rather full of tourists, the welcome is agreeable, and English is spoken. The *patronne* is Mme Francis.

Hôtel de Lille no stars
2 rue Montholon, 9e
Tel: 47 70 38 76
Métro: Cadet

Room with *cabinet de toilette*	1 or 2 persons	150F
with shower	1 or 2 persons	190
with shower and WC	1 or 2 persons	240
Petit déjeuner		16
Shower		15

Although the entrance looks a bit dark, persevere. The rooms are clean and tidy, though they don't provide twin beds, only doubles. And don't be put off by the aroma of garlic which may greet you as you come in – if this bothers you, go elsewhere. Or even leave Paris itself. Rates at the Hôtel de Lille have gone up in the past two years, but it is still inexpensive, and the transport is good. The neighbourhood which at first glance looks drab and commercial, will yield some interesting and unexpected places if you don't pass through it unseeing. No English spoken, but if you make an attempt at even hit-or-miss French you will be all right. No credit cards, but it's possible that American Express traveller's cheques will be accepted in 1992. The *patron* is M. Amir.

10e arrondissement

Hôtel Bonne Nouvelle
125 boulevard Magenta, 10e
Tel: 48 74 99 90
Métro: Gare du Nord

Room with shower	1 person	120F
with shower and WC	1 or 2 persons	140–200
Petit déjeuner		17

A very Parisian hotel, this, somewhat old-fashioned but remarkably well located, just down the street from the Gare du Nord where the train from the airport brings you. There are buses and Métro stops galore within a few minutes' walk. The prices are remarkably low, so the Bonne Nouvelle is certainly *bon marché* . . . good value, though there is only one room at 120F. All rooms have showers, and some have a WC as well. The boulevard Magenta is noisy, 18 hours a day, so take ear-plugs. The rooms are smallish but clean, without any attempt at good taste in decoration. Some English is spoken – but a little French does help. Because of the location and the low rates, it is heavily booked during the tourist season, so write for reservations. It's best to do so in French, basing your letter on the Tourist Office form letter (see page 13).

Hôtel du Centre 1-star NN
4 rue Sibour, 10e
Tel: 46 07 20 74
Métro: Gare de l'Est

Room with *eau courante*	1 or 2 persons	140F
with *cabinet de toilette*	1 person	155
with *cabinet de toilette*	1 person	165
and WC	2 persons	215
with shower or bath		
and WC	1 or 2 persons	210
	(twin beds)	273
Petit déjeuner		18
Shower		15

In this rather unpromising neighbourhood – notable mostly for its bargain shoe and handbag shops – we fell out of a cloudburst into the doorway of the Centre Est and turned up a little gem of a hotel. Five minutes from the Gare de l'Est, which is a centre of bus and Métro lines that will take you anywhere, the Centre Est has a lift, facilities for wheelchairs, even accepts dogs. The rooms are big, the bathrooms spotless, and it has reading lights. The reception is friendly and courteous. Recent renovations include more rooms with showers and WCs, though the carpets and wallpaper are not the newest. Many of the rooms have huge mirrors, wooden ward⸱obes and tables, and some have a view of the Église St-Laurent. No credit cards, but traveller's cheques in francs and Eurocheques accepted.

Hôtel Jarry 2-star
4 rue Jarry, 10e
Tel: 47 70 70 38
Métro: Château d'Eau

Room with *cabinet de toilette*	1 person	130F
	2 persons	160

with shower	1 person	170
	2 persons	200
with shower and WC	1 person	190
	2 persons	220
with bath and WC	1 person	220
	2 persons	250
	3 persons	300
Petit déjeuner		17

In the not very interesting 10e *arrondissement*, this hotel is a pleasant surprise: very clean, sober, nicely redone in considerable taste, and the *concierge* speaks good English. Conveniently located for the Gare de l'Est, and there are some goodish restaurants and brasseries in the neighbourhood. No lift, and no credit cards or traveller's cheques accepted. The *patron* is M. Mahfouf.

Hôtel du Jura 1-star
6 rue Jarry, 10e
Tel: 47 70 06 66
Métro: Château d'Eau

Room with *cabinet de toilette*	1 person	140F
	2 persons	185
with shower	2 persons	210
	3 persons	250
Petit déjeuner		included
Shower		20

A more modest place, but comfortable, neat and respectable, and a remarkable bargain with well-arranged rooms and breakfast included. It can be a bit noisy and is beginning to need redecoration and repairs, but they're on the way, we're told. And while the 10e isn't one of the 'historic' areas of Paris, it has its own neighbourhood character, and some very good shopping. Those who run the hotel are kind, helpful, and willing to speak English of a sort and to help you with your French. No credit cards or traveller's cheques.

Little Hôtel 2-star NN
3 rue Pierre Chausson, 10e
Tel: 42 08 21 57
Métro: Jacques-Bonsergent, close to République

Room with shower or bath
    and WC   1 person   275F
                         2 persons   330
Petit déjeuner   25

A clean and pleasant place, which has been completely renovated. All the rooms have showers or baths, telephones and TVs. The hotel has a homelike feeling, and the *patron*, M. El Baz, is a sociable man who likes to take care of his customers. VISA, Eurocheques and traveller's cheques accepted.

11e arrondissement

Auberge de Jeunesse Jules Ferry
8 boulevard Jules-Ferry, 11e
Tel: 43 57 55 60
Métro: République, Parmentier

Dormitory room (sleeping 2, 3, 4 or 6) 82F per person
Shower and breakfast included

For more notes on Youth Hostels, see page 95. The Jules Ferry is an excellent example. You're expected to bring a *drap de couchage jettable* (sheet liner), though you can hire one here. Still, it's obviously better to have your own sleeping bag. Also, if you're not a Youth Hostel member, you pay a daily extra fee as a Guest.

The Jules Ferry Hostel is an old building, with some renovated rooms (all have basins and running water), not very fresh paint, but a pleasant atmosphere and a feeling of safety. The *patron*, M. Fischer, is co-operative and kind, no matter how busy he is – and he speaks English. In summer it's advisable to reserve two weeks to a month in advance, *by mail*, and reservations for more than one night must be accompanied by a cheque in francs and an international postal reply coupon. You can check in anytime between 8:00 a.m. and 9:00 p.m. and the building is open from 6:00 a.m. to 2:00 a.m. Rooms are accessible round the clock.

Hôtel des Arts 1-star NN
2 rue Godefroy de Cavagnac, 11e
Tel: 43 79 72 57
Métro: Charonne, Voltaire

Room with *eau courante*	135F
with *cabinet de toilette*	145–160
with shower	225
with shower and WC	250
Petit déjeuner	25
Shower	25

Here, in this so far ungentrified part of the 11e *arrondissement*, is an unpretentious hotel on a really great street. Rooms are inexpensive, not much to look at, comfortable enough. The welcome is very friendly and English is spoken. Prices are the same for one person or two, in most cases, which can make it a real bargain for couples. If you want to save even more, breakfast at any of the neighbouring cafés, for half the price; and look up the address of the nearest Bains/Douches – see pages 244–5 for more about them. The hotel is walking distance from the place d'Aligre market (Marché Beauvau, see page 240). No credit cards, no cheques, and don't be offended if they ask you to pay for the first day or two in advance.

Cosmos Hôtel 2-star
35 rue J.P. Timbaud, 11e
Tel: 43 57 25 88
Métro: Parmentier

Room with *eau courante*	1 person	155F
	2 persons	170
with *cabinet de toilette*	1 or 2 persons	185
with shower	1 or 2 persons	200
with shower and WC	1 or 2 persons	260
with bath and WC	1, 2 or 3 persons	270
Petit déjeuner		22

Recently renovated, this 41-room hotel has a lift, and TV in each room, it's very clean and fresh, and the largest of its double rooms with bath can sleep four people, in two big beds. Add to that the pleasure of this Paris-village street – restaurants, several Chinese/Vietnamese places, cafés, brasseries, *junqueries*, small supermarkets, art shops. There are great street markets Tuesdays and Fridays, one in the boulevard Richard Lenoir and the other in Belleville at the north end of the street. Transport is excellent; the 96 bus stops almost at the doorstep takes you straight to the Marais, to the Left Bank, to the Gare Montparnasse – and runs seven days a week.

Prices at the Cosmos are still low, as it's known only to the French. No English is spoken, so write or telephone in French. No credit cards, Eurocheques accepted but with a surcharge of 90F.

Hôtel Notre-Dame 2-star
51 rue de Malte, 11e
Tel: 47 00 78 76 (Fax: 43 55 32 31)
Métro: République

Room with *cabinet de toilette*	1 person	140–170F
with shower	1 person	200
	2 persons	260
with shower and WC	2 persons	300
with bath and WC	2 persons	310
Petit déjeuner		28
Shower		20

We are very fond of this hotel, which is getting well-known to English and American and German visitors to Paris. Close to the great square at République, with its shops, restaurants, and several Métro lines, it couldn't be more conveniently located. The hotel itself is so pleasant. The reception area has been beautifully redone, and the breakfast room is full of fine posters and fresh roses. The atmosphere is peaceful (though the rue de Malte is far from quiet in daylight). You're advised to book well in advance from late spring through early autumn. VISA, Access cards and Eurocheques with a Eurocard are accepted, also American Express traveller's cheques. The new *patrons* are M. and Mme Ades.

Hôtel Plessis 2-star
25 rue du Grand-Prieuré, 11e
Tel: 47 00 13 38 (Fax: 43 57 97 87)
Métro: Oberkampf, République

Room with *cabinet de toilette*	1 or 2 persons	200F
with shower and WC	1 or 2 persons	275
	twin beds	320
and with TV	1 or 2 persons	295
with bath and WC and TV	1 or 2 persons	320
Extra bed		75
Petit déjeuner		32

Renovations were taking place when we last called, and the hotel has gained an extra star. It's very well run by an enterprising couple, M. and Mme Montrazat, who speak English and know a great deal about this quite interesting neighbourhood. Staying here, you are within brisk walking distance of the Musée Picasso and the charming small streets of the 11e *arrondissement,* yet the very busy place de la République is just down the street. The hotel now has double windows and new doors – quite efficient against the noise. Closed from mid-July to mid-August. All credit cards accepted.

Hôtel Printania
16 boulevard du Temple, 11e
Tel: 47 00 33 46
Métro: Filles du Calvaire, République, Oberkampf

Room with *cabinet de toilette*	1 or 2 persons	160F
and WC	twin beds	230
with shower and WC	1 or 2 persons	250
with bath and WC	1 or 2 persons	280
	twin beds	350
Petit déjeuner		25
Shower		18

The Printania has been revamped, gradually, in fresh, pleasant colours, even to the corridors and stairs, and the extra touches are refreshing. Our friend who looked at it this year found the atmosphere unlike any Paris hotel she'd ever seen, and liked the green plants and birds cooing in their cage. However, if you don't like small animals the Printania is not for you, as a pair of well-behaved dogs are usually lying placidly near the reception desk. Bedspreads and curtains are very French in taste, the rooms are kept clean and tidy, the bathrooms adequate. The *patronne,* Mme Cochennec, is warm and friendly although she speaks no English. The rooms facing the boulevard are double-glazed, but even so it can be a touch noisy on that side. Best of all, there's a lift. Very convenient for the Métro, and for a base to explore the small streets both north and south. VISA, Access cards accepted, and Eurocheques with a 35F surcharge.

Hôtel Rhetia 1-star
3 rue Général-Blaise, 11e
Tel: 47 00 47 18
Métro: St-Ambroise

Room with *eau courante*	1 person	110F
with *cabinet de toilette*	1 or 2 persons	160
with shower and WC	1 or 2 persons	200
	twin beds	220
with bath and WC	3 persons (2 beds)	250
Petit déjeuner		included
Shower		10

The Rhetia is a hotel we discovered more than ten years ago, and a very good choice for those who like to explore parts of Paris that never make the guidebooks. The rooms have been redecorated in the past few years, there's an efficient new manager, and the prices are still moderate. The atmosphere is quiet and friendly, and once you get to know the neighbourhood, it's easy to put down roots. The pretty square opposite is bubbling with children after school. The Rhetia is well run, unpretentious, known to the French rather than tourists. It doesn't take credit cards, but will take traveller's cheques in francs.

Hôtel Sans-Souci 1-star NN
113 boulevard Ménilmontant, 11e
Tel: 43 57 00 58
Métro: Ménilmontant

Room with *eau courante*	1 person	100F
with shower	1 person	140
	2 persons	180
Shower		15

Basic, but clean and respectable. Most of the rooms are off the boulevard, hence quiet, and the hotel is just five minutes' walk from the green peace of beautiful Père Lachaise. We know this neighbourhood well and like the mixture of races, types, good little shops, restaurants of all kinds almost within arms' length. The managers say that renovations are in the offing, so the classification may change, but we have to say we didn't see much sign of it on our last visit. You must book well in advance, writing in French on the hotel-reservation form on page 13. These low rates mean that there are many long-stay tenants, students and young people working in Paris. Edith Piaf was born near here, in the rue Crespin-du-Gast. The very French street market on the boulevard Ménilmontant is on Tuesday and Friday mornings from about 8:00 a.m., while the

Belleville market, more raucous and rambling, runs west from the Ménilmontant Métro stop. Eurocheques with a Eurocard are accepted, no credit cards. The *patron* is M. El Djama.

12e arrondissement

Hôtel de Marseille
21 rue d'Austerlitz, 12e
Tel: 43 43 54 22
Métro: Gare de Lyon

Room with *cabinet de toilette*	1 or 2 persons	150F
with shower	1 or 2 persons	220
Petit déjeuner		20
Shower		18

The Marseille is close to the Gare de Lyon, in a short street of hotels. We think it is a very good buy, although fairly simple and basic. The rooms are well kept, and although none of them have private lavatories, the communal ones are clean. Very little English is spoken, but general willingness and good will helps make up for any linguistic difficulties. As you might expect from the low rates, no credit cards or traveller's cheques accepted. The *patron* is M. Soumar.

13e arrondissement

Hôtel Pacific 1-star
8 rue Philippe-de-Champagne, 13e
Tel: 43 31 17 06
Métro: Placé d'Italie

Room with *eau courante*	1 person	125F
with *cabinet de toilette*	1 or 2 persons	170
	2 beds	220
with shower	2 or 3 persons	250
with bath and WC	1 or 2 persons	235
Petit déjeuner		22
Shower		no charge

A hotel with an old-fashioned air, and with a lift – not all that common in 1-star establishments. We have always liked the neighbourhood, a well-to-do bourgeois one, only a few minutes from the good shopping of the place d'Italie. The reception is polite and efficient without noticeable warmth, but the comfort of the rooms and the good tiling and plumbing in the small bathrooms makes up for this slight drawback. There's a *gendarmerie* almost at the door, so the crime rate in this quiet area is probably low! No credit cards or traveller's cheques. The *patronne* is Mme de Roode.

Hôtel Rubens 1-star
35 rue de Banquier, 13e
Tel: 43 31 73 30
Métro: Campo-Formio

Room with *cabinet de toilette*	1 person	110F
	2 persons	130
with shower or bath and WC	2 persons	200
Petit déjeuner		20
Shower		12

This hotel never seems to change – it is remarkably good and the rates are still low, even though it has a lift. The rooms are delightful, and every bathroom we have seen here has been comfortable. The street is very quiet with no through traffic, but the hotel is within close reach of good restaurants (Lebanese, Vietnamese, South East Asian). The neighbourhood has an interesting life of its own which one can happily settle into – if you yearn for the bright lights and bustling streets, there's very quick transport by bus and Métro into the centre of Paris. The Rubens provides reading lights, something not always found in 1-star hotels. No credit cards or traveller's cheques. The *patrons* are M. and Mme Gourdal.

14e arrondissement

Hôtel des Bains 2-star
33 rue Delambre, 14e
Tel: 43 20 85 27 (Fax: 42 79 82 78)
Métro: Edgar-Quinet

Room with shower and WC	1 or 2 persons	290F
Suite (can be divided)	1 or 2 persons	330
	(double and two small beds)	420
Petit déjeuner		35

The Hôtel des Bains has been renovated over a period of many months, and the results are good – every room now has a shower and WC, and the larger ones are economical for several people travelling together. Everything is shining clean, and the staff speak several languages. It has always been much loved by visitors, and it's in a very interesting street which offers food, antiques, boutiques. The hotel is a short distance from the Tour Montparnasse, where many Métro lines and several bus routes take you all over Paris. The view from the 56th floor of the tower is unbelievable. The *patron* is M. André Regis.

Hôtel du Parc 1-star
8 rue Jolivet, 14e
Tel: 43 20 95 54
Métro: Edgar-Quinet, Montparnasse-Bienvenue

Room with *cabinet de toilette*	1 or 2 persons	200F
with shower and WC	1 or 2 persons	290
	2 beds	340
Petit déjeuner		20

While the building is old, it has been well maintained and improved by the owners, who plan to install a lift next (which will send the prices up). We like the view across the little triangular park which adjoins the busy boulevard Edgar-Quinet, or the very Parisian roof-scape seen from the rear windows. Double-glazing means the rooms are quiet, and they're clean, cheerful, pleasant to stay in. The street is a nice backwater of Montparnasse, with small shops, and restaurants ranging from Japanese sushi bars to inexpensive family-run Italian bistros; and there's a big Galéries Lafayette just around the corner on the rue Départ. The *patrons* are M. and Mme Jacob.

Hôtel de la Loire 2-star NN
39 bis, rue du Moulin-Vert, 14e
Tel: 45 40 66 88
Métro: Alésia, Plaisance

Room with *cabinet de toilette*	1 person	195F
with shower	1 or 2 persons	240
with shower and WC	1 or 2 persons	295–330
with bath and WC	1 or 2 persons	315–350
	3 or 4 persons	450
Petit déjeuner		27
Shower		15

The atmosphere here is almost like a country town rather than a street on the edge of an international metropolis. The Hôtel de la Loire has a range of small but efficient rooms set along the edge of a pretty little garden. Upstairs, larger rooms provide accommodation for a family of three or four. The Alésia neighbourhood is a good shopping area, and exploring it will give you a view of how Paris really runs. Mme Noël, the *patronne*, has a welcoming manner and really seems to enjoy running her 'village inn'. VISA cards accepted, but no Eurocheques.

16e arrondissement

Hôtel Stella 1-star
133 avenue Victor Hugo, 16e
Tel: 45 53 55 94
Métro: Victor Hugo

Room with *cabinet de toilette*	1 person	140F
	2 persons	150
with shower	1 or 2 persons	200
with bath and WC	double bed	250
	twin beds	270
Petit déjeuner		17
Shower		20

The Stella has a marvellous location on the elegant avenue Victor Hugo, and it has a good standard of furnishings, bedspreads, pretty chairs. The bathrooms with WC aren't large, but they are well arranged, and all the showers have curtains. It's usually heavily booked during 'peak seasons', so reserve a month or so in advance for those periods. If there's an exposition or trade fair, you shouldn't even hope to get a room; at other times, you may need only a few days' notice. Usually someone on the staff available will speak English, but not always, so reserve in French (use the form letter on page 13). Considering its prices and advantages, it is, as it has been for years, one of our best choices. No credit cards or traveller's cheques, and 'probably' no Eurocheques. The *patron* is M. Abderahman.

18e arrondissement

Hôtel André Gill 2-star NN
4 rue André Gill, 18e
Tel: 42 62 48 48
Métro: Pigalle

Room with *eau courante*	1 person	210F
with *cabinet de toilette*	1 or 2 persons	240
with shower and WC	1 or 2 persons	300
	3 persons	440
Petit déjeuner		included
Shower		25

Although the André Gill is just up the hill from the racket of Pigalle, it is tucked away in a sort of courtyard backing onto the rue des Martyrs. It's an oasis of peace and calm, yet very easily reached by Montmartrobus from the Métro. The neighbourhood is a complete delight, with attractive restaurants and food shops, and although the hotel is just five minutes' walk from Sacré Coeur, it's a world away from the *hurluburlu* of Montmartre. It has a lift, a reception room, and many of the 32 rooms have private baths or showers. Some rooms have delightful coloured glass windows dating back many years. Visa, Access and traveller's cheques accepted. The *patron* is M. Brahim Lounis.

Hôtel du Bouquet de Montmartre 2-star NN
1 rue Durantin, 18e
Tel: 46 06 87 54
Métro: Abbesses

Room with *cabinet de toilette*	1 or 2 persons	190F
with shower or bath	1 or 2 persons	290
with shower or bath and WC	1 or 2 persons	310

Petit déjeuner		25
Bath or shower		15

This is a hotel located in the centre of Montmartre, and here you are paying for the location. The bathrooms are small, the wallpaper clashes gaily with the bedspreads, the furniture is bargain warehouse. But the neighbourhood has vistas that remind you of Utrillo paintings wherever you look, and a lot of good small inexpensive restaurants within walking distance. To cut costs, try the Bains/Douches, the public baths of Paris (see pages 244–5) rather than pay the fairly high price for a shower here. And take your morning café au lait and croissants at the nearest coffee-bar for considerably less than 25F. English is spoken here, and all major credit cards are accepted, except for American Express. The *patronne* is Mme Gibergues.

Hôtel Central Montmartre 2-star
37 rue Hermel, 18e
Tel: 46 06 09 13
Métro: Jules Joffrin, Simplon

Room with *eau courante*	1 or 2 persons	150F
with shower or bath	1 or 2 persons	205
with bathroom and WC	1 or 2 persons	230

The Central Montmartre is in an area we're very fond of. The Montmartrobus stops at the door, the rue Ordener at the corner is wonderful for food shopping, restaurants, flowers, or just wandering. There's a pretty park nearby, and if you are lucky, on a summer's night you may hear a band playing. The hotel itself is modern and charming, with a telephone in each room, and prices which are really reasonable. Those staying in the quite luxurious double bedrooms with baths can have a TV in the room for only 25F a night extra. The furniture is good and the décor tasteful. There are no tourists in this slightly out-of-the-way neighbourhood, yet a bus will take you down the boulevard Ornano to the Champs-Élysées in a surprisingly short time. VISA, Access, and American Express cards are accepted, also Eurocheques with a Eurocard. English is spoken. The *patronne* is Mme Lam.

Other options

Bed and Breakfast: B & B on the English plan is slowly catching on. 'Café Couette' is an organization which operates all over France and has recently started up in Paris. Write to, or visit, them at 8 rue de l'Isly, 75008 Paris. Their office is at the back of a courtyard and hard to find, but persevere; an English-speaking representative is usually there.

Rooms to let: check the notice-boards at the American Church, 65 quai d'Orsay, 7e (*Métro*: Alma-Marceau, Invalides). They are plastered with notices by English-speaking residents who want to let rooms and flats. Most holiday lets are for two, three or four weeks; rooms to rent may be offered for longer periods. You will see ads for studios, or for bedrooms with use of bath and kitchen in a flat. Take a notebook, a lot of franc pieces or a Télécarte (see pages 277–8). St Michael's Church of England, 5 rue d'Aguesseau, 8e (*Métro*: Madeleine) has a similar service, and very helpful people who can tell you everything about living in Paris.

Student Housing: students are well catered for in Paris. Take your International Student Identity Card, or if you don't have one, a current photograph and proof of your full-time student status with 38F, to CIEE, 49 rue Pierre-Charron, 8e (*Métro*: Alma-Marceau).

The Cité Universitaire, in the quiet southern part of Paris, often has rooms to let during university holidays. Contact them at 18 boulevard Jourdan, 14e (*Métro*: Cité-Universitaire), where you may find someone who speaks English.

A very useful organization for the young is **UCRIF** (Union des Centres de Rencontres International de France), which has 11,000 beds on offer all over the country. Find them at:

> Office de Tourisme
> 127 avenue des Champs-Élysées 8e
> Tel: 47 23 61 72

> Gare du Nord
> Tel: 48 74 68 69

> Siège Social UCRIF
> 21 rue Béranger, 3e

Also first class at finding accommodation for young people:
> **Accueils des Jeunes en France:**
> 139 boulevard St-Michel, 5e
> *Métro* (RER): Port-Royal
> Tel: 43 54 95 86
> Open from March to October, Mondays through
> Fridays, 9:30 a.m. to 6:30 p.m.

Near the Bastille at:
> 151 avenue Ledru-Rollin, 11e
> Tel: 43 79 53 86

Gare du Nord, near the Halle des Arrivés
> Tel: 42 85 86 19
> Open 8:00 a.m. to 10:00 p.m.

Near the Pompidou Centre at:
> 119 rue St-Martin, 4e
> *Métro*: Rambuteau, Hôtel de Ville
> Tel: 42 77 87 88
> Open 9:30 a.m. to 6:30 p.m.

In the Marais at:
> 16 rue du Pont Louis-Philippe, 4e
> *Métro*: Pont-Marie, St-Paul, Hôtel de Ville
> Open June to September, Mondays through Fridays,
> 9:30 a.m. to 6:30 p.m. These hours are changing
> at the time of writing; they may be open on
> weekends in summer 1992.

There are four beautiful and historic converted houses in the Marais, 4e, given over to housing students. Check at the Maubuisson Hôtel des Jeunes, 12 rue des Barres, 4e (*Métro*: Hôtel de Ville, Pont-Marie).

Youth Hostels: *the Ligue Française des Auberges de Jeunesse (LFAJ)*, 38 boulevard Raspail, 7e (*Métro*: Sèvres-Babylone) is *the* address to use if you have a YHA card, no matter what age you are. Paris hostels are not comfortable, not very well located, and certainly offer little privacy, but at their prices who can complain? A three-day stay is generally the limit, but that's probably all you would want. For a more detailed look at one of the better hostels, see page 83, Auberge de Jeunesse Jules Ferry.

If you want to stay longer than a week or two, check the notice-boards near the restaurants, cafeterias, and in the entrance halls of the universities. One young friend, on a year's foreign study from Cambridge, found lodgings free. He had a room in a Left Bank flat in exchange for tutoring the flat's owner in English, all the while polishing up his own French. For such good deals, check these sources:

CROUS, 39 avenue George Bernanos, 5e *Métro*: Port-Royal

Assas, 92 rue d'Assas, 6e *Métro*: St-Placide

Cité Universitaire, 19 boulevard Jourdan, 14e *Métro*: Cité-Universitaire

CIDJ, 101 quai Branly, 7e *Métro*: Bir-Hakeim

Your own college or university may be able to add to this very brief listing of student-type places to stay.

Renting a flat in Paris, for a family or group planning to stay a long time, can work out cheaply: the best source we know is the Offres Meublés column in *Le Figaro*. But take a French-speaking friend when you negotiate any agreements! Several agencies which advertise in the *International Herald Tribune* are said to be efficient: they charge a finder's fee, of course.

Exchanging: perfect for paupers. A French person or family occupies whatever you have to offer, from a bed-sit to a house, and *you* go to their room/studio/flat. An experienced 'exchanger' has these tips to offer:

1 Make your arrangements through an exchange agency which lays down certain well-established rules. Or check the Announcements column in *The Times*, London.

2 Be specific about what you are offering – number of bedrooms, baths, equipment, use of telephone, daily help, linen, washing machine, car, motorbike, exact dates when you plan to leave and return.

3 Be sure you understand what you are getting: same as above, but with such important extras as how many flights of stairs, lift, concierge, etc.

4 Pets and plants can be catered for in exchanges, but specify *that* early on; some exchangers may be allergic or not willing to tie themselves down.

Everyone we know who has done exchanges has been satisfied, and plans to do it again. Most have had happy surprises: one family thought it was getting a four-room house and found they had four *bedrooms*: another was invited to spend the weekend in a Normandy cottage during their Paris stay; a third has established a long family friendship which includes the free use of a Paris flat over Christmas week. *Not* so great: the exchanger who arrived late at night and found the cupboard bare, not so much as a teaspoon of instant coffee or a slice of bread for breakfast, in an intimidatingly clean kitchen!

Agency exchanges cost about £35 a year, but work well because they are managed by experienced people who have a good set of guidelines for you and your prospective exchangees. The one we have used, which has many Paris members longing to do swaps in the UK and North America, is INTERVAC, 6 Siddals Lane, Allestree, Derby, DE3 2DY. Our family has done exchanges through them for about nine years, with 99 per cent great success and the occasional comic episode. One such was a Paris Christmas a few years ago, which included a temperamental front door lock and only one key for three people, a very nervous electrical system which blew fuses constantly, a bath/shower room with no door, bizarre linens, an invisible concierge. The plus points were – a perfect location one minute from a good Métro stop, a library of paperback thrillers in French, a fridge full of exotic foods, a bottle of wine, a dishwasher and washing machine, a lift, and a Christmas tree.

There are other exchange agencies: look in the telephone book or read about them in newspaper and magazine articles. INTERVAC is the one we know personally and use often.

La nourriture *(Eating well)*

What to expect

For anyone coming from a country where even 'alternative' magazines don't shrink from saying that a lunch costs 'only £16', and recommending wines at £9–11 a bottle; where only Indian, Chinese or Greek food is inexpensive: Paris seems like the bargain paradise of the world. True, prices have gone up sharply in the past few years, since most price controls have come off. But you can still eat well, as the Parisians do, in interesting surroundings, for roughly half what a comparable meal would cost you in London, Manchester or Edinburgh.

The great Paris restaurants, admittedly, can cost you a month's salary at one sitting, but that's not what this book is about. Everywhere in Paris there's an immense range of affordable and very good food. There's no equivalent whatever in English cuisine at any price that can compare with Paris food today. To eat well in England in 1990s comes far too high for the likes of travelling paupers.

Our basic requirement in setting out this list is what is called *le menu*. It is price-fixed, posted in the window (even some of the 3-star restaurants will publicly display their menu, but these will be from 400F up). Some offer a three-course menu, with a quarter-litre of wine, beer or mineral water and service (at 15 per cent) included. Others will include service, or will say *prix net* which means the same thing, but will not include drink. In most cases wine will be modestly priced at from 7F to 12F for a quarter-litre, two good glasses.

Some restaurants we have chosen do not offer three courses, but have opted for a two-course *formule* – starter and main course. A few have no set menu, but their *à la carte* choices seem so good, and the total is not staggering, that they are included here.

Now for the good news: almost every one of the restaurants here will feed you well, with a glass or two of drink, for not more than 80F – as this is written, you'll get 9F60 for your pound, so a meal to enjoy will be about £8.50. A few go as high as 95F, all inclusive, but they have been chosen as special occasion meals despite their extravagant prices. Only one is above 125F.

Best news of all: quite a number of new restaurants, and old favourites, have menus at from 45F to 60F including service, and often drink as well. As this book was being re-edited, and reports were flooding in from our diligent eaters in Paris, we were pleasantly amazed to see how many said 'the menu is 56F', or 'a very good meal for 48F'.

In no case has any restaurant been included just because it is cheap. Our reporters like to eat well, and in many places we've had to edit out some of their enthusiasms simply for the sake of space. In order to keep on offering really good food at affordable prices, many restaurants will offer their special menu only at lunch. Others have dropped *boisson inclus*, so you pay for what you drink, or skip it if that suits you better. A few offer food that is conventional, not particularly distinguished – but always of good quality, well cooked, and probably making up for a somewhat banal menu with fun, atmosphere, the always Parisian flair for making a meal an event. In these cases, we've set down exactly what you can expect in the most forthright terms: no one who contributes to *Paupers' Paris* owes any obligations to any establishment, so what you read is what you get. Unless of course a restaurant has changed hands, changed character, upped its prices between press time and reading time.

Now about drink: follow the lead of many Parisians. If wine, beer or mineral water is not included in the menu price, feel free to skip it. Contrary to what you have heard, not all Parisians drink wine with every meal. Ask for 'une carafe d'eau, s'il vous plaît', and you'll get a jug of clean, safe, very cold drinking water, which you'll probably like as much as pricey mineral waters.

We have grouped these restaurants by *arrondissements* (see page 33 to find out how these work), so that if you find your first choice is packed, another won't be far away. Many of these places hardly ever see a tourist, because they are good bourgeois eating-places patronized by serious eaters, and no one eats more seriously than the French. Each year, more and more accept credit cards, but see page 12. In the main they are clean, simple, usually with a spotless paper tablecloth put down over a longer-lasting cotton one; paper napkins – but sometimes linen ones – endless baskets of fresh, good

French bread, and undistinguished but palatable wine, beer, or mineral water.

Sanitation (*le lavabo*) varies from spotless to mildly squalid, and a few places still have *toilettes à la turque* reminiscent of the Dark Ages. Not once in our experience has the bill been padded in any way, and only one restaurant, described on page 161, made any sort of mistake on the bill. That small mix-up was quickly settled. However, we advise you always to run an eye down the bill before you pay. Although service is included in all prices, it's good manners to leave any small change on the little tray. Coffee is almost never included in the menu prices, and ordering it in a restaurant can bump up the price by as much as 9F. You'll sleep better without it anyway.

Many Paris restaurants close on Sundays, and some are open only for lunch or only for dinner. Most close on public holidays, some close Christmas Eve and New Year's Eve. Many which open on Sunday are closed one other day during the week, and a surprising number are now open in August, the traditional month when all Paris is supposed to close up like a clam. They take their holiday in off-season months, so that visitors in the summer have many more choices than in years past.

We found as we re-edited the book that Paris restaurants are changing their hours of opening, weekly and annual closing times with the speed of light, far more flexible to the demands of their customers than ever before. What we set down here is as accurate as possible as of autumn 1991, but please don't send us thunderbolts by post if a good little French restaurant has become an expensive chilli parlour or South-East Asian café!

Have the occasional snack lunch or dinner in your room (or outdoors), which can save you 18–20F on a restaurant meal (see page 60, about hotel eating). Or go to one of the very good value 'Selfs' (pages 163–6), where three courses with your choice of drink can be as little as 40–50F.

Café eating – those alluring little corner spots with outdoor tables and awnings – can tear a carefully calculated budget wide open. But if you're exhausted in mid-morning or late afternoon, sit down and spend 8F for a cup of coffee, or 12F for a *citron pressé* (real lemonade). The chance to rest your weary feet, write your post-cards, read the newspaper, and sit as long as you like, is worth the money.

For breakfast, if you choose not to eat at your hotel (often over-priced and not nearly as enjoyable as mingling with the French on their way to work), take your coffee and croissants at *le zinc* (the counter), not sitting down at *la terrasse* (a table) which ups the bill by about 30 per cent. And never order tea in Paris! You get a cup, a teabag, and a jug of water that's hottish but never boiling, and you'll pay about 8F. Brandy would be cheaper.

All Paris tap water – in hotels, flats and restaurants – is safe to drink. But if you worry about what a change of water can do to your digestive system, it's good to know that you can buy small bottles of good mineral waters to put in your carry-around bag. And huge (1½-litre) plastic bottles of Vittel, Evian, and private-label *still* mineral water, at supermarkets for about 2–3F. *Eau gazeuse* – Perrier and the like – are usually available only in glass bottles, but they are still cheap. What's more, you get back 1F when you return the bottle to the shops.

Restaurant manners

Restaurants – except for 'Les Selfs' (pages 163–6) – are run by a *patron* or *patronne*, with waiters and waitresses. All very human, all very connected to their clients. We're not talking here about McDonalds or their like. Contrary to myth, those who work in restaurants are not to be addressed as 'Garçon!'. If you want fast, friendly service, and advice if you need it, it pays to be polite. As you enter the restaurant it doesn't hurt to say 'Bonjour', or 'Bonsoir, Monsieur'; as you leave, 'Au revoir, m'sieur/m'dame'. In between, you should fill out your sentences with 's'il vous plaît', and 'merci bien', and such. In very small family-run restaurants, it's usually polite to include the entire clientele as well as the management in your goodbyes: 'Au revoir, messieurs-dames'.

French restaurants – especially the ones you'll find listed here – don't give you a lot of elbow room, and curiously enough you find that you don't need it. You may find yourself just barely able to squeeze into your seat; or seated opposite a stranger instead of with a table to yourself, and seated very snugly at that. Yet, such is the general air of *politesse* and enjoyment, that such tight spacing doesn't seem like encroachment on your personal living space.

You'll find it easy to adapt to. Your neighbours are absorbed in their food, or each other, and there is no lack of privacy. A 'Bonsoir' or 'Bon appétit, Madame' will not be taken amiss if you happen to catch someone's eye. If no one wants to get into conversation, it will be obvious; if everybody does, this soon becomes known. In any event, there is no stuffiness or awkwardness about your proximity. Best of all, women who eat alone in restaurants need not worry about being put at the worst table, near a draughty door, or in a forgotten corner. They are never ignored, and are always treated with respect, and even a little encouragement.

Recommended restaurants

1er arrondissement

Auberge du Palais Royal
10 rue Jean-Jacques-Rousseau, 1er
Tel: 40 26 51 53
Métro: Louvre, Palais-Royal

The Auberge is nicely hidden away in a narrow, crooked street, and further hidden behind brown curtains, which give it privacy and atmosphere. Most of its patrons, at lunch, are government or business people who talk quietly, there's a subdued hum of conversation rather than a noisy chatter. The décor too is subdued in tone but cheerful in feeling, the room is decorated with theatre posters, fresh flowers, candle-lit at night. The *patron* is friendly and welcoming. The menu is 65F at lunch and 70F at night, both including wine and service, and, which is unusual, the menus are identical at both meals. The *terrine de campagne* had a good winey taste, and the *faux filet* was well cooked and flavoured with bundles of herbs, the crisp potatoes roasted with rosemary. Other choices of starters would have been *fromage blanc* with garlic and herbs, garlic sausage, or lentil salad. In the winter, you can have soup as a first course. Main courses are few, each is good: *escalope panée*, grilled chicken, *brochette* of tender lamb pieces. For dessert, the cool fruit salad, plum, apple, grape and banana was lightly spiked with some unidentifiable liqueur. Their chocolate mousse has a light texture and is made with care, not the usual dense commercial mousse. Good cheeses and fruit tarts are on the menu too. Service and a quarter-litre of wine are included. Open noon to 3:00 p.m., 7:00 to 10:00 p.m. Closed Saturdays and Sundays, 14 July to 1 August, and Christmas. Open Easter and New Year's Day.

Au Petit Ramoneur
74 rue St-Denis, 1er
Tel: 42 36 39 24
Métro: Châtelet, Les Halles

Having known this restaurant, so conveniently located near the Forum des Halles and quite close to Beaubourg, for almost 10 years, we always wonder if this is going to be the year that the proprietors retire? Or that the overhead awnings finally give way in a cloudburst? Will one of the tightly packed clients knock over the communal bottle of rouge? But all is still well. One of our eaters, a Paris-based Englishman, ate there for the first time, and said that it's a real treasure – a *Paupers' Paris* special, the kind of place most tourists would pass without noticing anything but the sleazy street. Inside there's a noisy little room lost in a happy time-warp. Photographs of Les Halles-as-it-used-to-be are everywhere, and the *patrons* can remember the time of the great market, its little restaurants, and the market-porters, butchers and early-morning revellers who were their clients.

The menu is ridiculously good value, 58F including a half-litre of red wine or a half-bottle of mineral water and service. First courses might be: *terrine de campagne*, fillets of marinated herring, *pâté de foie* with green peppercorns; then a choice of *petit salé* with lentils – a very Les Halles dish – and so forth. Desserts are conventional and the pastry is fine. The menu is offered at both lunch and dinner. Open 11:30 a.m. to 2:30 p.m., 6:30 to 9:30 p.m. Closed Saturdays, Sundays, major holidays, and 15 August to 1 September.

Chez Fernand
81 rue Rambuteau, 1er
Métro: Les Halles

Not easy to find, a restaurant of this quality so near Beaubourg and Les Halles! The menu is 56F for two courses: and our report from Paris friends is 'very good food, very French cuisine. The duck baked with cider was excellent, and who could be unhappy with a *chèvre* salad to start?' Other choices would be onion soup (getting rarer in Paris), grilled *entrecôte* with herbs, or an *entrecôte marchand de vin*. This is all very filling, but if you want to add a dessert it will cost about 12–15F for the usual *tartes* and crème caramel. Service is included, beer is 12F and wine is 15F for a quarter-litre. Chez

Fernand is open noon to 2:30 p.m., and 7:30 to 9:30 p.m. Closed Sundays and two weeks in August.

La Fauvette
46 rue St-Honoré, 1er
Tel: 42 36 75 85
Métro: Louvre, Les Halles

When the market of Les Halles packed up, it left behind some semi-wholesaler meat businesses, many *charcutiers*, and a very few characteristic small 'market' restaurants. Fortunately, the crowds of tourists who swarm around the new Halles haven't noticed this one. It's a good filling station bang in the centre of Paris. The food is nothing special, but it's a prime site for French-watching. The noise! The speed! Clients include bourgeois businessmen in sharp suits, porters from the remaining meat packers, paint-spattered workmen slurping up red wine. Here, you can see how much interest the average Parisian working-man takes in what he eats.

The menu at 55F costs only a little more than it did two years ago: a choice of three main dishes – the *cervelles de veau meunière* (brains cooked in butter with shallots and garlic) was very good, although the potatoes were boiled to pieces – and, usually, roast beef, steak with *frites*, or a fillet steak with shallots for a 10F supplement. Starters are the standard ones; for dessert a rice cake, *île flottant*, crème caramel – or unexpectedly good cheeses including *chèvre* and gruyère. Service included, drink extra – a quarter-litre of red wine only 7F, beer or mineral water 8F50. Open for lunch only, 11:15 a.m. to 3:00 p.m. Closed Saturdays, Sundays, August and holidays.

Le Galtouse
Corner of rue de la Grande Truanderie and rue Pierre Lescot, 1er
Tel: 45 08 04 61
Métro: Les Halles, Étienne-Marcel, Châtelet

Somehow this one has slipped past the guidebooks. The two-course *formule* at 65F, service included, is amazing value, especially because as we write (1991) the price is the same as it was two years ago. It's one of the best meals you can find in an area which can be rather hit-or-miss when it comes to eating. This confident little restaurant has a touch of old-fashioned French class to it. The *à la carte* menu is impressive and rather high-priced, usually a good sign that the *prix-fixe* dishes will be cooked by people who know what they are doing.

Le Galfouse offers a first course choice of *salade aux fruits de mer*, a rabbit *terrine*, onion soup, a big salad with cheese and walnuts, then a main course of *faux filet*, grilled trout, or, for a 10F supplement, lamb chops, all with baked potato with chives, and two other vegetables. Desserts are *à la carte* and range from 23F for crème caramel to 35F for profiteroles. The cheeses are 25F. A meal of such quality for 65F, or the minor extravagance of three courses for under 100F, is really rare. The dining-room is very attractive, with fresh flowers, big mirrors, candles, a luxurious air. A woman friend who has eaten there says they are kind and thoughtful to a lone female client. Service is included in prices, drink extra and not cheap – 25F for a quarter-litre of good red. Open noon to 2:30 p.m., 6:30 to 11:30 p.m., every day except Christmas.

L'Incroyable
26 rue de Richelieu, 1er
Tel: 42 96 24 64
Métro: Palais-Royal

It is still literally incredible, this famous little place. People working and living nearby come here week after week, year after year, as do members of our 'extended family' in Paris. The three-course menu is 53F including service! The restaurant is perched on either side of stairs that join the rue de Richelieu and the rue de Montpensier – entrances in both streets. On a cold winter night it's warm, and on a baking August day in 1991, it was almost the coolest place in Paris even without air-conditioning. The menu gives you six starters, six or seven main dishes which could include squid *provençale*, and duck breast with freshly made pasta and gruyère cheese, finishing with a choice of four or five desserts and cheese. Their fruit tarts are made in their kitchen, and cost 8F extra. A quarter-litre jug of wine is 9F, as is Vittel water. This is an early-hour place, opening at 11:30 a.m. to 2:15 p.m., when it is usually empty. Dinner is 6:30 to 8:30 p.m. – eat early, go home early. Closed Saturday nights, Sundays, Monday nights.

Le Palet
8 rue de Beaujolais, 1er
Tel: 42 60 99 59
Métro: Palais-Royal

This restaurant is secreted in a pretty little street very close to the Louvre, and so far it has escaped the notice of tourists, who stick to the more obvious places. We liked the rustic atmosphere, the stone walls, and the changing art exhibitions which customers enjoy wandering around to gaze at between courses. On the ground floor there's a bar and some tables, and downstairs a room converted from a vaulted wine-cellar, with tables tucked in between the arches. The *formule* is 55F, with a main course and either a starter or a dessert, all chosen from the slightly more expensive 65F three-course menu. First courses included a *tartine*, a big salad with walnuts, *crudités 'du marché'*, mushrooms *à la grecque*, *cervelas*, etc. Main courses: *faux filet* with a choice of shallot or black-pepper sauce, poached turkey liver, lamb fillets, and what they call *'l'idée du jour, selon l'humeur du Chef!!!'* All are served with crisp *frites* or a selection of vegetables. The dessert list is copious, including a flan with coconut, sorbet, lemon tart. Try *Coupe Damnation* which includes chestnut purée, *crème fraîche*, and hot chocolate sauce!

Wine such as a Touraine rosé, the house red or Bergerac Blanc is served in *pichets*, 16F for a quarter-litre or 30F for a half-litre. Service is included, so you could eat well there for 81F, or 71F if you opt for the 55F *formule* and a *pichet* of wine. Open noon to 2:00 p.m., 7:30 to 10:00 p.m. Closed Saturday lunch, Sundays, and one week over Christmas. On other holidays, Le Palet closes for lunch, and opens for dinner. No annual closing.

Pasadena
rue du 29 Juillet between rue de Rivoli and rue St-Honoré, 1er
Tel: 42 60 68 56
Métro: Tuileries

For 90F including service, the menu offers flavoursome home-made fish soup, or *oeuf en gelée*, a seafood salad or vegetable soup, then extremely good salmon in a saffron sauce, scallops in puff pastry, steak and veal dishes. Desserts may include sorbet, chocolate cake, fruit tart, or specials of the day. The Pasadena is also called Au Bon Accueil; however, Madame who runs the house can be distinctly un-*accueillante*; she's temperamental, moody, speaks only French and can be sharp-tongued. Best to go there prepared to speak at least some French while ordering. You will enjoy the distinguished cooking, which at this price is a distinct rarity in this very pricey *quartier*. Wine is 14–16F a quarter-litre, and mineral water 10F. Open noon to 2:30 p.m., crowded and lively at lunch, with Madame kept very busy, reservations recommended. Dinner, from 7:00 to 9:30 p.m., is a quieter time. Closed Saturdays and Sunday evenings. A Sunday lunch here after a morning of museums is an inexpensive luxury. Closed July and holidays.

Le Relais du Sud-Ouest
154 rue St-Honoré, 1er
Tel : 42 60 62 01
Métro: Louvre, Palais-Royal

Year after year, the Relais goes on being a delight – nearly 10 years ago, we discovered it one rainy day when we were foot-weary from a morning at the Louvre just around the corner. Most tourists never get as far as the rue St-Honoré for lunch, and are probably intimidated by the grandeur of such an address. What they are missing! It's unaffected and traditional, packed at lunch and dinner by the locals, almost entirely French. The service is brisk, friendly, and the stone walls, old photos and wall panels painted to look like wood never change. At lunchtime, the menu for 57F includes service and drink, and has a choice of six starters, such as artichoke hearts, good *crudités*, tuna salad, fillet of herring, etc. Main dishes change every day, always include good steaks and usually a fish dish. Desserts could include *gâteau Basque*, pastry – or cheese. This menu is available only at lunchtime. A more expensive one, still only 80F service included, is served at lunch and dinner – with such goodies as a duck mousse, *cassoulet*, fresh salmon steak, saddle of lamb, duck with plum sauce, and a selection of desserts. Drink is extra – a quarter-litre of the house red only 15F. Open 12:15 to 2:30 p.m., 7:00 to 11:00 p.m. Go early at lunchtime – if you arrive after 12:30 you may have to wait for a table, or be courteously told the house is full. Closed Sundays, for three days over Easter, and for Christmas; open New Year's Day and 14 July. Closed August.

Le Stado
150 rue St-Honoré, 1er
Métro: Louvre, Palais-Royal

The *patron* of Le Stado is a former rugby player, and the stone walls are hung with mementos of his career and many of the teams of the Tarbes (south-west) region. The cooking is extremely good, hearty Pyrénées food, and the service is warm and welcoming. Starters are the usual *crudités*, *charcuterie* and *pâté*, with a fine garlicky *rillette du pays* or a salad with nuts; typical main courses are beef *brochette*, rumpsteak, *lapin chasseur*, veal kidneys. We are fond of the sporting, rather noisy ambiance and the back-slapping, chatting owner. The cheeses are brought to you on a plate for your choice; and one member of our family always goes for the coffee dessert, Moka St-Michel. Service and wine included, a feast of a lunch comes to just 80F. At dinner the price goes up to 100F. Open seven days a week, noon to 2:30 p.m., 7:00 to 11:00 p.m. Open August, but closed major holidays, 14 July, Christmas, New Year's Day.

2e arrondissement

Anadolu
rue de Turbigo, corner rue Volta, 2e
Métro: Sentier

One of the very unpretentious little cafés which stand on every street corner in the business section of Paris. On the edge of the wholesale jewellery/leather goods/luggage area, the Anadolu is a godsend: it serves huge sandwiches of spit-roasted lamb (*shawarma*) shaved into slivers and put into a giant 'pocket bread', like a monster pitta. Then in go onions, lettuce, tomato slices, seasonings, and a dollop of very hot sauce. Sandwiches at the table are 22F, at the bar or 'to go' are 20F. The set menu is 52F, with the usual Middle Eastern starters of *tarama*, vine leaves, feta cheese, and salad, then lamb *brochette*, steak, lamb chops, and a choice of ultra-sweet desserts. All prices include service, and wine and beer are inexpensive. The one or two waiters are genial and handle a constant stream of customers. Open early morning for coffee, pastries, croissants; sandwiches are served all day. The 52F menu is available for lunch and for dinner from 6:30 p.m. until about midnight. Open seven days a week, closed some holidays – no annual closing, as far as we could make out.

Note: the loos are unisex and really should be used only in real necessity.

L'Auberge Hongroise
52 rue Ste-Anne, 2e
Tel: 42 86 00 37
Métro: Opéra, 4 Septembre

In restaurant terms, L'Auberge Hongroise is a newly fledged bird, opened in May 1991. It should fly forever! The energetic owner and his wife have turned a disused TV salesroom into a countryish Hungarian inn with trellises, woven cane chairs and rustically tied lace curtains. And it produces cooking that is real 'Puszta style' – chicken paprikash, *choucroute de Transylvanie*, pork chops gypsy-fashion. Home-made flaky pastries are strong on poppy seeds, apricot fillings, prune jam (*lekvar*). Can you believe that at lunch-time, for 45F, you will be served a starter, a *plat du chef*, and a dessert, with service included? A quarter-litre of red wine 12F, beer 15F. They also offer two buffet-style lunches at 59F and 82F – the less expensive one has two courses from a buffet table, then pastry or cheese. The higher-priced one gives you hors d'oeuvres, main course, pastry *and* cheese. At night, the menu is 95F for a meal which starts with a Hungarian aperitif, then a choice of six starters including strudel pastry with chicken livers, main dishes such as veal paprika, and ends with Hungarian pastry, cheese, and coffee – service included, drink extra. Wednesday and Saturday evenings, there's live music from a trio of *gitanes*. Open noon to 2:30 p.m, 8:00 p.m. until – as the proprietor said, 'Bof! On ferme quand on ferme!' Closed Saturday lunchtime, Sundays, Christmas Day and August.

Le Drouot
103 rue de Richelieu, 2e
Métro: Richelieu-Drouot

The same management as Chartier (page 140), it's large, too well-known. Normally we wouldn't include it here, but if we don't we'll get a postbag full of letters telling us about how good it is, what excellent value. All true. It's near the Opéra, hence useful for pre- and post-Au Printemps and Lafayette excursions. A three-course meal with wine recently was 49F, plus 12 per cent service – leek salad, *boeuf bourguignon* with steamed potatoes, and *tarte tatine* (caramelised apple tart), with a quarter-litre of slightly better than ordinary wine. A cheese or ham omelette was only 8F50! Open 11:30 a.m. to 2:30 p.m., 6:30 to 11:00 p.m., seven days a week. No annual closing, but closed major holidays.

Restaurant Kurde Dîlan
13 rue Mandar, 2e
Tel : 42 21 46 38
Métro: Sentier

If you're near Les Halles, walk away from crowded and costly places, into the streets around rue Montmartre, where we found this gem, one of the few Kurdish restaurants in the Western world. The character of the food is unmistakably from the old Ottoman empire: *bostanê balcara*, aubergine purée with red and green peppers, garlic, olive oil; *tarator*, spinach with garlic and yoghurt; grilled lamb marinated in lemon, yoghurt, diced red pepper and parsley. An exotic soup called *sorba* is made with rice, lemon, yoghurt and mint. There are 19 cold starters, and a dozen grilled dishes, served with salad, rice, and superb Kurdish unleavened bread. Desserts are lush: try *firini*, fine semolina baked with a sugar syrup, pistachio nuts and butter. No set menu, but prices are not high: soups 16–18F, starters 20–26F, main dishes from 38F, desserts 18–22F. Beer is 12F. A delicious three-course dinner in autumn 1991 came to 72F without drink. The Dîlan is suffused with a most remarkable, relaxed, convivial atmosphere so that those who eat here are at once taken into the hospitable arms of the Kurdish family. We hear their New Year's Eve celebration is a party to remember! The Dîlan is open noon to 3:00 p.m., 7:00 to 11:30 p.m. Closed for lunch on Sundays and holidays but open in the evening. Closed Christmas. No annual closing. VISA, Access and Diners' Club cards accepted.

Pavarotti
8 rue de Hanovre, 2e
Tel: 47 42 78 98
Métro: Opéra, 4 Septembre

We were looking for a travel agent, and found instead the Pavarotti in a narrow street just a few minutes from the crowds, the noise and the petrol fumes of the Opéra. We took a chance on the menu at 49F – and our usual luck held. This small, pretty restaurant is run by an Italian family, and it's clean, fresh, green and white. There's music in the air, but muted. Our meal, and what a good one it was, cost about what you'd pay for a main dish in one of the local brasseries! We chose antipasto, then a plate of veal *piccata*, cooked as the Italians do so well, pounded very thin, quickly done in butter and finished with a splash of lemon juice and herbs. The cooking was above average, the pasta fresh and tender, obviously home-made. The Italian ice-cream was very good, and the cheeses at the next table seemed to be an unusual selection. It's very 'family'. We were the only outsiders, it seemed, yet the manager, who said he spoke only a little English, was in fact quite fluent, and served us with care and attention. Our fine lunch, including a beer and strong Italian coffee, was only 62F. At night, a longer and more expensive menu is served. Open noon to 2:30 p.m., 7:00 to 9:30 p.m., Mondays through Saturdays. Closed holidays, no annual closing.

4e arrondissement

La Canaille
4 rue Crillon, 4e
Métro: Sully-Morland

One of our student scouts of years past wrote 'Very cool – *assez sympa, décontracté*', another in 1989 called it 'sort of campy'. It's a good night out in a thronging place with a really optimistic atmosphere – big, imaginatively decorated with trendy lights, and a youngish, very talkative crowd. Go early, or brace yourself for a wait. Everything runs on greased wheels here – you write out your order, it is whisked away, and eventually your meal will come, although service can't be very fast in a place so popular, so packed with appreciative eaters. The menu at 78F is short; attention is paid to quality rather than variety. Unusual starters: pumpkin mousse with a green sauce, a *terrine* of fresh and smoked salmon with a creamy lobster sauce – 'almost unbearably good, and certainly the dish of the week'. Main course choices were sautéed rabbit with mustard sauce, chilli, or a lamb *brochette* with couscous and 'desperately hot' sauce. Desserts are quite ordinary, sorbets (commercial, not home-made), several pastries, a small selection of cheeses. Service is included, drink extra – a quarter-litre of wine 10F, mineral water 12F. Open noon to 2:00 p.m., then 7:30 p.m. to midnight. Closed for lunch Saturdays and Sundays. Closed Easter, Christmas, New Year's Day. No annual closing.

Le Châteaubriand
6 rue de la Bastille, 4e
Tel: 42 72 05 23
Métro: Bastille

'I recommend this place with all my heart', commented the Paris friend we sent to eat here. The menu is wisely kept short, and everything is perfectly prepared. The 75F lunch menu had some wonderful choices – mushroom *terrine* with tarragon, and fish with the classic French sauce, *beurre blanc*, tricky to cook but completely successful here. The crème brûlée to finish was caramelized to a turn and made with real vanilla bean, not synthetic essence. A quarter-litre of wine is 18F, so your meal, service included, could come to 94F, less if you skip the drink. As the Bastille neighbourhood changes almost day to day, it's good to find a restaurant so confident and relaxed that it keeps its 1950s décor of wire chairs and coat racks. At night, Le Châteaubriand is expensive, 135F for a more elaborate menu. Open noon to 2:30 p.m., 7:00 to 11:30 p.m. Closed Mondays, Christmas, New Year's Day, and August. Open Sundays and 14 July unless it's a Monday.

La Comète
6 rue des Archives, corner of rue de la Verrerie, 4e
Tel: 42 72 10 27
Métro: Hôtel de Ville

The elegant upstairs dining-room is open for lunch, and it's a place for a leisurely meal at a very special price – 58F50 for three very satisfying courses. The tables are nicely set, with good linen, and there's no feeling of the elbow-to-elbow jostling you'd expect in a popular and well-known restaurant. This *prix-fixe* menu is served at dinner as well, and in the evening the downstairs room is open too. The menu isn't going to surprise you with its originality, but the cooking is good and the servings really large. First courses are *terrine, crudités*, mackerel fillets, *oeuf mayo*; main courses included grilled *bavette* (steak), sautéed chicken, *boudin* or *calamares* in a good sauce; the apple tart is reported as remarkable. Instead of a three-course meal, you can have a *formule* of salad and *brochette* of beef, 18F, or steak and salad, 62F. Another day, a good lunch was made of two starters, each 18F, avocado salad and a slice of *pâté*, then a lovely pastry and a quarter-litre of wine, 6F50, the whole meal only 62F50. At night, La Comète is open from 7:30 p.m., and serves meals until midnight. Closed Sundays, and one or two weeks in August at the *patron*'s discretion - open 'most' holidays, but check by phone first.

Le Cristal
13 rue Beautrellis, 4e
Métro: St-Paul, Bastille, Sully-Morland

Le Cristal is in one of the prettiest streets of the Marais, and it's small, with space for only about 24 people. We and our friends have been going there since 1982, through several changes of management and menu. A French girl we know who had a meal there for the first time, liked the décor and the food – with one reservation noted below – the room is attractive, with bare stone walls. Two menus: one at 69F, fairly routine, with *pâté* or salad as starters, then fish, pork chop, chicken or steak for the main course, with dessert or cheese. The 89F menu is longer, and certainly not expensive for what it gives you – cold salmon with dill sauce as a first course, or *oeuf en gelée*, then good choices like duck breast with green pepper-corn sauce, goulash, and salmon with cranberry sauce, which sounds awful but is very good. Desserts were fairly conventional but excellent – lemon tart, *tarte tatin* and créme caramel. The one reservation? The main courses were accompanied, on a spring night, not with superb fresh vegetables nor with a salad, but with 'awful vegetables straight from the tin, a real shame'. Service included in prices, wine is available only in half-bottles at 40–48F, mineral water 25F, so anyone eating alone must either spend real money for wine, or ask for the usual carafe of fresh cold water, free. Open noon to 2:30 p.m., 7:00 to 11:30 p.m. Closed Saturday lunch, Sundays, and 'some time in September'. Open holidays including Christmas (unless it falls on a Saturday or Sunday), Good Friday and Easter Monday.

Le P'tit Comic
6 rue Castex, 4e
Tel: 42 71 32 62
Métro: Bastille

This little place has a new manager, Marie-Thérèse, who has kept the *bande dessiné* (comic book) décor. She cooks, serves and keeps an eye on everything. In addition to crêpes, there are salads, such as the delicious 'Sirène', seafood and salad greens, for 35F, or 'Gourmande', tuna, baby corn, tomato and so forth, a big bowl for 49F. Among the crêpes are 'Tyrolienne', which is a savoury affair with ratatouille and minced steak; and 'Bigoudine', a substantially filled Breton crêpe, both 45F. The most inexpensive main-course crêpe, 'La Pleuveuse', rolled around sautéed onions, is 40F. For dessert, try the 'Négresse', 30F, an incredibly rich choc-mint crêpe, covered in dark chocolate with two scoops of mint ice-cream. 'Bonne Maman', 20F, is more basic, jam-filled. Ideal, as *Le Monde* commented, after you've been to some theatre event around the Bastille Opéra. Cider, usually drunk with Breton food, is available only in bottles, which three or four could share, 35F. Wine and mineral water are over-priced, we think. Service is included in all prices. Open 11:30 a.m. to 3:00 p.m., 7:00 to 10:00 p.m. Closed Sundays and Christmas Day. Open Good Friday and Easter Monday, New Year's Day, and 14 July.

Le Petit Gavroche
15 rue Ste-Croix de la Bretonnerie, 4e
Tel: 48 87 74 26
Métro: Rambuteau, Hôtel de Ville

'An odd, scuzzy little restaurant, with *zinc* bars upstairs and down, peeling paint, toilets to avoid, a revolting stuffed deer in one corner, radio music – and one redeeming quality: good food,' reported an American in Paris a few years back. Add to that the location, in the depths of the now-fashionable Marais. Somehow it has managed to remain unchanged in the nine or ten years we and our friends have been going there. Le Gavroche rambles over several floors, with tables fitted in wherever. Astonishingly, in late 1991, you could still have a really good lunch for 49F, service included. A reasonable red wine was just 10F a quarter-litre. The menu changes all the time. At dinner, the *à la carte* prices are not exorbitant – *faux filet* with roquefort sauce, for example, was 45F recently, veal escalope Normandy-style in cream and cider sauce 44F. Starters such as *jambon de Bayonne* are 22F, desserts from 14F to 16F. Service is not very fast, but extremely amiable. Although this restaurant has been in a number of (French) restaurant guides, tourists don't seek out it, perhaps put off by the faded street entrance, or the look of bar as they glance in. Appreciate it for what it is, an old-style Marais restaurant before yuppification set in. Open noon to 2:30 p.m., 8:00 p.m. to 2:00 a.m. Closed Saturday lunch, and Sundays. In August, open for dinner only, from 4:00 p.m. to 2:00 a.m.

Les Piétons
8 rue des Lombards, 4e
Tel: 48 87 08 45
Métro: Châtelet, Les Halles, Hôtel de Ville

Undeniably one of the best restaurants near Beaubourg and Les Halles – the interior looks like any Paris café and it will never win a prize for décor, so perhaps it's most enjoyable on a warm summer day or evening when you can enjoy the outside tables on the old cobblestone street. Good food, friendly service, and our waiter was amusing and informal. The two-course menu, for 58F, is served at both lunch and dinner, and while there were no surprises in the starter list – grated carrots in a good vinaigrette, *oeuf en gelée*, and *pâté* – we liked the very tender steak *au poivre* with superbly cooked fresh vegetables. Apricot tart for 16F was spectacular, and wine only 8F a quarter-litre, so three courses with wine and service came to just 86F! One friend made an *à la carte* meal of ripe, thin-sliced tomatoes lavishly scattered with fresh basil, 16F, and a plate of good country *pâté*, 14F, finishing with the irresistible fruit tart, and wine, for just 54F. Open early, 11:30 a.m. to 3:00 p.m., and 7:00 to 10:30 p.m. Closed Sunday evenings and Christmas Day, but no annual closing. Open Easter Sunday, New Year's Day, Bastille Day. Lovely place to lunch on Sundays the year around, and 'perhaps' it will be open all day Sundays in summer months, but check by phone.

Le Quidam (Le Relais St-Gervais)
13 rue François Miron, 4e
Tel: 40 29 07 52
Métro: Hôtel de Ville, St-Paul

The name and the proprietors of this fine restaurant have both changed, but the mid-14th century building is the same, and the cooking is still superb. So far, although it is popular with the lucky people who live in the historic Marais district, it has attracted few tourists, except for a delightful couple from Scotland we encountered there last year, who came in with *Paupers' Paris* in hand. The food has more of an Italian slant than in past years, and the value is still remarkable: a menu at lunch only is 59F. Another, for lunch or dinner, at 90F, offered eight choices of first course which included a huge bowl of fish soup with *croûtons* and *rouille* sauce, *feuilleté au roquefort* –. puff-pastry layers enclosing morsels of cheese – and seven main-course dishes, such as *aigrettes de canard à la catalane*. Desserts are unusual and good. Prices for a three-course meal include service, drink is extra. Carafe wines are not too expensive, but better bottles can run into real money. You may want to have Perrier, l0F, or merely ask for a carafe of water. Open noon to 2:00 p.m., 7:00 p.m. to an incredible 1:30 a.m. Closed Sundays and holidays. Major credit cards accepted.

Relais de L'Île
37 rue St-Louis-en-l'Île, 4e
Tel: 46 34 72 34
Métro: Sully-Morland

This lovely restaurant was described as 'shoebox-small with little gallery' by the Bramhalls, who discovered it for us. It's remarkable value, astonishing in this very up-market street. There are two good short menus at lunch, both at 55F. One has a choice of two huge main-course salads followed by a selection of five or six sweets. The price included a big basket of very good bread and a quarter-litre of red or rosé wine. The second menu offers a starter and main course, with wine, but with no dessert.

Friends living in Paris were enthusiastic about the food and the setting – paintings everywhere, soft music. They liked the *salade fraîche*, a platter of varied greens with tomato, egg, *salade russe*, and the thick slice of coarse country *pâté* with a generous serving of salad greens. The main courses that day were grilled chicken marinated in lemon and honey, and a big plate of lamb steaks sprinkled with fresh herbs. Desserts are *à la carte* at 25F, and extraordinary – home-made crème brûlée in shallow saucers, strawberry melba made with real vanilla ice-cream. But their pleasure in the meal was marred by the cool treatment – the waitress brought mineral water when asked for 'Une carafe d'eau', and charged them extra for it on the bill. The special menus are served only at lunch, and Le Relais is closed Sundays and holidays. Credit cards accepted.

Le Temps de Cerises
31 rue de Cerisaie, 4e
Métro: Bastille, Sully-Morland

There's a poster of Jacques Brel on the wall of this friendly little corner restaurant in the Marais, and it's likely that he would have been at home here. You'll be caught up in the flow of talk from the workers in overalls and the young Parisians of the *quartier*, and Gérard, the *patron*, really does keep the lively spirit of the place going. The food, as a Breton friend, Patrick, remarked a year or two ago, is honest and correct. But the quality is variable, and the best bet is to stick to simple dishes such as cold beef salad with ratatouille, or roast pork with *haricots verts*. The first courses are usually very good – smoked fish with potato salad, or *charcuterie*, or *crudités*, and excellent desserts, fruit compote, *gâteau fourré*, ice-cream. If *Far breton*, a pudding made with prunes and raisins, is on the menu the day you're there, choose that. All this, and walls papered with photographs of the Marais as it once was, comes to just 46F, service included. A quarter-litre of house wine is 10F, but a better bet for two might be the Côtes du Rhône at 28F the half-bottle. Open as a café from 7:30 a.m. to 8:00 p.m., but serving lunch only from 11:30 a.m. to 2:30 p.m. – go before 12:30 or after 1:30 to be sure of a table. Closed Saturdays, Sundays, holidays and August.

Vancouver
64 rue de la Verrerie, 4e
Tel: 42 72 67 63
Métro: Hôtel de Ville

Once again, we're glad to report that prices in this much-liked restaurant have crept up only a few francs in two years. The two-course *formule* is only 58F at lunch, with half a dozen choices of starters – rabbit *pâté* with hazelnuts, quiche made in their own kitchen, avocado with a sprightly sauce; then various steaks including our favourite with roquefort sauce, escalope of veal

Normandy-style, or *andouillette* with sharp mustard sauce. Desserts — an irresistible chocolate charlotte 30F, *tartes* 28F — will up your bill a bit, but as wine and service are included, a fine lunch could be as little as 88F. Dinner prices are higher, but if you can content yourself with an escalope of salmon for 65F and a huge bowl of three sorbets for 30F, with a carafe of water instead of drink, you'd have a lush meal for under 100F. Wine or beer at night is 16F. All prices include service. Open noon to 2:30 p.m., and 7:00 to 11:00 p.m. Closed Sundays, Christmas Day and August, but open other holidays — a good place to know for New Year's Day, when most Parisian restaurants are tightly shuttered. The outside tables get taken up early; the service is outstandingly pleasant and fast, and the rooms inside are serene and lights are low. Don't go if you're allergic to dogs, as a large friendly fellow wanders around to greet guests.

5e arrondissement

Aux Savoyards
14 rue des Boulangers, 5e
Tel: 46 33 53 78
Métro: Jussieu, Cardinal Lemoine

Aux Savoyards, like many other restaurants around this 'street of restaurants' is, and always has been, a place for students. They eat here, or wait outside for a table to clear, or often work part-time on the staff — it all adds up to a somewhat hectic and very 'in' feeling. Don't expect to linger, or have a quiet meal. The service is lightning fast — otherwise they could never cope with the crowds that want to come in. A meal, with service and perfectly passable wine, costs just 62F. Ask for the menu as you enter, tell whoever is behind the bar what you want. It may be a philosophy student from the University of Paris, but even if he's thinking Kierkegaard he can write legibly, and somehow your order will emerge from the kitchen. The food is basic, very French, somewhat slapdash in presentation. A plate of *crudités* is a mound of roughly arranged grated carrots, beetroot, lettuce and so forth. Steaks, hamburgers, chicken, sausages — all cooked well, rural fashion, with no fancy sauces or names. A Cambridge student living in Paris met it head-on for the first time in summer 1991. His report: 'This isn't the place for a romantic soirée, but if you want to soak up a bit of old Paris atmosphere, and have a chatty commiseration with Madame about the yobbos who sprayed her friend's wall with graffiti . . . this is for you. Everything's rough and ready, and very enjoyable.' Open noon to 2:30 p.m., 7:00 to 10:30 p.m. Closed Saturdays and Sundays, Easter weekend, Christmas, New Year's Day, and 'probably' in August.

Le Baptiste
11 rue des Boulangers, 5e
Tel: 43 25 57 24
Métro: Jussieu

A beautiful little room with provincial decoration on stone walls; copper jugs, plants and so forth. Lovely food. Menus are written on wooden paddles, and include, at 62F, *chèvre* on salad greens, *pâté*, fresh *cervelas* sausage vinaigrette, herring fillets served with potato salad. Main dishes are few but well cooked, such as sirloin steak *au poivre*, fish, and a *plat du jour*. Cheese or fruit salad or the usual crème caramel follow. Service is included, wine extra at 14F the quarter-litre. *À la carte*, a three-course meal could cost as little as 80F, or as much as 140F, service included, drink extra. Recently, one of our 'Paris family' liked the eggs baked in tomato sauce, and chicken-liver *pâté* in a cream and cognac sauce. Main courses included duck breast cooked in honey sauce (overdone, said the French girl), and cod fillet in cream sauce. Other choices were veal fillet in mushroom sauce, kidneys cooked with cassis. For dessert, profiteroles, apple tart, fresh fruit salad. A quarter-litre of drinkable Côtes du Rhône was 15F. Go before 8:00 p.m., as it's popular. Service is brisk, not chatty, but friendly, the manager keeping things moving during the busiest times. Open noon to 2:00 p.m., 7:00 to 10:30 p.m., and 11:00 p.m. Fridays and Saturdays. Closed Saturday lunch, Sundays; on holidays closed for lunch, open for dinner, unless the holiday falls on a Sunday. No annual closing.

Le Blé d'Or (Freddy Gosse) (*boulangerie–pâtisserie*)
243 rue St-Jacques, 5e
Métro: RER Port Royal (B-line)

This delightful shop is not a restaurant – it is one of the best of those *boulangeries – pâtisseries* that make Paris a paradise for the greedy. The classic Paris-Brest pastry is almost beyond words – go and try it for yourself. 'Airy pastry, the filling made with pure Normandy butter, creamy, praliney and almost overflowing', one of our resident reporters describes it. At Freddy Gosse's, a short walk from the Sorbonne, in the Latin Quarter, all their cakes and crusty bread are made in purest French tradition. The staff is warm, interested, and even the smallest fruit tart is wrapped and presented with a flourish. We'd suggest that if you have had a two-course *formule* without dessert in a Left Bank restaurant, walk up to Freddy Gosse's for a pastry that is almost literally out of this world. Their croissants, too, are superb – rich, but not too buttery. From here, it's a short stroll with your sweet course to the tree-shaded, fountain-playing gardens of the Luxembourg where you can eat as Parisians do, from the 'designer paper' wrappings. Freddy Gosse is closed Saturdays, Sundays, two weeks in August, open most holidays.

Le Bouche Trou
20 rue des Boulangers, 5e
Tel: 40 51 73 25
Métro: Jussieu

The name of this favourite restaurant in the heart of the student district translates, roughly, 'Stuff-your-face', and never a truer word was spoken. It's one of the most genial of restaurants, always crowded. Visitors to Paris know this and walk up from the more touristy parts of the 5e *arrondissement*. It serves some of the tastiest food we know at such good prices. The lunchtime menu, 64F for three courses including service and wine, changes every day – one day there was a *méli-mélo de choux*, like a superlative coleslaw made with cider vinegar, or *rillettes*, then a grilled *faux filet*, roast pork with *herbes de Provence*, fish fillet in a vermouth sauce: ending with cheese, pastry, *crème praliné*. The menu at night is 95F, including service but not drink, and is certainly one of the great values of the Left Bank. An English friend who dined here had a first course of sliced avocado with crabmeat, his companion had 'voluptuous fish *terrine* with asparagus tips', then *entrecôte* with roquefort sauce, and *confit de canard* with garlicky potatoes. Desserts, by which time they were feeling faint with food, were sorbets (coconut, chocolate mint, lime or pear), and '*le concours orange chocolat*'. Drink, at dinner, is extra, a quarter-litre of red wine 9F, mineral water 12–14F. Open noon to 2:30 p.m, 7:00 to 11:00 p.m. Closed Saturday lunch,

Sundays, and August. Closed major holidays but open 14 July, Good Friday and Easter Monday, and New Year's Day. VISA cards accepted.

La Brouette
41 rue Descartes, 5e
Métro: Cardinal-Lemoine

La Brouette seems to have a slightly grasping hand out for tourists, but it's included here for its out-of-ordinary offerings. For 70F you can start with snails or leeks in vinaigrette; then frogs' legs, or mussels in garlic butter, or *colin meunière*, followed by an excellent tart, or prunes in wine or profiteroles – and the price includes wine *and* coffee. Unbeatable for quantity and quality, but slow on service even when uncrowded. Go there some evening when you feel like spending a leisurely hour or two watching the street scene. Open 12:30 to 2:30 p.m., 7:00 to 10:00 p.m. Closed Saturdays and Sunday nights, open holidays and August.

Les Degrés de Notre-Dame
10 rue des Grands Degrés, 5e
Métro: St-Michel, Maubert-Mutualité

Les Degrés announces on its card 'Petite restauration à toute heure', and it does serve food from 7:00 a.m. to 2:00 a.m, every day of the year. They offer two menus, one at 95F and another with more choices, at 105F. These prices have gone up sharply since we last wrote about Les Degrés, so perhaps this is the last time it will appear here. There isn't anything very distinctive about the menu at 95F, but everything is well prepared and servings are large: herring fillets with potatoes in oil-and-vinegar, *crudités, oeuf mayo*; and tender steak and wonderful *frites*, or roast chicken, *andouillette*, followed by chocolate mousse, fresh fruit salad or fruit tart. The bread is the *pain poilâne*, coarse and flavoursome peasant loaf, served with a crock of butter, and they keep refilling the basket as you eat it up. The room is pretty with real 16th-century exposed beams, truly old stone walls, big windows looking out on the peaceful, narrow little street. After your meal, turn the corner and gaze over the stone parapet above the Seine, to the great grey walls and the new gardens of Notre-Dame, while the rush and swish of boat traffic goes on below. While not very cheap, the Degrés is open very long hours, every day, and major credit cards are accepted.

La Maison de Verlaine
39 rue Descartes, 5e
Tel: 43 26 39 15
Métro: Monge

This restaurant is new to us, drawn to our attention by the fact that Verlaine, the Symbolist poet, once lived in a room upstairs (where was Rimbaud?). It's typical of the good little unfussy traditional restaurants in this popular street. Two menus are on offer, 50F and 78F, both including service but not drink. The less expensive has two kinds of *pâté*, *museau vinaigrette* (this translates as pig's nose in oil-and-vinegar dressing, much better than it sounds), sardines, *oeuf mayo*, then fish fillet *à la Normande* – cream and cider sauce – or *steak au poivre*, or some highly spiced sausage, with the usual crème caramel, ice-cream, pastry, as dessert choices. The more expensive menu is worth the extra 23F, according to one of our reliable Paris eaters: snails, mussels, fish soup, quail *pâté* among the starters; as main dishes, frogs' legs, grilled steak, escalope Viennoise, or lamb cutlets, with profiteroles, sorbets, and chocolate mousse to follow. The 50F menu is served at lunch only, the 78F one is for both lunch and dinner. Wine is expensive at 20F the quarter-litre, and beer is 19F. The *carafe d'eau* is fresh, cold, and free. Open noon to 2:30 p.m., 7:00 to 10:30 p.m., Mondays through Thursdays. Friday and Saturday nights, open until 11:30 p.m. Closed Saturday lunchtime, open on Sundays. Open most holidays, but check by phone for Easter, Christmas, New Year's Day.

Le Pavé aux Herbes
43 rue Mouffetard, 5e
Tel: 43 31 77 88
Métro: Monge

A very amusing place to eat, a good mixture of Greek and French food – and we're saving the news of the menu price for later. Courses could be *taramasalata* or *pâté de campagne*, squid in a tomato sauce or steak with a big heap of *frites*, loukoum from the Middle East and apple tart from France. The *patron*, from Crete, has painted a scene from his home on the wall and added artifacts and photos. There's always an amiable fussing going on – the owner keeps it open every day of the year, while the chef talks about taking a real holiday. Clients are evenly divided between French who know a good meal when they find it, and tourists who long ago sussed it out from the many other restaurants of the Mouff'. Now for the real news ... three courses with wine for 45F, at least as this book goes to press. And even if the prices rise slightly in 1992 and 1993, it will always be great value. A more elaborate menu including *escargots* and *champignons à la grecque* for starters, and calamares and moussaka as main courses, is 75F. Open noon to 3:30 p.m., 6:00 p.m. to midnight, every day.

Restaurant Lÿ
4B rue des Écoles, 5e
Tel: 43 54 93 25
Métro: Maubert-Mutualité

The Lÿ has the appearance of any Paris café from the outside, but inside, the Vietnamese owners have given it an Eastern air with some Oriental touches. The food is unusual and very delicious: there's no menu, but the *à la carte* prices are not high, especially considering the distinctive nature of the cooking. The pork with bamboo shoots and rice, 39F, was among the best we have had in a restaurant serving this piquant, delicate South East Asian food. As a first course, the Vietnamese *nems* (spring rolls – *rouleaux de printemps aux crevettes*) were stuffed with shrimps and fragrant with mint, served with a dipping sauce of tantalizing flavour, 25F. Other starters were chicken broth with lemon grass, 28F. Service is rather formal, correct, but friendly. Chopsticks are provided, but the really hamfisted can ask for knives and forks. Beer and wine are expensive, desserts not very interesting. If you really want to finish with a sweet taste, we suggest you drop into a nearby *pâtisserie*. Open noon to 2:30 p.m., 6:30 to 11:00 p.m. Closed Sundays, annual closing not set at the time of writing. VISA, Access, Eurocards accepted.

Taverne Descartes
rue Descartes, 5e
Tel: 43 25 67 77
Métro: Cardinal Lemoine, Monge

An old and faithful friend, where you can lunch on a two-course *formule* of hors d'oeuvres and a main dish and wine, *service compris*, for 37– 48F, prices which have crept up only slightly since the last edition of this book. Choices might be mussels in garlic sauce or a good *terrine* or salad, then lamb or various steaks or *andouillette* sausages. More ambitiously, climb up to the 76F menu which gives you a dozen mussels, or six snails, or avocado with crab and several other starters, then grilled lamb with garlic butter, baked potato with cream, or fish in wine sauce, or an aubergine and lamb and tomato dish, then a choice of cheeses *plus* dessert – orange salad, *tarte tatin*, sorbets and several more. Service is included on this menu, and another 12F will give you a half-bottle of wine. The interior is imitation-old: dark wood, dim lights; and fast and friendly service of really generous proportions. No annual closing, and open every day except for Saturday lunch, from noon to 2:00 p.m., 7:00 to 11:30 p.m. which on Saturday night stretches to midnight. Open most holidays, except Christmas and New Year's Day. You'll like the ambiance of the street, full of off-beat shops, boutiques of zany clothes, families out for a stroll on warm summer evenings, the smoky smell of chestnuts on winter nights, a street life that never stops.

La Trattoria
5 rue d'Arras, 5e
Tel: 43 29 51 28
Métro: Cardinal Lemoine

A newish Italian restaurant, this, which is a pleasant find in one of the small streets that surround the University of Paris. Already colonized by enterprising students, it seats barely two dozen people, but makes up in personal attention for what it lacks in size. The 'Trat' is run by a lively Italian couple, and the menu, at 50F, is much like that you'd find in southern Italy – nothing very startling, but everything good, and lots of it. Also, this inexpensive menu is served until 8:30 p.m. They'll feed you on tomato and lettuce salad, or Italian *charcuterie* such as mortadella and salami, with good crisp-crusted bread, then tagliatelle, spaghetti Napoli, lasagne, or *scallopine* of veal. Cheese, chocolate mousse, apple tart or ice-cream round off the meal. Service is included, wine is extra – 16F for a quarter-litre. So for 66F you will have dined well *alla casalinga* – Italian home-style. After 8:30, everything's *à la carte*, and main dishes such as lasagne or tagliatelle will cost you about 42F. So an early supper here is one of the bargains of the neighbourhood. Open noon to 3:00 p.m., 7:00 p.m. to 1:00 a.m. Closed Saturdays and Sundays at lunchtime. Open most holidays, and in August when many other restaurants in the university area are closed for the month. VISA, Access, and Eurocheques are accepted, and it's possible AMEX cards will be too, by the time you go there.

6e arrondissement

Restaurant B.E.P. of the École Ferrandi
11 rue Jean Ferrandi, 6e
Tel: 49 54 29 33 or 49 54 28 00
Métro: St-Placide

This just has to be the best-kept culinary secret of Paris, according to our friend Gloria Girton. It's actually the training school run by the Paris Chamber of Commerce. It opens only at lunch, and only during the academic year, so it's closed in summer, on all holidays and during school holiday periods. But if you can fit it into an off-season holiday in Paris, don't miss it. The tables are most attractively set, and would that all Paris waiters and waitresses were as nice as the ones training here. The menu is a *prix-fixe* at 73F, service included, and it's a feast. For instance, fillet of *flétan Dieppoise*, fish in a sauce of cream, shrimps and mussels; or the best roast beef in France, sliced very thin and served with a *marchand devin* sauce and very delicate roast potatoes. Other main courses looked equally inviting. After that, you are offered a choice of seasonal salad or an exquisite cheese tray, and then dessert – four courses in all. *Crêpes suzette* were prepared at the table with great élan, but there were also fresh strawberries, pastries, fresh fruit in *eau de vie*. Half a bottle of very good Beaujolais was only 19F, and the rest of the wine list is excellent. The B.E.P. is open 12:15 to 4:00 p.m., Mondays through Fridays. Not to be missed.

Bistro de la Grille
14 rue Mabillon, 6e
Tel: 43 54 16 87
Métro: Mabillon

Be prepared to spend real money here, as the menu is 130F, service included, drink extra – even so, that's only about £13.50 at present rate of exchange, less than you'd pay in many an English restaurant recommended as good value for money. Le Bistro is one of the most 'branché' – plugged-in to the BCBG circuit – of Paris restaurants. (BCBG's are the French equivalents of London's Sloanes, fun to watch and listen to.) The walls are adorned with photos of film stars you'll probably half recognize. The welcome is warm, the service friendly, and, even if you have to wait for a table, you never get parked and forgotten in a corner. The dining-room is pure 19th century, the cooking true French traditional. Starters can include marrow-bones with toasted French bread, salad with hot *chèvre*, calf's foot vinaigrette, a big plate of *charcuterie*, fresh asparagus, turtle soup, poached seafood. Main courses recently included *daube à l'ancienne*, a sublime beef stew, a duck casserole, and, for a 20F supplement, *pot au feu*. For dessert, beautiful cheeses such as *brie de Meaux*, *chèvre*, *Bleu de Bresse*; or *tarte tatin*, chocolate cake, or a plate of pastries. A quarter-litre of wine is only 12F, and beer a very reasonable 8F – a good choice with something like the *daube*. Open all day, from coffee and croissants at 7:00 a.m., until about midnight, every day of the year. For holiday dinners, however, phone first. Reservations are really necessary. At lunch, try to arrive before 12:30, or wait at the bar for a table.

La Bolée
25 rue Servandoni, 6e
Tel: 46 34 17 68
Métro: Odéon, Luxembourg

Une bolée is the word for a bowl of real Breton cider, the correct accompaniment for the many kinds of crêpes and pancakes and galettes offered here. For times when you want a light but satisfying meal, perhaps when you've had a lavish lunch or are planning a splurge dinner, make for La Bolée. You can tuck into the traditional cheese-, ham-, tomato-filled crêpe, or go for the mildly outrageous – Le Hot Dog with sausage, mustard, gruyère; *L'Americaine*, hamburger, ketchup, gruyère and fried egg; or *Le Maritime* with fish, spinach and cream, all between 25F and 35F. There are several kinds of salads available too. For dessert, there's a really wild choice: *La Normande*, home-made apple compote with caramel and cream, or flambéed with Calvados, for 27F, or *Le Bleuet*, filled with vanilla ice-cream, blueberry jam and whipped cream, for 22F. More conventional sweet crêpes are priced from

16F to 22F. Coffee, 5F, beer 12F, and Breton cider, a half-litre for 18F, are comfortingly cheap. Open Mondays through Fridays from 11:00 to 3:00 p.m., 6:30 to 10:00 p.m. Closed Saturday nights, Sundays, and 13–30 August; open most holidays, closed Christmas Day.

Les Byzantins
33 rue Dauphine, 6e
Tel: 43 26 47 85
Métro: Odéon, St-Michel

The neighbourhood is packed with Greco-French restaurants, all with similar menus. Les B. is 'banal but honest', with stuffed vine leaves, salad, *taramasalata*, and so forth as starters, then *calamares* or *brochettes*, and various predictable desserts, to provide a filling meal for 58F at lunch. A slightly more ambitious menu at 78F is served at lunch and until 8:00 p.m. – after that, everything's *à la carte*. Service is included, drink is extra – a quarter-litre of rather ordinary red wine is an expensive 18F. Jonathan Browne, who lunched there for the first time last summer, was put off by the arrogant manner of the waiter, and the 'rubbishy piped pop music', but said the food was typically Greco-French and good value at the price. It's very popular at night, and a reservation is necessary. Open noon to 2:00 p.m, 7:00 to 10:30 p.m., every day of the year except Christmas and New Year's Day; usually open Easter Sunday and 14 July, but this can vary. VISA, AMEX cards accepted.

La Cabane d'Auvergne
44 rue Grégoire de Tours, 6e
Tel: 43 25 14 75
Métro: Odéon

La Cabane is described as 'warm, cosy, welcoming, really French and rustic, not touristic at all.' Here is a restaurant where you never feel rushed, even though it's one of the better-known streets of the *Quartier Latin*. The atmosphere is that of an *auberge* deep in the country, far from the crowds of the Left Bank. Auvergnat food is 'serious' food, and here it's authentic, not pastiche. No *prix-fixe* menu is offered here, but servings are huge – a main-course dish of *confit de canard* with cèpes (wild mushrooms) would do for two, and is 75F. *Coq au vin, cassoulet, petit salé* with lentils – ranging from

69F to 75F – all these dishes will serve two people. First courses may
be home-made game *pâté* – venison, quail, wild boar, duck; or a
salad of frisée lettuce with strips of sautéed bacon. There's an
old-fashioned bar in the corner, for a glass of wine while you wait.
The crowd is friendly, talkative, and enjoys both the food and the
country-inn atmosphere. You must reserve for dinner. Open noon
to 2:00 p.m., 7:30 to 11:00 p.m. Closed Sundays, one week at
Christmas, one week in May, and all of August. Open some holidays, but check by phone before going.

Claude Valentino
5-7 rue Guisarde, 6e
Tel: 43 29 53 04, 43 29 34 04
Métro: Mabillon

A very smart restaurant indeed, wonderful place for a candle-lit
dinner for two, or three, or four, as both the service and the décor
are elegant and discreet. Claude Valentino offers a lunch menu at a
very reasonable 60F, and actually goes on serving it until 9:00 p.m.
– at least at the moment of writing, but how long they can hold this
is anybody's guess. It's two minutes from St-Germain, just down the
street from St-Sulpice, and a million miles from the tourist-
pandering found in most restaurants in the area. The food is a good
mix of traditional French and some interesting Italian. You may
have to ask to see the 60F menu, but do so: if red peppers with hot
anchovy sauce are being served that day, they're great. We have
enjoyed their unusual steak tartare, served with parmesan and
fennel; chicken with a *cacciatore* sauce, and desserts – lemon and
orange tarts. The restaurant is usually full at night, but the service is
always good, and there's no feeling that they'd like you to hurry.
After 9:00 p.m. everything's *à la carte* and pretty expensive. Drink is
extra to the 60F menu but not too dear; a bottle of wine will be
about 28–30F. Open noon to 2:00 p.m., 6:00 p.m. to about midnight. Closed Sundays, open most holidays except Christmas Day.
At the moment, no annual closing is planned, but it might be wise to
phone first before going in August. If Claude is full, explore the rue
Guisarde – it's jam-packed with good places to eat, though you
should check the prices on the outside menus, as some are more
expensive than they look.

L'Écaille de PCB
5 rue Mabillon, 6e
Tel: 43 26 73 70
Métro: Mabillon

In 1990, our restaurant reviewer gave this restaurant 8 out of a possible 10, and we still can't find one point on which to fault it. The décor is fresh and light, with pure white tablecloths and crockery, and a light hand with the food. It's a spin-off of the very pricey Les Charpentiers, and the same fine spirit is at work here. Fish is the strong point, and they offer a 99F three-course menu, including a small *pichet* of wine or mineral water, and service . . . you must look for this menu, as it is set out in fine print in the bottom corner of the *carte*. It might include fish soup, or some other fishy starter, then a main dish such as *aiguillette de St Pierre*, dessert or cheese. If *tartare de poisson* is on the menu, don't miss it – raw fish 'cooked' in lemon juice, very fresh and delicate in flavour. The menu is served at both lunch and dinner, except on Saturdays. *À la carte*, L'Écaille can run into real money. At night, you must book a table. Open noon to 3:00 p.m., 7:00 to 11:30 p.m. Closed Sundays and major holidays, and 'probably' two weeks in July or August, so check by telephone to avoid being disappointed.

Les Frères de la Côte
12 rue du Cherche-Midi, 6e
Métro: Rennes, St-Placide

This tiny place, with room for only about 20 people, was one of our most fortunate finds of the year: it serves superb fish dishes, and also features a range of distinguished wines by the glass, priced from 6F up. The menu at 79F astonished one of our more experienced (and gluttonous) Paris friends: first courses included *taramasalata* unlike the usual pinkish paste, ripe Charentais melon, a huge salad of ripe tomatoes and good salad greens, or radishes served with butter and coarse salt. Next: turkey escalope with a mysterious *sauce chien*, a *faux filet* steak cooked with thyme, and 'perfect salmon *en papillotte* cooked with sliced tomatoes, butter, white wine and herbs', all served with two vegetables, rice or potatoes. Desserts are things like coconut cake, cheese, or *île flottante*, a towering cone of poached meringue adrift on a pool of creamy vanilla sauce. Servings are very large, and our glutton suggests that two people should order different starters and share them. Don't come here unless you are hungry! The service is greatly praised for friendliness, the one waiter speaks good English. The *à la carte* choices looked wonderful – fish soup at 45F, mussels, squid, marinated cuttlefish, grilled fresh tuna, from 60F to 90F. Open noon to 2:30 p.m., 8:30 p.m. to 2:00 a.m. Closed Sundays. No annual closing. Visa and Access cards accepted.

La Godasse
38 rue M.-le-Prince, 6e
Tel: 43 26 54 14
Métro: Luxembourg, Odéon

When this restaurant first appeared in the 1990 edition of this book, our restaurant spy called it 'a fashionable place in a fashionable area', with handsome stone walls and wooden beams. It attracts a good mix of people, from joking students to prim old ladies with dogs, to a certain number of knowledgeable tourists. The kitchen is open, and everything's cooked within sight. It is a place for carnivores, not for veggies or semi-veggies. And surprisingly enough, there's still a menu for 69F, offered both at lunch and dinner. The choices are few but good: salad with *chèvre*, a flavourful *terrine*, or *oeuf mayo*, then lamb chops, grilled *faux filet*, pork chops; and cheese, or a dessert which changes every day. A second menu is a steepish 120F, and has some remarkable choices. First courses included a salad with *lardons* (crisp slivers of bacon), and a plate of *carpaccio* – the thinnest slices of raw fillet steak. Main dishes were salmon with sorrel sauce, *confit de canard*, a thick juicy steak with béarnaise sauce, and lamb cutlets. The crème caramel was made with *real* caramel; other desserts were a charlotte with fruits, crêpes, pastry, sorbets. Service is included in all prices, but drink is extra: a *pichet*, one-third of a litre, enough for two to share, is 28F. Open from noon to 2:30 p.m., 7:00 to 11:30 p.m. Closed Sundays and most holidays, open 14 July. Closed the last two weeks in July and the first two weeks of August – these dates are not immutable, so if you're looking for a very good place on the Left Bank at that time, telephone – they might be open.

Marco Polo
8 rue de Condé, 6e
Tel: 43 26 79 63
Métro: Odéon

Full of Italians, which means good food, Marco Polo will give you an excellent two-course lunch for 85F, which is a considerable jump from the prices a year or two ago . . . but it's worth it. You must go there for lunch as in the evening everything's *à la carte* and you'd pay between 85F and 125F for main dishes. However, in this popular neighbourhood, food of this quality at this price is rare. And it's perfect for vegetarians, as both starters and main courses can be meatless. Begin with tomato and mozzarella salad, or *carpaccio* (raw beef sliced transparently thin), progress to big plates of pasta served with various sauces – walnut, mushrooms-ham-and-cream, gorgonzola, *carbonara*, *bolognese*. Service is included, and a quarter-litre of nice red wine is 15F. Open noon to 2:30 p.m., 7:00 to 11:30 p.m. Closed Saturdays and Sunday lunch, open (as we write) for dinner on Sundays. Closed major holidays but usually open 14 July, closed first week in August.

Orestias
4 rue Grégoire-de-Tours, 6e
Métro: Odéon

A wonderful little restaurant run by a troupe of manic Greeks who operate on the 'always room for one more' principle. The tables are long and open, offering minimum privacy and maximum chance to get to know people. They are very obliging: one steamy summer day we arrived at nearly 2:30, for lunch, and were fed with speed and amiability. Unbelievably, the menu is only 42F, service included: vine leaves, salad or *tsatsiki* (yoghurt beaten up with finely chopped cucumber, garlic, salt and lemon juice), then lamb on a skewer, roast chicken, lamb chops, etc., and fruit, yoghurt, pastry to finish. *À la carte*, you could have a big plate of assorted Greek hors d'oeuvres which include *taramasalata*, vine leaves, feta cheese, *tsatsiki*, lettuce and tomatoes, for 22F, and as a main dish moussaka, stuffed peppers with rice, various grills and *brochettes*, all immense portions, and ranging from 28F to about 40F. Wine is inexpensive, about 7–8F for a quarter-litre. It's an entertaining, noisy, crowded, hospitable place and once you've discovered it you will probably want to return again and again. Open noon to 2:30 p.m., 6:30 to 11:30 p.m. Closed Sundays, but open holidays and August.

Osteria del Passe Partout
20 rue de l'Hirondelle, 6e
Tel: 46 34 14 54
Métro: St-Michel

This beautiful little restaurant is tucked away in a lane under an
arch, just off the raucous boulevard St-Michel. It's a real find, in this
vastly over-priced and over-crowded district. Work your way
through the spidery handwriting of the menu, and you find a very
well-chosen selection of Italian and French dishes. There are two
menus at lunch: 56F and 66F, each including service. On the less
expensive one, first courses may include a salad of fennel, oranges
and black olives, a *terrine* of courgettes with tomato *coulis*, ricotta
with tomatoes, etc. Then pasta with most unusual sauces, such as
macaroni with guinea-hen, orange rind and cream, or spaghetti
with tomatoes, *petits pois*, spring onions and slivers of bacon. Desserts are very Italian, very traditional – have the *tiramisu* – a very
special Italian cake. The 66F menu is even more special – a remarkable mousse of herring with lemon, and then *carpaccio* (paper-thin
slices of raw fillet of beef) with salad, and the *tiramisu* of course. At
dinner, the menu prices go up to 75F and 115F, with such delicacies
as *tagliatelle alla panna e funghi gorgonzola* (thin noodles with cream,
wild mushrooms and gorgonzola cheese), and *fricassée* of guinea-
hen in a red-wine sauce. Drink is extra, a small *pichet* of wine is 14F,
beer or mineral water is 12F. L'Osteria is open noon to 2:30 p.m.,
7:30 to 10:45 p.m. Closed for Saturday lunch and Sundays. Usually
open on holidays, but telephone first to make sure. No annual
closing, at the time of writing.

Le Polidor
41 rue M.-le-Prince, 6e
Tel: 43 26 95 34
Métro: Odéon

Polidor is really Vieux Paris, extremely popular and usually packed,
so best to go early when daily specials are still available. A two-
course menu – starter and main course, or main course and dessert
– at 50F is offered at lunchtime Mondays through Fridays. The
starters are fairly conventional, but there's a a different main course
each day. Thursday, it might be kidneys with a Madeira sauce,
Wednesday, chicken with a creamy sauce *suprême*, Monday, *boudin*

noir (a black pudding-like sausage) with puréed potatoes. Desserts are quite remarkable, *baba au rhum*, ice-cream, good sorbets, rice gâteau, *tartes*, chocolate mousse. Le Polidor has been here since 1845, but with its elegant décor of mirrors, lamps, chairs, the feeling is that of a 1930s film set. At night and weekends, everything's *à la carte*, but the prices are reasonable – veal in a creamy sauce with white wine, or sirloin, or rump steaks, are the most expensive at 60F, tripe 40F, and so forth. Lemon tart, 14F, is superlative. Wine is not expensive, available by the glass, carafe or bottle. The establishment has many delightful quirks, such as the huge bottle of champagne displayed all year long, then opened with a bang on New Year's Eve. The dining-room has beautiful old floor tiles, and little drawers where the rolled napkins of long-gone patrons were kept for them. The courtyard *toilettes* are *à la turque* and ancient, be warned. Open every day, noon to 2:30 p.m., then 7:00 p.m. to 1:00 a.m., except Sundays when it closes at 11:00 p.m. This is our choice for Christmas lunch in a true Parisian family setting.

Restaurant des Arts
73 rue de Seine, 6e
Métro: Odéon

Here's something rare in this very touristy area, a restaurant that seems to stay the same year after year and indeed generation after generation. It has been here since 1921, it's family-run, and always full of people chattering, waving forks, eating heartily. And most of them are French. It's good simple food, a three-course menu for 64F including service, as we write, the same price it was two years ago – it may go up a few francs in the near future. There are large *salades composées* such as tomatoes, rice, sweetcorn, crunchy lettuce, or *salade niçoise*. Main dishes could include grilled salmon steak, or veal escalope, chicken in a sauce of cream, white wine and tarragon, or steaks (not very tender). Always a big selection of good fruit tarts, or several cheeses. Wine is inexpensive, only about 7F a quarter-litre, but as it isn't very special we usually skip it in favour of the free *'carafe d'eau, s'il vous plaît'*, instead. No reservations, no credit cards. Open noon to 2:00 p.m. (after that they will courteously refuse to serve you), and 7:00 to 9:00 p.m. Closed Friday nights, Saturdays, Sundays, holidays, and August.

Restaurant des Beaux Arts
11 rue Bonaparte, 6e
Tel: 43 26 92 64
Métro: St-Germain-des-Prés

Everyone knows this restaurant, and it has been in guidebooks for
years, but nothing has changed its busy bustling character or the
quality of the food. There's an amazing variety of choices – 12
different starters and as many main courses to pick from – all for
56F, which includes service and wine! Year after year, the *boeuf
bourguignon* gets praise. You can usually find a non-meat dish on the
menu, fish is well cooked and served. Desserts are conventional but
the quality is never less than good. The high-speed shuttle service of
the waitresses is something to see, and a wave of noise hits you as
you open the door. In winter, there's usually a great *pot-au-feu* with
marrow-bones. There are perpetual queues, and you aren't encouraged to dally for long periods over choosing, so consult the menu
posted outside and be ready to give your order quickly. Open noon
to about 2:00 p.m., 7:00 to 11:00 p.m. Don't be disappointed if you
go late in the evening and many of the best choices are gone. Open
every day of the year, including holidays.

Le Sybarite
6 rue du Sabot, 6e
Métro: St-Germain des Prés, St-Sulpice

The rue Sabot is a beautiful, narrow, short street on the Left Bank,
near St-Germain des Prés and St-Sulpice, with several boutiques
and *dépôts de vente* – elegant resale shops where rich women leave
their gently-worn clothes to be sold at lowish prices. Le Sybarite is
garlanded with mentions in the Gault-Millau guide and magazine,
the *Guide Deuzère*, the Touring Club de France, etc. It's an experience in what the French can do to produce really superb food for a
meal at a price that would barely buy you one course in a London
wine bar or restaurant – 75F, service included. Their secret is to
keep the choices few, and offer only a short selection of what is best
in the market each day. First courses could be *mesclun aux noix* –
tender little leaves of several kinds of salad greens, with walnuts – or
an *entrée du jour*, possibly *pâté*, or an egg dish. Steaks are a speciality,
such as *pavé grillé avec thym*, or a *plat du jour*. End with cheese, pastry,
ice-cream or sorbet. A half-litre *pichet* of red wine from the Gard

area of the Midi is only 15F; so two people could eat and drink well for 165F, about £17. They accept Visa cards. Open noon to 2:00 p.m., 7:30 to 10:00 p.m. Closed Saturday lunch, Sundays, holidays and August.

7e arrondissement

Au Pied de Fouet
45 rue de Babylone, 7e
Tel: 47 05 12 27
Métro: St-François-Xavier

Straight out of the late 1940s in décor and ambiance, this tiny, friendly restaurant is not for the claustrophobic. Don't come in a crowd, the five or six tables cannot take a large group. And come early, or be patient and wait. Coffee after the meal is served at the bar, so you don't have to hang about in the doorway while people sit over their cups. Everything is *à la carte*, but inexpensive – *entrées* 11F, main courses between 38F and 48F, desserts 12F. The choices are interesting; *rillettes* and *tabbouleh* as well as soup or salad, with main courses including ravioli in cream sauce, sautéed chicken livers, beef *terrine*. The fruit tarts are famous, plum, gooseberry, cassis, lemon; cheeses include St-Nectaire and very good brie. If you are there on a rare quiet evening, Andrée or Martial may show you the napkin rings kept for their regulars, but don't ask if you blush easily. Adam Steinhouse and a young French friend, Benoit, warn that the toilets are 'indescribable'. Open noon to 2:00 p.m., 7:00 to 9:00 p.m. – last serving at 8:45 p.m. Closed Saturday nights, Sundays, holidays, and from the last week in July to the first Monday of September.

Cam Mach
21 rue de la Comète, 7e
Tel: 45 55 10 36
Métro: Latour-Maubourg

A pleasant little Vietnamese–Chinese–Thai restaurant, a pretty street, an elegant neighbourhood, two minutes to the rue St-Dominique for shopping (see pages 216–18) – and an interesting menu somewhat out of the usual run of Oriental food. For 75F, including service, you can choose from crab and asparagus soup, papaya and chicken salad, steamed *dim sum,* or Vietnamese spring rolls *(nems),* then *porc laqué,* which is glazed roast pork with bean-sprouts and mushrooms; or sweet and sour chicken, curried fish, or beef with satay sauce – very tender thin strips of fillet steak in a spicy but not overpowering sauce – all with rice. Desserts are unusual too: preserved ginger in syrup, *beignets* of fruit, or *flan gelée aux amandes,* cool and refreshing after the spiced food. The restaurant is quiet and the service unobtrusive. Open noon to 2:30 p.m., 7:00 to 11:00 p.m., every day. Visa, Access and Eurocards accepted.

Chez Germaine
30 rue Pierre Leroux, 7e
Tel: 42 73 28 74
Métro: Vaneau

You *must* go early, otherwise prepare to queue for 10 minutes to half an hour – it is that good, and that popular. The gregarious atmosphere will draw you into conversation that could last all evening if you weren't aware of hopeful eaters peering through the windows. Everyone at Chez Germaine knows exactly what you've chosen for your meal, as it is bellowed across the room to the kitchen. M. Babkine says *interdit de fumer,* and he means it, so this is a great place for non-smokers. The menu is an astonishing 40F including service. But even the *à la carte* list is inexpensive, so you'd find it hard to spend more than about 60F. The *prix-fixe* menu is short, but the food is really traditional, well cooked, satisfying. In late years the clientele has become somewhat more BCBG (Paris Sloanes), but the restaurant still has its own atmosphere of innocent enjoyment. Open 11:30 a.m to 2:30 p.m. – go early or you'll have to wait; and at night from 6:30 to 9:00 p.m. Closed Saturday nights, Sundays and holidays, and August.

Le Roupeyrac
62 rue de Bellechasse, 7e
Tel: 45 51 33 42
Métro: Solférino-Bellechasse

One of the few affordable places within walking distance of the Musée d'Orsay, Le Roupeyrac changes little over the years. At lunch, it's crowded with people from nearby ministeries, so go early. Saturday lunchtime is a wiser choice. This is a simple restaurant in an elegant neighbourhood, and does not attempt to give you a long menu. For 65F, it offers starters such as *pâté*, mushrooms *à la grecque, crudités*; then brains in black butter, which we always enjoy, or steak, or grilled pork chop, all with good *frites*. End with cheese, or extremely good chocolate mousse, ice-cream, crème caramel. The *à la carte* menu is really good, with several choices which usually incl. de a very distinguished fish dish such as marinated and grilled fish, at 48F, and a great choice of desserts. A three-course meal could be about 100F. Wine here is served in a small *pichet*, 22 cl, and depending on the quality costs from 6F50 to about 14F. All prices include service. Open noon to 2:45 p.m., 7:00 to 9:30 p.m. Closed Saturday night, Sundays, holidays, and August.

8e arrondissement

L'Assiette Lyonnaise
2l rue Marbeuf, 8e
Tel: 47 23 53 94
Métro: Franklin-D.-Roosevelt

L'Assiette is a real, authentic Lyonnais *bouchon*, a place that serves not only lunch and dinner, but also welcomes you to drop in for a substantial snack anytime between 9:00 a.m. and 11:30 p.m. – a snack such as the traditional *Mâchon* (a platter of *charcuterie* and salads with cold roast meat), and a glass of Beaujolais. L'Assiette is the real thing, friendly and bustling, just what you'd find in the narrow streets of Lyon itself. There are no *prix-fixe* menus, but the *à la carte* choices are interesting and inexpensive: *tripe Lyonnaise* with a *gratin* of macaroni, at 44F, or *andouillette* in a mustard sauce with *gratin dauphinoise* (potato baked in a casserole with cream and cheese), 48F are typical. That very Lyonnais delicacy called *tablier de sapeur* (the fireman's apron), tripe breaded and sautéed, is served with steamed potatoes and tartare sauce for 48F. For starters, you could have a salad of tomatoes and real mozzarella, 32F, or *oeuf en gelée*, 24F. Their cheeses include the famous *cervelle de canut*, a soft cheese with herbs, garlic and a dash of vinegar, 20F. Desserts such as *tarte tatin* or crème brûlée are all 24F. Service is included in the prices, drink is extra – a carafe of Côteau de Lyon is a reasonable 26F. Lunch is from noon to 3:00 p.m., dinner 7:00 to 11:30 p.m., seven days a week and all year around. However, in July, August and September, L'Assiette is closed on Sundays. Reservations are advisable, even for lunch.

Galerie Point Show
66 Champs-Élysées, 8e
Métro: Franklin-D.-Roosevelt, St-Philippe-du-Roule

Fast, frantic and a complete contrast to Le Moka just down the street – here's a Chinese snack bar inside this big gallery of shops. It's the best place to have a quick and satisfying bite to eat on the Champs-Élysées. Try to get there well before 1:00 p.m. or go after 2:00 p.m., because at the height of the lunch rush you'll be queueing for an appreciable time. While the food isn't typically French, the people who eat there are. The menu changes quite frequently, depending on what was in the market on the day, but usually you'll find favourite Oriental dishes like sautéed prawns with bean-sprouts, stir-fried beef with oyster sauce, various kinds of spring-rolls – thin pancakes wrapped around various fish or shredded meat and vegetable fillings. All the main dishes are about 30–35F. Everything's quickly cooked to order, fresh and crisp, and we like the shrill shouting that goes on from the horseshoe-shaped bar where you sit to the chefs at the back. Open mid-morning to 9:00 p.m., every day of the year.

Hyotan
3 rue d'Artois, 8e
Tel: 42 25 26 78
Métro: Franklin-D.-Roosevelt

The entrance to this remarkable Japanese restaurant is so underplayed that you could easily miss it – look for an unassuming white sign with the name in black letters. At the top of the stairs, you see an old Japanese drinking-gourd, the *hyotan*. Inside, it's as if a corner of Tokyo had landed in a street just off the Champs-Élysées. Nine out of ten of the patrons here are Japanese, and it's run by a husband and wife who do all the cooking. Bottles of Japanese 'Scotch' whiskey and *sake* line the walls, labelled with the names of the regular customers for whom they are reserved. Shoji screens at the windows, and totally authentic Japanese food – extremely fresh ingredients, labour-intensive preparation, everything done by hand – and so not cheap. But it is superb; try the *tonkatsu* (deep-fried pork nuggets in batter with a 'fantastic' sauce), or *taki sakama* (baked fish), noodle dishes like *udon*, *soba* and *ramen* which come in a bowl of soup with vegetables, seaweed and shreds of pork. The *miso* soup is very good. Everything's *à la carte*, nothing more than 48F. You could eat well here for between 90F and 100F, including service. Keep the cost down by not ordering wine, which doesn't go well with Japanese food, or beer, which is a steep 18F for a small bottle. Tourists haven't found the Hyotan yet, perhaps because the entrance is so unobtrusive. Open evenings only, 7:00 p.m. to midnight. Closed Sundays, one week between Christmas and New Year's Day, and two weeks in late July and early August.

Le Moka
28 rue d'Artois, 8e
Métro: George-V, St-Philippe-du-Roule

Here's the perfect alternative to lunch in one of the expensive restaurants on or near the Champs-Élysées – where you'll probably have been stricken by the prices and the banality of the food in the touristy places. Le Moka is open for lunch only, and is the sort of restaurant that only the locals know about. It's a typical working-man's place, packed and noisy, full of building workers in paint-spattered dungarees, all eating and joking and shouting at each other. The menu is slightly different every day, well thought out and always well cooked – otherwise its clients would have deserted Le Moka long ago. There's no set-price menu, but the *à la carte* choices are value for money. For a starter, we like the coarse *terrine* or the alternative of a good salad, 17F, and the *plat du jour* is almost always veal or chicken, 43F. *Tournedos*, tender fillet steak cooked to your order, is the most expensive, at 50F. Desserts – fruit *tartes* in flaky pastry, crème caramel, rice pudding – are about 20F, and couldn't be better. Wine bottles stand on every table, and you help yourself. So for 80–5F, you can lunch in the most French way, and be delighted by the atmosphere. Open only from 11:30 a.m. to 3:00 p.m. Closed Saturdays, Sundays and 'probably' two weeks in August.

9e arrondissement

Chartier
7 Faubourg Montmartre, 9e
Métro: Montmartre

A cliché restaurant, listed in all guidebooks, but the value is so good it must be included. It's possible to eat a really superb meal for 61F, everything included: *terrine de lapin, cassoulet parisienne* or *escalope de veau forestière,* and *gâteau St-Sylvestre* or *mousse au chocolat,* and a quarter-litre of wine – just to give you the gist. Service is quick, not too much Gallic charm, but the customers are always an interesting mixture of students, tourists and impecunious Parisians. Look for the *menu conseillé,* which is always good value, but note that 12 per cent service is added to its basic cost. The 1920 décor alone makes Chartier worth a visit. Open 11:00 a.m. to 3:00 p.m., 6:00 to 9:30 p.m., seven days a week, no annual closing.

Le Choron
9 rue Choron, 9e
Tel: 48 78 58 97
Métro: Notre-Dame-de-Lorette

This restaurant is also called Chez Said, and has had a considerable amount of success since it was mentioned in our last edition. But even with more tables, new tablecloths, the disappearance of the pinball machines, and the appearance of a waiter, it's just as winning as before. The menu, served at both lunch and dinner, is now up to 38F from its former 30F, and has expanded to a choice of three main dishes. The first course of hors d'oeuvres is a help-yourself buffet spread with vegetables, salads and egg dishes. Main dishes are simple, grilled pork chops, chicken, steak, fish on Friday, or an escalope of veal, all with good vegetables. If you go on Thursday or Saturday, do have the couscous. You can choose from two desserts such as fruit salad or *crème maison,* or cheese. One couple ate here five nights running, and on their last night in Paris brought M. Said flowers to thank him. If you go there at night, try to arrive early, to admire the fantastic food shops of the street before they close at 8:00 p.m. Open noon to 3:00 p.m., 7:00 to 9:30 p.m. Closed Sundays and August. Open Good Friday, New Year's Day, 14 July, closed Easter and Christmas.

Duhau
32 boulevard Haussmann, 9e
Tel : 47 70 80 01
Métro: Chaussée d'Antin

Open for lunch only, with two menus at 60F and 90F, this is an offshoot of one of Paris's best-known *traiteurs*, famous for their luxurious prepared takeaway dishes. The less expensive menu one day offered quiche, *charcuterie* and *crudités*, then steak, grilled ham, or a *plat du jour* such as Basque chicken, with cheese or dessert – fresh fruit salad, and a glorious chocolate mousse. The 90F menu changes each month, and in July 1991 you could have had prosciutto ham with Charentais melon, served with a glass of Côteau du Layon white wine, and chicken baked with spices, or grilled fish. For dessert, a rich and wonderful *île flottante* or cheese. It's a cool retreat from the great boulevard outside, very welcome after strenuous shopping at the Galéries Lafayette. The service is leisurely. After lunch, look into Duhau's main shop, and see what Parisian chefs make of food when they are really trying. Service included, wine only 6F50 a quarter-litre, and half a bottle of mineral water 8F. Open 11:30 a.m. to 2:30 p.m. Closed Sundays, holidays, and Saturdays from the weekend of 14 July to the last week in August. No annual closing.

Picpain
2 boulevard Haussmann, 9e
Métro: Richelieu-Drouot

Here's a breath of fresh air in the fast-food world! 'It should be a criminal offence to eat in the best-known hamburger-chain restaurants when there's something like the Picpain,' according to a Paris-based friend. It's clean, fresh-feeling with white latticed walls, small pretty tables, cane chairs, staff who actually smile. You stand at the small counter to give your order and wait while it's cooked on the spot. Picpain is open from 8:00 a.m. for a 'Pic-Oeuf', a freshly cooked egg with a crusty roll, orange juice, excellent coffee; later, you could have a sandwich made with breast of chicken, salad, tomato, *frites*, and crusty roll, for 18F20. The burgers of various types are made as you watch, and have none of the steam-table taste of other eat-and-run places. Salads are crisp and fresh. Their *menu grillé* is a cheeseburger, a bag of *frites*, and a big glass of a soft drink, for 23F50. All their bread is made in their own bakery, and is a treat. Closed Mondays, but open every other day until midnight, and until 1:00 a.m. Fridays and Saturdays.

Pupillin
19 rue Notre-Dame de Lorette, 9e
Métro: St-Georges

A stylish neighbourhood restaurant, under gay management and catering to a mixed crowd. Its bar salads are much recommended – there are at least six, each enough for a full meal: avocado stuffed with fresh cheese, lemon, orange, ham, olives, and dill, for example; or a pasta salad with peas, hard-boiled egg, bananas, pineapple, tomatoes, ham, fresh cheese and seasonings, each 33–35F. The fare varies with available produce. The imaginative 69F menu features chicken-liver or vegetable *flans*, zucchini quiche or cold spinach soup for starters, and kidneys in Madeira sauce, squid *à la armoricaine* or *carpaccio* with salad to follow. Wine is available only in demis, at 32F50; beer is much cheaper. Desserts, says our delighted critic, are divine. Open 11:30 a.m. to 2:30 p.m., 7:30 p.m. to 1:00 a.m. Closed only Christmas Day.

Le Relais Savoyard
13 rue Rodier, 9e
Tel: 45 26 17 48
Métro: Cadet, Notre-Dame-de-Lorette

The same family has run the Relais Savoyard for the past quarter of a century, and it has its quota of regulars from the neighbourhood – visitors from the outer world, so to speak, are looked upon as rather an oddity. Service is efficient and polite. The chef, if he has time to talk, is very friendly and chatty. In this simple pine-panelled restaurant, the food is good bourgeois cooking, very, very French. The menu is 72F, including red wine and service – only about 8F up in price from two years ago. Among the hors d'oeuvres, *cervelas* salad, *crudités*, herring with potatoes in oil, grapefruit, and black radish – a huge radish is brought to your table and you cut off the slices you want. Main courses recently included *poule au pot*, chicken in cream sauce, *boudin* sausage with sautéed apples, a plate of cold country ham with salad. The home-made apple tart was exceptionally good;

other choices are crème caramel, cake or cheese. Open noon to
3:00 p.m., 7:30 to 10:00 p.m. or possibly a little earlier or later,
depending on how busy they are. Closed Sundays, holidays, and
August.

Xavier Gourmet
21 rue Notre-Dame de Lorette, 9e
Métro: St-Georges

Serendipitously next door to Pupillin, another notable find, Xavier
is a rather sophisticated blend of tea-room and restaurant, always
busy, always good. Examples: trout in aspic with smoked salmon
sauce and a green salad, 35F. A crêpe stuffed with raw mountain
ham, raclette cheese from the Savoie, with green salad and
tomatoes, 30F. A sandwich, on wonderful chewy *poilâne* bread, of
tomatoes, mozzarella, fresh basil, and olive oil, served with a green
salad, 30F. Best of all are the pastries. A glass of good wine is 9F,
service is included, and it's easily possible to walk out satiated for
55F. Open 9:00 a.m. to 10:30 p.m., seven days a week, including
holidays. No annual closing. They have another branch, as yet
untested, at 89 boulevard de Courcelles, 8e.

10e arrondissement

Au Gigot Fin
56 rue de Lancry, 10e
Tel: 42 08 38 81
Métro: Jacques Bonsergent

A bistro in 1920s style, popular with the local working population –
you must go early in the evening to get the best choices, as everything is freshly cooked each day and represents what the chef liked
in the market that morning. There's a menu at 50F for lunch only,
and three others, at 85F, 105F, and 170F, served at lunch and
dinner. Our eaters opted for the 85F menu and were offered some
good choices as starters – *mousseline* of duck liver (very tasty and a
good portion), hot *chèvre* with salad (over-seasoned and rather oily),
or herring with potato salad or a cold meat salad. Main courses were
roast turkey, tender and very good, sliced and served with sautéed
potatoes, leg of lamb redolent of garlic, *brandade de morue* (salt cod in

a rich, creamy, garlicky sauce), and always a *plat du jour*. It was an opulent meal, and they chose fruit sorbet, raspberry and lemon, for dessert. Service is included in all prices, and drink is fairly reasonable – wine from 12F to 20F a quarter-litre, mineral water 12F, beer 15F. Open noon to 2:00 p.m., (the 50F menu is such a bargain that it gets crowded by 12:30), 7:30 to 10:00 p.m. Closed Saturday lunch, Sundays, holidays and August.

11e arrondissement

Au Trou Normand
9 rue Jean-Pierre Timbaud, 11e
Tel: 48 05 80 23
Métro: Oberkampf, or a brisk walk from République

Not fancy, but attractive in its simplicity, and its *à la carte* prices are astonishingly low: a potato salad with smoked salmon for 11F, *calamares* in tomato sauce with rice 26F30, chocolate mousse 10F, a quarter-litre of house red wine 7F: a whole meal, with an apéritif before dinner, only 62F including service. Other choices on the menu were various country *pâtés*, salads, *tabbouleh*, very tender *tournedos* steaks, *brochettes*, all quite inexpensive. This is the perfection of village Paris, run by two nice women. The service is leisurely and friendly, the clients obviously very local and very happy. The restaurant spy who discovered this for us several years ago, remarked 'I peeped through the steamed-up windows one winter evening and saw that all the clients were dancing.' A small, friendly dog has the run of the place. Open noon to 2:30 p.m., 7:00 to 11:30 p.m. Closed Saturday nights, Sundays, holidays. Usually they're closed the day before and the day after Christmas and New Year's, Good Friday and Easter Monday, and 'probably' in August.

Bois et Charbons
8 rue de la Main d'Or, 11e
Tel: 48 05 77 10
Métro: Ledru-Rollin

It takes persistence to find this small gem, as it's on a short street off a narrow alley of furniture-makers' shops that runs beside no. 133, faubourg St-Antoine. It serves good home cooking from Lyon, the native city of Patrick Cormillot, the *patron*. At first glance, the place looks unpromising, with half a dozen workmen drinking at the bar. Go through into the little dining-room, still very unpretentious, with the occasional unpainted patch on the wall, and the smell of good cooking will lift your spirits. The menu at lunch, for 52F, has few choices, written on a blackboard. Every dish is a winner. At night, everything's *à la carte*, but not expensive. Starters were all 25F: the home-made *terrine beaujolais* was a thick slice, with a delicious taste of red wine. The Lyonnais speciality *cervelle de canut* is soft white cheese sparked up with fresh herbs. Calves' liver as a main dish was thinly sliced, with vegetables and sautéed potatoes liberally sprinkled with parsley, 72F. A dish of *tripe gratinée* was only 52F. Desserts are all 25F, the chestnut cake served with *crème fraîche* and a thin icing of bitter chocolate is exceptional. Service is included in all prices, wine quite expensive at 21F for a quarter-litre *pichet*. The hours are eccentric: noon to 2:00 p.m. for lunch all year; in the summer months, dinner at 8:00 p.m. to 10:00 p.m. on Wednesdays, Thursdays and Fridays only; in the winter, open for dinner only Thursdays and Fridays. Closed Saturdays, Sundays, August, and holidays (closed for a week from Christmas to New Year's). If you plan to dine here, phone early in the day, so the friendly cook/waitress will know how many to expect.

Les Cinq Points Cardinaux
14 rue Jean Macé, 11e
Tel: 43 71 47 22
Métro: Charonne

We have known this little place for more than ten years, when our friend Rory Cellan Jones found it in a dilapidated alleyway off the rue St-Antoine. Now that the street has been bulldozed, the restaurant has re-appeared at this pretty and peaceful spot. It still serves simple, well cooked food, and most of its patrons are still the working people of the neighbourhood. The owner has decorated the plain walls with the original tools used by the artisans of this craftsmen's area, brought from the old site. Don't be misled by the ordinariness of the bar as you come in, you are here to eat, like everyone else. Everything's *à la carte* at lunch, and the prices are exceptionally low: duck mousse 10F, a thick *tournedos* steak with bordelaise sauce, 28F, and cheese or dessert – wonderful redcurrant tart, 7F50. The meal cost just 45F50, service included. A quarter-litre of wine is 7F50, and a half-litre of a light, pleasant Beaujolais-style wine is 16F. Les Cinq Points is now open for dinner, with a more imaginative menu at 95F. Open noon to 2:00 p.m., 7:00 p.m. onwards. Closed Sundays, holidays and August.

Nini Peau d'un Chien
24 rue des Taillandères, 11e
Métro: Bastille, Place Voltaire

A line from a French popular song gives this very unusual restaurant its unusual name. It was one of our best discoveries in the late summer of 1991. 'Nini' is a small room, decorated with theatrical posters, photographs, sheet music, cool fresh greenery. In summer, French doors open to a street short on glamour but long on very French neighbourhood life. At lunch, the menu is short, but the food distinguished – and the cost is an incredible 56F, including service. For that you get a buffet table for starters, five or six choices of main dish, and dessert. The buffet offers freshly prepared artichoke hearts, Charentais melon crescents, tomato and fresh basil salad, frisée lettuce, two dressings; then grilled chicken, omelettes with cheese or ham, various meat and vegetable dishes. Desserts can be rich, or as simple as fresh fruit salad. You can even have an eat-as-much-as-you-like buffet table lunch for 32F. Wine is inexpensive, and they serve 1930s-type cocktails – Gin Rickeys, White Ladies, Tom Collinses, Whiskey Sours. The clientele is a good mix, women lunching here after shopping, older people with small dogs on leads, all sorts of couples dining before the theatre, family groups at tables for four or six. At night, a more elaborate menu is 109F, service included, drink extra. Open 11:30 a.m. to 2:30 p.m. 8:00 to 11:00 p.m. Closed Sundays, Mondays, holidays. Open August, but closed for a short holiday in autumn or winter, so check by phone. VISA, Amex credit cards only.

Palais de la Femme
94 rue de Charonne, 11e
Tel: 43 71 07 07
Métro: Charonne

One of the many surprises in the long list of good restaurants in the 11e is in this fine building, a residence for young women alone in

Paris. The hotel is open to women only, but the superb self-service restaurant in its magnificent high-ceilinged room is open to everyone. In addition to the main room, there's a new pizzeria in the basement, and a tea-room in the lobby. Everybody eats here — writers from a smart magazine down the street, fashion models from a shoot in the place d'Aligre, elderly locals who love it for the fine food and the low prices. You can heap a plate with *crudités* for 6F20; steak *haché* with leeks, peas and *frites*, 24F50; pastry from 7F80 to 10F30; mineral water 4F a small bottle, beer 12–15F. Service at the counter is very friendly, and you're asked only to take your tray to the service hatch after your meal. What a place! Open 11:30 a.m. to 2:30 p.m., 6:30 to about 9:30 p.m., every day of the year including all holidays.

Pizza Tavola
10 rue de la Roquette, 11e
Tel: 47 00 20 85
Métro: Bastille

In a magical street just a few steps away from the place de la Bastille, there's one of the best of the many Italian restaurants we know. Although it calls itself a pizza place, it's more than that. They do make real Sicilian pizzas, thin-crusted, irregular, spread with home-made pizzaiola sauce, and toppings put on with a generous hand. But they also do pasta, freshly made, with sauces tasting as though *mammina* is standing over the cooker in the kitchen. And their non-pasta main dishes are said to be as good as their *canneloni* and *fettucine alla crema*. Pizzas cost 28F to about 40F, main dishes are 40–60F. We like their big servings of cassis, lemon, or mango sorbets from one of the best Parisian ice-cream makers, 14F. An *à la carte* meal here, lunch or dinner, could be as little as 65F including drink and service. The delightful owner has been decorated by several gastronomic groups. He loves to chat, and speaks good English. Open 11:00 a.m. to 2:00 a.m., seven days a week. Major credit cards accepted.

La Ravigotte
41 rue de Montreuil, 11e
Tel: 43 72 96 22
Métro: Faidherbe-Chaligny

This restaurant is a real find, tucked away in a part of Paris which saw a lot of goings-on in the French Revolution – there are plaques commemorating this or that event, in all the surrounding streets. This is one of our top-priced restaurants, but very much recommended for serious eaters – plan to go there one evening when you've had only a snack for lunch and are feeling adventurous, and mildly rich. It's in an area with real character, and owned by the original proprietor's charming grand-daughter. She will suggest the evening's best choices. The menu is 115F, service included: among the dishes, a salad with *foie gras* and smoked duck breast, or a fricassée of snails, then a choice of *tête de veau*, home-made *cassoulet* (excellent), veal with tarragon, steak with shallots, and a delicious fish called *eglefin*. For dessert, try the bitter chocolate mousse, or profiteroles with chocolate sauce, or have cheese. Service is included, drink is extra – a quarter-litre of wine is really pricey at 28F, so have mineral water or 'une carafe d'eau'. Open for lunch Mondays through Saturdays, noon to 2:30 p.m. Dinner is served only Thursdays, Fridays and Saturdays, 7:00 to 9:30 p.m. Closed Sundays, holidays and August.

Relais du Massif Central
16 rue Daval, 11e
Tel: 47 00 46 55
Métro: Bastille

We have known this simple family restaurant for years. Now, since the Bastille area is changing and up-grading so fast, we asked a friend living in Paris to visit it for us. As we hoped, the warm welcome and 'really splendid food' is unchanged. Even on a Monday night, the place was full. There are three menus: one at 58F had such starters as red cabbage vinaigrette, *pâté de campagne*, egg mayonnaise, followed by veal escalope *milanaise*, grilled steak or half a chicken, with dessert or cheese. The most expensive at 95F was praised; first courses included a seafood pie packed with goodies, and frogs' legs with rice in a *provençale* sauce, with lemon-scented wipes to clean up sticky fingers, or snails or fresh asparagus vinaigrette. For a main course, our friend had scallops *provençale* with rice, so good that she wiped the plate clean with crusts of bread. Another choice was a dish of big, juicy, grilled prawns served with crisp potatoes. Even if you're full (the portions are large), you'll find the desserts tempting: cake with lashings of whipped cream, three kinds of fruit tart, and chocolate mousse. Service is included, wine extra but inexpensive, 9–13F for a quarter-litre. Open noon to 3:00 p.m., 7:30 to midnight. Closed Sundays, holidays, and August.

12e arrondissement

Le Limonaire
88 rue de Charenton, 12e
Tel: 43 43 49 14
Métro: Ledru-Rollin, Gare de Lyon

This good little neighbourhood place hasn't changed in years. A tiny restaurant on a tree-studded corner, in turn-of-the-century style, decorated with musical instruments on the walls, plants, old photos, a piano in the corner and an old *orgue de barbarie*. The ceiling is pressed tin, the bar is beautiful, traditional *zinc*. There is no *prix-fixe* menu, but 85F will see you beautifully fed, and another 9–16F will get you excellent wine, Côtes du Rhône or fruity red Visan. Starters include a variety of *terrines*: tuna, or chicken livers with blueberries, or a Basque *terrine*, 22F, or *friton de canard de Lot*, also 22F. The *plat du jour* comes with a glass of wine, and could be an unusual veal dish cooked with lemon and herbs, or chicken done in any number of imaginative ways, with potatoes and salad, about 52F. If you are lucky, their famous chocolate/hazelnut cake, with *crème anglaise* will be on the menu for 25F. Wine is available by the big glass for about 9F. Open noon to 2:30 p.m., 8:00 to 10:00 p.m., seven days a week. Closed August and major holidays.

13e arrondissement

Bangkok-Thailand
35 boulevard Auguste-Blanqui, 13e
Tel: 45 80 76 59
Métro: Corvisart

Pure Thai restaurants, unalloyed with Vietnamese or Chinese influence, are rare in Paris, which is why we like this one – although the décor has to be seen to be believed, with plastic bric-à-brac, amazing paintings, a plethora of Buddhas (there must be a collective noun to describe these, perhaps a Smile of Buddhas?), insistent music. Never mind: enjoy the food, the smiling welcome, the good service. The food is subtly spiced and has a tantalizing flavour that owes much to coriander leaves. At lunch the menu is 60F, including service, and offers a variety of Thai soups, *nems* (spring rolls with an irresistible thin sauce), or Thai salad. Then beef with basil, pork with spices, beef with sautéed onions, all served with rice. Fruit, or a deep-fried *beignet* of fruit, are the desserts, served with tea or coffee. At night the menu price soars to 100F – a lot of money for the fairly restricted choice of dishes. Open noon to 2:30 p.m., 7:00 to 10:45 p.m. Closed Sundays and holidays, and for two weeks or so, in July or August – dates not set, so telephone first.

L'Espérance
9 rue de l'Espérance, 13e
Tel: 45 80 22 55
Métro: Corvisart

Don't turn and walk away when you see the rather dingy exterior of L'Espérance, or the run-down look of the neighbourhood. As soon as you go up the few steps to the restaurant itself, the atmosphere alters at once. The waiter and the other diners give a smiling welcome, and you can join in the conversation if you're so minded. The price is hard to believe: 41F50, including service and drink! There are three or four choices of starters. The leeks vinaigrette are home-made and very good, or you might have anchovies, sardines or herring. For your main course, steak with shallots is very good, with thin crisp *frites* freshly made and hot. Roast chicken, sausages, and roast pork are usually on the menu. Desserts sound banal, but are really fine: mocha cake and fruit tart especially. As well as the standard brie and camembert, the cheeses include gruyère and *chèvre*. How do they do it? If you're looking for elegance, you won't find it here, but it's simple and satisfying. Open seven days a week, noon to 2:15 p.m., 7:00 to 10:15 p.m., and Christmas, Easter, New Year's Day. Closed one month in summer, dates not yet decided.

Hawai
87 avenue d'Ivry, 13e
Métro: Tolbiac, Porte d'Ivry

In the heart of Le Quartier Chinois of Paris, this restaurant combines Vietnamese, Chinese and Cambodian food, and was highly praised by a Chinese student living in Paris and by one of our most experienced eaters. They tried a variety of dishes, and report that you can eat well for 60–65F, or have a real splurge for 125F; and they suggest that you have a soup and two other dishes, perhaps steamed spring rolls and a hot rice dish, or the spring rolls and a cold noodle dish. For those not familiar with South East Asian delicacies, a 'soup dish' like the Tonkinese *xelua*, *nho*, or *taubay*, 26F–28F, gives you a big bowl with 'everything' in it. Steamed spring rolls – a Vietnamese speciality quite unlike the Chinese ones – are 24F, with an irresistible dipping sauce. *Riz au porc grillé et émincé*, for 34F, was delicious. One order of fresh fruit, mangos and papayas, at 35F, is enough for two. The menu is heavy on meat, so the Hawai is no place for vegetarians. Service is included in all prices, drink is extra – a quarter-litre of wine is 12F, beer 14F–16F, and jasmine tea 5F. Hawai is clean and the service is friendly, fast and attentive, but no one minds if you linger over dinner. Open 10:30 a.m. to 3:00 p.m., 6:00 to 11 p.m., 365 days a year . . . great idea for an offbeat Christmas lunch.

14e arrondissement

Au Vin des Rues
21 rue Boulard, 14e
Tel: 43 22 19 78
Métro: Denfert-Rochereau

This adorable little restaurant changes its menu daily, but a typical selection might be a plate of Lyonnaise salads which includes marinated anchovies, pigs' ears vinaigrette, pickled lambs' feet, 30F; crayfish with home-made mayonnaise, 45F; or marinated salmon with a salad of potatoes in olive oil, 45F. If you are still able to eat another mouthful after that, cherry *clafoutis* (thick pancake from Limosin) and lemon tarts, among other choices, are 30F. They always have a nice selection of Beaujolais red at about 12F a quarter-litre. Without dessert, you'll be spending about 87F, service included, for a superb meal, in a very pretty room embellished with pictures, posters, maps and drawings. Except for readers of the 1990 edition of *Paupers' Paris*, it's undiscovered by visitors. It's near the lively and attractive rue Daguerre where a street market bubbles and sparkles. Open 1:00 to 3:30 p.m., dinner Wednesdays and Fridays only, 9:00 to 11:00 p.m. On other evenings it's a wine bar presided over by the owner. Closed Sundays, Mondays, and August.

Crêperie de St-Malo
53 rue de Montparnasse, 14e
Tel: 43 20 87 19
Métro: Montparnasse

The rue de Montparnasse has always been rich in Breton restaurants, and this is one of the choicest, very 'sympa'. It's much more than a crêperie, offering three menus. Even the least expensive, the Menu Forestière at 56F50, gives you such choices as a frisée salad with chicken livers and bacon, then a Breton galette (a big flat pancake) wrapped round ham, cheese and egg or mushrooms, finishing with a crêpe with chocolate, honey or lemon. The Menu Marin at 58F50 offers a saucer of *taramasalata*, a smoked salmon or seafood galette, and sweet crêpes as above. For the top price of 68F50, luxuriate in *moules marinière* for a first course, or homemade fish soup, thick, delicious and partnered by a very good *rouille* – then grilled salmon with Béarnaise sauce, luscious grilled sardines in season or *dorade* – finishing with a sweet crêpe or crème caramel. Service is included in all prices, and Breton cider at 13F50 is a must. The St-Malo is open 365 days of the year, 11:30 a.m. to 3:00 p.m., 6:00 p.m. to 2:00 a.m.

Le Jéroboam
72 rue Didot, 14e
Tel: 45 39 39 13
Métro: Plaisance

A lovely little bistro which offers three *formules* at lunch. One, 49F including service, is an excellent cold buffet which one day in 1991 included glazed salmon, *charcuterie*, vegetables in a vinaigrette, and *tabbouleh*. A second *formule*, at 53F, added a hot vegetable plate to the cold buffet. For 59F, you could have a lavish dish, the buffet *and* a lush chocolate cake. A quarter-litre of wine is 15F. At night, there's a two-course menu at 89F including service. The last time one of our most food-loving friends was there, the first courses were smoked salmon salad, consommé with sherry under a puff-pastry dome, fried camembert with a salad; then *pot-au-feu* with marrow-bones, among other hearty dishes, all very well cooked. Servings of dessert are huge: the chocolate cake was big enough to divide in two, 30F, and a real OTT dessert, armagnac soufflé with prune-caramel sauce, the same price. Open noon to 2:30 p.m., 7:30 to 10:00 p.m. Closed Sundays and Monday evenings. The annual closing is usually from the last Sunday in July to the end of August. Open some holidays, but ring first to check.

Kenavo
20 rue d'Odessa, l4e
Tel: 43 20 72 62
Métro: Montparnasse

Kenavo isn't the kind of place most people would ever find, but once discovered it becomes a sort of addiction. The nearby Breton centre sometimes overflows in here on a Sunday night, and you might be treated to an impromptu concert. One musician played his diatonic accordion so infectiously that the diners left their places and danced among the tables. And the crêpes are splendid. There are two menus at 68F70 and 78F50 – on the more expensive one, the first course was a big salad with lardons and preserved duck livers, then a main-course crêpe, and a sweet pancake for dessert. Other choices on this menu were a cheese and fresh mushroom crêpe, or one with egg, ham, cheese and mushrooms. If you order *à la carte*, a wonderful crêpe with leeks, crème fraîche and cheese is the most expensive at 48F50, other main-dish crêpes are as low as 14F50. Some dessert crêpes are real fantasies, like the thin lacy one rolled around fresh pineapple or banana, and flamed with rum, 36F50. Breton cider is costly at 22F50 a quarter-litre. Try *lait ribot*, a yoghurt drink, 14F50. Open noon to 3:00 p.m., and from 6:00 p.m. to whenever the owners decide to close, typically sometime between midnight and 2 a.m. Open seven days a week, the year around, except either Christmas or New Year's Day as the mood takes them.

Le Luma
64 rue Daguerre, 14e
Tel: 43 35 16 92
Métro: Denfert-Rochereau, Edgar-Quinet

70F buys you a remarkable dinner in this charming Montparnasse restaurant. First courses one night included seafood salad, vegetable soup, and an Easter *pâté* of egg, meat and herbs. Main courses: the salmon with spinach was outstanding, and other dishes included roast kid, and turkey in curry sauce. For dessert, if *poire bourdaloue* – pear with an almond-flavoured cream base – is on the menu, have it; other choices are crème caramel, ice-cream and fruit tart. À *la carte* prices climb swiftly out of most people's reach, but here many of the dishes from the expensive menu appear as choices on the more modest *prix-fixe* one, always a good sign. 'A group of my father's friends, ten sleek, rich, choosy businessmen who hate a bad meal more than anything in the world went there for dinner,' our French restaurant spy told us, ' and one sent me a note of thanks for the recommendation!' Open noon to 2:30 p.m., and 7:00 to 11 p.m. Closed Saturday lunchtime and Sundays, holidays and 15–31 August. Open Good Friday and Easter Monday, and 14 July unless it falls on a Saturday or Sunday.

Midi-Trente
56 rue Daguerre, 14e
Métro: Denfert-Rochereau

We got a superlative report on this café/restaurant, found by a Paris friend when strolling around Montparnasse. Its odd opening hours make it possible to have a late breakfast with coffee and remarkably good pastries, or a very special lunch, or to drop in after lunch elsewhere for coffee and dessert, or real tea. The *à la carte* prices seem rather high, at first, but you can lunch there for about 62F, with a wonderful starter such as *pâté* with *confiture d'oignon*, a delicious onion marmalade, 18F, and a main course like the salad of broccoli, walnuts, cantal cheese, prosciutto and salad greens, 44F. Or have a main course and a 'fabulous dessert like cherry flan', for only a little more. If you let yourself go, you could have three superb courses and wine for about 125F, but that's real extravagance. It's a good place for vegetarians; try courgette quiche with *chèvre* and salad, or a platter of anchovies, ripe tomatoes, basil, real mozzarella and curly lettuce, each 48F. Prices include service – the house wines are well selected but expensive. You are recommended to sit on the terrace under an awning in summer, or if indoors, get a table near the bar. In the afternoon, Midi-Trente stays open as a tearoom with a selection from a famous Paris tea-merchant. Open 11:00 a.m. to 6:00 p.m. only. Closed Sundays, holidays, and the third week in August.

Le Plomb de Cantal
3 rue de la Gaité, 14e
Tel: 43 35 16 92
Métro: Gaité

It would be easy to pass by the Plomb de Cantal, it's such an unassuming little place not far from the theatres on the rue de la Gaité. But if you miss it, you will not have experienced a very characteristic Auvergnat restaurant of Paris. There's an air of great friendliness here, and although there is no set menu, prices are low and servings large. Our friend who knows her way around the Auvergnat and Breton world of Paris, says that she can make a meal from one dish. The gratinéed 'Bougnat' soup is topped with bread and cheese, 30F. A potato casserole from the Auvergne is made with potatoes, garlic, cream and *tome* cheese. Their main-course salads, such as the one with duck livers, *croûtons*, eggs and frisée lettuce, are 50F. After that, if you can face it, try the chestnut flan, 28F. Wine is pricey, stick to mineral water or a carafe of water. Sometimes you hear Auvergne bagpipes moaning and wailing in the cellar where musicians practise. Crowded, popular, either book, go early, or brace yourself to wait for a table. Open noon to 3:00 p.m., 7:00 p.m. to midnight. Closed Sundays and August. Open most holidays unless they are on a Sunday, but as usual it's safest to phone first.

15e arrondissement

Bistrot Bourdelle
12 rue Antoine Bourdelle, 15e
Tel: 45 48 57 01
Métro: Montparnasse (use the Bienvenue exit)

A simple restaurant, with its own circle of habitués, oil-cloth covered tables, posters on the walls, a couple of tables outside in good weather, a cordial *patron*, and excellent, imaginative food. The two-course menu of 74F includes a number of salads to start (mushroom and cabbage, lentil salad, cucumbers in cream, salad with warm chicken livers, *fromage de tête*), followed by a *plat du jour*, or *andouillette* in mustard sauce, *quenelles de brochet* in nantua sauce, steak in a choice of sauces, *boeuf bourguignon*. Desserts are extra at 26F, among them *île flottante* and chocolate mousse. There's a good house Côtes du Rhône, 12–15F. Open noon to 2:00 p.m., 8:00 to 10:00 p.m. Closed Saturdays, Sundays, and an unspecified three weeks in August.

17e arrondissement

Formula Uno
28 rue de Vernier, 17e
Tel: 40 54 05 39
Métro: Porte de Champerret

This restaurant in the far reaches of the 17e is worth the Métro journey – yet most people would walk on by. It was a serendiptous find one hot Saturday, when a much better-known restaurant was unexpectedly closed: a very small delicatessen/pizza parlour/restaurant with a few tables on the pavement, rare cheeses in the window, a big piece of *prosciutto* ham on a carving board. Expecting nothing but a so-so pizza, what we had was a remarkable meal for 68F: a mozzarella/tomato/anchovy/caper salad, then fresh home-made pasta with a choice of sauces, finishing with a huge serving of chocolate mousse, dense dark rich chocolate lightly fluffed with egg whites, enough for two to share. Another member of the party ate what he called the best mortadella sausage this side of Palermo, and said that even he had never tasted a pizza as good as the 'Carrietera', baked to a crisp darkness in a charcoal oven. His dessert was real Italian vanilla ice cream. A half-litre of good rough red was 30F. The owners are a Sicilian family, and long may they reign over the rue de Vernier. Open from 11:30 a.m. to 2:30 p.m., 7:00 to 9:00 p.m., every day except Christmas, Easter and January 1. No annual closing.

Tanger
16 boulevard des Batignolles, 17e
Métro: Place de Clichy

This tiny neighbourhood restaurant specializes in Moroccan food and is always packed with locals and people from other neighbourhoods who come to have excellent couscous or *tagines*, the North African casseroles of chicken with prunes and almonds, or chicken with olives and preserved lemons. The menu at 85F includes service and Moroccan wine or beer, and is served at lunch and dinner. We liked the aubergine purée as a starter, and the spicy but not over-hot *brochette*; another choice was ratatouille with spiced *merguez* sausage. A fresh fruit cup was a cool finish to a highly-flavoured meal. À *la carte*, the *tagines* and immense servings of couscous with chicken (garnished with chick peas and raisins in a flavoursome broth with fiercely hot harina sauce served alongside) are each 71F. Homemade almond pastry is 24F. Service included, drink extra – beer is the thing to order. Open noon to 2:30 p.m., 7:00 to 10:30 p.m. Closed Sundays and August. Open 'some' holidays. Service is really slow, so be prepared for a long lunch or to sit around most of the evening.

18e arrondissement

Les Chauffeurs
11 rue des Portes Blanches, 18e
Tel: 42 64 04 17
Métro: Marcardet-Poissonières

Our latest visit found this restaurant as appealing as ever. The owner is chatty and friendly, his wife is still the chef, the only waitress is still helpful. The *à la carte* menu is well-priced and a good meal could cost as little as 89F, including service and a quarter-litre of wine. The dishes change every day, often using fresh produce from the family farm in the Touraine. Our first courses included pork *confit* or smoked pork fillet, both 12F, rabbit *terrine*, 16F, asparagus vinaigrette, and a large plate of paper-thin slices of Auvergne country ham, the most expensive starter at 42F. Main courses that day were roast lamb with *flageolets*, 48F, *pot au feu* with leeks, turnips, potatoes and carrots – a real country dish,

big and hearty, for 38F, sole *meunière* and roast chicken. The profiteroles are special; choux pastry shells made at the restaurant are
filled with rich ice-cream and swamped with hot, bittersweet
chocolate sauce, 25F. The 25F ice-cream sundaes with fresh fruit,
liqueurs, sauces and whipped cream, are topped with ridiculous
campy little paper umbrellas and figurines. Open noon to 3:00
p.m., 7:00 to 10:00 p.m. Closed Wednesdays and Thursdays, and
July, August and most holidays.

Restaurant Ephèse
58 rue Doudeauville, 18e
Métro: Château-Rouge

This Franco-Turkish restaurant is in a really tacky neighbourhood
full of cheap-luggage shops, about ten minutes' walk north of the
boulevard Rochechouart. If you've been prowling for bargains at
Tati or in the rue Séveste (page xx), head for Ephése. It's small,
friendly, and has really good mid-Eastern food: lentil soup for
16F, stuffed vine leaves or *taramasalata*. Servings are large. The
very tender lamb *brochette* is served with *burghul*, couscous, or rice.
There's a *plat du jour*, 30F, on weekdays. Or have a plate of various
starters, followed by a sweet treat. If you enjoy your desserts sweet,
rich, very Turkish, they cost 16–17F. The young men who cook,
wait on tables, and help you sort out the Turkish/French menu,
are very kind. Service is included in all prices, drink extra; beer
10F, wine 13F a quarter-litre. Open noon to 3:00 p.m., 7:00 to
midnight. Closed Sundays, open most holidays but closed Christmas, and for about two weeks in mid-August.

Le Fait Tout
4 rue Dancourt, 18e
Tel: 42 23 93 66
Métro: Anvers, Pigalle

The rue Dancourt is a short street leading into the peaceful and
pretty place Charles-Dullin, and it has several little restaurants. Le
Fait Tout (full name: À Napoli ... On Fait Tout) looks from the
outside to be a run-of-the-mill pizzeria; inside it's simple, clean and
pretty, with wooden tables and benches, flowers on tables. For 46F
you can have a salad with walnuts, or *pâté*, or onion tart to begin;

then grilled *châteaubriand* steak, or pork with black peppercorns, followed by cheese or a *tarte*. The 59F menu includes salads with crisp bacon slivers, and onion soup, then steak with mustard sauce, fish, veal escalope *normande* (in a rich cidery sauce). The sweets run to richness too, with pastry puffs filled with good ice-cream and topped with dark chocolate sauce. Everyone says the same thing about this little place – quiet and convivial, the cooking simple but not undistinguished. And everyone likes the low price and its closeness to Pigalle. Service is included; the house wine is 16F a quarter-litre. Open noon to 2:30 p.m., 6:00 to 11:00 p.m. No weekly or annual closing, and open holidays.

L'Homme Tranquille
81 rue des Martyrs, 18e
Tel: 42 54 56 28
Métro: Abbesses

New to us, and very welcome in this neighbourhood where so much is over-priced AND over-crowded. It is well named, with a calm and beautifully soothing feeling, very welcome after a long day of sight-seeing. At 98F for three courses, service included but wine (moderate-priced) extra, it's crowding the top of our price range, but worth every franc. The small room seats only about 30 people. Table linens are really linen, napkins are big, music is soft and classical. When we were there, the waiter was relaxed, efficient and unhurried; when he wasn't serving, he sat with a glass of Bordeaux and a salad – now *that's* style. The food is inventive, beautifully cooked, the menu changes every day, everything is obviously *fait à la maison* and fresh. The *terrine* of tuna as a starter was faultless, with salad and a tangy dressing – other choices were vegetable *terrine* with a creamy herb dressing, and a salad of warm St-Marcellin cheese on a plate of assorted lettuces. As main courses, there's chicken with basil in a cream sauce (great), lamb chops poached with fresh thyme (ditto), or trout with smoked bacon, and pork chop with honey and curry. Desserts range from very rich – redcurrant crumble with thick Normandy cream – to simple, pure lemon sorbet with a twist of lemon rind. Booking is imperative; people were being turned away on a Sunday evening. Open only for dinner, 7:00 to 11:30 p.m. Closed Mondays, August, and Christmas Day. Open Easter, New Year's Day and 14 July.

19e arrondissement

Au Rendez-vous de la Marine
14 quai de la Loire, 19e
Tel: 42 49 33 40
Métro: Jaurès, Stalingrad

Don't come without a reservation. The Rendez-vous is always full –
a very good sign indeed. In fact, you may want to book a few days
ahead. It's on the Bassin de la Villette, in a neighbourhood which
is rapidly going up in the world. The utterly absorbing river traffic
is seen through the big glass windows. But the real reason for
coming here is dishes like scallops in a heavily garlicked sauce,
salmon steaks, *magret de canard*, steak with various sauces – everything wonderfully cooked, and served with a green salad, rice
pilaff, and fresh vegetables. There's no *prix-fixe* menu, but you
could eat and drink well for about 90–100F, including service.
Main dishes cost 40–60F, starters are 20–40F, and include mon-
kfish in green peppercorn sauce, snails, leeks vinaigrette, or duck
pâté. Dessert choices are good, but after two courses you may not
have room for any more food. The restaurant is always busy.
Service is friendly but on the leisurely side of slow, so spend time
on your meal. Drink is extra: wine 15–25F a quarter-litre, mineral
water a reasonable 12F. Open noon to 2:00 p.m., 8:00 to 9:45 p.m.
when last orders are taken. Closed Sundays, Mondays and August;
open holidays unless they fall on a Sunday or Monday.

Le Chaumont-Laumière
20 avenue Laumière, 19e
Métro: Laumière

This very French and very friendly neighbourhood restaurant is in
the street that leads to the beautiful, quiet and relaxing parc des
Buttes-Chaumont (pages 172–3). It changed hands not too long
ago, and according to our young student researchers, things have
not really settled down yet. The *prix-fixe* menu is extraordinary:
pâté or garlic sausage or mackerel with potato salad are usually
available as starters, then a wonderful dish of pork fillet with mustard sauce and mini-noodles, or rabbit, roast chicken, or an
omelette *parmentier* stuffed with potatoes; orange pudding and
fresh fruit salad are among the dessert choices, or three kinds of

cheese. Both wine (or beer or mineral water) and service are *included*, a rarity these days; and when you check your bill, you'll find it cost only 51F! For 65F the 'house couscous' with lamb, chicken and spicy *merguez* sausage is a special treat. The new owners have changed the name from Le Petit Laumière, but not the atmosphere or the friendly polite service. Open noon to 2:30 p.m., 7:00 to 10:00 p.m. Closed Sundays and August. Open holidays unless they fall on a Sunday.

Duthil (*pâtisserie/traiteur*)
4 rue de Meaux, 19e
Tel: 42 05 41 51
Métro: Laumière, Bolivar, Jaurés

It is worth travelling up to this very, very French and interesting neighbourhood to find Duthil, one of the most famous *pâtissiers/ traiteurs/épiciers* of Paris – and to our taste, far better than many of the more highly publicized ones in central Paris. It combines a super pastry shop, great take-away prepared dishes, and even some very fancy groceries. A beautiful shop, staffed by remarkable people who treat a customer buying a single portion of lemon cake with the same friendly, helpful, interested demeanour as the one ordering a complete banquet. 'The cakes explode with cream,' reports one of our more gluttonous Paris eaters. Ice-cream is home-made and perfect. Pastries cost from 10F to 25F, and there's an irresistible mint and chocolate cake with a little tree on top. On a sunny day, you might choose something from their ready-cooked foods, plus some crusty *petit pains*, a raspberry tart, a half-bottle of wine, and take off for the little-known park of Buttes Chaumont (see pages 172–3) for the picnic of the world. Afterwards, check out the fascinating Marché Sécretan street market nearby. Duthil is open Mondays through Saturdays, early morning until late evening, and on 'some' holidays, but phone first if you're in doubt.

20e arrondissment

Crêperie La Rozelle
4 place Martin-Nadaud, 20e
Métro: Gambetta, Père Lachaise

If you've ever tried to find a good place to eat after dropping in to call on Chopin, Colette, Piaf and company at Père Lachaise, you'll know that this isn't an easy neighbourhood to find special food. But now a Breton crêperie has escaped the traditional location of the 14e *arrondissement*, and is almost at the Gambetta Métro stop. The *patronne* welcomes you heartily, and will probably tell you about her daughter's experiences as an au pair in England. Musthaves: buckwheat crêpes – galettes – filled with asparagus, mushrooms, ham, cheese, eggs, hamburger, sausage, smoked salmon (the most costly at 40F), or just plain melted butter (15F). Dessert crêpes are about 30F, rolled around chocolate, honey and walnuts, various jams, and a big swirl of chocolate chantilly (whipped cream), for the foolhardy. Two three-course menus, at 52F and 70F, have limited choices. This is a good place to take children, as crêpes range from simple to epicurean. À *la carte*, you can have a two-course meal, plus Breton cider, for about 80F. Open 11:30 a.m. to 2:30 p.m., 6:30 to 10:00 p.m. Closed Sundays and holidays, and from 15 July to 15 August.

'Le Self' – yes or no?

As the pace of Paris life becomes faster, self-service restaurants are proliferating, and they're a very good bet if you want to eat *à la carte*, inexpensively, and without the usual hour and a half over lunch. The great advantage of 'Les Selfs' is that if you have a fancy for making a meal of starters instead of a main dish, it's easy and cheap: ideal for vegetarians. The disadvantage is that if you let yourself go among the rather dazzling choices you can spend as much in a 'Self' as in a prettier, more comfortable restaurant with some character.

The best-known 'Selfs' in such fashionable venues as the rue de Rivoli and around the Louvre are distinctly *not* good value for money. They are over-praised, over-crowded and over-priced, and especially at lunchtime can be more of an ordeal than a pleasure.

However, there are some lesser-known 'Selfs' which can be an agreeable surprise to anyone whose idea of a self-service place is based on McDonald's. Can you believe a meal that begins with a salad of frisée lettuce with *chèvre* 10F, goes on to beef in a rich red wine sauce, 46F, a cool plain yoghurt (4F), or real ice-cream with fresh fruit and whipped cream (12F)? A quarter-litre of drinkable wine will be about 6F. These were the most expensive choices in a really nice 'Self', so the whole excellent meal was only about 46F. The quality was higher than many neighbourhood restaurants could have provided on *prix-fixe* menus. In another 'Self', a complete meal – starter, main course, salad, bread, dessert and wine, beer or mineral water – was less than 50F, in a clean, bright, air-conditioned room.

'Les Selfs' are, on the whole, quite attractive. At lunchtime, they are lively with chatter and laughter; not so much so in the evening when those who eat there, tend to be, as in any big city, people who haven't much else to do. But they are well worth considering, when you want a good meal or a hearty snack without spending the whole afternoon eating, or when you're planning a splurge on museums, perfumes, gifts.

Samaritaine
19 rue de la Monnaie, 1er
Métro: Louvre, Pont-Neuf

For lunch or snacks in the big department store, go early and get a table near the window, for the astounding view across the river and over the city. The food is fairly standard; don't expect a gastronomic miracle. The setting is the thing. Mushrooms in a spicy tomato sauce for a starter, a beefsteak hamburger with *frites* at 38F, and a fruit pie with whipped cream for 10F made a satisfying and inexpensive meal for an English student studying 'and trying not to starve' in Paris last spring, but an American visitor was disappointed, saying the food was not very tasty. Open 11:30 a.m. to 6:30 p.m., but the earlier the better at lunchtime as it gets very crowded and the best choices go early.

La Petite Bouchée
24 rue de la Pépinière, 8e
Métro: St-Lazare

A good place to know about if you are shopping around the boulevard Haussmann is this lovely small 'self', a charming little room up the stairs from the useful snack bar Pomme de Pain. It is wall-to-wall with well-dressed young secretaries and office workers from the *quartier*, who are both value- and figure-conscious – good salads for about 25–35F, well-prepared grills and vegetables, light desserts, good coffee. A three-course meal, without wine, would cost less than 50F. Open 11:30 a.m. to 3:00 p.m. Closed Sundays, holidays.

Le Balthazar
corner of boulevard St-Martin and rue René Béranger, 10e
Métro: République

After a year or two's absence, we returned for a meal at this out-of-the-ordinary 'Self', set on a triangle just west of the place de la République. It's as good as ever, and as attractive, with beautiful wallpaper reproduced from the *Plan Turgot*, the bird's-eye view of Paris in the 18th century. You can lunch outside on a terrace with garden tables, trellises with vines, plants in tubs. Starters such as *pâté*, salads, plates of *crudités*, are from 8F50, and main dishes, moussaka, lasagne, steaks, grilled lamb chops with sautéed potatoes, cost 29F50–48F. The dessert choices are beautiful, always fresh chilled fruit, 'Bio-B Yoghurt', 8F, or a mountain of ice-cream, fresh fruit, strawberry sauce and whipped cream, 18F. Quarter-litre bottles of good red Beaujolais are 8F50, and coffee brought to your table is 5F. Couscous is served on Thursdays. Open 11:00 a.m. to 10:00 p.m., every day of the year, including holidays.

Take-away
all of rue de la Huchette, rue de la Harpe, 5e
Métro: St-Michel

The centre of take-away food: almost every restaurant or store-front along these streets will treat you to delicious charcoal-grilled *souvlakia* (skewered lamb and vegetables) or *shawarma* (barbecued, thinly sliced spiced lamb), both in pitta pockets. Walk a little further, and you find sweet Mid-East pastries to eat from the hand. At various times we've enjoyed *sandwich tunisien*, with tuna, olives, tomatoes, peppers, lettuce drenched in a hot sauce and overstuffed into a hard roll, at El Hammamet; and a giant *pan bagna*, a huge roll crammed with *salade Niçoise*, at Au Gargantua. They'll cost between 18F and 22F wherever you find them. The names change constantly in these streets but it's still a pocket of the

Mediterranean world, charcoal fumes drifting from every door. The crowds are good-natured, enjoying life in the open air. Even in dark or rainy weather, a spicy hot sandwich and a mug of beer is very cheering. Food's available all day long, from 10:00 a.m. or even earlier. Nothing doing on Christmas or New Year's Day, as far as we know.

M. Benvisti and others
boulevard de Belleville, near rue Ramponeau, 20e
Métro: Belleville

Food in the extraordinary quarter called Belleville – the Arab and old Jewish Paris – is dealt with at greater length in 'Getting around', (pages 51–2). Our favourite is a big Tunisian-Jewish take-away, Benvisti. You tell the cashier whether you want a *sandwich tunisien*, about 20F, or an *assiette tunisienne*, about 24F: take the ticket to the counter, where your order is slapped together at speed. You will get a big thick roll or pitta bread, crammed with olives, tuna, capers, cucumber, tomato, with a fiery sauce, in a paper napkin or a plastic bag, or the same thing on a plate, with crisp lettuce and a hunk of *baguette*. Or have *brik à l'oeuf*, a delicious crumbly Tunisian pastry enclosing a fried egg, and get crumbs all over you and your clothes as you eat it, for about 20F. You can, of course, have a sandwich to take away and eat from the hand, sloppy and delicious, as you watch all Belleville sauntering by. Also available: 12 kinds of olives, capers, hot peppers, many other highly spiced foods, sold by weight in plastic bags, to take away for a picnic lunch or supper with some thick crusted North African bread. Open about 10:00 a.m. to 9:00 p.m. Closed Friday evenings from sundown until sundown Saturday. Open all day Sundays.

Ouvert le dimanche *(Open on Sundays)*

1er arrondissement
Le Galtouse
Pasadena (lunch only)
Le Stado

2e arrondissement
Anadolu
Le Drouot
Restaurant Kurde Dîlan

4e arrondissement
La Canaille (evenings)
Les Piétons (lunch)

5e arrondissement
Les Degrés de Notre-Dame
La Maison de Verlaine
Le Pavé aux Herbes
Taverne Descartes
La Trattoria (evenings)
All the take-aways of the rue de la Huchette, rue de la Harpe

6e arrondissement
Le Bistro de la Grille
Les Byzantins
Marco Polo (evenings)
Le Polidor
Restaurant des Beaux Arts

7e arrondissement
Cam Mach

8e arrondissement
L'Assiette Lyonnaise
Galerie Point Show

9e arrondissement
Chartier
Picpain
Pupillin
Xavier Gourmet

11e arrondissement
Palais de la Femme
Pizza Tavola

12e arrondissement
Le Limonaire

13e arrondissement
L'Espérance
Hawai

14e arrondissement
Crêperie de St-Malo
Kenavo

15e arrondissement
Formula Uno

18e arrondissement
Les Chauffeurs
Le Fait Tout
L'Homme Tranquille (evenings)

19e arrondissement
Most of Belleville

Ouvert en Août *(open in August)*

1er arrondissement
Auberge du Palais Royal
Au Vieil Écu
Chez Fernand (for two weeks)
Le Galtouse
L'Incroyable

Le Palet
Pasadena
Le Petit Ramoneur (1st two weeks)
Le Stado

2e arrondissement
Anadolu
Le Drouot
Pavarotti
Restaurant Kurde Dîlan

4e arrondissement
La Canaille
Le Châteaubriand (1st two weeks)
La Comète (two weeks)
Le Cristal
Le P'tit Comic
Le Petit Gavroche (dinner only)
Les Piétons
Le Quidam

5e arrondissement
Le Baptiste
Le Blé d'Or (two weeks)
Le Bouche Trou
Les Degrés de Notre Dame
La Maison de Verlaine
Le Pavé aux Herbes
Taverne Descartes
La Trattoria
All the take-aways of rue de la Huchette, rue de la Harpe

6e arrondissement
Bistro de la Grille
La Bolée (1st two weeks)
Les Byzantins
Claude Valentino
L'Écaille de PCB (two weeks)
Les Frères de la Côte
La Godasse (last two weeks)
Marco Polo (closed first week)
Orestias

Osteria del Passe Partout
Polidor
Restaurant des Beaux Arts
All of rue de la Huchette, rue de la Harpe

8e arrondissement
L'Assiette Lyonnaise
Galerie Point Show
Hyotan (three weeks)

9e arrondissement
Chartier
Duhau
Picpain
Pupillin
Xavier Gourmet

11e arrondissement
Nini Peau d'un Chien
Palais de la Femme
Pizza Tavola

13e arrondissement
Bangkok-Thailand
Hawai

14e arrondissement
Crêperie de St-Malo
Kenavo
Le Luma (1st two weeks)
Midi-Trente (three weeks)

15e arrondissement
Bistrot Bourdelle (open one week)
Formula Uno

17e arrondissement
La Bonne Cuisine

18e arrondissement
Le Fait Tout
Restaurant Ephèse (two weeks)

19e arrondissement
Duthil
Most of Belleville

20e arrondissement
Crêperie La Rozelle (open last two weeks)

Les spectacles
(Sights and sounds)

The number one attraction in Paris is Paris. A little footwork can provide all the entertainment you need. Parisians have always relied on their feet for diversion – there's a Parisian art of strolling – the city is inexhaustibly explorable. For a few possibilities, see the chapter on 'Getting around' (pages 32–55).

For incomparable theatre, there are the Parisians themselves. They dress distinctively, and carry themselves with a certain air: they have a highly developed vocabulary of gesture; their voices range from a croak to a twitter; they love to see and be seen. Almost any place will do for Paris- and Parisian-watching: park benches, Métro stations, the *zincs* in local cafés, outdoor markets. It's up to you to be receptive.

Should street-life pall, there are other, more organized entertainments – a surprising number of them free, or very cheap.

Paris parks

There are dozens of parks scattered through the city: tiny, intimate parks in the shadow of churches; parks that are 'wild' and rambling in a curiously artificial and very French way; vast, arid, formal parks consisting of gravel and neoclassical sculpture. All are meticulously kept. Here are a few (you'll find many more yourself):

Jardin des Plantes

bounded by the Seine and the rue Geoffrey-St-Hilaire, 5e
Métro: Jussieu, Gare d'Austerlitz, Monge

Part formal garden – minimal grass – part botanical station, with some lush peripheral areas. Contains the Natural History Museum and the Ménagerie. The latter, like every other 'caged' zoo in the world is dismal, smelly, and to be avoided.

Parc de Monceau

boulevard de Courcelles, 8e
Métro: Monceau

Large, full of artificial waterfalls and ponds, glades, romantic statuary. Like most upper-echelon Paris parks, good nanny territory. Two steps away, at 63 rue de Monceau (southern edge of the park), is the Musée Nissim de Camondo: an 18th-century mansion, preserved inside and out (see page 190).

Square des Batignolles

directly behind Église Ste-Marie-des Batignolles, 17e
Métro: Brochant, and a fair walk

A charming, unpretentious park in a quiet neighbourhood, with duckponds and a population of elderly park-sitters. The low iron fencing along the paths resembles a lattice of bent twigs – a reminder of the French love for 'natural' artifice.

Parc des Buttes-Chaumont

bounded by the rue Manin and the rue Botzaris, 19e
Métro: Buttes-Chaumont

This is a park which most tourists miss because it is so out of the way – a pity, because it is charming. Set on a hillside in the not very fashionable 19e, it was created by Baron Haussmann in response to his monarch's love for anything English. It was once a much more sinister place, where corpses blackened on the gibbet of Montfaucon in the Middle Ages; later a slaughterhouse for horses, finally a general rubbish-heap. Haussmann had the idea of making rock gardens *à l'anglaise*, and there it is, a perfect and peaceful park.

It's rich in waterfalls, grottoes, rustic chalets, a fake-Greek temple, even fishponds (to fish, you need a permit from the *gendarmerie*). It's 60 acres of lovely strolling and picnicking ground, with a fresh breeze always blowing. If you have been in Belleville in the neighbouring 20e, and have collected a sandwich and a bottle of beer for lunch, get on the No. 26 bus heading towards St-Lazare, step off at the Botzaris-Buttes-Chaumont stop, and find a sheltered grotto for lunch. Even the local dogs, which run to neatly clipped poodles and brushed spaniels, have good manners, and despite the English look of the park, people walk lightly, if at all, on the tidy grass.

Bois de Boulogne

from Porte d'Auteuil to Porte Maillot, 16e
Métro: Porte de Neuilly, Porte Dauphine, Les Sablons

When Parisians say 'Le Bois', they are referring to this park. It's a 19th-century creation, roughly modelled on Hyde Park, at the suggestion of that passionate Anglophile Napoleon III. Its history as a green wooded space dates back centuries, to the days when it stood just inside the fortified boundary of Paris. It was a favourite duelling-ground until, and even after, that sport of the court was outlawed by Louis XIV. Now it is 2000 acres of beautiful, varied, country-like terrain: with one museum, two world-famous race courses, a small zoo, a rose garden, a polo ground, a 'Shakespeare Garden' where grow all the plants mentioned in his plays, two lakes, broad avenues for riding, paths for biking. One can literally live in the Bois – there are camping grounds for tents and caravans.

Of the Métros which serve the Bois, Les Sablons takes you closest to the charming Jardin d'Acclimatation with its little zoo and playground. And one of the most delightful of Paris museums is nearby: the Musée des Arts et Traditions Populaires. This is great for a rainy day; a compendium of everything from country crafts (butter moulds, bee-keeping), to games (*boules*, royal tennis) to bagpipes, Breton headdresses, lace, 16th-century toys – the list is endless.

Boats in the Bois can be hired by the hour, at an office near the Lac Inférieur, and the pretty little man-made islands can be visited. Take a picnic: and stay away from the restaurants, which are calculated for the rich.

The exquisite park of Bagatelle, within the Bois, is nearly 60 acres surrounding a fairy-tale palace, and in June it is a paradise of roses. Sir Richard Wallace, said to have been the illegitimate son of the Marquis of Hertford (and a passionate lover of Paris), lived here.

In the daytime the Bois is peopled with strollers, dog-walkers, kite-flyers, riders, cyclists, lovers, and dreamers. But at night it's a different story. Stay away. It's not romantic even in moonlight, and it's very, very dangerous. For years it was the pickup place for certain kinds of Paris prostitutes, and at least some of *les girls* are South American transvestites. Vandalism and violent crime have taken over the Bois at night.

Bateaux-Mouches

Glass-enclosed excursion boats glide up and down the Seine for about an hour, under various names but generically called Bateaux Mouches.

Bateaux-Mouches: from the Pont de l'Alma, right bank (*Métro*: Alma-Marceau), every 30 minutes. From 10:00 a.m. to noon, then 1:30 p.m. to 8:30 p.m., 30F; under 14s, 15F

Bateaux-Vedettes Pont Neuf: from the Square du Vert-Galant on the Île de la Cité, (*Métro*: Pont Neuf): every 30 minutes from 10:00 a.m. to noon, then 1:30 to 6:30 p.m. Evening cruises 8:30 to 10:30 p.m. in the summer, 35F.

Cemeteries

A taste for these is not as macabre as you may think (but it does help to go on a rainy day. If you're depressed, they're great places to wallow in despair). There are at least 13 within the city limits. The best known, and the best for browsing, is **Père Lachaise** (you could win bets as to its real name, which is Cimetière de l'Est).

Bounded on two sides by the avenue Gambetta and the boulevard de Ménilmontant (*Métro*: Père Lachaise) it consists of 19th- and 20th-century tombs and sepulchres: some mouldering and decrepit; some sprucely cared for; some distinctly spooky; others – shiny granite and plastic photographs – very sentimental. Here lie Colette, Proust, Wilde, Chopin, Hugo, Balzac, Piaf, Gertrude Stein. And Jim Morrison. On sunny days the cats come out to bask on the *tombeaux*. A map of the cemetery is 2F from the *gendarme* at the gate.

If you haven't exhausted your taste for the illustrious dead, your next stop should be the **Cimetière de Montmartre** in rue Caulaincourt, 18e; *Métro*: Place de Clichy or La Fourche. Contents: Dumas *pére* (where is *fils?*), Stendhal, Berlioz, Fragonard, Baudelaire.

Markets

As you must have gathered by now, food is an object of worship in Paris. It's appreciated on the plate, and almost as much on the hoof. Paris abounds with open air and covered markets where everything is displayed to perfection: fruits and vegetables placed just so; incredible conglomerations of fish and shellfish; poultry and game hung disconcertingly at eye level. There's nothing antiseptic about the markets, and nothing haphazard – the stall proprietors are there to sell (voices that can be heard streets away), and those who come to buy are determined to get the best. It's hard to know whether to look at the sellers, the clients, or the merchandise.

The 'moving markets' of Paris are almost unknown to the casual visitor. But they are essential to understanding Parisians, from elegant matrons of the 8e *arrondissement* to the women in *djellabas* of the 11e.

Open air. Try these, 8:00 a.m. to noon only:
Carmes, 5e: At Maubert-Mutualité Métro. Tuesdays, Thursdays, Saturdays.

boulevard Raspail, 6e: between rue de Cherche-Midi and rue de Rennes. Upper-class food, beautiful people. Tuesdays, Fridays.

Belleville, 11e: rue Oberkampf to Belleville Métro. Huge, mainly run by North African French – everything from wild strawberries to Bleu d'Auvergne cheese to plastic sandals. Tuesdays, Fridays.

Père Lachaise, 11e: begins at the Ménilmontant Métro and runs east along boulevard Ménilmontant to rue des Panoyaux. Next to Belleville, but completely different – very French, very classy, beautiful fish, cheese, and the best olives and dried fruits at Pierre Blanc's English-speaking stand.

avenue de Président Wilson, 16e: between rue Debrousse and place d'Iéna. Even more BCBG. Wednesdays, Saturdays.

Covered markets. Weekdays, 8:00 a.m. to 1:00 p.m., 2:00 to 7:30 p.m. Sundays, 8:00 a.m. to 1:00 p.m.
St-Honoré, 1e: place du Marché St-Honoré.
St-Germain, 6e: 3 rue Mabillon.
Europe, 8e: 1 rue Corvette.
St-Quentin, 10e: 95 bis boulevard Magenta.
Passy, 16e: corner of rue Bois-le-Vent and rue Duban.
Ternes, 17e: rue Lebon.
La Chapelle, 18e: 10 rue d'Olive.
Sécretan, 19e: 33 avenue Sécretan.

Window-shopping

Food

For museum-quality displays, go to Fauchon, *the* de luxe shop which faces two sides of the place de la Madeleine, 8e (*Métro*: Madeleine). Early morning is best, when the *terrines* and *pâtés* are arranged in the window, the crayfish and lobsters set out. Unbelievable *gelées*, *pâtisseries*, arrangements of bread, displays of wine, cheeses you never dreamed of. On the opposite side of the Madeleine is Hédiard – smaller, more compact, and just as expensive. Michel Guérard, known for *nouvelle cuisine*, has a glamorous shop nearby, and, unbelievably, a cafeteria.

Exquisite *pâtisseries* and *charcuteries* can be found all over Paris, in the most surprising *quartiers*, some that are nearly slums. No one hesitates to spend five minutes or more peering in the window, choosing one pastry or a *tranche* of a wild boar *terrine*. One wonders how all this intricately decorated food ever gets eaten, never mind prepared from day to day. A partial answer is the restaurant trade: the thousands of restaurants large and small rely on the shops of their *quartier* for the day's *terrines* and *tartes*. Somehow, Parisians have overlooked the idea of mass-marketed, prefabricated victuals, and they do seem to be happy in their ignorance.

Clothes

As you know, they are of vital importance to the French sense of self-esteem and to their economy. The couturiers' windows are accordingly magnificent. Whether sedate or outrageous, they display their wares beautifully, imaginatively, both inside and in the windows of the great houses. The smaller boutiques, too, have a fresh and lively approach to display. The department stores, however, in comparison to almost any American store and some English ones, are a dead loss – frozen in the display techniques of the 1950s. The only worthwhile window among them is the dome of the Galéries Lafayette, and that's spectacular.

Walk up the rue Royale, along the rue du Faubourg-St-Honoré, along the side streets and avenues of St-Germain-des-Prés, along the avenue Matignon, the avenue du Pierre-Premier-de-Serbie, the rue Boissy d'Anglas, and you come away reeling with the great inventive talent and daring of Hermès, Cardin, Chanel, Dior, St Laurent, Givenchy. It costs nothing to look in the windows of Cartier, Bulgari, Van Cleef and Arpels, and unconsciously you are absorbing what makes for elegance, quality and flair.

Antique shopping

The pleasure of 'antiqueing' in Paris, too, is for the eye only. Prices are high and rising, as the rich take their panic money out of gold and put it into irreplaceable objects of beauty and luxury. So consider the time you dally in front of windows or in shops as part of your education in what constitutes value in craftsmanship and materials.

If you love antiques and want to see an incredible collection all under one roof, an obvious but good answer is Le Louvre des Antiquaires, in the place Palais Royal, 1er. This three-storey building is a mass of showrooms run by some of the best-known dealers of Paris. Unless you are conspicuously well dressed, don't expect much attention or friendliness from the dealers: they know their customers, and are fairly sure as soon as they set eyes on you that you're not a prospect.

The back streets of the Marais, around the rue des Francs-Bourgeois, are beginning to be lined with elegant small antique shops, but here again you will find few if any bargains. Look, too, at the Village St-Paul, in the rue St-Paul near the Seine (4e), a beautifully reconstructed cluster of grey stone mansions now housing some lovely shops. Then cross to the Left Bank, and wander around the side streets that make up the St-Germain-des-Prés area: rue Jacob, rue Furstenberg, rue du Bac, rue des Beaux Arts, rue de l'Université.

In the more rarefied reaches of the 7e, you'll find the Village

Suisse – a collection of rather expensive dealers – at 78 avenue de Suffren (*Métro*: La Motte-Picquet), open Thursdays through Mondays, 11:00 a.m. to 7:00 p.m.

What is conspicuously missing in Paris is fine antique silver: much of the best table silver and decorative pieces owned by the aristocracy and the rich bourgeoisie were melted down to pay for the wars of Louis XIV, and most of what remained went into the fires of the Revolution. The few pieces that escaped are now in museums. You will now find that the best silver on offer is elaborate late-19th-century work, a few fine Art Nouveau pieces, and – more available – some of the chic, stark creations of the 1930s, at prices about one-third *more* than a London or New York dealer would charge. You may be lucky in a flea market or a small semi-junk shop, but don't count on it.

Again, all this comes under the general heading of education. Remember, too, that if you find anything you like and can afford, and it's too big to go in your luggage, you will have to deal with shipping, insurance, customs, and collection at the other end, which can easily double the original price.

The flower markets

If it's not food, clothes, paintings that separate Parisians from the rest of the world, maybe it's their intoxication with flowers. The flower shops and stalls are fantasies of scent, colour, life, and the sort of instinctive flair for arrangement of even quite humble flowers that is absolutely French. The markets are found on the Île de la Cité, at the back of the Madeleine (8e, *Métro*: Madeleine), and at the place des Ternes. The first two are thick with tourists in high summer, but don't let that deter you. The place des Ternes is well off the tourist beat and has a fine street-market as well as flower stalls. A few blossoms in a water glass or Perrier bottle will cheer up your hotel room.

Plants: walk along the quai de la Mégisserie, 1er (*Métro*: Pont Neuf), if you want to see how the French approach the whole question of gardening, with an emphasis on window-box plants, kitchen and herb gardens, small-scale city adornment. One of the great seedsmen of Europe, Vilmorin, has a big shop here. A packet of real French basil grown from their seed seems to have a special flavour which may be more in the imagination than in reality (but check to see if your country allows you to import seeds). Weekdays only.

Ducks, deer, swans: also on the quai de le Mégisserie are the caged animals, birds, tortoises, domestic and wild fowls – which can break your heart. Two swans in a cage; a miniature deer for some rich child's private zoo; even the chickens are pitiable. Don't look.

Museums

Paris glories in the existence of nearly 100 museums: from the largest in the world (the Louvre) to one of the most specialized which displays only the crystal of Baccarat. Many are in the area of central Paris (see museum map, pages 300–1), others within half an hour's travel on the Métro, bus or RER express lines. Some are small and exquisite and so highly specialized that in their best week they get no more than a dozen visitors. Some are great private houses now open to the public, worth seeing even if you didn't look at the contents. One of the most extraordinary, the Musée Nissim de Camondo, is a frozen slice of 18th-century France, created by the grieving parents of a World War I hero. Still another has an enticing collection of mechanical toys and clockwork gadgets. There are not one but *two* modern museums in Paris, while poor London struggles on without any.

Many of the major Paris museums are free or half price on Sunday. Some give discounts to students (an International Student Identity Card helps) and to those under or over a certain age. Details under each museum mentioned. If you're under 18 or over 60 (women) or 65 (men), show your passport and ask for *demi-tarif* which cuts museum charges in half. Two elderly friends of ours were admitted free to the Petit Palais on production of passports.

It's true that almost every museum charges an entrance fee, and if you are a conscientious pauper used to the generous free museums of Britain, this comes as a shock. Brace yourself, do without lunch if you must, but either pay the sum asked or wear yourself out on Sundays. You will be rewarded in every sense by the thrill of the beautiful, the odd, the heart-warming or the blood-chilling.

Most museums close on Tuesdays, a few on Mondays, some both

days. A few are open on public holidays but most are closed. All are near a Métro stop or within five minutes' walk. All have free cloakrooms (obligatory) for carrier bags, umbrellas, briefcases, but they won't take anything that holds money, jewellery, passport or camera. Some let you take photographs, some forbid flash equipment. Check for rules when you go, as they change from time to time.

Most Paris museums, as one would expect from the general French attitude towards civilized comfort, have benches or chairs on which to fall when your feet, eyes and mind give out. The attendants on the whole give good directions as to what's where, and will do their best to answer questions in English. They have eyes in the back of their heads and voices that when raised can cut like a laser beam. Don't touch, don't breathe on, don't put a finger near the surface of a painting or a sculpture unless you are prepared for a loud metallic French shout.

Be prepared to queue for admission to the Louvre, and to the Musée d'Orsay (Impressionists, Post-Impressionists), and to any major exhibitions which may be open. For these, take along a thermos of coffee and sandwiches to sustain you: for the 'Corot to Impressionists' in spring and summer 1991, people began queueing with camp stools, folded blankets, pillows, at 6:00 a.m. Sellers of hot coffee and croissants from heated carts made a good franc or two. One couple we spotted were sharing a small bottle of wine and a bag of sandwiches at 8:00 a.m. Waiting so long in hot weather, or cold rain, can leave you too exhausted to enjoy what you came to see. Sometimes queues are shorter at lunchtime, or when an exhibition has just opened, or during the last ten days when crowds are minimal.

One way to beat the queues is the fairly new *Carte Inter-Musées* (see opposite) which gives you free entry to the dozens of museums and historical sites in Paris. It costs 50F for one day, 100F for three consecutive days, 150F for five consecutive days. You'd get your money's worth if you are a real museum buff and can cope with three or four a day; and it allows you to bypass queues, enter by 'group admission' doors, and sail past the ticket offices. At the Louvre, for example, you don't stand in the endless line inching towards the new Pyramid, but go to the escalator in the arcade leading from the Palais-Royal Métro, normally reserved for groups. Work it out for yourself if the convenience is worth the money. We think the three- or five-day investment is a better buy than the one-day pass. Our thanks to Howard Rye of London, who used the

Carte Inter-Musées with pleasure and profit. This expensive but useful admission *carte* can be obtained in the UK from Voyages Vacances, tel. 071-581 5111, as well as at museums and at the main Paris Métro stations.

The museums listed and described in this section include our own personal guide to the lesser-known ones as well as the more popular leaders.

1er arrondissement

The Louvre

Métro: Palais-Royal, Louvre

Hours: 9:00 a.m. to 6:00 p.m. Wednesdays to 9:45 p.m. Certain rooms open to 9:45 p.m. Mondays. Closed Tuesdays.

Admission: 30F; 15F reduced price for 18–25s and over-60s; under-18s free. 15F after 5:00 p.m. Thursdays, Fridays, Saturdays and all day Sundays.

The Pyramid! It's been called 'an architect's megalomania', 'a magical machine', 'violation of the historic Louvre', 'a triumph of the imagination', and a litany of phrases ranging from violent denunciation to ecstatic praise. Go and see for yourself. It is now the main entrance to the museum, and is attracting queues of the curious. This elegant airy structure is 71 feet high, surrounded by three baby likenesses. It has freed many of the superb rooms from the clutter of ticket-windows, postcard racks, gift shops and whatnot. Access to the museum's unbelievable treasures is now astonishingly easy, and you could spend half a day playing with the computerised information service below the Pyramid.

Perhaps the best thing is that as you move out of the high-tech underground entrance hall, you find the great crypt, revealed during the excavations, which now displays the original walls of palaces of past centuries. Beyond that, the Louvre stretches forever. It's still in the process of being transformed, and in years to come more rooms will be opened, more wonders revealed. At the moment, so many things are going on in what Mary Blume of the

International Herald Tribune once called 'the uncomfortable, dingy, distinctly user-unfriendly Louvre' that it's almost impossible to sum it up here.

Obviously, if you had but one day in Paris (or one lifetime), the Louvre would be the one indispensable museum. The Big Three (Winged Victory of Samothrace, Venus de Milo, Mona Lisa) may have been over-exposed, but you must see them, at least on your first visit. A guided tour, booked in the entrance hall, could be a good way to learn your way around: after that you'll find your own personal treasures, the Poussins, the Chardins, the Rembrandts, the Egyptian hoard, the Italian primitives.

A sophisticated Parisian recommends sauntering around the Pyramid, hoping to see the daring Alpinistes who abseil around it to clean its glittering panes (apparently little account was taken in the planning for the ravages of rain, dirt, city pollution and seagulls); the best time, really, is on a still, moonlit night when reflections dance and shimmer in the triangular reflecting pool. After your first visit to see the Pyramid, she says that if you are in a hurry to get into the Louvre, make for the Pavillon de Flore, westward of the main block (Métro: Tuileries). Be wary of a very hot or very cold day at the Pyramid: there is neither shade nor shelter as you wait for security checks and single-filing into the entrance, and in summer the sun beats down relentlessly on the entry-level platform before you descend to the gloriously lit *sous-sol*. Apparently, the great central pillar in the Pyramid was meant as a base for the Winged Victory, but cooler heads prevailed.

The Louvre itself is set on the site of royal palaces that date back to the 12th century, and stretches over acres along the Seine. Much of the present structure is 'new', as things Parisian go. Both the great Napoleon and the later, lesser Louis-Napoleon had a hand in building or reconstructing. François I was the first royal collector – or looter – in the 16th century. He picked up trifles like Giottos, Leonardos, Veroneses on his way through Italy and Spain.

The incredible Egyptian collections owe their existence to the Napoleonic campaigns. Louis XIV housed most of his 'finds' at Versailles, but after his death they were dispersed, some to the Luxembourg Palace but most to the royal palace of the Louvre. After 1789, the Louvre became the Central Museum of the Arts of the infant republic, and was almost at once opened to the public.

This is a sketchy description of what may be the world's greatest museum: to do it justice, the rest of this book would have to be dropped. Go early in the morning, go often, leave before you develop visual fatigue. Remember that if you are lucky you will return to it many times in the future.

The Jeu de Paume

place de la Çoncorde, 1er
Métro: Concorde, Tuileries

Hours: 12:00 to 9:30 p.m. on Tuesdays. 12:00 to 7:00 p.m. Wednesdays through Fridays. 10:00 a.m. to 7:00 p.m. Saturdays and Sundays.

Admission: Prices will vary for each exhibition, from 30F up, with concessionary rates, and under-13s usually free.

The lovely little Jeu de Paume, whose treasures crossed the Seine to new and airier premises in the Musée d'Orsay some years ago, has been redecorated and opened as a showcase for major temporary exhibitions. It has a beautiful small art bookshop, and great windows letting light in from the Tuileries gardens, a dramatic long staircase, and a lift. In 1991, it launched its new career with a big show of work by Dubuffet. Tickets cost 40F. The usual queues ensued. Check for the current exhibition and the cost of admission in *Pariscope*, or watch for posters in the Métro. And be prepared to queue for quite long stretches, as security checks and ticket-taking is necessarily slow.

The Orangerie

place de la Concorde, 1er
Métro: Concorde

Hours: 9:45 a.m. to 5:15 p.m., every day except Tuesdays and major holidays.

Admission: 23F; 12F Sundays. 12F every day for under-18s, students under 26, and over-60s.

A hundred yards closer to the Seine from the Jeu de Paume, this is a museum with (so far) no queues. It houses the Walter Guillaume collection, mostly early 20th-century paintings, reflecting the highly personal choices of Mme Walter and her two husbands (Paul Guillaume and Jean Walter). There are 14 ravishing Cézannes, some fine Picassos, many Derains and Soutines, some unusual Douanier Rousseaus – and areas of creamy, satiny, plushy Renoirs. Certainly worth seeing – many critics hated it; those who find out about it seem to love it. The great Monet water-lily paintings in the Salle des Nymphéas are not to be missed.

The Museum of Decorative Arts

107 rue de Rivoli, 1er
Métro: Palais-Royal

Hours: 12:30 p.m. to 6:00 p.m., Wednesdays through Saturdays; 12:00 a.m. to 6:00 p.m. Sundays. Closed Mondays and Tuesdays.

Admission: 20F; 15F reduced price for students and over-60s.

A magnificent collection of furniture, tapestries, arts and crafts, books about the decorative arts. It often has fine special exhibitions such as the 1991 show called 'Poupées d'hier, créations d'aujourd'hui' (Dolls of bygone days, creations of today) which had 300 dolls from all parts of the world, some almost 200 years old, plus work by contemporary fashion designers and artists from Japan, the United States, and all of Europe. In addition, there was a startling show of furniture of the decade 1980–90 from Italy's avante-garde designers.

Musée de la Publicité

107 rue de Rivoli, 1er
Métro: Palais-Royal

Hours: 12:30 to 6:00 p.m. Closed Mondays and Tuesdays.

Admission: 20F; 12F for the unemployed, for students and *Carte Vermeil* holders or over-65s with passport. The ticket admits you to their little *cinémathèque*.

The poster and advertising museum has moved from its beautiful old Art Nouveau building in the 10e *arrondissement* to a more modern space. It shows every form of advertising, including signs, prints, cinema posters and ads, and always has an interesting special exhibition to do with advertising. In 1991, they featured Le Grand Prix Byrhh, posters dating from the first competition organized by this celebrated apéritif, with such artists as Maurice Denis, Felix Valloton, other beginning-to-be-famous painters. The museum's own *affiche* is well worth buying for the pleasure of the graphic design. The French have been doing this with wit, flair and irony for a 100 years. Look at the postcard reproduction of the original posters advertising the great French liner *Normandie*, queen of the Atlantic before World War II.

The museum has reduced its admission fee since moving, and we urge a visit – it sells postcards and reproductions of some of the very unusual French advertising material of the past century. In 1991 there was a spectacular show of posters from an unexpected place – Venezuela. We have heard, but can't verify at the time of writing, that the museum may be printing postcards of the poster that made all Paris hoot with laughter in 1990 – the *affiche* for the film *Il gèle en enfer* (Hell Freezes Over), which showed two little black-winged angels falling out of heaven, the lady angel in black fishnet tights, her partner well-displayed.

3e arrondissement

Musée Carnavelet

23 rue de Sévigné, 3e
Métro: St-Paul, Chemin-Vert

Hours: 10:00 a.m. to 5:35 p.m. Closed Mondays and holidays. Open Thursday evenings to 8:00 p.m.

Admission: 15F; 8F50 for reduced price tickets.

The Bicentenary year of 1989 saw a long-overdue renovation of this exquisite 17th-century building which houses the museum of the City of Paris. Once the home of Madame de Sévigné, it has been extended and joined to its next-door neighbour, the Hôtel Le

Peletier de St-Fargeau. All the history and beauty of Paris right back to Roman times is beautifully displayed here – with a most remarkable feeling that it has all been assembled by one ardent collector. A fantastic collection of revolutionary artefacts is in the Le Peletier house – fans, buckles, proclamations, warrants for arrests and executions; drums, flags, Louis XVI's razors, Napoleon's travelling *toilette* set, the little notebooks of the imprisoned Dauphin. Beautiful period rooms have been reconstructed throughout both buildings; don't miss the Art Nouveau room from the old Café de Paris, and a 1920s ballroom.

Musée Picasso

5 rue de Thorigny, 3e
Métro: Chemin-Vert, St-Paul

Hours: 9:15 a.m. to 5:15 p.m. weekdays, Saturdays and Sundays. Thursdays to 8:00 p.m. Closed Tuesdays.

Admission: 28F; 16F reduced price tickets.

All we can say is Picasso, Picassissimo: if you are a fan, go. If not, skip it. In addition to Picasso *in excelsis*, it includes work by other painters which he owned, treasured, and kept all his life. Great photographs of himself at work, on the beach, with friends; and usually a film in the little cinema high up under the roof of this beautiful and historic palace on the edge of the Marais.

4e arrondissement

The Conciergerie

1 quai de l'Horloge, 4e
Métro: Hôtel de Ville

Hours: 10:00 a.m. to 5:00 p.m., Mondays through Fridays. To 6:30 p.m. Saturdays and Sundays, and to 9:00 p.m. Thursdays. Closed holidays.

Admission: 30F; 15F reduced price tickets.

Don't go unless you feel fairly strong. Deep in the huge and pretty formidable Palais de Justice, the Conciergerie puts the Terror of 1789 right at your throat. No matter how you feel about the pre-revolutionary aristos, the sight of Marie Antoinette's cell, and the rooms where philosophers, writers, artists and the nobility waited for death, cannot leave you unaffected.

Beaubourg: Musée National d'Art Moderne

Centre National de l'Art et de Culture Georges Pompidou, 4e (this mouth-filling title is usually shortened to *Beaubourg*)
Métro: Hôtel de Ville, Rambuteau

Hours: Noon to 10:00 p.m. weekdays, 10:00 a.m. to 8:00 p.m. Saturdays, Sundays, and holidays. Closed Tuesdays.

Admission: 23F; 17F reduced price tickets. Free on Sundays from 10:00 a.m. to 2:00 p.m. Day pass for the museum and all other exhibitions, 50F; reduced price pass 45F.

A dazzling collection of every important modern painter and sculptor of the 20th century. Sit down from time to time to rest and stare, because this art is not meant to soothe the eye or the spirit.

Beaubourg itself is like a great museum on its own, and much of it is *free*, including the escalator that snakes up the front of the building and gives you an unmatchable view of the city. But the *small* escalator that leads to the big one is narrow, short, and often jammed with queues that even crowd the huge entrance courtyard.

5e arrondissement

Musée de Cluny

6 rue Paul-Painlevé, 5e
Métro: St-Michel

Hours: 9:30 a.m. to 5:15 p.m. Closed Tuesdays.

Admission: 15F; 8F reduced price tickets. Under-18s, free.

Utterly fascinating medieval monastery buildings which now house one of the world's great collections of arts and crafts of the Middle Ages. Spurs, chastity belts, sculpture, ivories, bronzes – and, except in the high summer months, almost empty of visitors. Often you find yourself in a small dark room staring at some endearing little object that no one has bothered to document or catalogue. And of course, the high point is the haunting tapestry series called, collectively, *La Dame Aux Licornes*. Bonus: when your feet finally give out, you can hobble 100 yards to an inexpensive good restaurant near the boulevard St-Michel ... L'Osteria del Passe Partout (see page 132).

L'Institut du Monde Arabe

1 rue des Fossés St-Bernard, 5e
Métro: Jussieu, Cardinal Lemoine

Hours: 1:00 to 8:00 p.m. every day except Mondays.

Admission: 40F.

The price is high, the building is spectacular inside and out. It's a treasure-store of archaeology, history, calligraphy, decoration, books, photographs of the world of Islam. There's a cafeteria, a restaurant, a *salle image et son* for films, music. At the very least, go and see the exquisite façade, even if you'd rather have an inexpensive lunch than pay the 40F admission fee.

7e arrondissement

The Invalides

Esplanade des Invalides, 7e
Métro: Invalides, Latour-Maubourg, École Militaire

Hours: 10:00 a.m. to 6:00 p.m.

Admission: 27F; 14F for students and *Carte Vermeil* holders. This ticket entitles you to all three of the museums and to Napoleon's tomb, and can be used on two consecutive days.

The Invalides is a catch-all name for the complex of museums which deal primarily with Napoleon, but also with everything to do with French armies from the shot-torn battle flags of Louis XIV to more modern armour. Napoleon's tomb, under the dome of the Invalides, is majestic, solemn, and always surrounded by a silent, circling group.

Musée d'Orsay

1 rue Bellechasse, 7e (at the quai Anatole France)
Métro: Chambres des Députés, Solférino

Hours: 10:00 a.m. to 6:00 p.m. every day except Thursdays, when it is open to 9:45 p.m. Closed Mondays.

Admission: 30F; 15F reduced price tickets. Sundays, 15F for everyone, under-18s free on that day only.

Built for the Great Exhibition of 1900, the old, derelict Gare d'Orsay has been joyously transformed into a palace of 19th- and early 20th-century French art: Ingres and Delacroix, Daumier, Moreau and Degas; Manet, Monet, Renoir; Seurat, Redon, Toulouse-Lautrec; Bonnard, Vuillard and Vallotton . . . the entire contents of the Jeu de Paume, with generous helpings of the Louvre and the Palais de Tokyo, are ranged among three floors of galleries and halls. The light is for the most part natural – filtered through the glass roof – and the internal architecture has a curious King Tut's Tomb effect – at once airy and monumental, in muted tones of grey. It's a stunning success. As well as its permanent collections, it usually has a special show of interest, such as the Neo-Impressionist drawings, and the Circus Posters, of summer 1991.

Hang on to your ticket, you can go in and out of the museum as often as you like in the course of one day.

Musée Rodin

77 rue de Varenne, 7e
Métro: Varenne

Hours: 10:00 a.m. to 6:00 p.m. Closed Mondays, open holidays.

Admission: 20F; 10F reduced price tickets.

This old and beautiful house in a rather pompous part of Paris holds many of Rodin's most superb works – their power and vigour fairly burst the walls. More sculpture in the remarkably beautiful garden. And a place to eat in the museum. A nice Paris touch: on the Métro platform at Varenne, lifesize reproductions of the greatest Rodins, and some small ones in a dramatic spotlit glass cage.

8e arrondissement

Musée Nissim de Camondo
63 rue de Monceau, 8e
Métro: Villiers

Hours: 10:00 a.m. to noon, 2:00 to 5:00 p.m. Closed Mondays, Tuesdays and holidays.

Admission: 15F; 10F reduced price tickets.

Very quiet: most tourists pass it by, which is their loss. A museum dedicated to the memory of a young aviator shot down in World War I, which sounds both dull and depressing. Not so. His father, a wealthy art collector, recreated the interior of a house as it would have been done by an 18th-century tycoon. French furniture, *objets d'art*, then were of a luxury and perfection seen nowhere else in the world, and there they are, gleaming with care, love, and polishing, and waiting for the minuet to begin.

Musée du Petit Palais

avenue Winston-Churchill, 8e
Métro: Champs-Élysées-Clemenceau

Hours: 10:00 a.m. to 5:40 p.m. Closed Mondays and holidays.

Admission: 20F; 15F reduced price tickets. Free for under-18s and over-60s.

This museum, also often neglected by Paris visitors, has some fine works bequeathed by private collectors – beautiful Manet pastels, Berthe Morisot, Mary Cassatt, Toulouse-Lautrec pastels, Bonnard, Vuillard, Cézanne – and historic French furniture, *bibelots*, clocks and so forth. The peaceful, flowering circular garden is usually deserted; a good place to rest, read, meditate. However, they courteously discourage picnicking, so don't try it. Often there are fine temporary exhibitions: check *Pariscope* or street posters.

12e arrondissement

Musée des Arts Africains et Océaniens

293 avenue Daumesnil, 12e
Métro: Porte Dorée

Hours: 10:00 a.m. to 12:00 p.m., 1:30 to 5:30 p.m. weekdays: 10:00 a.m. to 6:00 p.m. Saturdays and Sundays. Closed Tuesdays.

Admission: 23F; free for under-18s. 13F Sundays.

It's worth trailing all the way out to this fairly remote part of Paris to find an almost unknown treasure. The arts of black Africa – bold statements in wood, bone, leather, brass – the delicate beauty of carvings and leather from Moslem North Africa – and some gem-like artifacts from the Pacific islands colonized by the French. Poster collectors: don't miss the museum's own magnificent *affiche*.

16e arrondissement

Musée Guimet

6 place d'Iéna, 16e
Métro: Iéna

Hours: 9:45 a.m. to 5:15 p.m. Closed Tuesdays and holidays.

Admission: 25F.

The exact opposite of the Beaubourg Modern Museum: calm, soothing Far Eastern art. The Asiatic Art Collection of the Louvre, and worth return visits if you can afford it – save money with picnic lunches. Japanese and Chinese masterworks, irreplaceable sculpture from parts of Cambodia that have vanished for ever in wars, art of India and Pakistan, and an important exhibition on Japanese Buddhism. An annexe, to which your Musée Guimet ticket admits you, is at the Hôtel Heidelbach-Guimet, 19 avenue d'Iéna, just up the street.

Musée Marmottan

2 rue Louis-Boilly, 16e
Métro: La Muette, and about 10 minutes' walk through a park

Hours: 10:00 a.m. to 5:30 p.m. Closed Mondays.

Admission: 25F; 10F for students and over-60s.

Rejoice! The stolen Monets which have been missing for several years have been found and are now back where they belong, on the walls of the renovated Marmottan. One, *Impression at Daybreak*, is the painting that gave Impressionism its name. For many years the Marmottan was little visited – now you can expect a queue down the 10 steps and into the street. Be patient and you'll get in. For the less mobile, there's a narrow lift to take you down to the beautifully lit underground room with everything from a cool Scandinavian farm scene to the dazzling and baffling water-lily paintings that became the nucleus for the famous Nymphéas collection in the Orangerie (page 184). There are many other works by friends and contemporaries, and some treasures from the Renaissance. Don't miss the touching exhibition of Monet's letters and postcards to friends: a haunting record of difficulties, illness, lack of money, broken promises from patrons and dealers.

Art Moderne de la Ville de Paris

11 avenue du Président-Wilson, 16e
Métro: Iéna

Hours: 10:00 a.m. to 5:30 p.m., Wednesdays to 6:30. Closed Mondays and holidays.

Admission: 28F; 18F reduced price tickets.

Much of the Musée Moderne's contents have been moved to the Musée d'Orsay, across the river on the quai Anatole France, and to Beaubourg – but there is still an impressive permanent collection on exhibit, and it installs great temporary shows: retrospectives, private collections, and thematic exhibits. This is the place to find Cubist, Fauve and École de Paris paintings. Check *L'Officiel des Spectacles* for current events.

18e arrondissement

Musée de Montmartre

12 rue Cortot, 18e
Métro: Lamarck-Caulaincourt
Bus: Montmartrobus

Hours: 11:00 a.m. to 6:00 p.m. every day except Mondays (closed).

Admission: 25F; 15F reduced price tickets.

An 18th-century house crammed with souvenirs of the legendary artists' quarter. The Toulouse-Lautrec posters may have been reproduced on cheap paper a million times, but the originals can still stop you in your tracks. Many drawings, relics, and costumes of the days when Montmartre was a place to be enjoyed, not where one is ripped off as at present.

This list of museums, of course, is the merest scratching of the surface. We have missed out (but you don't have to) such esoteric delights as the Musée Bricard (locks and keys from Roman times to the 1950s, some as fine and intricate as jewellery), the Delacroix and Balzac houses, the Victor-Hugo Museum in the place des Vosges, the Grévin (waxworks to make Madame Tussaud melt with envy), and a great crazy one devoted entirely to the art of the counterfeiter. Would you believe a Rock'n'Roll Hall of Fame? Go to the Forum des Halles, Porte du Louvre. A Musée de la Vie Romantique, with souvenirs of Georges Sand? A Hunting Museum, at the Hôtel Guénegaud at 60 rue des Archives? If you can read French and want details of every museum in Paris and the surrounding area, get the brochure *Musées, Expositions, Monuments de Paris et de l'Île de France*, published every two months by CNHMS, Hôtel de Sully, 62 rue St-Antoine, 4e (*Métro*: St-Paul), and often available from the Tourist Office at 127 avenue des Champs-Élysées.

Galleries

Welcoming and forbidding, worthwhile and not to be bothered with – for a century or more galleries have been a keystone of Paris life. For the visitor, they are the best way we know to let you see the world through other eyes, without paying entrance fees to museums, or scrambling to see as many as you can in one, three, or five consecutive days with the good but fairly expensive *Carte Inter-Musées* (see page 181).

Paris is lavish with art for paupers, from inexpensive art posters available in bookshops, to postcards given away by CarteCom in bars and tourist offices. The galleries are scattered all over the city, from the luxurious 15e and 16e *arrondissements* to the small streets leading to the Gare de Lyon in the plebeian 12e *arrondissement*. Since they tend to cluster by kind, here's an *arrondissement* by *arrondissement* guide.

The 8e *arrondissement* has 'Establishment art'. Work by the famous dead, Boudin, Jongkind, Pissarro, Dufy, Redon, Seurat, and by the million-dollar living artists, is at home all the way down the avenue de Matignon, rue Miromesnil, rue de la Boëtie, rue St-Honoré.

The Left Bank, in the 5e, 6e and 7e *arrondissements* is where you'll find Picasso – mostly sculpture, ceramics, etchings, lithographs –

Braque, Mirò, the greats from before World War I until well into the 1970s. A good art-walk is along the *quais* from St-Michel, westward to the Musée d'Orsay. Smaller galleries range around St-Germain and St-Michel in the narrow streets to the Seine.

Across the river, in the burgeoning 3e and 4e *arrondissements*, there are interesting, sometimes controversial, young rising stars in galleries centred on the place des Vosges, rue du Pont Louis-Philippe, around Beaubourg.

Newest of all is found in the vital and fascinating 11e *arrondissement*, and the 12e from the Bastille *quartier*, a web of streets going north and east – rue de Charonne, rue de la Roquette, rue Keller, rue du Faubourg St-Antoine. Where furniture-makers, framers, joiners, junk shops once stood, galleries are popping up.

Many galleries, especially the grand ones around the rue de Seine, St-Germain des Prés, Latour-Maubourg, avenue Matignon, and the rue St-Honoré, estivate in August – that means they're closed. Galleries often open only Tuesdays through Saturdays, or Mondays through Fridays. Some in the newer art-areas have Sunday morning openings, or *vernissages* the night before a show is to begin, when the doors may be open for the passing art-prowler to walk in, meet the artist, have a glass of wine, try to see the pictures. The grander ones are invitation-only, but around the 3e, 4e, 6e and 11e *arrondissements*, try your luck. Check *Pariscope* or *L'Officiel des Spectacles*, *Figaro*, and all handouts from the Champs-Élysées Tourist Office, for specific shows.

The galleries listed here are a sampling: many established for 30, 40, even 50 years; with others, the printing-ink is almost still wet on their posters. All were open in the summer of 1991, and we hope all will be doing well for years to come.

Note: we have not listed the really world-famous galleries – such as Louise Leiris, Galerie Maeght, the Galerie des Naïfs et Primitifs, the Galerie du Chat en Majesté – because you can't miss their posters, displayed like works of art themselves in shop windows all over Paris.

1er arrondissement

Christian Siret, Arcade Colette, Jardins du Palais Royal. 134–7 Arcades Valois. Specializes in Colette-iana: posters, photographs, original manuscripts, postcards. Open 2:30 to 7:00 p.m.

Galerie du Jour Agnès B., 6 rue du Jour. Work of new, young, promising artists.

Anne Blanc, 158 galerie de Valois, Jardins du Palais Royal.

Schmitt, 396 rue St-Honoré. l9th- and 20th-century masterpieces – Vuillard, Delacroix, Manet, Bonnard, Rouault, and others.

3e arrondissement

Daniel Templon, 30 rue Beaubourg. Top-ranking, top-price American and international, Roy Lichtenstein *et al.*

4e arrondissement

Médart, 109 rue Quincampoix. Works by gallery artists, often accompanied by photographs, personal appearances.

ADAC Galerie-Atelier, 21 rue St-Paul. Youngish, progressive artists' group.

Baudoin-Lebon, 38 rue Ste-Croix de la Bretonnerie. Avant-garde paintings, photos.

Zabriskie, 37 rue Quincampoix. Many famous magic-realists and surrealists, and 20th-century photographer 'names'.

6e arrondissement

Philippe de Hesdin, 46 rue du Bac. Group shows of 'house' artists.

Daniel Pons-Jeanne Debord, 9 rue de l'Epéron. Many non-objective and abstract painters.

Nicole Ferry, 57 quai des Grands Augustins. Collective shows, some modern Eastern European work.

Cimaise de Paris, 74 rue Notre-Dame-de-Champs. Interesting, offbeat. Sometimes has one-subject exhibitions – e.g. butterflies.

Galerie Claude Bernard, 7–9 rue des Beaux Arts. Always fine and famous artists on show. Superb Bonnard show in summer 1991.

Isy Brachot, 35 rue Guénégaud. High Surrealists, Magritte, Delvaux, Mesens.

Callu-Mérite, 17 rue des Beaux Arts. Very modern, interesting gallery.

8e arrondissement

Alain Daune, 14 avenue Matignon. Well known artists, velvety atmosphere.

Artcurial, 9 avenue Matignon. Big group shows, established artists, kind welcome to wandering visitors.

Galerie 1900–2000, 9 rue de Penthiévre. The great surrealists, including photographers – Man Ray, Masson, Mirò, Picabia.

Daniel Malingue, 20 avenue Matignon. Very famous artists of the 20th-century.

11e arrondissement

Le Gall Peyroulet, 18 rue Keller. Works by artist-architects.

J. and J. Donguy, 57 rue de la Roquette. Near the new Opéra, in a street that is a living, walking, talking art display of its own.

Nicole Bellier, 25 rue de Charonne. Charming gallery, worth visiting for itself.

Carpe Diem, 60 boulevard Beaumarchais. Paintings, glass designed by artists, very modern.

12e arrondissement

Michel Vidal, 56 rue du Faubourg St-Antoine. Artists under 30, very provocative work. Vidal is one of the first to open in this interesting and blossoming area.

Cultural centres

You can take advantage of nationalistic self-promotion by attending free, or almost free, events at various cultural centres. Some are dull beyond belief; others – among them the ones listed here – are full of life, even explosive.

Centre Culturel Américain

261 boulevard Raspail, 14e
Tel: 43 21 42 20
Métro: Raspail

Concerts, courses and spectacles, exciting and well organized, with emphasis on the contemporary.

Centre Culturel Britannique

9–11 rue de Constantine, 7e
Tel: 45 55 54 99
Métro: Invalides

Lectures, films and concerts, and a good library. Closed Saturdays and Sundays.

Centre Culturel Canadien

5 rue de Constantine, 7e
Tel: 45 51 35 75
Métro: Invalides

Art galleries, a sculpture garden, a library, and an auditorium for concerts. Monthly children's concerts. Admission free. Closed Sundays.

Centre Culturel de la Communauté Française de Belgique

7 rue de Vénise, 4e
Tel: 42 71 26 16
Métro: Les Halles, Rambuteau

Theatre, films, concerts, art shows and dance – burgeoning activity, from 5F to 30F.

Centre Culturel Latino-Américain

6 rue des Fossés-St-Marcel, 5e
Tel: 43 36 56 04
Métro: St-Marcel

Exhibitions, concerts and conferences.

Institut Néerlandais

121 rue de Lille, 7e
Tel: 47 05 85 99
Métro: Rue du Bac

Classical music concerts, and Dutch jazz and contemporary music. Free. Closed Mondays.

Centre Culturel Portugais

51 avenue d'Iéna, 16e
Tel: 47 20 86 84 and 47 20 85 94
Métro: Étoile

Classical music concerts.

Centre Culturel Suédois

11 rue Payenne, 3e
Tel: 42 71 82 20
Métro: St-Paul

Exhibitions, concerts, theatre, film – usually free.

Goethe-Institut

17 avenue d'Iéna, 16e
Tel: 47 23 61 21
Métro: Iéna

German music, film, and art.

Check also (if your interests run in these directions) the cultural centres of Yugoslavia, Egypt, Mexico, Spain, Italy, and Brazil. They're all in the phone book.

Concerts

The French are not the most musical nation on earth, and the dearth of classical music in Paris seems to be worrying quite a lot of people. Compared to London, New York, Manchester, Chicago, Cleveland, it's a bit of a desert. The 'major' composers rank as minor compared to Germans, Austrians, Italians. French popular music is unoriginal, not even a good copy of American or English. But there is music to be found, and more of it every year. Much of it is vastly overpriced, but we've tracked down a number of concerts that are either free or very nearly so.

In churches

You can hear some of the finest organ music in the world, played in the incomparable settings of Paris churches, often on Sunday afternoons, and it's free. For current listings, check the magazine *Pariscope*, published every Wednesday.

Maison de la Radio

An orchestra organized by the French National Radio Service (ORTF) often gives free, or very inexpensive, concerts. For details, send a self-addressed stamped envelope to Radio France, 116 avenue du Président-Kennedy, 16e. Or drop in and see what you can find out. *Métro*: Ranelagh, Passy.

Grande Hall de la Villette

place de la Fontaine aux Lions, 19e.
Métro: Porte de Pantin

Free 'pre-concerts', two hours before big Jazz Festivals. Impromptu music, shows, etc. Check 'Jazz-Pop-Rock' listings in *Pariscope* and the free English-language newspapers (page 270).

Métro music

Classical music students at the Conservatoire National are encouraged by their teachers to learn to perform, not just to practise, and a very good way for them to do so is to pick a spot in a Métro corridor and play for the passers-by. It's a neat way to pick up some change, too. The quality is often exceptionally good, although the acoustics may leave something to be desired. Some fairly good Irish bands, accordionists, provincial flute-and-drum ensembles, and even expatriate American blues and jazz singers also make use of the Métro, and are not to be sneezed at (they're impossible to ignore, anyway).

Beaubourg

The cobblestoned vastness in front of the Georges Pompidou Centre, 3e (*Métro*: Hôtel de Ville, Rambuteau) often plays host to musicians of very good standard, mixed in with the mimes and fire-eaters.

Rue de Provence, 9e

Of all unlikely places, a pedestrian square between Au Printemps, the department store, and Prisunic frequently has chamber groups, soloists, or blues or pop singers performing to people sitting on the steps of the nearby church. *Métro*: Havre-Caumartin.

Discounts

Student discounts: reduction in ticket prices for classical music in the big concert halls is usually available. Check listings in *Pariscope*, or apply with student card to COPAR, 39 avenue Georges-Bernanos, 5e (*Métro*: Port-Royal).

Senior citizens: with the *Carte Vermeil*, which the French generously provide for women over 60 and men over 65 *of any nationality*, discounts for musical events are given. See pages 250–1 for details of this marvellous card. Look for the initials 'CV' in the price listing of any event. Or show your passport at the box office.

Free music – a typical week's offerings*

Festival of the Golden Muses of Paris: young, talented musicians in the parc de Choisy

Music at the Louvre: soprano and piano in the new Louvre Auditorium

Fête de Musique à l'Hôtel de Sully: a whole afternoon of concerts in one of the historic mansions of the Marais

Jacqueline and Jean-Pierre Carrière, pianists, playing two-piano classics at the Institut Hongrois

The Rosamonde Quartet at the Grand Théâtre, boulevard Jourdan

The American Boys' Choir, American Church, quai d'Orsay

Music of the Middle Ages, at the Église St-Merri

Festival de la Butte Montmartre, Musée Montmartre

Pariscope and *L'Officiel des Spectacles de Paris*, out every Wednesday, list all the musical events of the week. Look for the words *Entrée Libre* or *Gratuit* in the listings, which mean you get in free.

Spectator Sports

Racing

If you can resist betting, a day at a French track with the sun shining, the crowd shrieking and stamping on losing tickets, is an experience not to be missed. You'll also see some very classy animals, hot competition, and a mix of people from working-class to the truly elegant racehorse owners and followers.

The two racecourses at the southern end of the Bois de Boulogne are enchanting. **Longchamp** is by all odds the smartest and most modern. It's the world's longest track, and said by horsey people to be one of the most difficult. The Prix de l'Arc de Triomphe and the Grand Prix are the great social events – go very early if you hope to get in. However, on other days, go for the fun, and the beauty, and try to refrain from betting as, unless you really understand the monumentally complicated French system, you may find that in the end you didn't have your money on the horse you chose at all.

To get to Longchamp, take the Métro to Porte d'Auteuil, then the special bus which costs 9F (*Carte Paris Visite* and RATP tickets not valid). Inside the Bois, on the bus route, you will see several gates marked *Pelouse*; entrance here is to the infield, standing among the crowd, and costs least. If you choose the gate marked *Pesage*, you enter the grandstand which costs more for unreserved seats on wide bare stone steps. Take a newspaper to sit on, they're dirty.

Here, we recommend splurging on the higher-priced entrance fee, as the surroundings are beautiful and comfortable, and you can follow the knowledgeable to watch the horses from above the saddling enclosure behind the stands. Take the lift to one of the towers marked 'Restaurant Panoramique' for a most lovely view over the course and the park, and some extremely posh lavatories, free.

Racing at Longchamp goes on from early April to October.

Auteuil, the other racecourse in the Bois, is for steeplechasing, and gets a very mixed crowd (i.e. pickpockets). If you can get there for the Prix des Draggs in early summer, it's one of the best almost-free sights of the world. Again, admission to the *pelouse* is cheap, to the grandstand more expensive.

Vincennes, in the Bois de Vincennes at the other end of Paris, is another city track, this time for trotters, which look like something out of Degas. There's daytime racing all year around; night racing from the end of March to the first week in December – a great way to spend a spring or summer evening. Don't believe anyone who tells you it is a ten-minute walk from the Château; it's 50 minutes' dusty or muddy foot-slogging. Get there by RER to Joinville-le-Pont (free with your *Carte Paris Visite*, or a ticket), then about 15 minutes walk.

The **Hippodrome** at St-Cloud is reachable in either of two ways: quickly by RER to Rueil station, then by bus No. 431 to the stop 'Laboratoire Débat' for the *pesage*, or 'Champ des Courses' for the *Pelouse*; more slowly, the Métro to Pont de Sèvres, then bus No. 431 to the stops as above. St-Cloud is the place for flat-racing, a lovely track which attracts lots of fashionable people and famous horses at certain classic races. Last week in February to end of July, then from late September to the end of November.

Tennis

Tennis generates immense interest in Paris, where quite a lot of tournaments with some of the world's great players competing are held. The scene changes so fast that it is impossible to make an accurate listing here, so check the newspapers if you're a fan. The Stade Roland-Garros (*Métro*: Porte d'Auteuil then – during major tournaments – special buses to the stadium) is world famous, but the prices are high, especially for big events, so don't say you weren't warned.

Cinema

For many film buffs, France leads the world in appreciation of the cinema, and Paris leads France. No matter what your taste in films – recent release, art-house, cult movie, retrospectives, Third World – some cinema in Paris will be showing it. *Pariscope* and *Officiel des Spectacles* have complete listings. 'V. O.' means the film is shown with its original sound-track (and so its original language). 'V. F.' means a French sound-track has been dubbed in.

A big difference in cinema-going is that in France, the usher who shows you to your seat should get a tip – 1F per person.

Circus

The circus is having something of a revival in Paris – a great place to take the kids when walking around Paris palls. One of them actually offers a whole day with the circus artists who will show you rehearsals in the morning, then sit with you at lunch, and perform the full spectacle in the afternoon.

The listing below is necessarily provisional, as places, times and dates change with the seasons and circuses come and circuses go. Check with *Pariscope* or *Le Figaro* for up-to-date listings. Fortunately, you don't need to understand or speak French to enjoy these spectacles.

Circus Alexandra Franconi

parc de St-Cloud
Tel: 46 02 84 14
Tickets 40–80F. Performances Wednesdays, Saturdays, Sundays, and holidays, at 3:00 p.m.

Cirque de Paris

corner of avenue Commune-de-Paris and avenue Hoche, Nanterre (it's in the suburbs, and you get there by RER to Nanterre)
Tel: 47 24 11 70

Here's where you can spend the day with the circus people, if you telephone first. Performances Wednesdays, Sundays, and holidays, 3:00 p.m.

Puppets

Marionetterie, if there is such a word, is a very old French art, and although the shows are nominally for *les jeunes*, parents and hangers-on love them too. They are seasonal; the ones noted here are among the old favourites, others will be performing during your visit. Have a look at *Pariscope* for up-to-the-minute listings.

Marionettes des Champs-Élysées
Rond-Point des Champs-Élysées, at the corner of avenue Gabriel and avenue Matignon, 8e.
Métro: Champs-Élysées-Clémenceau, Franklin-D.-Roosevelt

The *guignol* horror show that has entranced kids for ever. Tickets 10F. Wednesdays, Saturdays, Sundays, holidays, 3:00, 4:00 and 5:00 p.m.

Marionettes du Champs-de-Mars
Champs-de-Mars, 7e
Métro: École Militaire

During school holidays, every day at 3:15, 4:15 p.m. Otherwise Wednesdays, Saturdays, and Sundays only, same times. Tickets 10–14F.

Marionettes de Montsouris
avenue Reilles-rue Gazan, near the lake, 14e
Métro: Cité-Universitaire, Glacière

Mondays, Tuesdays, Wednesdays, Saturdays, Sundays, 3:30 and 4:30 p.m. Tickets 14F.

Théâtre Guignol Anatole
parc des Buttes-Chaumont, 19e
Métro: Laumière

Wednesdays, Saturdays, Sundays, holidays, 3:00 and 4:00 p.m. Tickets 10F.

Théâtre du Petit Ours
Tuileries Gardens, 8e
Tel: 42 64 05 19
Métro: Concorde

Wednesdays, different shows at 3:30 and 5:30 p.m. Tickets 8F.

Children's Theatre Paris is extremely rich in children's theatres which do magic shows, straight plays and pageants. Often there are extra performances during Christmas and Easter holidays. Some theatres close for five to eight weeks during the period mid-July to mid-September, so it's best to refer to the current *Pariscope* for last-minute information. Two of the best which usually have something going the whole year:

Cité des Sciences et de l'Industrie
30 avenue Corentin-Cariou, 19e
Métro: Porte de la Villette

Closed Mondays.

Musée en l'Herbe
Jardin d'Acclimatation in the Bois de Boulogne, 16e
Métro: Sablons

Wednesdays, Saturdays, Sundays, 3:00 p.m. Tickets 30F which give you entry to a theatre performance and the museum itself.

Television

French TV is *very* French. If your hotel has a set in the office, breakfast-room or lobby, linger and look. When a big soccer match, race or (best of all) the Tour de France, is on, make for the nearest TV dealer and join the crowd which will stand there for ever with boos, whistles, groans and some racy French language. The TV news 'speakerines' are chosen for intelligence and wit; they sparkle – eyes, teeth, lipstick and intellect – in the hard, brilliant studio lights.

Paris, plus

Versailles

Some of the most alluring places to visit are within an hour or two of Paris by public transport or by fast train. It would be almost illegal to be in Paris and not see Versailles. This vast complex of parks, palace, and the pavilions known as Les Trianons, is almost impossible to comprehend when you are on the spot. It's wise to collect and study a good small guidebook before you go. The *Blue Guide* (page 254) has a very good, succinct and easily followed section on the Château, the park and gardens, and if you have already invested in it you really won't need another book. Versailles is easy to reach, and if you have the time to do it, go for a few hours three or four times, rather than wearing yourself out mentally and physically by one long visit.

You can reach Versailles free with your *Carte Paris Visite* (Zones 1 to 4). Métro to Pont de Sèvres, then bus No. 171, but it takes about an hour. SNCF trains from the Invalides station go every 15 minutes and take about half an hour, but be prepared for long queues at the ticket windows, and make sure you go to Versailles Rive Gauche (RG), nowhere else. *Aller-retour* (return) tickets cost 30F; make sure you get both tickets when you buy.

Half-day all-inclusive tours, by coach, including transport, entrance to major attractions, and guide, are 220–250F from many ticket agencies, but in our view to be avoided. You are shoved through at a brisk trot, told where to look, never allowed to lag or sit down, and returned to Paris more dead than alive. You can do the whole thing at your own pace for half the price.

The main treasures of Versailles – the Chapel, the State Apartments of the King and Queen, and the Hall of Mirrors – must be seen by every visitor. The fee for them is 31F, reduced to 16F if you are between 18 and 25 or over 60. Under 18, it's free. On Sundays, everyone gets in for 16F – but NEVER go then, as queues for tickets can stretch half a mile.

The King's Private Bedroom and the Royal Opera, the Queen's Rooms, and Madame Du Barry's Rooms, can be seen only by guided tours, lasting an hour and a quarter, and are 24F each.

The Grand Trianon costs 16F, the Petit Trianon 6F, or 20F for both.

The Lenôtre gardens carved out of the swamp, and the Mansart fountains, a marvel of hydraulic engineering, are 'musts'. If you can visit more than once, don't miss two of the smaller delights: the Musée des Voitures, with its perfectly preserved state coaches, wedding carriages and hunting *calèches*; and the extraordinary Hameau, the rustic village where Marie Antoinette went on playing at being a country wife up to 1789.

Guided tours of the Versailles park and grounds are available; information from the Versailles Tourist Office, tel: 49 50 36 22.

The Château and the Grand Trianon are open Tuesdays

through Saturdays, 9:45 a.m. to 5:00 p.m., the Petit Trianon 2:00 to 5:00 p.m. only. Everything is closed on Mondays and public holidays.

Chartres

Again, it can be done by taking a fairly pricey tour bus, which gives you cosy shepherding; or, cheaper, more fun, and infinitely more flexible, take the train from Gare de Montparnasse as early as you can and wander round on your own. Trains run about every 45 minutes from 6:26 in the morning, with the last train back at 10:53 at night. Return fare is 125F (or free with Eurailpass).

Wander around the town, which is a delight in itself, and absorb the miracle of the cathedral by yourself, through your own eyes, and not blurred by tour-guide patter. Then find a small neighbourhood restaurant, which will be half the price and twice the pleasure of any suggested by an organized group, and eat what you want at a price you want to pay. Or take a picnic. Get a small, good guidebook to Chartres before you leave Paris, and read it on the train. Henry Adams, the 19th-century American writer, did rather a good job on both Chartres and Mont-St-Michel.

A coach tour to Chartres costs 250F, takes five hours (and since it's 88 miles from Paris, travelling time eats into Chartres time); it gives you a view of Rambouillet and Maintenon châteaux on the way, and a guided tour of the cathedral. Various companies do tours on different days, so check with a travel agent for details.

The Monet Gardens – Giverny

A coach tour to the famous water-lily gardens of Monet now costs about 275F for half a day from Paris – don't do it, as the bus trip out is intensely boring and the commentary more so, with piped music all the way back. Instead, take the train from St-Lazare to Vernon for 104F, and bus to Giverny, pay about 35F for admission to the house and gardens, wander freely, picnic, and come back when you choose. The ponds and bridges and flowers are *exactly* as they were painted. Closed 31 October–1 April.

Mont-St-Michel

Once a month, the RATP (Paris Transport) runs a day trip to this dreamlike village rising on its mount from the sea. It's not very expensive, it's all in French, and it's an experience you'll never forget. Coaches leave at 7:00 a.m., and it's a long day. Get brochures about this and other day trips from RATP, 52 quai des Grands Augustins, 6e (*Métro*: St-Michel).

Malmaison

The RATP has half-day excursions four times a year to these two châteaux, which are curiously neglected by visitors to Paris, unless they are passionate about Napoleon. The cost is 165F, or 135F for those (over 65, students, etc.) entitled to a concession.

However, if you are willing to take the time, you can do-it-yourself by public transport, with a guide at Malmaison. Take the RER from Charles de Gaulle-Étoile to La Défense, five minutes away, then the No. 158A bus to the Malmaison-Château stop. Buses run about every 15 minutes and take about 25 minutes to the bus stop nearest the Château, then it's about an eight-minute walk.

The RER station at the Charles de Gaulle-Étoile Métro stop is huge, eerie, depopulated, and if you get lost you'll find yourself asking directions from a weary flower-seller. If you have a *Carte Paris Visite*, travel on the RER and the suburban bus line is free. Otherwise, take a ticket from the automatic dispenser (one way). Follow signs marked 'St-Germain-en-Laye' for trains to La Défense. On the No. 158A bus, if you're travelling without a *Carte Paris Visite*, the fare is one ticket.

Malmaison is the Château bought and furnished by Napoleon for Josephine, set in most lovely grounds. Across the park is the Bois-Preau *petit château* which has souvenirs of Napoleon's final exile at Ste-Helena, and the Church at Reuil-Malmaison has the tombs of Josephine and Queen Hortense. Entrance to the château is 27F (13F for 18–25 and over-60s; under 18, free), and you can't wander around: when a little group has collected, a guide appears. The tour takes about an hour and a quarter, it's all in French, so if you are a true Napoleon fan, read the very good entry in the *Blue Guide* (page 254). At the end of the tour (which tells you more than you want to know about the history of the porcelain plates and the very banal paintings), give the guide one or two francs. The Château is unexpectedly small for such a great man (and the beds are tiny); but for those who expect Napoleon to rise from the dead and take over France, it's very touching. Open 10:00 a.m. to 12:30 p.m., 1:30 to 5:30 p.m. (last visits noon and 5:00 p.m.). Closed Tuesdays, public holidays.

For information about the RATP tours (in French), get the folder titled 'Les Bus Decouverte' from RATP offices.

À bon marché
(The shops)

What are paupers doing shopping anyhow? Generally speaking, you've got a much better chance of picking up bargains on your home territory. Still, there are things that the French and French shops do better than almost anyone else. And if we have to put a label on what that *je ne sais quoi* is, we'd say it was attention to detail. So you'll find it in the cut of clothes, or the choice and display of foods, or in accessories for you or your home. With space and weight of your luggage in mind, we'd suggest small things that show individuality: if you wear specs, look at French frames; or think about replacing your watch, or buying a new fountain pen, or finding just the right piece of jewellery, or tie or belt. If you're a seamstress, look at the vast range of buttons. If you're houseproud, this could be your chance to buy the door-knobs or finger-plates that will make the difference to your home.

Shopping is distinct from window-shopping, though you can combine the two. What you crave in Lanvin or Kenzo can be duplicated or approximated elsewhere at a discount; or found 'once-worn'. You can use Paris to stock up on often outlandish items of food: pickles and conserves that would cost a mint in Soho, available for next to nothing at the Prisunic. Second-hand books, cheap but thrilling gifts, museum prints, and every kind of flea-market hand-me-down. But remember, you've got to fit it all into your luggage and get it home.

Manners: as everywhere, you can go farther and faster on a few elements of *la politesse* and a smile. In some situations, however, no amount of manners will do you the least bit of good. Salespeople in large establishments tend to be more abrupt than in small ones, less willing to help. Solution: know what you're looking for; find out the correct terms (the name of the article, the colour, the size, the brand); do not be browbeaten into buying something you don't want; if one person won't tell you where to find it, try another.

If you can, pay for everything in cash. A bank will always give you a better exchange rate than a shop (or for that matter, a hotel or restaurant) for traveller's cheques or foreign currency. However, even really small shops now take VISA/Access and Mastercard cards, which are a considerable convenience if cash is low and you've *got* to shop.

Bargains

Here we include cheap shops – not resale. Paris is a mine of good clothes at less than Paris prices – if you know where to look. The rue St-Placide in the 6e is lined with shops plastered with signs: 'Dégrif-fés', 'Soldes Permanents', 'Les Prix Dingues'. The rue St-Dominique, in the 7e, is a magnet for bargain hunters. However, be warned that shops in both these streets have a mushroom growth and disappear just as fast. A big vacant shop can be stocked up with clothes for men, women and children, from various sources, do a roaring trade and vanish in six months or less. La Clef des Soldes was a biggish place in the rue St-Dominique a few years ago, specializing in de luxe ready-to-wear for men and women (Cardin, Hechter, etc). Then it went completely over to sports and ski-wear, the next year it was gone, and now it's back, full of racks and bins.

This listing is the current crop of good cheapies, all over Paris. Don't write us a letter of reprimand if they've disappeared. We would rather have a letter from you telling us of *your* discoveries, so that we can look them over ourselves and possibly include them in a future edition.

These shops can be fun to fish around in. They often have bins of oddments, or racks of clothes that can be just what you are looking for (equally good chance of nothing but monster coats and dwarf dresses). With patience you can turn up something.

6e arrondissement

rue St-Placide

Métro: St-Placide, Sèvres-Babylone
Bus: No. 96

Hours: mostly Mondays through Saturdays, 10:00 a.m. to 7:00 p.m. See specific shops for any variation in these basic hours.

The whole of this street is lined with shops which either offer a) fine value at average prices, or b) real cheaperinos varying from a silk scarf at 11F to an Alligatored or Centaured T-shirt for 75F or so. We have concentrated on just one length of the street, between no. 32 and no. 60, at which point our *meute des magasins* – which roughly translates as shop-hound – gave up and fell into a very expensive tea-room for restoratives. There are many more shops to be discovered. These she found on one single day in mid-1991:

Philomène: no. 34   A favourite shopping place of ours for about eight years, very good stock, mainly raincoats. They have good winter coats, sometimes handsome tailored shirts for women, classic styles, under 100F.

Miss Girl: no. 35   Belts, bags, clothes, smart, well-priced, good for gifts.

Boba: no. 37   Very House-and-Garden gifty things – from gadgets for 25F to such beautiful items as a porcelain lemon dish for 59F, oversized heavy glass stemmed 'sundae' dishes, 29F; a magnificent chrome-and-wood fish-shaped tray, 195F, and silk flowers, pot-pourri, little flowered boxes, telephone pads, wicker, porcelain, glass, crystal, wooden things at all prices. Major credit cards accepted.

Discount R: no. 37A   Lots and lots of dresses, two-piece summery-type suits, all for less than 100F.

Vu d'Ici: no. 42   Sportswear for men and women, and very smart too – look for well-made T-shirts for 59F, jogging outfits, trainers, sweatshirts.

Dexter: next door to Vu d'Ici   More elegant sportswear at half the prices you'd pay at Galéries Lafayette or Au Printemps.

Sale Shop: no. 43   If you're prepared to spend 250F for a single beautifully styled shirt or skirt, make for Sale Shop, and hope it is still there.

Moda: no. 45   A shoe shop that has stayed at the same address for several years, featuring shoes labelled with every famous French and Italian couture name, all at discount prices.

Bargains de Mansfield: no. 47.   End-of-range shoes for men and women, elegantly conservative styles, about half the original prices of this expensive brand.

Boutique Stock: no. 48   Velours *caleçons* (pantalons) 199F, and a range of cotton sweaters 'in colours to die for', same price.

Insolence: no. 54   Very high fashion, and prices higher than the average in rue St-Placide shops – a linen skirt marked 'For the Caribbean Winter', 340F, and worth it.

La Bazardière: nos. 54–6   Irresistible! Handsome jackets in beautiful fabrics, high-style colours for women, 199–250F.

Parizzi: no. 58   Wonderful value: they are makers as well as sellers of leather jackets and skirts, good jeans, skin-fitting *caleçons* in dramatic colours, bicycle shorts à la André Agassi in fluorescent pinks and greens.

L'Annexe: no. 48   Inexpensive and for the most part fairly well-made men's casual clothes: jackets from 69F, shirts 119F. VISA, Mastercard and American Express cards accepted. Open Mondays through Saturdays, 10:00 a.m. to 7:30 p.m. but sometimes inexplicably closed.

Le Train Bleu: no. 55   A big shop with several floors of toys and games and models, but the only place our shopper has come across that sold a hexagonal chess set (three sets of chessmen play on a hexagonal board).

CRAC: no. 60   Racks marked 'Everything 50F', or '100F' or up to '200F', and here is where our shop-hound seems to have gone wild, buying a 'chic Chanel-type striped cotton jacket with brass buttons' for 100F, a 'white-dotted black skirt' for 60F, a 'great blouse' for 100F. Visa, Access, Eurocards accepted. Open 10:00 a.m. to 7:30 p.m., Mondays through Saturdays.

Magic Kids: no. 60   Formerly Magic Soldes, this shop now caters to children 0 to 16, and the prices are remarkable value for jeans, shirts, trainers, some little girls' dresses; a few boxes and racks for young mothers of their primary customers. A size 8 (American) friend bought a small wardrobe of cotton trousers, shirts, dungarees, straight off the teenage racks.

If you start at the 'Train Bleu' end of the street, near the St-Placide Métro stop, you can zig-zag along to no. 32, La Campagnarde, which provides sandwiches, quiches, mini-*baguettes*, to eat while recovering strength to go on. Or turn right, into the rue Cherche-Midi, and have a wonder-lunch at Les Frères de la Côte restaurant (page 129).

7e arrondissement

rue St-Dominique

Métro: Latour-Maubourg

We've seen this street of bargain shops go up market and down in the 10 years we've been shopping here. This year we had the help of our *meute des magasins* who has the flair of a truffle-hunter when it comes to smart buys. Now (1991) it seems to have settled into a good mix of gentrified and low-low priced shops. It's very busy, cheerful, full of people enjoying bargain-hunting. In between shops, you will be able to eat well, have superb coffee and pastries. Several good places are: Thoumieux, at no. 79, for an inexpensive lunch (52F in the summer of 1991); or a favourite Oriental one, Cam Mach, around the corner in rue de la Comète; and a much-liked bistro, Au Petit Paname, in the rue Amélie. Most of the shops here now take credit cards. They are usually open Mondays through Saturdays, about 10:00 or 11:00 a.m., until 6:30 or 7:00 p.m. Some are closed on Mondays.

Myc: no. 54   Upmarket, and rather expensive women's clothes, but compared to the rue St-Honoré, they are *not* high-priced. For example, a magnificent wool suit, with a finely detailed blouse, at 1000F, was less than half the price you would expect to pay. Major credit cards accepted.

Meli Melo: no. 60   Linens, pillows, duvets, duvet covers, Pierre Cardin bedlinens, 'Les Baux de Provence' designs for bed and table. A Ted Lapidus towelling dressing-gown was recently seen for 299F – you could pay more than that elsewhere for one much less stylish, commented our demon shopper. Also furnishing fabric, chairs, small gifts. Major credit cards accepted.

Gisquet: no. 62   One of Paris's great *boulangeries/pâtisseries*, with pastries in the window as exquisite as jewels. Gisquet is not cheap, but it will give you an idea of what Paris is all about. Presentation as well as taste matter, from paper-lace mats, to the smell of real chocolate, real vanilla, and the final flourish of the ribbon that ties up the smallest package.

Fil à Fil: no. 81   Beautiful shirts for men and women, beginning at 315F up, up, up. Some fine costume jewellery, links, studs, for about 250F. Prices are not low, but the quality is fine. Fil à Fil shirts seem to last the wearer a lifetime. French girls buy the men's shirts to wear as beach cover-ups.

Safari: no. 83   A shop which displays some of its wares in the window, and keeps many more in the back room. Great shoes at good prices, many with famous designers' names.

Tutticolori: no. 85   The name is very apt for a shop that imports and sells smart Italian sportswear for men and women in sun-splashed colours that shine out even on a dark day.

Bookshop: no. 78   International books: French, German, Italian, English, all at cut prices, a rarity in Paris. This well-stocked shop sells postcards, as well as guidebooks, art books, serious novels, some pop best-sellers.

L'Espace des Griffes Couture: no. 100   'L'Espace' is a long-established, high-fashion shop which has clothes for men and women from the good Paris ready-to-wear and 'diffusion' houses. Rather 'serious', no fantasies, at prices far below those of Right-Bank shops.

La Clef des Marques: no. 99   The 'Key' has changed its name from La Clef des Soldes, but it's still a huge bargain bazaar crammed to the rafters with bins and racks for all ages and sexes. At various times, our bargain-wise friends have bought: 'racing' *maillots* for serious swimming, 75F, Indian silk handkerchief-scarves, two for 10F, Dior fancy tights, 10F the pair, Ellesse cotton blouses 59F, shoes for under 100F, furry-lined anoraks 150F, huge down-padded ski jackets 200F, packs of baby-pants, 10 for 60F. Major credit cards accepted. Open Mondays, noon to 7:00 p.m.; Tuesdays through Fridays, 10:00 a.m. to 2:00 p.m, 3:00 to 7:00 p.m.; Saturdays, 10:00 a.m. to 1:45 p.m., 2:15 to 7:00 p.m.

Near the front door is the famous notice-board for personal ads: lifts to the Riviera, English-speaking babysitters, motor-scooters for sale, contents of a flat, skis and tennis rackets going cheap, lonely-hearts groups, news of cheap student flights.

9e arrondissement

boulevard Haussmann

Métro: Havre-Caumartin

If you're a serious shopper, here is where to start. Not as smart as the avenue de l'Opéra, it is still a Paris must. There's Galéries Lafayette, Au Printemps, Prisunic, Monoprix, Marks and Spencer – all within one fair-sized *endroit*. Dozens of discount and specialist shops are tucked away behind and between these giants.

Au Printemps: no. 64, at rue du Havre   Go on a Saturday to enjoy the fun of the stalls outside this elegant department store – but go inside as well, to admire the vast range of goods and the building's architecture. In Printemps-Maison, there are both chic and practical goods: a lampshade for a candle (it fits over the top and sinks as the candle burns), beautiful paper goods, a corkscrew for 10F, a set of six cocktail glasses for 39F. In the Printemps main building, for clothes and fashion, you'll see a very good selection of what's in style. Men have their own shop, Brummel, just behind the main store.

Parallèle: rue Joubert, corner of rue de Caumartin   Behind Au Printemps, there's a pedestrianized area facing the Église St-Louis. Parallèle is one of the long-stayers – a discount shop with casual clothes for women – racks outside, with Naf-Naf jumpsuits from 175F, suits and wool jackets for 399F, and bright, cool summer clothes even in August.

Jigger: no. 58 rue Caumartin, and nos. 56 and 66 bis rue de la Chausée d'Antin   While you're wandering around here, listening to street musicians, see what's on offer at Jigger, you never know what you will find. T-shirts for 39F, shirts from 50F up. An ever-changing stock of inexpensive and fashionable clothes, even dresses for about 100F. Around the corner in the rue Chausée d'Antin, there's more to select from, in two more Jiggers. All open Mondays through Saturdays, 10:00 a.m. to 7:00 p.m.

Prisunic: rue de Provence   The enterprising Prisunic chain is the French – very French – equivalent of what Woolworths once was, but there the resemblance ends. You can buy a light-bulb, or saucepans in high-fashion colours, food-processors, lamps, waffle-makers. Year after year, smartly dressed Parisian girls and young men shop early to find 'the' rugby-stripe jersey, good jeans, a perfect copy of a couturier silk scarf in silky polyester for only 42F, lambswool sweaters for men from 125F, Chanel-adaptation wool jackets 420F, school satchels that double as handbags, or shoes from trainers to velvet espadrilles.

Check out the food department for herbs, mustards, wines, olive oil flavoured with basil – 85 kinds of cheese – *pâtisserie*, freshly baked whole-grain bread. The cafeteria serves quick snacks, pastries, drinks at half the price of a brasserie. Cheap photocopy machine, ½F per copy. Open Mondays through Saturdays, 9:00 a.m. to 7:30 p.m. Closed Sundays.

Tissus Bouchara: corner of rue Charras   Next door to Printemps, this huge fabric shop has a remarkable range: Indian cottons in summer colours at 50F a metre, washed silk pongee 70F. Magnificent linen fabrics, wide widths, from a couture house, were 165F a metre, and cheerful ginghams only 16F. They also sell buttons, zips, yarn, threads, paper patterns – everything.

11e arrondissement

---

rue de la Roquette

Metro: Voltaire, Bastille

The maze of small ancient streets around the Bastille has been disrupted by the construction of the Opéra. But though the whole texture of the neighbourhood has changed irrevocably, there is still one wonderful street, the rue de la Roquette, which retains its old character. Most of the shops mentioned here are closed on Mondays.

Start midway, at the Voltaire Métro and the sprawling shopping square shaded by big trees. Walk south towards the Bastille. The first shops sell handsome, inexpensive shoes – this was the *quartier* of the shoemakers. Then **El Indio Feliz**, at no. 69, has a Peruvian owner, who imports painted masks, toys, *serapes*, rugs, tapestries, reed pipes, and covetable hand-made jewellery. Prices from 15F to about 90F.

On a side street to the east, **Tonkam-Bastille** no. 29 rue Keller, has an incredible collection of *bandes dessinées*, 'BDs' to the French, and comic books, posters, *fanzines*, badges, pins.

Verrerie, no. 62 rue de la Roquette, has expensive porcelain, crystal, silver, and table settings – but some beautiful inexpensive things like a chrome whale-shaped bottle opener for 29F, a bread-knife in a *baguette*-shaped and coloured case for 100F, and padded cotton travelling mules in a drawstring bag, 142F.

Atou-Mome, no. 55 (a punning name which roughly means The Ace of Kids), has delightful children's clothes. **Mappemonde**, no. 78, sells all brands of jeans, from Levis to our favourite Arthur. Next door is a very small bookshop selling new and used books, and a stack of bargain-price paperbacks, 'The Owner's Mistakes'. **Le Comptoir du Désert** at the corner of rue Keller sells tropical-style clothes and the occasional low-priced find.

ModE Moi at no. 60 is getting towards the chic end of the street – gorgeous clothes in gorgeous colours, and sometimes great sales. **Épigramme** is a big, eclectic shop, with art books and postcards, hard-to-find guidebooks and helpful, English-speaking staff. **Nota Bene**, no. 42, has witty jewellery, straw hats, accessories.

Down a side street, at no. 21 rue Daval, is **Duelle** which sells jewellery miraculously made from wood, bronze, seashells, driftwood, tin, iron. Another side street, rue St-Sabin, houses **Meli-Melor** at no. 1, quite new, but in a short time everything they sell has become sought-after: huge silk squares big enough for a beach cover-up, handbags, scarves, astounding hand-made jewellery of sea-glass and pebbles netted in gold wire, 'ear jewels', miniature clusters of grapes in fantasy colours, starfish in a gold mesh, for as little as 55–85F.

Last stop is **Ambia**, at no. 9 rue de la Roquette. It sells: leather sofas and chairs, computer desks, mirrors, pencils, bathroom accessories, shelving, glass and plastic barware, futons, and everything in the place has flair. Things to take home: pencil boxes with Chinese flower designs, multi-striped heavy plastic glasses, small tapestries, geometric puzzles in wood and brass.

There are so many good places to eat along rue de la Roquette that we can't list them all. Check our recommended restaurants, and keep your eyes peeled for the brasserie, bistro, or take-away that appeals. But we have to mention the **Bar des Bières**, just round the corner in the boulevard Beauharnais, famous for its incredible range of beers, including the overpowering Belgian *Kriek*, known as Sudden Death.

12e arrondissement

Square 26 rue Charles Baudelaire, 12e

Métro: Ledru-Rollin

Near the market in the place d'Aligre, this funny little shop goes on being sought out, year after year, by beady-eyed bargain hunters. It specializes in 'Retro' clothes from the 1950s and 1960s, and the last time we snooped, there were tight-waisted, full-skirted cotton dresses for about 150F, dinner jackets and tailcoats from 250F, striped Breton jerseys – the real thing, not copies – for 80F, and sometimes new or very slightly used cheapies. Browse as long as you like, the amiable owners don't mind. Open Tuesdays to Saturdays from 10:30 a.m. to 1:00 p.m., 3:00 to 7:00 p.m., and Sundays 10:00 a.m. to 1:00 p.m. Closed Mondays.

18e arrondissement

rue Séveste–rue de Steinkerque

Métro: Anvers, Barbes-Rochechouart

Between the boulevard Rochechouart and the Butte Montmartre there's a warren of streets given over to discount clothes, shoes, luggage, fabrics. Many of the goods are Third World imports, but if cheap and cheerful is what you want, the choice here is vast. The rue Séveste is a street market, with stalls outside, and some very inexpensive clothes indoors – perfect impulse shopping.

Tati: 4–28 boulevard Rochechouart, 18e   At the Barbes-Rochechouart Métro stop, this complex of big, untidy and very cheap shops deserves a small book of its own. One of a chain, this Tati is paradise for those who have the time and the knack of picking through racks, shelves, and bins of clothes despite being jostled and overheated. If you can manage this, you'll get smart clothes, often copies of rue St-Honoré fashions at incredibly low prices. Alaïa, the young designer, has even designed huge canvas bags and beach towels using the pattern on Tati's carrier bags – a giant hound's-tooth check: the monster-size travelling bag is only 49F.

Tati is divided into several shops: **Tati Hommes** for men, **Tati Femmes** for women, and, especially good value, the children's shop. Most men won't go in. Most women, including some of the *richissimes* of Paris society, love to find silk-look dressing-gowns for 59F. Other Tatis are in the rue de Rennes and in Belleville, and that one's open on Sundays.

Jordy: 36 boulevard Rochechouart, 18e   Up-market (compared to the rest of the neighbourhood), but still inexpensive: men's shirts and suits, sometimes very convincing fake-leather jackets. What you find here depends on the season – some are good buys and others very questionable quality, so use your common sense. Open Mondays through Saturdays, 9:30 a.m. to 5:00 p.m.

Club Rochechouart: 50 boulevard Rochechouart, 18e   A fashion editor told us about the Club a number of years ago – an unexpected shop in this very raffish street of cheaper-than-cheap shops. It has some very smart clothes for women, few of a kind, and you may have to go back several times to find what you want. A striking navy and white print dress, probably a quick copy of one shown in the summer Paris collections, was 280F – 'très Ascot', said the friendly manager. Summer suits in flowery crush-proof 'linen' for 299F, in plain colours, 199F. Open Mondays, noon to 7:00 p.m.; Tuesdays through Saturdays, 10:00 a.m. to 5:00 p.m. Open the year around, even in August. VISA cards accepted.

Sympa: corner of rue de Steinkerque and boulevard Rochechouart, and on rue d'Orsel   Sympa seems to go on for ever – let's hope it doesn't suddenly vanish. Every spare inch is packed with rails and bins, to rummage through for clothes at ridiculous prices. Cardin T-shirts, Lycra-type swimsuits, cotton leggings, cycling shorts, underclothes, children's wear. This is only for those who can take their time, and not be tempted just because it's cheap. Around the corner, another Sympa shop has briefcases, bolsters, pillows, shoes of all kinds, tacky kitchen knick-knacks. Plastic sandals 8–15F, shoes about 50–75F, every kind of carrier bag, suitcases from airline carry-ons to small trunks, from 10F to about 100F. Open Mondays through Saturdays, 10:00 a.m. to 7:30 p.m. Open August.

Dalya: rue de Steinkerque   Worth having a rummage around for inexpensive casual clothes which will last at least one summer. T-shirts for 35–40F. Open Mondays through Saturdays, 9:30 a.m. to 7:00 p.m. Open August.

Paname: rue de Steinkerque   A small shop, but have a look, sometimes you find startling buys such as facsimiles of some of Paris's greatest names in design – ankle-length cotton jersey skirt in candy pink, 85F, a wide-striped beach shirt, 52F, unisex jerseys.

Bonnes Éstoffes: rue de Steinkerque   Less crowded than Sympa or Tati, and with a more sober range of clothes (for men, women and children) but still at bargain prices. Raincoats, suits, jackets, swimsuits. A fully lined Madras cotton jacket for a man was 240F one summer; the following year Madras was out, and a very good 'dupli' (in plain English, a copy) of a 'B——y', was in, 290F.

Tissus Laik: 1 bis rue de Steinkerque   Fine fabric buys begin here at the shop with the sign 'TAM'. From here, if you have the time and interest, work your way around the neighbourhood – rue d'Orsel, rue Briquet, rue Séveste, to find some of the most attractive, most French materials imaginable. Stock changes rapidly, but last time we saw linens at 99F a metre, all colours of stretch fabrics, crushed velours, shiny satins, beautiful lace, and even net with flock motifs. Look out for upholstery and curtain fabrics capable of being transformed into spectacular clothes. Open Tuesdays through Saturdays, 9:30 a.m. to about 6.45 p.m. Usually closed August.

Bis! Bis! *Second-hand*

It's *encore, encore* for clothes, handbags, jewellery, scarves, shoes which rich people wear four or five times, then pass on to be resold.

Paris abounds in shops featuring 'gently used', very good-quality stuff; this is how all the pretty girls of Paris who carry Vuitton bags and wear Charles Jourdan shoes manage to buy them on their salaries. It's one of the great features of city life.

If you're lucky, you can find a timeless black wool Chanel suit from the ready-to-wear collection of last year, for about 2000–3000F, roughly one-third its original price. The one we saw was buttoned in gilt, lined with silk, from hem to braided edge. Or a fine polished leather or reptile handbag, under 500F, instantly recognizable as originally bought in a famous shop in the Palais Royal arcade.

More rarely, you can find superb men's clothes and beautiful, once-expensive children's clothes.

Some of these shops have been going for years, and have well-established connections not only with the elegant women of the *quartier*, but with the couturiers themselves. Often there are superbly finished, luxurious silk and brocade evening dresses, worn only in the seasonal collections, or shoes that have only walked on carpeted catwalks. They are almost always model sizes (for which read tall and thin), and the shoes are apt to be narrow. If your taste runs to the extreme of fashion, these shops can be a joy. But it takes time and the patience to return several times if you don't find your little Yves St Laurent treasure at first visit. Most of the shops are closed on Mondays, and almost always in August. Usually they have a clearly posted sign (in French) about their policy on returns or exchanges, and some of them have salespeople who speak excellent English and are almost always very helpful.

Most clothes are legibly labelled with the selling price (sometimes with original price). In the few that we found where garments were shown without price tags, we had the feeling that the owner of the shop matched the price to the customer. In these cases, feel free to raise your eyebrows, say something like 'Un peu trop cher' (a bit too expensive), and put the garment back on the rack. This tip was passed on by a friend who buys every year in one well-known shop, and never pays the asking price. Keep a steady nerve. Be prepared to leave the shop without buying anything. Check seams, hem, buttons, linings in men's suits and coats, insides of shoes and hand-bags. Look for small spots, dust, or face powder in a luxury bag. Point out any defects which might bring the price down. In every resale shop we checked, however, the merchandise was in fine condition – having been cleaned, brushed or polished before being put on view.

These vendors of de luxe merchandise sometimes have a few rails of women's and men's clothes that come from the better French ready-to-wear manufacturers at the end of a season – special purchases in small quantities. They're often worth going through carefully, as what you take home – colours, fabrics, fine finish, the general air of Parisian smartness – will delight you when your Paris visit is only a memory.

Some resale shops spring up hopefully in fashionable parts of Paris, buying fairly ephemeral clothes from the young and capricious. By their nature, these rather tentative shops may not be very long-lived. Their survival hangs on their supply of customers to bring in clothes, as well as those who come in to buy them.

It is hoped that all the addresses below will still be in business for a while: they are the best-established and most trusted by the more fashion-minded of our Paris friends. But don't lose your cool if you find they have moved or gone out of business. Most of the neighbourhoods where they are located are worth a visit if only for local colour; and if one shop is gone, another one 100 yards away may catch your eye.

2e arrondissement

Rétro Activité
38 rue du Vert-Bois, 2e
Métro: Temple

In the wholesale-clothing district, a 'second-hand Rose' blossoms in a tiny crowded shop. Go! Great 1930s–1940s–1980s clothes, clean, smart and good quality – men's Burberrys sometimes, silk nightgowns at about 100F, now the thing to wear to smart parties. Anna Rago, an English girl, is often there, and is most helpful. Open Tuesdays through Saturdays, noon to 7:00 p.m.

4e arrondissement

Vertiges
85 rue St-Martin, 4e
Métro: Rambuteau

At the edge of the renovated Halles, Vertiges has racks and stands and piles of authentic 1940s–1960s' American and French clothes for men and women. In August 1991, padded silk Chinese kimonos, unisex, were 300F, and ruched and shirred American 1960s' bathing suits, under a basket of fur hats. Old clothes can sometimes be hired. Open Mondays through Saturdays, 10:00 a.m. to 8:00 p.m.; Sundays, noon to 8:00 p.m.

6e arrondissement

Linda Noël
2 rue de Sabot, 6e
Tel: 45 44 51 16
Métro: St-Germain-des-Prés

There's always a warm welcome from Noël, the *patronne*, who not only sells very slightly used high-fashion women's suits, dresses, blouses, evening gowns, but designs and has made to her rigorous specifications some superb clothes. She was discovered for us by a French fashion writer who praised the fine fabrics, buttons, lining and finish of some classic light wool suits for less than 1000F – about £98 – and dateless. Names spotted here one day were Kenzo, Georges Rech, Alaïa. Open Tuesdays through Saturdays, 11:30 a.m. to 7:00 p.m.

Chlorophyll
2a rue de Sabot, 6e
Tel: 45 44 02 44
Métro: St-Germain-des-Prés

Side by side with Linda Noël, another delicious shop which specializes in the highest of Paris fashion clothes, some worn only a few times during the 'collections' showings. Yves St Laurent Rive Gauche, Sonia Rykiel, Chanel Boutique suits, Georges Rech coats, Giorgio dresses, Courrèges silk blouses, all 50 per cent off new prices. Open Tuesdays through Saturdays, 1:00 to 7:00 p.m. Closed August.

8e arrondissement

Anna Lowe
35 avenue Matignon, 8e
Métro: St-Philippe-du-Roule

Investment clothes, according to our Paris shop spy, sell for a fraction of the price they might command around the corner in the rue du Faubourg St-Honoré. Anna Lowe was a model and has connections with the couture houses, from which she gets end-of-season clothes. From the best ready-to-wear lines, she buys fashions only two months after they first appear. At various times, you'll find Yves St Laurent Rive Gauche, Alaïa, Comme des Garçons, Karl Lagerfield, Kenzo, Guy Laroche, Hermès. Ms Lowe also has handsome clothes made especially for her shop, and to *her* taste which is perfect. Simple alterations are free! Open Mondays through Saturdays, 10:30 a.m. to 7:00 p.m. Closed the first two weeks in August.

Le Troc des Trucs
50 rue Colisée, 8e
Métro: St-Philippe-du-Roule

This is a 'dépot-vente' where well-heeled women leave their last season's clothes to be resold. You'll find superb-quality women's fashions for as little as one-quarter of their original price. Open Mondays through Saturdays, 3:00 to 7:30 p.m.

11e arrondissement

Les Compagnons d'Emmaüs
54 rue de Charonne, 11e
Tel: 48 07 02 28
Métro: Ledru-Rollin

A resale shop run for the benefit of the Community of Abbé Pierre. Here be treasures. One day in July 1991, a crocodile handbag for 79F, a flowered silk Courrèges blouse for 32F, a man's ski-suit for 95F, a fine make of shoes for men, polished, for 90F; a silk foulard square for 15F. Lace, linens, porcelain, watches, jewellery, all donated, in perfect condition, and ridiculously priced. There's fine luggage, too, but the Vuitton shoe-carrier for 125F went out with our *meute des magasins* (shop-hound, that is). Open Mondays, 2:30 to 6:00 p.m.; Tuesdays through Saturdays, 10:00 a.m. to 12:30 p.m., 2:30 to 6:00 p.m. Possibly closed in August: phone and ask Chantal, who lived in England for several years.

15e arrondissement

Troc-Eve
25 rue Violet, 15e
Tel: 45 79 38 36
Métro: La Motte-Picquet, Dupleix

Very small, very friendly, and packed with fashionable women's clothes. Some are new, ends of ranges, all chosen with a fine hand; others are carefully maintained high-quality *encore* clothes. Also little antiques such as a toy-size, working carriage clock, silver-plated, 395F; porcelain, crystal, jewellery, picture-frames. Run by delightful women, it's open Tuesdays through Saturdays, 10:00 a.m. to 7:00 p.m. Closed August.

Trocanelle
35 rue de la Croix-Nivert, 15e
Tel: 43 06 34 15
Métro: Cambronne

Slightly worn, high-style clothes for women – not bargain prices but good buys. Also some new dresses, blouses, suits. Many superb-quality accessories, shoes, handbags, scarves. Open Tuesdays through Saturdays, 11:00 a.m. to 7:00 p.m. Closed August.

16e arrondissement

Catherine Baril
14–16 and 25 rue de la Tour, 16e
Métro: Passy

These two long-established resale shops are well stocked with designer clothes, some quite clearly recognizable even with the labels cut out, others still labelled. Whatever we mention now will have gone by the time you read this, but there will be more – the Chanel Boutique clothes, Azzedine Alaïa, even Hartnell and Vivienne Westwood! Have a look at the bargain rails: last year's model clothes, 320F up. Open Mondays, 2:00 to 7:00 p.m.; Tuesdays through Saturdays, 10:00 a.m. to 7:00 p.m. Usually closed the first three weeks in August. Major credit cards accepted.

Réciproque
95, 101 and 123 rue de la Pompe, 16e
Métro: Pompe

Huge and with a tremendously wide selection, worth spending a morning wandering around these three shops. At no. 95, there are well-arranged racks of good couture clothes worn a few times, by private clients, or at fashion shows. There are always many well-made ready-to-wear things. At no. 101, excellent men's clothes and gifts. At no. 123, jewellery, scarves and miscellaneous clothes, even including fine gloves and hats. Open Tuesdays through Saturdays, 10:00 a.m. to 6:45 p.m. Usually closed for the last week in August.

17e arrondissement

Trocade
5 and 9 avenue de Villiers, 17e
Tel: 42 67 80 19
Métro: Villiers

A fashionable neighbourhood, a beautiful, tree-shaded street, rich surroundings, and the clothes for men at no. 5 reflect this ambiance. Prices are not low, but for *la haute couture masculine*, this is *the* place. For women, no. 9 has Chanel, St Laurent, Thierry Mugler, and beautiful furs in winter. Men's shop open Tuesdays through Saturdays, 10:00 a.m. to 7:00 p.m. Women's shop: Mondays, 2:30 to 7:00 p.m.; Tuesdays through Saturdays, 10:00 a.m. to 7:00 p.m. Probably closed August.

18e arrondissement

Derrière les Fagots
8 rue des Abbesses, 18e
Métro: Abbesses

Really priceless clothes from 1890 to late 1960s – plus jewellery, mesh coin-purses, crocodile handbags, hatpins, stick pins from the 1900s, and fine shoes, for women. For men, look at English tweed overcoats, grey Ascot-type toppers, walking sticks. Some of the best things are not on view, but Eliane will bring them out if you are a serious visitor. The windows are like jewel-cases, full of 1930s' and 1940s' costume jewellery worth a fortune, but gently priced here. Open Tuesdays through Saturdays, noon to 7:30 p.m. English is spoken.

Gift shopping

The shops of Paris are crammed with perfect gifts – at a price. Wander along the rue du Faubourg St-Honoré, or the rue de Rivoli, or rue Royale, or among the boutiques of the Left Bank, and you will begin to feel like a poor relation outside a rich man's door. But once you get your eye in, you can with some perseverance find an enticing selection of small portable presents at a fraction of the big-name shop prices.

The newest gift-shopping street in Paris is a very old one – rue de la Roquette, 11e, beginning at the Bastille. For full details, see pages 219–21.

Note: many shops close during August for the annual holiday; and hours can change, from time to time. If a shop has closed, or even disappeared entirely, it's not a disaster, you'll wander the neighbourhood and find places of your own.

Monoprix, Prisunic, Uniprix

These have turned up frequently in these pages as perfect hunting grounds for food, clothes, household gadgets. Consider them for gifts, too. Make for the larger shops, near the Opéra, in the Marais, near Galéries Lafayette, in the more fashionable areas of the Right Bank, which quickly seize upon the year's fashionable ideas and copy them down to a price. At 21 avenue de l'Opéra, 1er, *Métro*: Opéra, Monoprix usually has silk-look scarves in subtle colours for as little as 30–40F. In the late summer of 1991, their autumn fashions were arriving – a Chanel-type jacket with good lining, heavy gilt buttons, was 350F; a man's sweater in Scottish wool and mohair was 420F; shoes and slippers for both sexes were well designed, well made, and inexpensive. Their own cosmetic range, 'Miss Helen', is much used by models – inexpensive and 'innocuous' to the skin, they say.

Look in Prisunic for traditional French earthenware plates and cups, handsome oven glassware, well-designed and colourful plastic for the *micro-ondes* oven, a range of handsome Italian glass refrigerator jugs and boxes, *really* inexpensive.

Les Grand Surfaces *Supermarkets*

Supermarkets such as CODEC, ED (Épicier Discount), and GS-20, are a great and relatively untapped source of small, inexpensive and desirable household gadgets. A half-hour in a big, well-organized CODEC turned up a set of four clips with mini-weights to stop a table-cloth blowing around in the open, 21F; 'Pousse-Mousse' cream soap made with almond oil, in a decorative pink pump-action bottle, 15F; rough-cut Marseille soap, the newest craze for body-scrubbing, 14F for four; and a small, efficient, folding corkscrew, 7F. At ED, look for their Chocolat Supérieur Dessert, 200gm for 6F, and their inexpensive, very good *chèvres*, heavily wrapped so they won't contaminate your luggage, about 9F50.

Most supermarkets are closed on Mondays but many open on Sundays until the afternoon. Often they're closed at lunch, and open until about 7:00 p.m.

1er arrondissement

FNAC
1 rue Pierre Lescot, Forum des Halles, 1er *Métro*: Les Halles
136 rue de Rennes, 6e *Métro*: Montparnasse
26 avenue Wagram, 8e *Métro*: Étoile

These are big, crowded, incredibly well-stocked shops with books, magazines, records, cassettes, small gifts and gadgets. Great for last-minute buys. Open from 10:00 a.m. to 7:30 p.m., closed Sundays and Mondays.

Madame Bijoux
13 rue Jean-Jacques Rousseau, 1er
Tel: 42 36 98 68
Métro: Palais Royal, Louvre

A very small shop which specializes in 'retro' clothes and theatrical fantasies from the 1930s and 1940s. Masks, beads, 1920s shoes, costume jewellery, boas, buttons. Some junk, some gems. Open, usually, 11:00 a.m. to 7:00 p.m., Mondays to Saturdays, but phone first to make sure.

2e arrondissement

Centre Franco-Americain SA
49 rue d'Aboukir, 2e
Métro: Sentier

As it now seems the duty-free shops at Paris airports are among the most expensive in Europe, after Frankfurt and Heathrow, you might do well to check out this small place where perfumes, etc. are tax-free, and 25 per cent off the marked prices. They offer Dior, Chanel, Cartier, Givenchy Yves St Laurent, Hermès scents, non-allergenic skin and body treatment products and make-up. The *directrice*, Madame Nimhauser, is a great Anglophile. Open Mondays through Saturdays, 10:00 a.m. to 5:30 p.m., but closed on Saturdays in August. Prices are keener and the atmosphere more agreeable than in the very crowded shops of the rue de Rivoli, and it's strong on personal service. You can sniff around until you find exactly the scent that suits you, or to buy as a gift. VISA, Access, American Express cards accepted, and traveller's cheques.

Louis Chantilly
8 rue de l'Echelle, 2e
Tel: 42 96 67 89
Métro: Opéra

This tranquil little shop, painted in pale colours, is lined with international luxuries: jewellery from Van Cleef, handbags from Hermès, suits from Chanel, mink jackets from the *haute couture* houses, Dior, Rochas, Patou perfumes. That said, the entire ambiance is Japanese – calligraphy, staff and customers. Yet despite the rich surroundings and the exquisite courtesy, the prices are discreetly discounted and much is affordable, from little pieces of porcelain to perfume at about 20% less than airport prices.

Gil C. . .
36 avenue de l'Opéra, 2e
Tel: 47 42 40 65
Métro: Opéra

The small Gil C. . . is the nearest most people will get to being at the bottom of a rugby scrum. They discount perfume and skin-care products from 30–40 per cent, and at these prices, the shop is really crowded. The service is fast, expert, accurate, with no time for browsers, but if you know what you're looking for, hang in there. Our advice is to go early in the morning, and when the tourist season is over and the staff has time to advise the undecided. Open Mondays through Saturdays, 9:30 a.m. to 6:30 p.m. They take VISA, Access, American Express, Diners' Club, and traveller's cheques.

3e and 4e arrondissements

---

rue des Francs-Bourgeois (odd nos. are 4e, even 3e)
Métro: Rambuteau, St-Paul

Jean-Pierre de Castro
17 rue des Francs-Bourgeois

Silver, silver, silver. Napkin rings at 40F, bracelets made from forks and spoons 50F, repro Art Deco frames from 60F, tea strainers 120F, and old silver (spoons, knives, forks) sold by the kilo, about 15 pieces, for 450F! Open Mondays, 2:00 to 7:00 p.m.; Tuesdays through Saturdays, 10:30 a.m. to 7:00 p.m.; Sundays 11:00 a.m. to 7:30 p.m.

La Licorne
38 rue de Sévigné, near rue des Francs-Bourgeois

The shops in the Marais change almost overnight, and if this is still here it's a delightful place to find not very expensive costume jewellery. VISA, Eurocheques. Open Mondays through Saturdays, 9:30 a.m. to 6:30 p.m.

La Maison Rouge
45 rue de Sévigné

It's worth looking here for 1900s–1930s curios and trinkets, and sometimes you'll find some choice bits of jewellery. Open 10:00 a.m. to 7:00 p.m. Closed Tuesdays. Open Saturdays and Sundays from 2:30 to 7:00 p.m. Usually closed the last week in August but this can vary.

À L'Olivier
25 rue de Rivoli, 4e
Métro: St-Paul, Hôtel-de-Ville

The traditional place to find cold-pressed extra-virgin olive oil as well as walnut and avocado oils and a range of most unusual olives and olive-based soap. Open Mondays through Fridays, 11:00 a.m. to 7:00 p.m. In August, 11:00 a.m. to 1:00 p.m., 3:00 to 7:00 p.m. Major credit cards accepted.

Izrael, Epicerie du Monde
30 rue François-Miron, 4e
Métro: St-Paul, Hôtel-de-Ville

Spices, herbs, delicious goodies from all over the world in a very
crowded neighbourhood shop. Try a few ounces of their olives with
lime, coriander and sesame seeds. Open Tuesdays through Fridays,
9:30 a.m. to 1:00 p.m., and 2:30 to 7:00 p.m.; Saturdays, 9:00 a.m.
to 7:00 p.m. Closed Sundays and August.

Au Grenier du Marais
7 rue François-Miron, 4e
Métro: St-Paul, Hôtel-de-Ville

Gold earrings for about 200–300F which you wouldn't find anywhere else in Paris for under 500F, 1940s' and 1950s' spectacle
frames that can't be equalled. Choose a pair, and persuade your
optician to put in a pair of lenses that suit you. The owner is
cheerful, friendly, happy to bargain, and accepts VISA, American
Express and Eurocheques. Open Mondays through Saturdays, 9:30
a.m. to 7:00 p.m. Closed Sundays and August.

L'Oeuf de Colomb
23 rue des Blancs Manteaux, 4e
Tel: 42 72 21 22
Métro: St-Paul, Hôtel-de-Ville

Exquisite and off-beat: small, easily carried delights in marble,
crystal, and wood. Some quite inexpensive, others 'toys for a friend',
as our shop-hound said. Open Mondays through Saturdays, 10:20
a.m. to 1:00 p.m., 2:00 to 7:30 p.m. Carte Bleue, American Express
and Access accepted.

5e arrondissement

La Tuile à Loup
35 rue Daubenton, 5e
Métro: Censier-Daubenton

A shop scented with herbs, filled with beautifully designed, rather rustic gifts: wicker, wood, earthenware casseroles, baskets and cookbooks (in French). Old-fashioned wicker heart-shaped *coeur à la crème* baskets, classic glazed earthenware wine pitchers, breadboards. Open Tuesdays through Saturdays, 10:30 a.m. to 1:00 p.m., 3:00 to 7:30 p.m.; Sundays, 10:30 a.m. to 1:00 p.m. Open August.

6e arrondissement

Au Chat Dormant
13 rue du Cherche-Midi, 6e
Métro: St-Sulpice, Sèvres-Babylone

A minuscule paradise for cat lovers, with gifts ranging from postcards to antique silver boxes, everything saluting cats. Figures of cats in marble, metal, porcelain, plastic. Umbrellas whose handles are heads of cats. Paintings, prints, posters. Open Mondays, 2:30 to 7:00 p.m.; Tuesdays through Saturdays, 11:00 a.m. to 7:00 p.m.

9e arrondissement

Violine
12 boulevard Haussmann, 9e
Métro: Richélieu-Drouot

A beautiful shop that offers good discounts on perfumes, cosmetics, skin-care products, and also does beauty treatments including a make-up service, manicures, waxing. The staff are detached, professional, uneffusive – a far cry from the hyper sales people of the better-known *hors de taxe* shops around the rue de Rivoli. English is spoken, and the shop is open Mondays through Fridays, 9:30 a.m. to 7:00 p.m.; Saturdays, 10:30 a.m. to 6:30 p.m. Beauty treatments are by appointment. All credit cards accepted.

11e arrondissement

Miroiterie Brugnon
134 rue Amélot, 11e
corner of rue J.-P. Timbaud
Tel: 43 57 70 35
Métro: Filles du Calvaire

In a glazier's shop that does mirrors, double-glazing, picture-framing, and security installations, there is a surprising collection of beautiful, small, portable and well-priced things. Baccarat-style paper-weights, 35F, *faux* bamboo photograph frames, 35F, others in fine leather, chromium, fabric. Also crystal bowls and vases and pin trays, 50F up to real money for the bigger items. Open Mondays through Fridays, 8:00 a.m. to 12:30 p.m., 1:30 to 7:00 p.m. Phone to ask about weekend hours.

14e arrondissement

La Salle des Ventes
123 rue d'Alésia, 14e
Métro: Alésia

In this lively, very untouristed area, a real discovery: one big sales-room which specializes in huge pieces of furniture, and another with old jewellery, china, glass, silver. A wonderful place to browse – and you might find some delightful, very French *objet* to take home: a crystal-and-gilt *compotière* for 150F, and 1920s' Jazz Age mesh coin-purse, a Victorian beaded cushion, a rope of spiky coral beads for 200F. A girl who regularly drops in here made a great find in the spring of 1991 – a tortoiseshell-and-gilt piqué box that is perfect for stamps or earrings, for 195F. Open Mondays through Saturdays, 10:00 a.m. to 7:30 p.m. Closed holidays and August.

Brocante Montparnasse
62 boulevard Edgar Quinet, 14e
Tel: 43 20 79 91
Métro: Edgar-Quinet

An interesting shop in the rather touristy Montparnasse district, but so far unspoiled by antique- and junk-hunters. This *brocante* sells small pieces of fine real jewellery, but the best finds are authentic costume jewellery from the 1930s to 1950s, now beginning to fetch hundreds of pounds in the salesrooms of New York and London. Recently, there were also some 1900-ish porcelain bowls, silver picture frames, fans. And often, you will find bigger items such as an impressive walnut and marble mantel-clock topped with a bronze lion and a 'Vendu' sticker across the clock-face. Open afternoons only: Mondays through Fridays, 1:00 to 7:00 p.m.; Saturdays, 2:00 to 7:00 p.m. We are told that if you speak French, or have a friend who is fluent, you might phone and arrange with the dealer (if he is there and not too busy) to go some morning. You can try bargaining, but prices won't come down more than about 10 per cent if that. Probably closed in August, but date not set as we write.

Flea markets

Les Marchés aux Puces – one of those romantic conceptions of Paris, whose faded glamour lingers somewhat past its prime. As there are now 'flea markets' of sorts all over the world, your chance of finding a nice little precious object for almost nothing is not what it was even five years ago. You could probably do as well in a Sunday morning sale in Salford, as in the most famous flea market in Paris. However, if you like the fun of scrabbling through bins and tables on a summer day, before a good lunch, or enjoy watching Parisians striking bargains in rapid-fire slangy French – and you still hope to find something everyone else has missed – so be it. Here is the latest, most realistic information.

The flea market at St-Oeun

Métro: Porte de Clignancourt and a fair walk

Even on our most recent visit to look the market over again, nothing had changed. We can only repeat our words of 10 years ago: acres of sprawling market-stalls, crammed with people on the hunt for bargains or for 'the picturesque'. These days, this means German tourists photographing American tourists. It is the best-known market, and the most expensive. Much of the stuff you see is pure and simple junk, brought in to unload on the unwary. For the rest – the dealers know where the good buys are, and by the time you have reached here on a Saturday or Sunday morning, by public transport, they have come and gone. Most of the best-looking stalls are owned by merchants who also do business from flossier premises in the 1er, 8e and 16e *arrondissements*. The prices you see in the flea market will not be substantially lower than in the rue du Bac. However, it's an Experience. If you are willing to make the longish journey, go for it – rummage, and enjoy the bargaining. It could be fun, it will be tiring. Open Saturdays, Sundays and Mondays from dawn to about 1:00 p.m. *Please watch out for pickpockets!*

Despite the apparent haphazardness of the market, it is actually laid out in a comprehensible and sensible fashion. Outside, on the fringe, are the inevitable buses, station-wagons and hand-carts spilling over with second-hand jeans, Indian blouses, 'Afghan' rugs, damaged transistors, boxes of keys, much-used clothes. Inside this sprawl, you will find a number of individual markets, well signposted. Most interesting:

Marché Vernaison, 136 avenue Michelet. Everything from gilt buttons off Napoleonic tunics, to small walnut prayer-stools, toys, jewellery, lamps, glassware. Forget about any Art Nouveau *trouvailles*, the Paris, London and New York dealers got there 15 years ago. Go for the small pieces of the 1930s, 1940s, 1950s, even the 1970s. Fashion will catch up with you some day, and sooner than you think.

Marché Malik, rue Jules-Vallès. Mostly old clothes, umbrellas, walking-sticks, tatty fake-sheepskin coats, scratched records, bins of lace, 1920s-ish dresses, earthenware, glass, tin, perfume bottles – sometimes these are fun, smelling in a ghostly way of scents no longer made. The clothes will probably need washing, dry-cleaning, mending, new buttons.

Marché Biron, rue des Rosiers. Expensive, elegant furniture and *bibelots*, on stands run by professionals who know precisely the worth of everything they stock. You might beat them down 10 per cent, but as the original price is usually astronomical to begin with, you'll still end by spending real money, if you buy at all. However, everything is good value, and backed by reputable names in the business.

Marché Paul Bert, rue Paul Bert. Some really exquisite crystal, modern gilt, bronze, polished wood furniture, ornaments, mirrors. They could easily fetch double the asking price if put up at Christie's

– that is, if you can afford to pay what the sellers charge you in the first place!

Marché Jules-Vallès, rue Jules-Vallès. The most fun, and the most promising for finding something unusual and not too expensive, if you feel your stay in Paris isn't complete without something from the flea market. Look for small bisque-headed dolls, theatrical costumes, 1930s' shoes, decorative glassware, candlesticks, ashtrays, doll trunks. Bargain if you can. Most of the dealers speak a sort of English, and a little New York vernacular with some low German or Italian sometimes helps. Don't be disappointed if the final price is not really rock-bottom. No one forces you to buy.

The other flea markets

These are where the knowledgeable Parisians find their bargains. As they become better known, the quality of merchandise brought to them goes up, and prices are rising fast. A few years ago, these were true junk stalls, set up along the edge of an established street market. Some still qualify for this status. But the dealers are moving in to buy, and smart young professionals are setting up their stands, so go now, if you can.

Place d'Aligre, 11e
Métro: Ledru-Rollin

Six days a week, including Sunday – take the Métro, and follow signs to 'Marché Beauvau', one of the lesser-known and most delightful markets in Paris. In the square, about 20 tables, and many racks, are set up with odds and ends. Boxes of the most astounding old clothes – cracked leather shoes, a furry bowler hat, a pair of striped trousers, a stack of fourth-hand handbags. Keep looking. Old postcards, small pieces of silver or silver-plate, glassware, crystal, beautiful 1900s' embroidered linen shifts, lace-and-lawn night dresses, men's swallow-tail coats, cooking utensils of every age and condition, books, odd boxes of jewellery – mostly Woolworth stuff, but occasionally a fine and rare piece turns up. There's a table of buttons old and new that will send button-collectors wild. Everything is quite cheap, the atmosphere quiet, the dealers pleasant.

A few years ago, the market shrank abruptly, as the Mayor of

Paris apparently decided that it was bringing too much traffic to the surrounding streets. But now most of the long-established vendors have crept back. Don't miss our favourite 'Chineur' who sells astoundingly good blouses, shirts, sweaters, jogging trousers, for as little as 5–20F each (not there in August). The shops and stalls in the streets around the market are wonderful places to shop for fruit, flowers, North African olives and hot peppers, good breads, and the corkscrew you forgot to bring. Plenty of picnicking material, for a snack in the square bounded by rue Vollon and rue Trousseau. Open Tuesdays through Sundays, about 9:30 a.m. to about 1:00 p.m.

Porte de Vanves, 14e
avenue Marc Sangnier, 14e
Métro: Porte de Vanves

A very good small flea market is held here on Saturday and Sunday mornings – mostly junk, but if you have a quick eye you can still spot some real bargains. Look for oldish Dinky toys, copper jelly moulds, Art Deco compacts, empty 1930s scent bottles, old glass lamps, costume jewellery of the 1940s and 1950s, comics, postcards, pots, bottles. A few small (rather pricey) antiques. After lunch on Sunday it becomes a 'Marché aux Fripes' – real trash, lovely to pick through if you have a good eye, and can wash your hands after the rummage.

The grander end of this market in avenue Georges-Lefenestre, around the corner, is described below.

Marché aux Puces de la Porte Didot
Take the *Métro* to Porte de Vanves, walk through the tatty part, and in the avenue Georges-Lefenestre you find 'the real market of grandpapa'. This means delectable junk and little treasures, but not rock-bottom cheap. You have to be able to bargain in French if you want to get prices down. Good for pretty china, glass, silver, ornate little picture frames, small antique furniture. Not many (foreign) tourists yet, but a lot of beady-eyed young French couples and photographers hunting for props. On even the hottest summer weekend, it is agreeable to stroll under the trees and through the good-natured, ambling crowd. You can still find places to sit and have a picnic while your feet recover. Or find a café in the nearby

rue Raymond Losserand. Saturdays and Sundays, from 8:00 a.m. to
about 6:00 p.m., but best before lunchtime, as by mid-afternoon
most of the clients have peeled off for a rest, and the best stall-
holders have begun to pack it in. The Porte de Vanves/Porte Didot
market has been under threat of closure for the last six years. Local
shopkeepers complained that it takes away trade from them and
sometimes brings undesirable characters into the *quartier*. Police
show up regularly to chase away the unlicensed who spread their
odds and ends on newspapers on the pavement. But the market still
goes on. In fact, in spite of the extremely variable weather of late
summer 1991, and some spectacular lightning storms, the market
seemed to be getting larger every weekend, with many more good
things appearing.

Foire du Brocante St-Paul
quai de l'Hôtel de Ville, quai des Célestins, 4e
Métro: St Paul
Bus: Nos. 69, 96

At various times during the year, there's a mammoth 'Brocante'
Fair – second-hand goods from dining chairs missing their cane
seats, to comic books, to small bits of fine jewellery, lots of good junk
and plenty of portable small antiques – near the Seine in the Marais
area. On a sunny day it's crowded with strollers, tourists, just-
looking people – a lot of dealers from all over Paris hit this market
every month. The stalls are manned with a mix of professional flea
marketeers and amiable amateurs. The bargains aren't the greatest
in Paris, but it's fun to have a wander around and who knows, you
might find that missing Scalectrix train engine. Try making an offer
(in French if you can): prices are usually negotiable. Best buys are
found in the winter months when only real Paris-lovers are willing
to prowl in a grey, drizzly, bone-chilling morning. The Foire begins
about 8:00 a.m. and goes on until early afternoon. Check *Pariscope*
under the heading 'Fêtes Populaires' to see if it is happening when
you are there. It's such a crowd-magnet that the local buses have to
to be re-routed around the area! Again, look out for pickpockets,
don't carry a wallet in your back pocket, leave expensive cameras
and handbags under lock and key at your hotel.

Paris pratique
(Staying afloat)

The quality of your stay in Paris – reverie or nightmare – is going to depend on some very basic circumstances: the state of your digestion, your feet, your French. The amount of time you spend looking for a post office is stolen from the time you spend looking at paintings. The confusion you encounter when dealing with telephones, tipping and traffic detracts from your pleasure in everything else Parisian. The information that follows, alphabetically arranged, is simple and practical – it can make the difference between two weeks of fretting about mechanical details and 10 minutes of dealing intelligently with them.

Animals

Parisians are unsentimental about animals, but they like to have them around. Small dogs of peculiar breed on leads trail every other person – on the Métro, in restaurants, everywhere. The pavements are consequently treacherous. You can get entangled, or step in something, but you'll rarely be snapped or barked at.

Cats run wild in certain areas, notably the cemeteries, and are *not* to be petted. This goes for all animals in France, except those personally known to you. See Animal bites, pages 294–5.

Live animals for food are closely caged and brusquely treated. If this puts you off your feed, avert your eyes.

Babysitters

We recommend that you first ask your hotel if they can provide a *garde des enfants* service. If they can't, then try the American College in Paris, tel: 45 55 91 73. Their people charge about 30F an hour.

Or look for advertisements in the English-language newspapers (page 270), or contact the American and English Churches in Paris who often have a roster of English-speaking sitters.

Remember, if your baby-sitter travels to you, you must pay for his/her transport; late at night, this means a taxi-fare.

Other suggestions come from Paris friends. In most cases, you will find someone who speaks English at these places:

Alliance Française: Tel: 45 44 38 28 *poste* (extension) 277. The sitters are students and usually multi-lingual. 30F an hour, 35F after midnight. They'll also give French lessons to your littles for 50F an hour!

Kids' Service: Tel: 47 66 00 52. Trained nannies, young and expert: about 30F an hour plus 50F to the agency.

Petit Prince: Tel: 42 64 54 54. A subscription fee of 35F for each booking, and 25F an hour.

Institut Catholique: Tel: 45 48 31 70. A fee of 10F to the Institute, then 28F an hour with a 3-hour minimum. After midnight, 29F an hour.

Baby-Sitting Service: Tel: 46 37 51 24. Agency fee of 50F, then 30F per hour for the sitter.

Association Générale des Étudiants en Médecine: Tel: 45 86 52 02, from noon to 5:00 p.m. Our latest information is that you pay a subscription fee plus 25F per hour. You get a well-educated and responsible medical student sitter.

Baths, public

If your hotel doesn't provide a shower – or if it's too expensive – try the Bains-Douches Municipaux. Bring a towel, soap, shampoo, and slippers (the flip-flop variety). Cost 5F50. Open Thursdays, noon to 7:00 p.m.; Fridays and Saturdays, 7:00 a.m. to 7:00 p.m.; Sundays, 8:00 a.m. to noon.

8 rue des Deux Ponts, 4e

18 rue Renard, 4e

38 rue du Rocher, 8e

40 rue Oberkampf, 11e

188 rue de Charenton, 12e

34 rue Castagnary, 15e

18 rue de Meaux, 19e

place des Fêtes, 19e

27 rue de la Bidassoa, 20e

66 rue de Buzenval, 20e

148 avenue Gambetta, 20e

296 rue des Pyrénées, 20e

There are also 64 fountains donated to Paris by Richard Wallace (he tried to give Paris his furniture collection, too; it was turned down and wound up in London). The fountains are scattered throughout the city, contain clean water, and are good for a *toilette de chat* ('a lick and a promise').

Books (in English)

When French newspapers begin to give you indigestion, revert to English. Remember, though, that imported books are expensive – about double their home price. All stock *Paupers' Paris*, or can get it for you, if you've lost your copy or just need another one.

The Abbey Bookshop
29 rue de la Parcheminerie, 5e
Tel: 46 33 16 24
Métro: St-Michel

This Canadian bookshop says it is 'a quiet refuge for poet, scholar, pilgrim'. They have a children's reading hour on Saturdays from 11:00 a.m. to noon. And on Sundays they are open from lunchtime until late night. A very good place to look for new and second-hand books in English and other languages, after a leisurely Sunday lunch or dinner at one of the Rive Gauche restaurants. Open Mondays to Thursdays, 11:00 a.m. to 10 p.m.; Fridays and Saturdays, 11:00 a.m. to midnight; Sundays, noon to 10:00 p.m.

Brentano's
37 avenue de l'Opéra, 1er
Tel: 42 61 52 50
Métro: Pyramides

Very big, efficient, friendly; the staff speak about a dozen languages. Brentano's often have English language paperbacks *en promotion*, another way of saying 'marked down'.

Galignani
224 rue de Rivoli, 1er
Tel: 42 60 76 07
Métro: Tuileries

A well-stocked 'intellectual' bookshop long on art books, gorgeous postcards, superb guidebooks (mostly French); short on charm and helpfulness, we are told.

Nouveau Quartier Latin
78 boulevard St-Michel, 6e
Tel: 43 26 42 70
Métro: St-Michel

An eclectic international bookshop, with plenty of mixed fiction for the browser, and well-stocked academic bookshelves. Their true speciality, though, is in textbooks for foreign language teachers. Open 10:00 a.m. to 7:00 p.m. every day of the week.

Palacio de la Madeleine
11 rue Tronchet, 8e
Tel: 42 65 17 34
Métro: Madeleine

Beautiful *new* art books, great bargains – and knowledgeable people who speak good English. Open 9:00 a.m. to 7:00 p.m., Monday to Saturday.

Shakespeare and Company
37 rue de la Bûcherie, 5e
Métro: St-Michel

This little shop has earned its place as one of the sights of Paris. It sells old and new paperback and hardcover English books, has chairs outside for browsers, is next to a charming little park, and has a splendid view of Notre-Dame. And there are notices of flats to let, poetry readings, places to stay, summer jobs, share-the-cost rides to the U.K. and all points south and east.

Tea and Tattered Pages
24 rue Mayet, 6e
Tel: 40 65 94 35
Métro: Duroc, Falguière

We conquered our impulse to walk straight past any shop with such a twee name, and found a very useful place for books, browsing, looking over second-hand literature, and having tea and real American brownies. We hear their fudge is fine, too. They also do a mail-order service. Open Mondays through Saturdays, 11:00 a.m. to 7:00 p.m. Closed August.

W. H. Smith & Son
248 rue de Rivoli, 1er
Tel: 42 60 37 97
Métro: Concorde

W.H.S. is familiar, comfortable, and staffed by kind and helpful people who will nanny you in the nicest way. Every English-language book you might need, or just want to buy and read, is stocked.

Clothing sizes

Women:
Dresses/Suits

British	10	12	14	16	18	20
American	8	10	12	14	16	18
French	38	40	42	44	46	48

Stockings/Tights

	small		medium		large	
British/American	small		medium		large	
French	0	1	2	3	4	5

Shoes

British	4½	5½	6½	7½
American	6	7	8	9
French	37	38	40	41

Men

Suits/Overcoats

British/American	35	36	37	38	39	40
French	36	38	40	42	44	46

Shirts

British/American	15	16	17	18
French	38	40	42	44

Shoes

British	7	8	8½	9½	10½
American	7½	8½	9	10	11
French	41	42	43	44	45

Discounts – *for students*

Train travel: *Carte Carissimo*

The *Carte Carissimo* is for the under-26s. Valid for a year, it entitles you to a 20 per cent discount on two return tickets, or four single tickets during the 'White' (most expensive) hours of train travel, and 50 per cent in the 'Blue' (off-peak) periods. It costs 190F from main railways or travel agents.

International Student Identity Cards

For discounts on museum and film entrances, Eurail passes, and much more. You must have proof of full-time student status, a passport-sized photo, and 45F.

Using the card: Look for prices under 'Tarif spécial pour Étudiants'.

You get the card from:
Council for International Educational Exchange (CIEE)
49 rue Pierre-Charron, 8e

Tel: 43 59 23 69
Métro: Alma-Marceau

and from Council Travel, which is part of CIEE, at their 49 rue
Pierre Charron, 8e, and 51 rue Dauphin, 6e, branches. Other
branches may also issue the card by the time you read this: check
the Paris phone book for addresses.

Ligue Française des Auberges de Jeunesse (LFAJ)

38 boulevard Raspail, 7e
Tel: 45 48 69 84
Métro: Rue du Bac

For Youth Hostel card-holders. Hostels are cheap (75–90F per
night) but offer little privacy. Not for long stays. See 'Au lit', page
95, for more information.

Student restaurants *(les restos U.)*

About 23F per meal. You must, however, have a student ticket,
which you get by knowing someone enrolled in a Paris university.

Albert Châtelet
10 rue Jean-Calvin, 5e
Métro: Censier-Daubenton

Assas
92 rue d'Assas, 6e
Métro: Notre-Dame-des-Champs

Bullier
39 avenue Georges-Bernanos, 5e
Métro: Port-Royal

Censier
3 rue Censier, 5e
Métro: Censier-Daubenton

Cuvier
8 bis, rue Cuvier, 5e
Métro: Jussieu

Mabillon
3 rue Mabillon, 6e
Métro: Mabillon

Mazet
5 rue Mazet, 6e
Métro: Odéon

Discounts – *for those over 60*

Carte Vermeil

With great generosity, the French provide this discount card for
those of 'the third age' – a much nicer phrase than the unctuous
Anglo-American 'senior citizens' – available to anyone, of any
nationality, who is over 60 years of age (women) or 65 (men). It
entitles you to discounts galore on entertainment, travel, and many
museums. But it costs 165F, so if your stay in Paris is going to be a
short one, the *Carte Vermeil* may not pay for itself. Showing your
passport at cinemas, museums, theatres will often be enough to get
you the reduced rate.

However, if you're staying for a while, or returning often, do
consider investing in a *Carte*. Take proof of your age – your passport – to the *Abonnement* office in any major railway station, or to the
SNCF (French Railways) office in the lower ground floor of the
Office de Tourisme at 127 avenue des Champs-Élysées, 8e (*Métro*:
Georges-V). Pay them the 165F, and get in return the *Carte Vermeil*,
valid from 1 June to 31 May following.

The office at the Gare St-Lazare is an easy one to deal with, as the
station is served by several Métro and many bus lines, and the office
is not as crowded as the ones at the big Gare du Nord or at the
SNCF-Champs-Élysées. Don't expect anyone to speak English, but
you won't need much French to communicate your wishes, as they
are used to dealing with foreigners who have cottoned on to this
very useful offer.

As you look through *Pariscope* for theatres, music, cinemas, etc., note the price reductions available for holders of the *CV*; it can be 40 per cent or more. Most museums and special exhibitions (such as those at the Grand Palais and Petit Palais) give half-price admission to holders of the *CV*.

Even without this card, production of a foreign passport will usually (but not always) get you into museums, movies, theatres or concerts at a reduced price.

Holders of the British Senior Citizen Railcard should note that they will need the £7.50 Rail-Europ supplement card for discounts on rail/boat/hovercraft: check British Rail, in England, or at 55 rue St-Roch, 1er (*Métro*: Pyramides), for details of specific offers. Dates and hours may be restricted; read the small print to make sure you can get back from your holiday when you want to.

Dry cleaning

It's called *nettoyage à sec* or *le pressing*. Sample prices:

Trousers – 35F
Jacket – 40–60F
Dress – 45–90F (for silk, cocktail, or evening dresses, which no right-minded Pauper takes travelling)

Le pressing (your clothes are brushed and pressed) is also available everywhere for a touch-up – 15F up to 25F in 'good' neighbourhoods.

Electricity

Although the current in most modernized hotels is 220 volts, as in the UK (in a few older hotels it may still be 110 volts, so inquire before using any appliance), you must fit a *European* two-round-pin plug to the flex of electrical gadgets. Many hardware shops and ironmongers sell these (or get one in Paris). If you have an appliance with a three-cord flex, make sure the earth wire (green and yellow) is securely bound and covered with electricians' tape, so that it cannot touch the other wires nor the wall socket. Or buy one of the pricey but safe adaptors sold in ironmongers. Also do be considerate: you might check with the *concierge* about using a hair-dryer, which draws a lot of current.

Embassies

See 'Au secours', pages 295–7.

Emergencies

See 'Au secours', pages 283–297.

Entrances and exits

French doors open inward. This takes a while to get used to.

Entré = Entrance
Sortie = Exit
Tirez = Pull
Poussez = Push
Passage Interdit = No Admittance

For the less mobile

To be perfectly plain about it, Paris isn't the ideal city for anyone in a wheelchair or with serious walking difficulties. The Métro and the buses are only for those with a certain degree of mobility on their own two feet. Most museums, even the Louvre, are not user-friendly, although the new system of escalators and ramps in the Louvre itself does help to a certain extent. Remember, however, that you must be able to weather the unsheltered wait in the Pyramid courtyard to get in (see pages 181–3).

The Musée d'Orsay (page 189) makes up for it: easy to get into, easy to get around, wide aisles, very short flights of steps, escalators, easy-access loos. And of course it is crammed and jammed with wonderful things to see. The Jeu de Paume (page 183), newly renovated and reopened, has only a few steps at the entrance to be negotiated, but it has several flights of internal stairs; there is said to be a lift for those in real need – ask at the cashier's desk.

The Marmottan, in Passy (page 192), is manageable if you yourself can manage a short flight of steps up to the entrance, and now has a narrow lift which takes you down to the room full of breathtaking Monets. Beaubourg (page 187) is reasonably accessible: it has a short escalator up to the Main level, where you can transfer to a lift and go on to other floors (including the one with the Musée Moderne). There are platforms on each level, with all Paris spread out before you; and the Sculpture Terrace outside the museum is very visitor-friendly.

A French friend who walks with two sticks loves the Institut du Monde Arabe on the quai St-Bernard (page 188) for its easy access, elegant and soothing interiors, exciting architecture – and its mint tea and pastries!

For the less-mobile, the best time for Paris is late autumn or winter, or spring up to about the middle of June. Then you avoid the crowds and can manoeuvre, gaze, and enjoy at your own pace.

According to an article by Alison Walsh, in the *Telegraph* of 27 April 1991, driving in Paris with an automatic car is 'a doddle'. For holders of disabled badges, parking meter fees are waived, and charges in car parks are cut by 75 per cent. She also praises the facilities of the great science park at La Villette in the 19e *arrondissement* – everything accessible and pure enjoyment for children and adults alike.

Paris itself, its streets, beautiful parks like the Luxembourg and the Tuileries, tiny squares where you can watch the locals playing boules, sidewalk cafés, and its floodlit splendour at night, is infinitely accessible and always rewarding.

The official *Guide des Hôtels* indicates with a wheelchair symbol which hotels promise facilities for the less mobile, but in practice this is sometimes dicey. Many hotels with lifts are not as easy as they sound because there may be several steps to negotiate from street level to reception room, or additional steps inside before the lifts are reached. Check the hotel descriptions in this book: we have tried to indicate those which are really easy of access.

In France, there's a publication called *Voyager Quand Même* (Travel Anyway). It's published in French and English by Le Comité National Français de Liaison pour la Réadaptation des Handicapés (CNFLRH), 38 boulevard Raspail, 75007 Paris.

Association des Paralysés de France (APF), 17 boulevard Auguste-Blanqui, 75013 Paris, will furnish information about services and help available, and has representatives in various areas to help, as well as a magazine called *Faire Face* (in French) which often contains useful information. As far as we know now, some English is spoken, but it is primarily for the French; ask at the main Tourist Office in the avenue des Champs-Élysées, which always has the latest information.

Guidebooks

New guides to Paris come out every year, and you'd be wise to go to Brentano's, W. H. Smith, or the Abbey Bookshop and check out the current crop. These are the ones we like best, but remember that this is only an arbitrary opinion:

Blue Guide to Paris: In English, detailed information on museums and areas of historical interest.

Michelin Green Guide: In English, good overview, and excellent maps.

Gault-Millau: *Le Nouveau Guide*: In French, published monthly – 35F. About £4 in the UK, $8 in the US. An invaluable source of inside information on restaurants, wines, hotels, travel, holidays. Many of their restaurant recommendations are well above our price limits, but they often write about low- to medium-priced places too. Sometimes they make a find before we do, sometimes we get there first. They are utterly frank about the places they review, and they write wittily and often colloquially. One issue a few years ago had a feature on 'Restaurants to Flee From'. Restaurants weep with delight when Gault-Millau smiles on them, and start pulling down the shutters when the G-M score is 2/10 (meaning 'stay away').

Le Nouveau Guide is a country-wide or even world-wide magazine, and may not be of much use to the casual visitor to Paris. So have a look at the cover of the current magazine on the newsstands; if there is a Paris feature, buy it. Even if the restaurants are too high-priced for you today, who knows – in a future life you may come back as a rich Parisian.

Paris Pas Cher: In French. Superb for household bargains, cars, fridges, and consumer information, not as strong on more mundane things like hotels, restaurants, 'fripes' and 'bis! bis!'. For resident Parisians rather than tourists, but a good read.

Coping in French

You'll want to get to grips with the French language, and now the choice of books, cassettes, even videos, is vast. Decide if you want the simple ability to ask questions and understand the answers, or if you want to deliver a philosophy paper to the Académie Française, and pick the course that suits you. Here are a few that we've found useful:

Linguaphone Travel Pack. You get two 90-minute cassettes, one specifically for travel and full of hints and information, the other a general language cassette of fairly basic French, with phrases for most of the situations you'll encounter. In addition, there's a mini-dictionary, and a pack of 52 Panic Cards which give you instant phrases for emergencies . . . you could use them on a rainy day to construct some really gruesome games. £9.95

Get By in French. BBC. A quick course for beginners about meeting people, booking a hotel room, shopping, getting around in a French city – practical, concise information. £3.50

French in a Week. Hodder and Stoughton. Day by day, this takes you through travelling, booking a hotel, shopping, eating, everything you'd need for a week's stay. The book alone is £2.99; with cassettes, £9.99

Hairdressers

Le training – a first-class example of *Franglais* – offers you a chance to get a free or reduced rate haircut or styling in some very good salons. These sessions are popular with the young and broke of Paris, so you may have to wait or return another day. For women only (as far as is known now): although the trendier unisex salons may by now have 'training' sessions, too. You are sure of getting something smart and professional, as the cutter who works on your hair is actually employed in the salon at normal times, not just a learner-driver, so to speak; and there is always one of the top stylists of the establishment hovering near to criticize or comment or direct. Don't mind if you are treated as an object rather than a client to be flattered and soothed. And you will probably find that your own wishes are not paramount. Don't go in with long straight hair and expect to come out with just a trim. Get an idea beforehand of the general attitude of the salon before you put your head in their hands.

Note that although prices were accurate at the time of going to press, they may have risen by the time you read this book.

Michel Gregor
342 rue St-Honoré, 1e
Tel: 47 03 39 59
Métro: Pyramides

Every Wednesday evening, from September to June, and every weekday evening in July and August, from 6:30 p.m. By appointment only, in very elegant surroundings, at a cost of 40F.

Jean-Marc Maniatis 10 rue Poquelin, forum des Halles, 1e
Tel: 40 39 90 95
Métro: Les Halles

and 35 rue de Sèvres, 6e
Tel: 45 44 16 39
Métro: Sèvres-Babylone

Maniatis is a famous hairdresser, known for styling the hair of many film and theatre stars. One day each month, one of his senior *coiffeurs* or *coiffeuses* demonstrates at low cost. And one evening a week, students working under supervision try their hands; then your treatment is free, but book well in advance.

École Jacques Dessange 24 rue St-Augustin, 2e
Tel: 47 42 24 73
Métro: Opéra

Hair styling and make-up done by the trainees of this famous beauty academy. Free. From Mondays through Wednesdays, but closed during school holidays. Little English spoken, but try your luck.

École Jean-Louis David 5 rue Cambon, 8e
Tel: 42 97 51 71
Métro: Concorde

Jean-Louis David runs a chain of *coiffeurs*, and your hair will be cut and styled by experienced people who work in one of their 300 shops. Mondays to Fridays, from 10:30 a.m. to 7:00 p.m., and it's free – but advance booking is necessary.

Académie Rausch 16 rue St-Nicolas, 12e
Tel: 43 46 13 98
Métro: Bastille

Mondays through Thursdays, and sometimes Sundays – advance booking essential. We hear they adapt your cut to your personality. 40F.

Note: For a non-training (paid) coiffure, expect to pay about 80F for a cut, 30F for a shampoo, and blow-drying or setting, about 45–50F. All prices in Paris salons include service (tip).

Health

See 'Au secours', pages 283–91.

Holidays

1 January
Easter Sunday and Monday (Pâques)
1 May (French Labour Day)
Ascension Day

Whit Monday
14 July (Bastille Day)
15 August (Feast of the Assumption)
1 November (All Saints' Day – Toussaint)
11 November (Remembrance Day) and
Christmas.

The entire month of August is high season for tourists, low season for Parisians. The city trades its population in for a flock of provincials and foreigners. Stay out of town unless you don't mind being asked directions by passers-by. To us, Paris in August is close to Paradise – empty, quiet, little traffic, hundreds of restaurants eager to feed you, museums open and not too crowded. We are 'Aoûtiens', happy to be in one of our most familiar bistros on a hot, drowsy day, where lunch with wine can cost as little as 55–62F, and the owners are free to sit down and gossip.

Information sources

For basic information, consult the Offices de Tourisme. The *Hôtesses* speak English, and will provide information on hotels, transportation, sight-seeing, travel in France, and such.

Office de Tourisme

Main office
127 avenue des Champs-Élysées, 8e
Tel: 47 23 61 72
Métro: Georges-V
Hours: Mondays through Saturdays, 9:00 a.m. to 8:00 p.m.; Sundays and holidays, 9:00 a.m. to 6:00 p.m.

Branch offices

Gare de Lyon
Hours: Mondays through Saturdays, 8:00 a.m. to 1:00 p.m., 5:00 to 10:00 p.m., Easter to 1 November. Other months to 8:00 p.m.

Gare de l'Est
Hours: Mondays through Saturdays, 8:00 a.m. to 1:00 p.m., 5:00 to 10:00 p.m., Easter to 1 November. Other months to 8:00 p.m.

Gare du Nord
Hours: Mondays through Saturdays, 8:00 a.m. to 10:00 p.m., Easter to 1 November. Other months to 8:00 p.m.

Gare d'Austerlitz
Hours: Mondays through Saturdays, 8:00 a.m. to 10:00 p.m., Easter to 1 November. Other months to 8:00 p.m.

The Yellow Pages
The Paris telephone directories for offices, goods and services are yellow-covered, available at most hotels and all post offices. Ask for *Le Professionel*.

Language courses

Berlitz
29 rue de la Michodière, 1er
Métro: Opéra

Alliance Française
101 boulevard Raspail, 6e
Tel: 45 44 38 38
Métro: Notre-Dame-des-Champs

Office National des Universités et Écoles Françaises
96 boulevard Raspail, 6e
Tel: 42 22 50 20
Métro: Notre-Dame-des-Champs

Offers information on French language courses from French universities.

Lavatories, public

There are still one or two *vespasiennes* in Paris, but by the time you read this, there may be none. Métro stations frequently (but not always) have lavatories (marked WC-Dames, WC-Hommes); for once, correct vocabulary is *essential*. The attendant expects 1F in the saucer. Superb new automatic lavatories are sited on many street corners: a 2F piece gets you up to 10 minutes in an immaculate white cubicle.

Café and brasserie toilets offer various states of hygiene and civilization – about 25 per cent of the time, you'll find the *à la turque* variety, which can be very clean or very dirty, especially in the smaller out-of-the-way places. Most of our recommended restaurants, however, have clean, well-kept lavatories, usually well-equipped. However, we still say *never* leave home without a pack of humane loo-paper.

If your need for a lavatory doesn't quite coincide with your desire for a cup of coffee, find a café or brasserie and ask politely to use the phone – 'Le téléphone, s'il vous plaît?' Almost always, you will find the phone and lavatory next to each other. Don't use the phone. On your return to the *caisse*, smile politely and leave. Your party didn't answer.

Libraries

If you expect to be able to use the great French Bibliothèque Nationale, 58 rue de Richelieu, 2e, you will need some authoritative support: a letter from your university describing your research, or from your corporation. The more official the better. Count on bureaucratic resistance. The Bibliothèque Ste-Geneviève, 8 place du Panthéon, 6e, however, will issue you with a library card, no questions asked, in about 10 minutes, if you bring your passport.

Lost and found

We have found the Lost and Found charming and helpful, and they have at least one person who speaks good English.

Bureau des Objets Trouvés
36 rue des Morillons, 15e
Métro: Convention

Open Mondays, Tuesdays, Wednesdays and Fridays, 8:30 a.m. to 5:00 p.m.; Thursdays, 8:30 a.m. to 8:00 p.m.

Lost or stolen passport: see 'Au secours', page 292.

Maps

The best we know is the *Plan de Paris*, edition A. Leconte, red cover, 69F, and worth it. For details, see 'Aux alentours', page 32.

Mental Health

SOS Amitié (in English)

Tel: 47 23 80 80
Hours: 3:00 p.m. to 11:00 p.m.

For pouring out your troubles by phone. No advice given, no sides taken, but they lend a sympathetic ear and can recommend other sources of specific help or refuge. They are very busy, and simply trying to get through might drive you to despair.

Metric system

To convert centimetres into inches, multiply by 0.39
To convert inches into centimetres, multiply by 2.54

1 cm = 0.39 in
1 m = 39.4 in = 3.28 ft = 1.09 yd

1 in = 2.54 cm
1 ft = 30.48 cm = 0.304 m
1 yd = 91.44 cm = 0.914 m

1 kilogram (kg) = 2.205 lb
2 kg = 4.409 lb
5 kg = 11.023 lb
10 kg = 22.046 lb

1 lb = 0.45 kg
2 lb = 0.90 kg
5 lb = 2.25 kg
10 lb = 4.50 kg

To convert degrees Centigrade into degrees Fahrenheit, multiply Centigrade by 1.8 and add 32.
   To convert degrees Fahrenheit into degrees Centigrade, subtract 32 and divide by 1.8

Money

See also 'Preliminaries', pages 8–10, for an idea of how much to bring with you.

The denominations	Will get you
5 centimes	nothing
10 centimes	nothing
20 centimes	nothing
½F (50 centimes)	nothing

1F	tip for a lavatory attendant
2F	10 minutes in an automatic lavatory; one phone call
5F	coffee, drunk at the *zinc*; *Le Figaro*
50F	a lunch with wine and service at one of our least expensive restaurants
100F	a day at Malmaison *or* a meal for two with a carafe of wine; *or* a real splurge meal for one

French paper currency is whimsical. The portraits on the bills are not of politicians but of artists: Berlioz (on the now defunct 10F note), De La Tour (50F), Delacroix (100F), Pascal (500F). This is conclusive proof that the French value philosophy above literature, and literature vastly above music.

If knowing exactly what you are spending is important to you, consider the X-Changer, a gadget that instantly computes foreign exchange rates. £5.25 from larger branches of Boots, Rymans, Debenhams in London. (However, there is such a thing as carrying too many gadgets and worrying too much about whether the meal cost £6.50 or £7.00 when you should be concentrating on the *ris de veau*.)

Bureaux de change

Despite our wise words about sleeping cheap and eating well, within certain sets of limits, money does seem to drip through the fingers in Paris. And when you need it most – on weekends, or just before dinner – where do you go to get it? Even during banking hours on weekdays you can find yourself walking miles, past bank after bank of busy money-changing citizens, but barred to *you* by the inflexible sign *no change, no wechsel*. Every guidebook lists the exchange facilities in the railway stations: but we can only say that they are a foretaste of hell. Fearsomely crowded, jostling with impatient travellers barging themselves and their rucksacks past you to get to ticket offices and trains. But fear nothing, here are the life-saving addresses:

Banque Rivaud
boulevard St Germain, at the exit from the Métro

No commission charged, good rates, unsmiling staff. It was impossible to get accurate information on hours and days, but as it is a very
popular tourist area, they're probably open at hours convenient to
you, especially in the four summer months.

Chequepoint

The English chain of *bureau de change*, now have about 16 'changes'
in Paris, and in our experience give the best service, the best hours,
and *smile*, even at 3:00 a.m. And they cash personal cheques on
English banks, backed by your cheque card! For up-to-the-minute
information on their branches, etc., go to their main office, open 24
hours a day, every day, or telephone:

150 avenue des Champs-Élysées, 8e
Métro: Charles de Gaulle-Étoile
Tel: 49 53 02 51

Chequepoints open 7 days a week, 8:30 a.m. to 11:00 p.m.
134 rue de Rivoli, 1e *Métro*: Louvre
208 rue de Rivoli, 1e *Métro*: Tuileries
36 avenue de l'Opéra, 2e *Métro*: Opéra
9 boulevard des Capucines, 2e *Métro*: Opéra
23 rue Aubry le Boucher, 4e *Métro*: Châtelet les Halles
131 rue St-Martin, 4e *Métro*: Châtelet les Halles
18 rue de Buci, 6e *Métro*: Odèon

Chequepoints open Mondays through Saturdays, 8:30 a.m. to 11:00
p.m.
240 rue de Rivoli, 1e *Métro*: Concorde
274 rue St-Honoré, 2e *Métro*: Palais Royal
346 rue St-Honoré, 2e *Métro*: Tuileries
7 rue de la Cossonnerie, 4e *Métro*: Châtelet les Halles
19 boulevard St-Michel, 5e *Métro*: Place St-Michel, Cluny
21 rue St-Severin, 5e *Métro*: Place St-Michel
134 boulevard St-Germain, 6e *Métro*: Odèon
1 rue Scribe, 9e *Métro*: Opéra

CCF (Crédit Commercial de France)

115 avenue des Champs-Élysées, 8e
Métro: George-V
Hours: Mondays through Saturdays, 8:30 a.m. to 8:00 p.m., and in July, August and September on Sundays from 10:15 a.m. to 6:00 p m.

Currency Exchange du Rond-Point

Inside the Galerie Élysées Rond-Point, 8e
Tel: 42 25 91 36, 42 25 91 37
47 avenue Franklin D. Roosevelt, 8e
Métro: Franklin-D.-Roosevelt, St-Philippe du Roule
Hours: Open seven days a week in summer months (1 June to 30 September) 10:00 a.m. to 8:00 p.m.; off-season days and hours not posted as we write, so check on the spot.

No commission charge here, many languages spoken, notes and traveller's cheques, credit card advances, and the rates seem good.

Barclays Bank

33 rue 4 Septembre, 2e
Métro: Opéra
Hours: Mondays through Fridays, 9:30 a.m. to 4:00 p.m.

Rond-Point des Champs-Élysées, 8e
Métro: Champs-Élysées-Clemenceau
Hours: as above

Barclay cheques only, and traveller's cheques.

Beaubourg

Centre Pompidou, 3e
Métro: Les Halles, Rambuteau

A *bureau de change* has been opened on the ground floor of Beaubourg – open during the Centre's daytime hours and on

Saturdays and Sundays. The exchange rate is fairly standard, but note that a fee of 12F50 is charged on each transaction.

Citibank

30 avenue des Champs-Élysées, 8e
Métro: George-V, Franklin-D.-Roosevelt

A small, busy and newish bank in this very convenient location, with good exchange rates and useful opening hours: Mondays to Fridays, 9:00 a.m. to 6:45 p.m.; Saturdays 10:30 a.m. to 1:15 p.m., 2:30 to 6:30 p.m.

Banco Borges

30 rue du 4 Septembre, 2e
Métro: Opéra, 4 Septembre
Hours: Mondays to Fridays, 9:30 a.m. to 6:30 p.m., Saturdays 9:00 a.m. to 5:00 p.m.

Bureau de Change

9 rue Scribe, 9e
Métro: Opéra
Hours: Mondays to Fridays, 9:00 a.m. to 5:15 p.m. No exchange fee charged.

Melia Travel Agency

31 avenue de l'Opéra, 1er
Métro: Opéra
Hours: Mondays to Fridays 9:30 a.m. to 6:30 p.m., Saturdays 9:30 a.m. to 6:00 p.m. Days before holidays (e.g., 24 and 31 December): 9:00 a.m. to 4:00 p.m.

Banque Portugaise

5 rue Auber, 9e
Métro: Opéra
Hours: Mondays to Fridays 9:30 a.m. to 6:15 p.m., Saturdays
9:00 a.m. to 5:00 p.m.

An American living in the 9e says 'Inefficient, disobliging, while
smiling continually – but their rates are good, no exchange fee, and
open all day Saturday. Queues are *long*, paperwork from before the
war – be patient and take a book if dealing here!'

Banks and *bureaux de change* have varying charges for cashing
traveller's cheques, or notes, so shop around. American Express
traveller's cheques are best cashed (no fee) at their office, otherwise
you pay at least 1 per cent. Barclays' traveller's cheques cost you
nothing to cash at their branches.

Cheques, Credit Cards

Traveller's Cheques, of course, are the safest way to carry money,
as if lost or stolen they will be replaced with varying degrees of
speed. However, you pay in advance, you pay a commission when
you buy them, and sometimes you pay when you cash them abroad.
Most English banks, and major travel agencies like Thomas Cook,
charge 1 per cent commission for sterling traveller's cheques, and
1.25 per cent for foreign currency traveller's cheques. Be a little
wary of taking a lot of money in these last, as you'll lose on the
exchange if you bring them back unspent and want to cash them.
American Express and Barclays in Paris charge no fee for cashing
their own traveller's cheques. Incidentally, keep a record of the
cheque numbers, denominations, when and where cashed, separate
from the cheques themselves – this is a chore to do, but if the
cheques are pinched, at least you know what to tell the issuers.

Eurocheques are, in our experience, more trouble than they're
worth, at least in France. On the face of it, they seem a very good
alternative to carrying cash, which is lost for ever if stolen or
mislaid, or paying in advance for traveller's cheques. You pay your
bank a yearly fee (£4 at NatWest, £6 at Barclays), and get books of
ten cheques each and a Eurocheque card, and write them out in

local currency as needed. This saves you the petty annoyance of
queueing at banks or bureaux de change. BUT: many small hotels,
restaurants and shops will either courteously refuse to accept Eurocheques, or will add on a fee which can range from 5 per cent to 10
per cent, because *their* banks levy a surcharge on Eurocheques from
English banks. One French bank charges its account-holders a flat
fee of 100F (more than £9) for every Eurocheque, no matter how
small. In addition, you pay about 1.6 per cent of the sterling value
of the cheque when it clears through your account here, plus about
30p handling charge for each. Is it all worth it?

Personal cheques, backed by a bank card, or an Access or Visa card,
can be cashed at Chequepoint offices throughout the city. Barclays,
at 33 rue 4-Septembre, and at the Rond Point des Champs-Élysées,
will cash a Barclay cheque for up to £100 for a fee of 7F50; other
banks will ask you for two cheques of £50, and charge a fee for each.
NatWest at 18 Place Vendôme will cash cheques for its account
holders with the same fee as Barclays. French banks, which used to
cash cheques drawn on English accounts, now politely refuse.

National Giro will furnish its account holders with Post Cheques,
which can be cashed at any post office in francs – and this can be a
tremendous convenience for out-of-banking-hours emergencies.
These Post Cheques must be ordered in advance, take about a week
to ten days to get, and come in books of ten, each worth up to £50.
And – a real plus – you keep the money in your account until you
actually cash the cheque, unlike traveller's cheques which are
bought in advance. However, no shops or hotels or restaurants will
accept them, and French banks on the whole are baffled by them. A
charge of 50p is added in the UK when the cheque clears.

Credit cards can be used to draw cash from French banks displaying the appropriate symbol; the amount varies from year to
year, but you will be charged interest at the current rate – at this
writing, between 1.8 and 2 per cent *per month* – from the moment
you get the money. No interest-free grace period here. And again,
we have to warn that the exchange rate you will be charged will be
the company's own rate.

American Express charge-card holders can cash personal
cheques, backed by the AMEX card, for up to £500 every 21 days.
Diners' Club will advance up to 8250F to its card-holders every two
weeks, but as these are charge-cards, not credit cards, a sizeable

interest charge will be added if the account is not settled promptly when the bill comes in.

When it comes to using credit cards to pay for meals, hotels, and purchases, opinions differ. More and more shops, cafés and restaurants – even in such districts as Belleville, rue de Charonne, rue de la Roquette – will accept plastic. With VISA and Access, you'll have up to six weeks' free credit before you have to pay up. Diners' Club and American Express like their accounts settled promptly. See our warnings above for full details.

Protect the Plastic: for between £6 and £8 a year, you can insure all your charge and credit cards against loss or theft. Credit Card Sentinel (UK toll-free number 0800 414 717), CPP (071-351 4400), and CardWise (0702-362999) all run similar schemes. You report your loss with one phone call, they notify every organization you have specified, and get replacement cards under way. All have reverse-charge or toll-free facilities for overseas calls. All will advance cash, subject to certain restrictions, interest-free for a limited period, if your money has gone with your cards (£400 from Sentinel, £750 from CPP and £500 from CardWise). If you call in within 24 hours of discovering your loss, you're covered against any fraudster using your card (up to £500 with Sentinel, £1000 with CPP, unlimited with CardWise): once the loss is reported, all fraudulent use is covered. But make sure you keep your PIN (personal identification number) separate from your cashpoint withdrawal card. Otherwise, if a thief cashes a cheque on your account *before* you notify the card protection company, you're out of the cash.

If you don't use insurance, then note down the numbers, expiration date, and loss-notification phone number of your credit card issuers. Call them right away and tell them exactly when you discovered the loss, so they can issue a stop-order which protects you against someone booking a round-the-world flight on your VISA card. Each company has a slightly different policy on covering losses on credit cards, so be sure you know your rights when you make your call. If you get an automatic answering service, at night, Sundays, or holidays, say your piece slowly, and include the phrase, 'As of this moment, X a.m. or Y p.m., of reporting the loss, I am no longer responsible for any charges incurred on this card number: 0000 0000 0000.'

Newspapers

In French: *Le Monde*, marginally left of centre, is the most serious and well informed; *Figaro* veers right. Either will give you a morning's occupation if your French is slow. *France-Soir* leans toward the sensational, a good source of crime and scandal stories; *Libération* (*Libé* for short) is thoroughly 'in', very pointed, truly biased; *Le Canard Enchaîné* is a sort of French *Private Eye*, and requires a firm grip on French politics and *argot* to make any sense at all; *Paris-Match* is France's weekly picture magazine. A couple of hundred others, of all sorts and persuasions.

In English: the *International Herald Tribune* (daily) for comprehensive stock quotations, news, and American 'Op-Ed' features. Columnists syndicated from the *New York Times*, the *Washington Post* and elsewhere. *Guardian, Times, Telegraph, Independent*, available daily near the Hôtel Crillon, Odéon, St-Michel, place de la Concorde, Palais Royal, Opéra, place de la République and other central news kiosks.

And see 'Periodicals', pages 272–3.

Nuisances

Noise: hotel regulations specify quiet before 10:00 a.m. and after 10:00 p.m. Bang on the wall or call the manager if you have noisy neighbours. Try 'Il y a du bruit' (It's noisy), or 'C'est trop bruyant' (Too much noise).

Other complaints

Mosquitoes: *Moustiques*
Fleas: *Puces*
Lice: *Poux* (don't complain, leave the hotel)
Inedible: (mild) *Cela ne me plaît pas*
                (strong) *C'est dégoûtant, ça*
Odour (extreme): *Ça pue!*
Unwelcome advances: *Laissez-moi tranquille. Fiche-moi le camp!*

Beggars: if you're unwilling or unable to give handouts, the best defence is not to understand what they want. *Parle pas* will do in most cases – but Parisian beggars have been known to beg in English!

Thieves: see pages 293–4.

Smoking: Outside of Barcelona, all but invisible in a cloud of blue cigarette smoke, Paris must be the 'smokiest' city of Europe. If the smell of strong tobacco bothers you, leave the country. It's true that smoking is forbidden in some post offices, all Métros, buses, and certain other public places, but you can't spend all your time there. As Ian Irvine commented in *The Independent* in May 1990, the French treat the cigarette as a fashion accessory. Tobacco advertising has been taken off television and cinema, and many newspapers and magazines don't accept it, but the tobacco companies get around that in many ways. For instance, they produce matchboxes and lighters identical to their cigarette packs, and promote *them*. Classic advertising posters for cigarettes are reproduced on postcards, gift-wrapping paper, beach umbrellas, fabrics, anything which keeps the names alight. The cleverest ploy yet was an exhibition a year or two ago: the world's greatest photographers were commissioned to take photographs of gypsies – their fees were paid, the show sponsored, to enthusiastic reviews, by Gitanes, whose bright-blue pack features the negligently lounging gypsy dancer.

Numbers

It's absolutely necessary to understand the difference between, say, *quatorze* and *quarante*; between *cinq* and *cent*. When you can tell in an instant what *quatre-vingt dix-neuf* means, you've arrived. Memorize the following:

1	un	vingt-et-un	21
2	deux	trente-et-un	31
3	trois	quarante-et-un	41
4	quatre	cinquante-et-un	51
5	cinq	soixante-et-un	61
6	six	soixante-et-onze	71
7	sept	quatre-vingt-un	81

8	huit	quatre-vingt-onze	91
9	neuf	cent	100
10	dix	deux cents	200
11	onze	mille	1000
12	douze		
13	treize		
14	quatorze		
15	quinze		
16	seize		
17	dix-sept		
18	dix-huit		
19	dix-neuf		
20	vingt		

premier (ière)	first
deuxième	second
troisième	third
quatrième	fourth
cinquième	fifth

Unless you understand the numbers, you won't be able to ask information about bus routes; pay for a meal or a minor purchase without getting it in writing; figure out what the *gendarme* means when he says the Métro is *deux-cent cinquante* metres away.

Open and closed: abbreviations

TLJ – every day (*tous les jours*)
Sauf lundi – except Monday
S, D & F – Saturdays, Sundays and holidays (*samedis, dimanches et fêtes*)

Periodicals

Pariscope and *Officiel des Spectacles*, for weekly listings of cinemas, theatre, concerts, dance, music, cabaret, races and other sports, and art galleries. 3F50, every Wednesday.

France-USA Contacts (FUSAC), a fact-packed, lively, highly useful little glossy free-sheet published every two weeks, distributed wherever English or American is spoken; or from their office, 3 rue Larochelle, 14e (*Métro*: Gaité, Edgar-Quinet), tel: 45 38 56 57. It has a very American accent and slant, and an incredible amount of information about flats, sublets, hotels, restaurants, pubs, hairdressers, music, rides, flights, jumble sales, language courses, Fourth of July and Bastille Day parties – even therapy, health, AIDS and AA support groups.

Free Voice, a newspaper very much like the original *Village Voice* in New York. Ten issues a year, from 65 quai d'Orsay, 7e. Well-written, well-informed, rather serious-minded, strong on arts information including good new books, plays and films but not ignoring discos, jazz places; a range from mime festivals to the Paris-American Aids Committee. Good classified ads in their 'Bulletin Board' section; excellent 'Voice's Choices' page, highlighting the most interesting cultural events in Paris. Free from restaurants, book shops, brasseries, all over the Left Bank and now reaching out to other parts of the city. Or call 47 53 77 23.

Police (see also 'Au secours', pages 292–4)

Paris police come in different guises. The everyday cop, the *gendarme* ('*le flic*'), travels on foot, usually in pairs. He is to be addressed thus:

'*Pardon, Monsieur l'agent . . .*'

Any other means of getting his attention, short of falling in front of a bus, will get a chilly reception.

The CRS are a special anti-terrorist force who guard embassies, certain banks, some airline offices and the like. They wear blue windcheaters, carry guns, and look like thugs. Do not ask them what time it is.

If you are a foreigner, and are asked, for whatever reason, to show your *papiers* – your passport – to a *gendarme*, do so. If you don't have it on you, it's a fast trip downtown for you.

In general it would be unwise to break any laws while in Paris.

La politesse

Without which you might as well stay at home. Parisians – if you'll permit the generalization – are formal creatures. What they lack in rigid class distinctions they make up for in the personal carapace of manners that each carries around. While it is unlikely that any Parisian will adopt you into the bosom of his family, or spill his innermost secrets to you, Parisians can unbend to strangers. With the right approach you can at least penetrate the first line of defence.

The trick is to use the standard forms of *politesse: Excusez-moi, monsieur; s'il vous plaît, madame; pardon, mademoiselle* . . . and use the honorific (never the *tu* form unless a) you're a member of the family; b) you're a close friend or bitter enemy; or c) you're among the more casual student generation, who seem to have given up the second person plural). And say the polite words as if you mean them. As a rule, Parisians prefer to be spoken to directly; they are all for eye-contact; they enjoy shaking hands (brief – up-and-down only – but firm) on all occasions, once a relationship has been established.

And as a means of establishing relationships – even purely commercial ones – we suggest that you cultivate certain people and places throughout your stay. Even if you spend most of your days in the hinterland of the city, there should be a few characters – the *concierge* of your hotel, the owner of your neighbourhood café, the woman who sells you the newspaper, the staff of a restaurant or two where you return several times – who will get to recognize you, know you however slightly, welcome your appearance, bid you good appetite or good day. If you make the effort to communicate – in French, however stumbling – it will be appreciated. If you enjoy their food, their accommodation, their city, don't feel shy about showing it.

Post

Another exercise in bureaucracy: receiving parcels through the post office is said to be Kafkaesque.

Stamps (*timbres*) are available at post offices (*bureaux de poste*) and at tobacco shops (*tabacs*) for EC destinations only. Postboxes are oblong, about 2 feet by 3 feet, a pale, Dijon-mustard colour, generally attached to walls, and virtually invisible. In post offices you have a choice of three slots: Paris only, *Avion* (airmail), and *département étrangers* (anywhere outside Paris).

The French produce some of the prettiest (and biggest) commemorative stamps in the world. They're called *timbres de collection*, and are available at a special window in the post office.

A 24-hour post office is open Mondays through Saturdays at 52 rue du Louvre, 1er, (*Métro*: Louvre) but don't try it on a Saturday afternoon. Another 24-hour post office is at 71 avenue des Champs-Élysées, 8e, open seven days a week, but crowded on Sundays and holidays, for stamps, telephones and telegrams only – no other postal services.

Letters from Paris to the UK cost 2F50 for 20 grams (airmail envelope and two thin sheets of paper); postcards are 2F. Airmail letters to the US and Canada are 3F40 for 10 grams.

Postcards: it sometimes seems to take an abnormal length of time for a postcard to reach the UK from France, which is so close to our shores. It is possible that you can speed up the process by putting your card in an envelope and addressing that. It costs a few centimes more but it might be worth it.

Post codes: the postal code for Paris is 75, then 0, and then the number of the *arrondissement*. Most of the Marais is thus 75004. It's always written 75004 Paris, postal code first and town name second. The *Bureau des Postes* has even designed special envelopes with a box for the post code: decorative, sensible, available from most post offices.

Telegrams: via the telegram counter at any post office, or call 42 33 21 11. Seven word minimum; the address counts as part of the message.

Telex: public telex offices at 7 rue Feydeau, 2e. Tel: 42 33 20 12 or 42 33 20 13. *Métro*: Bourse. Open daily, 8:00 a.m. to 8:00 p.m.

Railway information

The great source of all knowledge about how to get from anywhere to anywhere in France is in the Information Bureau at Gare St-Lazare, near the entrance closest to the rue de Rome. It takes a few minutes to crack the code of how to work the timetables, mounted on rollers behind glass. But once you've done that, you're in clover. Also available: a certain number of printed timetables from a central stand in this office, each section labelled by the name of the station from which the train leaves. No one here speaks English, so equip yourself with your pocket dictionary to make sure you understand all the footnotes. And don't wait to do this planning until the last minute before a journey.

Slang

The current *argot* runs to Franglais, which you should have no trouble with (although it does change: jogging, a few years ago, was known as *le footing*, now it's *le jogging*). And abbreviation: you can go to *un resto très sympa* and possibly finish your meal with a liqueur or *un cogna*. Anyone in deep trouble is said to be *dans le chocolat* which is a delicate way to avoid saying *dans la merde*.

Most slang covers the world of pop culture: thus *un group* is a group, *le leader* is the lead musician; *le rap* and *le hip-hop* will be played by *le Dee Jay* while bright young things do *le break-dance* and *le looking* (acrobatic dance based on the fighting dances of the Brazilian slaves). *Le trainers* or *les baskets* are trainers, *le tagger* spray-paints scribbles on walls and the Métro, and *on est blacks* means 'we are, (or I am) black'. And everybody eats *le hamburger* (pron. *ang-boor-zhe*), *les bagels* and *le cheesecake*.

Taxis

Current prices in the City of Paris, as far as the Boulevards Périphériques:

From 7:00 a.m. to 7:00 p.m. 'Tarif A'

Pick-up charge 9F
Price per kilometre 2F62

From 7:00 p.m. to 7:00 a.m., and all day Sundays and Bank Holidays. 'Tarif B'
Pick-up charge 9F
Price per kilometre 4F08

(There's another rate for waiting time or if the taxi is held up in traffic and can go at only 24 km per hour or less)

Telephones

Run by France Telecom: public phones are widely visible, on streets, at airports, and always in post offices and telegraph offices which are identified by big bright signs PTT (Poste, Téléphone, Télégraphe). Otherwise, look for telephones in hotel lobbies, restaurants, bars, brasseries.

Pay phones: as in any big city, you will find that a certain number of these public phones are unusable. But it must be said that the French are rapidly making pay phones vandal-proof, mostly by limiting their use to *Télécarte* holders. If you have a phone card, you have quite a good chance of finding a kiosk when and where you need one. Queues are shorter at *Télécarte* points. It is now almost essential to buy a 40F *carte*, from post offices and many shops, including Le Drugstore at the Étoile. If you don't find a pay phone when you need one, you may have to do a bit of travelling – here's a list of peaceful venues.

The *sous-sol* (lower ground floor) of Galerie Rond-Point, 12 avenue des Champs-Élysées (*Métro*: Franklin-D.-Roosevelt), has three good working coin-fed phones, all with numbers where you can be called back.

Galerie Claridges at 74 avenue des Champs-Élysées has two phones, and wonder of wonders, complete telephone directories.

The Galerie des Champs, 84 avenue des Champs-Élysées, has three phones (free loos too, unlike other public places).

Most luxury hotels have public telephones, and a place to sit down. Although they are courteous, they do not welcome callers with backpacks or shabby clothes.

After you have put in your *Télécarte*, or coin, and dialled the number, you will hear a jumble of noise and then a 'ring' tone which sounds like the British 'number engaged' sound. Don't hang up – this is the French 'number ringing' noise.

Some cafés, *tabacs*, and bars may have a notice over the bar telling you that telephones and toilets are reserved for the clientele. If you don't see such a sign, ask politely at the bar to use the phone. They will point it out, and you either feed in coins, or pay for the metered time at the end of your call. A few places still use the *jeton* system, with special tokens. *Jetons* are not transferable from café to café, so if your party doesn't answer, get your money back. *Jeton* phones require you to press a rectangular button to the right of the phone when your party answers.

Long distance: outside the eight-digit area, time and distance come into play. In phone kiosks, there is a table listing the correct amount to pay for a call lasting a specified number of minutes. Consult the table, dial, wait for an answer, insert the money. When your time is almost up you'll be warned by a tone. Put in more change then, not before the tone.

International: the cheapest way to call the UK is to use a *Télécarte*, or amass a pocketful of 50-centime, 1F, and 2F coins and dial direct from any unvandalized coin-fed telephone kiosk. The instructions (in French) are clearly set out on a panel near the phone.

Don't, however, use British Telecom's 'Home Direct' service unless you're in dire need. When they advertise it, they don't tell you the cost – astronomical. Here's how the system works:

From France, you dial 19, wait for a second dial tone, then dial 00 44. This connects you to a London operator, who then makes a transferred-charge call to any UK number, or on request will put the charge on your BT charge card.

This is all very swift and convenient, but calls of even the shortest duration ('Hello, I'll be home Thursday at lunchtime, how's the weather, goodbye') are charged at the flat rate for three minutes. On your charge card, that's £3.11. If you're transferring the charge, it's £5.35. Each succeeding minute *or part thereof* costs 94p. Although these rates include the operator's fee, and VAT, they are exorbitant.

Travelling paupers should call home either through Paris PTT locations where an operator will put in the call for you and give you the charge when you're finished; or direct, with a handful of change. A one-minute call costs about 5F – roughly 55p at the moment. Why make British Telecom richer than it is?

We thank the *Independent* newspaper for calling our attention to this costly UK gimmick, and reader John Gallery for writing to us after he too discovered the cost of convenience calls.

International codes from France

UK: 19 44
USA: 19 11
Canada: 19 16
Australia: 19 61
New Zealand: 19 64

To use the 'Home Direct' services, dial 19, then 00, and the country code. But read our warning above about the cost of these calls.

Time

The French use the 12-hour clock, but run on 24-hour time. Hence, 5 p.m. is 17:00 (*dix-sept heures*); midnight is 24:00 (*minuit*); and so forth. It takes practice.

The days of the week, starting with Monday, are *lundi, mardi, mercredi, jeudi, vendredi, samedi*, and *dimanche*. The months of the year are easier to deal with: *janvier, février, mars, avril, mai, juin, juillet, août, septembre, octobre, novembre* and *décembre*. We narrowly escaped Napoleon's idea of *Germinal, Thermidor, Brumaire*, which, from 1793 to 1806, replaced the more familiar Gregorian Calendar.

France is one hour ahead of the UK; six hours later than the US (East Coast time). You should be aware of this before you call your friends in New York at 3:00 a.m., *their* time.

Tipping

The rules are clear-cut. Try not to deviate if you want to stay on good terms with your hosts.

Taxis: 10–15 per cent.

Lavatory attendants in public loos, where found: 1F or 1F50.

Waiters: 15 per cent is almost always included (you'll note the words *service compris* on the menu). When service is *non-compris*, prices will be itemized, with 15 per cent (rounded off either way) tacked on at the bottom of your bill, and the whole thing totalled.

Cafés: 15 per cent is included (as for waiters) for table service. If you eat or drink at the bar, leave some small change – the light-weight coins that rattle around in your pocket – to make up 1F or 1F50.

Hotels: Service is added onto the bill – but if the *concierge* or any other personnel have done you special favours (calling theatres, getting taxis), they should be rewarded. See pages 59–60.

Porters and Left Luggage: Set price, 10F per piece of luggage. No tip needed.

Hairdressers: Service is included almost everywhere, but a few extra francs at the end won't break you, and it's a nice gesture.

Theatre and cinema ushers: 1F for each person in your party.

Traffic

Since we assume you're not suicidal, we won't deal with traffic regulations from a driver's viewpoint here. As a *piéton* – a ped-estrian – you should know a few rules of the game.

If you're English, Scottish, Welsh, Irish or Japanese, you must never forget that traffic in France travels on the *right*, and fast. Therefore, before you step off the kerb, do *not* look to your right.

Look left. Then look right, left again, and in all directions as quickly as possible before you head out, or you'll be mowed down. Many Paris streets, though not all, are one-way.

For pedestrians, GO is a little green man in the traffic signal; sometimes a pinpoint of green or white light; sometimes nothing at all. STOP is a little red man. In both cases, it's very difficult to see the lights in bright sunshine. Your best bet is to wait for all traffic to stop, and ride on someone else's coat-tails across the street. All traffic lights, red or green, are called *feux rouges.*

Zebra crossings exist, but are usually ignored by all concerned. Traffic tends to go straight ahead even if a pedestrian is clearly out on the white lines. Be very careful of mopeds and motorbikes, especially the great roaring Harleys and Hondas.

Paris streets are either incredibly wide (the *grands boulevards*) and hence impossible to cross without feeling totally naked; or incredibly narrow, with cars parked halfway up the kerb, pedestrians walking with one foot in the gutter, single file, or edging along the wall. Either way, it's risky, so watch your step.

Women on their own

Word has it that women alone do just fine in Paris (the reverse has also been mentioned). Our sources say that women can eat alone in any restaurant (except around Pigalle and other obviously raffish neighbourhoods), drink alone at the counter or at a table in most bars, stay alone in hotels, walk alone in the daytime in parks, gardens and streets in almost every *quartier* without ever being disturbed or made to feel uncomfortable. None of this is true around Pigalle, boulevard de Clichy, or other obviously raffish areas: you must, in every case, use your head. Don't walk in parks or lonely dark streets at night – either alone or in company. You wouldn't do it in London, New York, Chicago; so don't do it in Paris. Some parts of Paris have had real trouble on the streets in the past few years, and the newspapers and television in Paris can keep you posted on where not to go in such cases. The woman (or man) who can't resist seeing what's going on is looking for trouble, and the Paris *flics* will toss you into the *panier de salade* (police van) no matter what gender you are, if you get in their way.

Any other advice applies all over the world. Don't be free with personal information, don't flash possessions or cash around, let the reception at your hotel know where you're going if you're going out with someone you don't know well, and keep your taxi fare back tucked up your sleeve.

Au secours *(Emergencies)*

Dealing with real trouble at home is bad enough. In a foreign country, and in a foreign language, it can be devastating. But there are resources.

Medical emergencies

If it's more than a minor ailment, you need an English-speaking doctor or nurse, or a supply of medicine dispensed by someone who can understand you and your problem without the aid of faltering French or a translator. Here are the numbers to note. Write them down in your pocket notebook for the times (we hope rare) when you don't have this book in your hand.

SOS Dentists

87 boulevard Port-Royal, 13e
Tel: 43 37 51 00
RER: Port-Royal

An English-speaking dentist is almost always at hand. Ask for a receipt, as your form E-111 (pages 24–5) covers only minimal repairs, and real emergencies such as raging toothache or a lost filling. You should claim on your Travel Insurance Policy for anything above the amount deductable.

SOS Médecins

87 boulevard Port-Royal, 13e
Tel: 43 37 77 77 or 43 07 77 77
RER: Port-Royal

As above.

Hospitals

British Hospital
3 rue Barbés, Levallois-Perret (in a suburb of Paris, reached by
Métro, but a long ride)
Tel: 47 58 13 12
Métro: Anatole-France
Hours: 24 hours, 365 days a year. Telephone first for an appoint-
ment. Medical only; no dental facilities.

American Hospital
63 boulevard Victor-Hugo, Neuilly
Tel: 47 47 53 00
Métro: Porte-Maillot, then bus No. 82 to last stop.

Telephone first for an appointment. *Hours*: Mondays through Saturdays, 9:00 a.m. to noon, 2:00 to 6:00 p.m. Sundays, emergency
treatment only, no fixed appointments. Dental as well as medical.

Pharmacists

Pharmacie Anglaise des Champs-Élysées
62 avenue des Champs-Élysées, 8e
Tel: 43 59 22 52 and 42 25 25 13
Métro: George-V
Hours: Mondays through Saturdays, 8:30 a.m. to 10:30 p.m. Closed
Sundays.

Well stocked with familiar English and American brands of medicines, or their French equivalents, and attended by professional

people who speak English. They will fill a prescription from a doctor, or can give you advice about a proprietary product for minor ills (headache, diarrhoea, streaming colds, strains and sprains, rheumatic pain).

Pharmacie Gagne-Petit
6 rue de Belleville, 20e
Métro: Belleville
Hours: Mondays through Saturdays, 8:30 a.m. to 10:00 p.m.

Pharmacie le Drugstore St-Germain
149 boulevard St-Germain, 6e
Métro: St-Germain des Prés
Hours: Mondays through Saturdays, 8:00 a.m to 2 a.m. Sundays, 9:00 a.m. to 2:00 a.m.

Pharmacie Derhy
84 avenue des Champs-Élysées, 8e
Métro: Franklin-D.-Roosevelt
Hours: 24 hours a day, 365 days a year.

Very small but well-stocked and the staff is proficient in many languages.

Pharmacie Finkel
133 avenue des Champs-Élysées, 8e
Métro: Charles de Gaulle-Étoile
Hours: Mondays through Saturdays, 8:30 a.m. to 2:00 a.m.

Pharmacie de la Place
5 place Pigalle, 9e
Métro: Pigalle
Hours: Mondays through Saturdays, 8:30 a.m. to l:00 a.m.

Pharmacie Caillaud
6 boulevard des Capucines, 9e
Métro: Opéra
Hours: Mondays through Saturdays, 9:00 a.m. to 1 a.m.

Pharmacie LaGarce
13 place de la Nation, 11e
Métro: Nation
Hours: Mondays through Saturdays, 9:00 a.m. to 10:00 p.m.

Pharmacie d'Italie
61 avenue d'Italie, 13e
Métro: Place d'Italie
Hours: Mondays through Saturdays, 9:00 a.m. to midnight. Sundays
from 8:00 p.m. to midnight.

Pharmacie du Départ
3 rue de Départ, 14e
Métro: Montparnasse
Hours: Mondays through Saturdays, 9:00 a.m. to 10:00 p.m.

British-American Pharmacy
1 rue Auber, 9e
Métro: Opéra
Hours: Mondays through Saturdays, 8:30 a.m. to 8:00 p.m. Closed
Sundays.

Staffed with bright, multi-lingual people.

Pharmacie des Champs-Élysées
84 avenue des Champs-Élysées, 8e
Tel: 45 62 02 41
Métro: Franklin-D.-Roosevelt, Georges-V

Open 24 hours a day, seven days a week – very small, but useful in
any out-of-hours emergency. They speak about 18 languages.

Poison Centre

Hôpital de l'Assistance Publique Fernand Widal
200 rue du Faubourg St-Denis, 10e
Tel: 42 05 63 29
Métro: La Chapelle

Burn Centre

Hôpital de l'Assistance Publique Trousseau
26 avenue Dr Arnold Netter, 12e
Tel: 43 46 13 90
Métro: Porte de Vincennes

Drug Crisis Centre

Hôpital Marmottan
19 rue d'Armaillé, 17e
Tel: 45 74 00 04
Métro: Argentine

Alcoholics Anonymous in English

Tel: 48 06 43 68

Opticians

Lissac Opticians
1 rue Auber, 9e
Tel: 47 42 57 80
Métro: Opéra

Lissac are said to be pricey, but good for emergency specs making
or repairing, and they speak English. Most Paris opticians will re-fix
a loose sidepiece (*une branche*) with courtesy and for free.

Chiropodists *Podologues*

Institut National de Podologie
7 rue du Marché-St-Honoré, 1er
Metro: Pyramides
Hours: 2:00 to 5:30 p.m.; Friday mornings, 8:30 a.m. to noon.
Closed during school holidays.

No appointments, you will have to wait, but if your foot trouble is minor, it's an inexpensive good thing. Students work under instruction, and you get your treatment and your feet soothingly massaged, for 35F. A little English is spoken, but not much.

Clinique de Pédicurie-Podologie
15 rue Cujas, 5e
Métro: Cardinal Lemoine
Hours: Mondays through Fridays, 9:00 to 12:00, 1:30 to 6:00 p.m.
Closed during school holidays.

Be prepared to wait for a treatment, which costs 35F.

André Legoff
12 rue de l'Isly, 8e
Tel: 43 87 19 18
Métro: St-Lazare
Hours: Mondays, 8:30 a.m. to 5:15 p.m.; Tuesdays through Fridays, 8:30 a.m. to 6:15 p.m.

By appointment only. Prices according to seriousness of foot problem, but expect to pay English prices.

VD Clinic

Ligue de Préservation Sociale
29 rue Falguiere, 15e
Tel: 43 20 63 74
Métro: Pasteur

Hours: Mondays through Fridays, 2:00 to 4:30 p.m., 5:00 to 6:45 p.m. Closed weekends.

AIDS and HIV Positive Counselling (FAACTS Anon)

American Church
65 quai d'Orsay, 7e
Tel: 45 50 26 49
Métro: Invalides

Thursday nights at 7:00 p.m. Telephone for information or an appointment. For English and Americans in Paris, who have AIDS (SIDA) or are HIV-affected, and for their families, friends, and lovers, this centre offers counselling, some therapies, and referral to therapy services. Complete confidentiality assured.

First aid

At night, Sundays, or holidays, your *concierge* or the hotel manager can telephone the nearest Commissariat of Police to get you the name of an emergency doctor. In case of a street accident or emergency, look for the automatic callbox marked *Services Médicaux*, at the nearest intersection of major streets.

Medical bills and insurance

Medical: Don't assume that because you are a citizen of an EC country, you'll get free medical care for the asking in France. Begin by getting the indispensable Form E-111 (see pages 24–5) and hang on to it like grim death. This provides rather minimal cover, and you'll still have to pay at least 20 per cent of the total cost. If you're unlucky enough to need a private ambulance to a private hospital or clinic, you pay the full whack. If you are ill enough to need bringing home by an air ambulance, or by a regular flight with someone to care for you, this can cost up to £5000. So take out insurance (through your travel agent, if you like, but even then read through before paying for the policy). Don't buy the first policy you are offered, and *check for exclusions*.

House calls in Paris by a doctor will cost from 100F, depending on the neighbourhood. Office calls are about 75F.

EuropAssistance is one of the best-known *au secours* systems, offering emergency help 24 hours a day, every day of the year. Their Medical Emergency Service *plus* Personal Travel Insurance covers practically every contingency you can think of. For five days, it costs £14.30, for six to 12 days, £17.80, up to 23 days, £23.00.

For this you are offered up to £1 million in medical expenses, unlimited cost of getting you home to the UK for urgent medical care, up to £1000 if your journey is called off for reasons beyond your control, up to £1000 for luggage lost or stolen, and so forth.

You pay the first £25 for any medical claim, for cancellation, or for loss of luggage or money. If you know there's a strike coming up on a certain day – as in the nerve-racking summer of 1989 – if you're delayed by riot, war or civil commotion, your policy won't shell out. But if your travel plans are wrecked by an unforeseen wildcat strike, you are covered, which is a great comfort. Policies from travel agents, or direct from EuropAssistance, 252 High Street, Croydon, Surrey CR0 1NF. Tel: 081-680 1234.

BUPA subscribers get up to £2 million in medical care, including the cost of bringing you home if necessary, and non-medical care which includes up to £1500 for cancellation or curtailment charges due to circumstances beyond your control, up to £1000 for loss of luggage, travel tickets, passports or whatever, and up to £500 allowance if you lose your money. These two policies will cost you up to £11.90 for five days, £14.70 up to 10 days, £16.30 up to 15 days. You pay the first £25 of any non-medical claim. There are no age limits on this policy for BUPA members. You must get your policy seven days before travelling. BUPA Head Office, Provident House, Essex St., London WC2R 3AC. Tel: 071-353 5212.

American Express has inexpensive, full cover policies to go with the travel tickets they sell: no age limits, few exclusions. Their charge of £17.80 for up to 17 days.

VISA and Access card-holders are protected by free death and injury insurance if travel is charged on these cards. But if you've taken out one of the all-purpose policies mentioned above, remember that you can't claim on two different policies if anything goes wrong.

Fine print department: As it is almost impossible to find a policy that will give you instant money to replace clothes, camera, luggage, etc., or pay urgent medical bills, one veteran traveller advises charging *everything* on credit cards. Save the receipts, photocopy them, send the originals to your insurance company within 48 hours of returning home, and hope that the payout arrives before you have to fork over to the credit card company. If medical or hospital bills are very high, the Emergency Number on your policy will guarantee payment.

Contact lens wearers must make sure their policy includes travel coverage.

Travel insurance

Everything you travel with – clothes, radio, watch, money, luggage, specs – can be covered by comprehensive travel insurance. This should, ideally, include cancellation insurance for plane, train, or boat tickets that may not be usable because of illness or accident. Try to get the kind of policy that provides you with instant money to get replacement clothes, luggage, camera, etc., without waiting months for reimbursement; or follow the advice above in 'Fine print department'. Check the policy very carefully. One friend who thought her fur coat was covered by her household policy had it pinched in a restaurant, and too late found that said coat was only covered in the house – not while being worn. Ask your travel agent for the best deals going.

Robbery, attack, rape

Or any other crime of which you are a victim – use the automatic callbox, marked *Police Secours*. Ask for someone who speaks English. We are advised by feminist friends in Paris that the police are notably unsympathetic to anyone claiming rape, as they seem to take the attitude that women who wear anything more provocative than an anorak are asking for trouble.

Lost passport

Wise words from a travel advisor in Paris who has helped bail out the unlucky, the feckless, the forgetful: photocopy the first few pages of your passport which show your vital details, when and where the document was issued, the French visa (if necessary), and keep it either with your travel tickets or in your wallet. If you lose the passport, report at once to the nearest police station (ask a policeman or a *pervenche*, the blue-clad meter maid), then go to your embassy (addresses on pages 295–7). They can issue you a new passport, or a travel document which will get you home or allow you to go on your way. In some parts of the Continent, this can mean at best a sour look and some questioning at immigration points; at worst a few hours of cooling your heels in airport or train station while they check up on you. Remember that your travel insurance policy will help pay the cost of replacing your passport (photos, embassy fees, etc.) which will at least ease the pain.

Lost money

Report it to the police, as for passports, then forget it. See Travel insurance, page 291.

Traveller's cheques

You *do* keep a record of those numbers in that notebook, don't you? Cross off each as you cash the cheques. If you lose the remaining ones, get in touch with the issuing company right away (their European addresses and telephone numbers are in the fine print that comes with the cheques). With varying degrees of speed, they will provide duplicate ones. Report this loss, too, to the Paris police.

Lost or stolen jewellery, camera, clothing, luggage

Report to the nearest police station (ask someone who speaks French, if you can't, to write out a brief description of the lost item in French). Last resort: the Lost and Found office (Bureau des Objets Trouvés), 36 rue des Morillons, 15e, *Métro*: Convention, (see page 261). File a report of what you lost and where you think you lost it. The chances of recovering anything are almost nil, but in dealing with such an emergency you'll be surprised at how your French improves, and you'll get to see the inside of offices and police stations that are right out of Maigret. At the Objets Trouvés office, English is spoken, but in the *gendarmeries*, functionaries are not really there to be linguists – it's not what they're paid for. So if you can chase up a French-speaking friend to go with you, it will help. And, of course, claim on your travel insurance.

Theft

Street theft

You can protect your serious money with an old-fashioned money belt, available from Youth Hostel and camping shops among others: or a more modern 'Hide-a-Pocket' in thin soft leather, on a short strap, to be looped over a belt and worn beneath trousers or skirt. It's about £5.95 from luggage shops and several mail-order houses; at 7 x 4 inches in size, it's big enough for passport, credit cards, traveller's cheques and cash. While this may sound fussy and grandmotherish, it is a neat, inconspicuous way to make sure that no alien hands are laid on your valuables.

The child thieves of Paris

If you find yourself surrounded by a posse of charming, laughing, appealing urchins jumping, patting and pawing you, *strike out with anything at hand*: rolled-up newspaper, magazine, umbrella, your fists. These pretty little fiends are carefully trained by local Fagins to surround the unwary tourist, and with small lightning darts at jacket and handbag, take *everything*. Passports, money, credit cards, tickets can go in a flash while you're wondering what hit you. Favourite venues are Notre-Dame, the Tuileries, the terrace outside Beaubourg, crowded Métro platforms, on the Left Bank, long queues at museums or anywhere. The kids race away laughing and jeering. Even if police pick them up, they cannot be held for more than an hour or two because of their ages, and in the meantime their *contrôleur* has received all the goodies. An American couple sat on a park bench to rest, and within two minutes were picked clean by kids who made a screen of newspapers around them. Two of the bandit band rifled pockets and handbag, and ended by snatching a gold chain from the woman's neck. If it happens to you, yell loud and harsh: *'Fiche-moi le camp! Voleurs! Va t'en!'* and lay about you with vigour. Forget about dignity. Get rid of these vicious kids.

Animal bites

Cat scratches, dog bites, a nip from a horse or a squirrel – don't shrug them off. The best we can advise is *not* to fool around with any animal on the Continent. Rabies is at large in Europe and coming closer to the big cities every year. No joke. The French call it *la rage*, and you will see warning posters in many places. If you are scratched or bitten, get a doctor at once, and report the incident to the police quickly. They will pick up the animal and hold it until it is proved to be either safe or rabid. And they will keep you under observation until the animal's condition has been thoroughly checked. At best, you will need an anti-tetanus shot and have a sore arm. If the animal is infected, you are in for a series of painful, costly, and time-consuming injections that will save your life but wreck your holiday. So don't feed squirrels or stray cats, and unless you know an animal and its owner personally, keep your hands to yourself.

Stranded

If you are without passport, money, traveller's cheques, or transport because of loss, theft, or other damage, call on your embassy. If they are convinced that you are a genuine victim without resources, they can arrange for your transportation home (the slowest and cheapest way). You have to pay them back as soon as you reach a source of funds. Each embassy has a different policy, so check with yours for the current rules. To get a temporary passport, remember you'll need photographs.

Claim on your insurance for all costs: photos, photocopies, transport, passport and visa fees, telephone calls. Keep every receipt and photocopy the lot before you send the originals to your insurers.

British Embassy

35 rue du Faubourg St-Honoré, 8e
Tel: 42 66 91 42
Métro: Concorde

It's a beautiful, historic house and worth taking a look at if you have legitimate reason to call. Nicer manners than at the American Embassy, and not so many guns in evidence, but the same basic approach: cool, business-like, efficient, good in genuine emergencies.

British Consulate

2 Cité du Rétiro, 8e
Tel: 42 66 91 42
Métro: Concorde

American Embassy

2 avenue Gabriel, 8e
Tel: 42 96 12 02
Métro: Concorde

Brusque but helpful. Don't expect much sympathy or offers of extra money, as they have had to deal with too many feckless tourists in the 1960s and 1970s who thought rich Uncle Sam was a soft touch. Take four *real* photos, not photo-machine pix, for a replacement passport, usually issued for six months only. (It's not a bad idea to carry a few extra prints of your original passport photo.)

American Consulate

2 rue St-Florentin, 1er
Tel: 42 96 14 88
Métro: Concorde

The embassies and consulates listed below have the same basic requirements as the British and Americans. Always phone first, and if possible make an appointment to see the right person to deal with your problem.

Canadian Embassy

35 avenue Montaigne, 8e
Tel: 47 23 52 50
Métro: Alma-Marceau

Australian Embassy and Consulate

4 rue Jean-Rey, 15e
Tel: 45 75 62 00
Métro: Bir-Hakeim

New Zealand Embassy and Consulate

7 rue Leonardo-da-Vinci, 16e
Tel: 45 00 24 11
Métro: Victor-Hugo

Maps

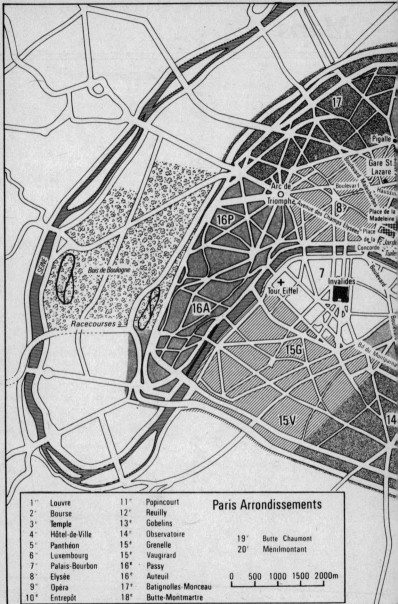

Paris Arrondissements

1ᵉʳ	Louvre	11ᵉ	Popincourt
2ᵉ	Bourse	12ᵉ	Reuilly
3ᵉ	**Temple**	13ᵉ	Gobelins
4ᵉ	Hôtel-de-Ville	14ᵉ	Observatoire
5ᵉ	Panthéon	15ᵉ	Grenelle
6ᵉ	Luxembourg	15ᵉ	Vaugirard
7ᵉ	Palais-Bourbon	16ᵉ	Passy
8ᵉ	Elysée	16ᵉ	Auteuil
9ᵉ	Opéra	17ᵉ	Batignolles-Monceau
10ᵉ	Entrepôt	18ᵉ	Butte-Montmartre

19ᵉ Butte Chaumont
20ᵉ Ménilmontant

0   500 1000 1500 2000m

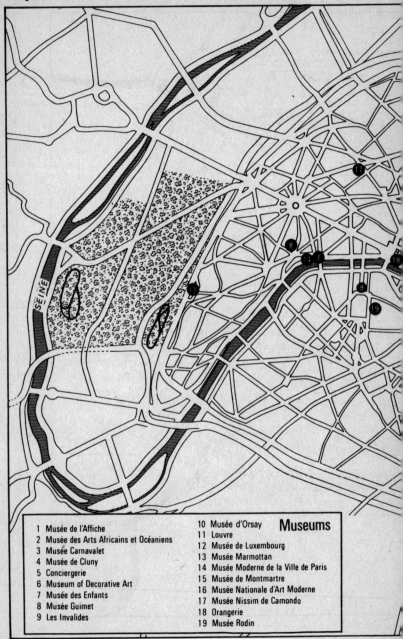

1 Musée de l'Affiche
2 Musée des Arts Africains et Océaniens
3 Musée Carnavalet
4 Musée de Cluny
5 Conciergerie
6 Museum of Decorative Art
7 Musée des Enfants
8 Musée Guimet
9 Les Invalides

10 Musée d'Orsay
11 Louvre
12 Musée de Luxembourg
13 Musée Marmottan
14 Musée Moderne de la Ville de Paris
15 Musée de Montmartre
16 Musée Nationale d'Art Moderne
17 Musée Nissim de Camondo
18 Orangerie
19 Musée Rodin

Museums

Index

Académie Française 41
Access cards 11, 213, 268, 269, 290
Acceuils des Jeunes en France 95
accidents, medical care 289
accommodation: bed and breakfast 94
  exchanging 96–7
  renting flats 96
  rooms to let 94
  student housing 94–6
  youth hostels 95, 249
  see also hotels
Adams, Henry 209
advertising, Musée de la Publicité 184–5
African art 191
African Museum 50
agencies: accommodation exchanges 96–7
  travel agents 18, 19–21
AIDS counselling 289
Air France 20, 26, 30
Air India 21
air travel 19–21
Air Travel Advisory Bureau 19
airmail 275
airport buses 25–6, 30
airports 25
Alcoholics Anonymous 287
ambulances 289
American Consulate 296
American Embassy 295–6
American Express 20, 267, 268, 269, 290
American Hospital 284
animals: attitudes to 243
  bites 294–5
  markets 179
antique shops 177–8
Arabs 51–2, 188
Arc de Triomphe 39
architecture, 53–5
arrondissement system 33–4
  5e (fifth) 47
  7e (seventh) 48
  8e (eighth) 48–9
  11e (eleventh) 50–1

art deco 54, 55
art galleries *see* galleries; museums
Art Nouveau 44, 54, 178, 186
atlases of Paris 32–3
attacks, violent 291
August, restaurants open in 168–70
Australian Embassy and Consulate 296
Auteuil 203
autobus *see* buses
automatic cash dispensers 12–13
'Axe Rouge' traffic scheme 40

babysitters 243–4
Baccarat 179
Bagatelle park 173–4
'bait-and-switch', travel agents 21
Balabus *see* Parisbus
Balzac, Honoré de 174, 194
Banco Borges 266
banks: automatic cash dispensers 12–13
  changing money in 264–7
Banque Portugaise 267
Banque Rivaud 264
BarclayCard 12
Barclays Bank 11, 265, 267, 268
bargains 213–23
Barye, Antoine Louis 55
Bastille 34, 41, 50
Bate, Elaine 12
Bateaux-Mouches 22, 174
Bateaux-Vedettes Pont Neuf 174
baths, public 244–5
baths and showers 58, 61–2
Batignolles 46–7, 172
Baudelaire, Charles 175
Bayeux Tapestry 46
Beaubourg 41, 187, 201, 253, 265–6
Beaune 46
bed and breakfast 94
beer 99
beggars 271
Belleville 51–2
Berlioz, Hector 175, 263

Bibliothéque Ste-Geneviève 47
bites, animal 294–5
Blue Guide to Paris 207–8, 210, 254
Blume, Mary 181–2
BNP 12–13
boating: Bateaux-Mouches 22, 174
  Bois de Boulogne 173
Bois de Boulogne 43, 173–4, 203
Bois-Preau *petit château* 210
Bonnard, Pierre 189, 191
booking hotels, in advance 13–14
books: bookshops 217, 245–7
  libraries 260–1
  see also guide books
bottles, mineral water 101
Boudin, Eugène 194
boulangeries 119–20, 217
boutiques 177
Braque, Georges 194
brasseries 29, 260
breakfast 57, 100–1
Brigade des Stups 51
British Airways 20
British Consulate 295
British Embassy 295
British Excursion Documents 23
British Hospital 284
British Midland 20
British Telecom 278–9
British Visitor's Passports 23
Bulgari 177
BUPA 290
Bureau de Tourisme 33
bureaux de change 27, 263–7
Burn Centre 287
bus travel 35–7
  Bus *24* 41
  Bus *29* 41–2
  Bus *32* 42
  Bus *52* 42–3
  Bus *63* 43
  Bus *72* 43–4
  Bus *83* 44–5
  from airport to city 25, 26
  leaving Paris 30–1
  Montmartrobus 45
  Noctambus 36–7
  Parisbus 40
  RATP 45–6
  sightseeing on 39–46
  tickets 36

Cabourg 46
'Café Couette' 94
cafés 100
  lavatories 260
  telephones 278
  tipping in 280

calendar 279
cameras, lost or stolen 293
Canadian Embassy 296
Le Canard Enchainé 270
Cardin, Pierre 177
CardWise 269
carnets, tickets 12, 38
cars 253, 280–1
Carte Carissimo 248
Carte Inter-Musées 180–1
Carte Orange 29, 30, 36, 37–8, 40, 45
Carte Paris Visite 25, 29, 31, 36, 37, 38–9, 40, 45, 208, 210
Carte Vermeil 202, 250–1
Cartier 177
cash 11, 262–3
cash dispensers 12–13
Cassatt, Mary 191
Cathay Pacific 19–20
cats 236, 243, 294–5
CCF (Crédit Commercial de France) 265
cemeteries 51, 174–5
Centre Pompidou 41, 187, 201
Cézanne, Paul 184, 191
Chambord, Château de 46
Champ-de-Mars 41–2
Champs-Élysées 45, 55
Chanel 177
charcuteries 176
Chardin, Jean-Baptiste-Siméon 182
Charles de Gaulle/Roissy airport 25–6, 30, 31
charter flights 19
Chartres 22, 209
chemists 284–6
Chenonceaux, Château de 46
Chequepoints 264, 268
cheques: Eurocheques 267–8
  personal 11, 268
  traveller's 11, 267, 292
Chevalier, Maurice 51
child thieves 293
children: babysitters 243–4
  circuses 205
  puppets 205–6
  theatres 206–7
chiropodists 288
Chopin, Frédéric 174
churches 53–4, 200
cigarette smoking 271
Cimetière de Montmartre 175
Cimetière de Picpus 42
cinema 204
  tipping ushers 280
circuses 205
Cité des Sciences et de l'Industrie 207
Cité Universitaire 94, 96
Citibank 266

City Express 16
City Limits 18, 19
Cler, rue 48
climate 6
clothes: bargains 213–23
   dry cleaning 251
   lost or stolen 293
   second-hand shops 223–30
   sizes 247–8
   washing 60–1
   what to take 6–7
   window-shopping 176–7
coaches, Euroline 15–16, 22
coffee 100
cognac 14
Colette 51, 174
Colombey-les-Deux-églises 46
concerts 200–2
The Conciergerie 186–7
concierges 59, 280
Conservatoire National des Arts et Métiers
   65
consigne (left luggage office) 62, 280
consulates 295–7
contact lenses 291
Cook, Thomas 267
Coupon Jaune 12, 30, 37–8, 39, 45
Coupon Orange 12, 37–8
couturiers 176–7
Credit Card Sentinel 269
credit cards 11–13, 213, 268–9, 290
Crédit Lyonnais 12
crime: child thieves 293
   pickpockets 239, 242
   robbery 292
   street theft 293–4
CRS (anti-terrorist police) 273
Cubism 193
cultural centres 198–200
currency 262–3
Currency Exchange du Rond-Point 265
customs and excise 24

Daily Telegraph 270
La Dame Aux Licornes (tapestry) 188
Dan-Air 20
Daumier, Honoré 189
days of the week 279
De Gaulle, Charles 46
deer 179
Degas, Edgar 189
Delacroix, Eugène 41, 189, 194, 263
Denis, Maurice 185
dentists 283–4
department stores 177
Derain, André 184
Deux Magots 43
dialling codes, international 279

Diners' Club 268–9
Dior, Christian 177
disabled travellers 252–4
discounts: concerts 202
   in museums 179
   rail travel 17
   for senior citizens 250–1
   for students 248–50
doctors 284, 290
dogs 243, 294
Domrémy 46
Drug Crisis Centre 287
drugs 51
dry cleaning 251
Dubuffet, Jean 183
ducks 179
Dufy, Raoul 194
Dumas, Alexandre *père* 175

Egypt 182
electricity 59, 251–2
embassies 295–7
emergencies 10, 14
   medical 283–91
entrances and exits 252
etiquette *see* manners
Eurocard 11
Eurocheques 267–8
Euroline coaches 15–16, 22
EuropAssistance 290
exchanging accommodation 96–7
excursions: Chartres 209
   Giverny 209
   Malmaison 210–11
   Mont-St-Michel 210
   package tours 22
   RATP 45–6
   Versailles 207–9
exits and entrances 252

fashion 176–7
Faubourg St-Honoré 42
Fauchon 49, 176
Fauves 193
feet, chiropodists 288
ferries: Hoverspeed 16–18
   Sealink 18
Le Figaro 96, 195, 270
films 204
first aid 289
Flamboyant Gothic architecture 53
flats, renting 96
flea markets 50, 238–42
fleas 270
flower markets 178–9
flying, cheap flights 19–21
Fontainbleau 22

food 98–101
  brasseries 29
  breakfast 57, 100–1
  cafés 100
  costs 9, 98–9
  eating in hotel rooms 60
  foreign 52, 108–9, 110, 122–3, 131, 135–6, 138–9, 149–50, 151, 159, 165–6
  markets 175–6
  menus 98–9
  sandwich tunisien 52, 165–6
  shops 217, 219
  take-away 52, 141, 165
  window-shopping 176
  see also restaurants
Form E-111 24–5, 289
form letters, booking hotels in advance 13
Formule 1 36, 37, 38
Foucault's Pendulum 65
fountains 245
Fragonard, Jean Honoré 175
France-Soir 270
France Telecom 277
France–USA Contacts (FUSAC) 273
François I, King 182
free-sheets 273
Free Voice 273
French Bookshop, London 33
Frochot, avenue 54
funicular, Montmartre 38

Galéries Lafayette 177
galleries 194–5
  ADAC Galerie-Atelier 196
  Alain Daune 197
  Anne Blanc 196
  Arcturial 197
  Baudoin-Lebon 196
  Callu-Mérite 197
  Carpe Diem 197
  Christian Siret 195
  Cimaise de Paris 196
  Daniel Malingue 197
  Daniel Pons-Jeanne Debord 196
  Daniel Templon 196
  Galerie Claude Bernard 197
  Galerie du Jour Agnès B. 196
  Galerie 1900–2000 197
  Le Gall Peyroulet 197
  Isy Brachot 197
  J. and J. Donguy 197
  Médart 196
  Michel Vidal 198
  Nicole Bellier 197
  Nicole Ferry 196
  Philippe de Hesdin 196
  Schmitt 196
  Zabriskie 196
  see also museums
Gallery, John 279
gardens *see* parks and gardens
Gare d'Austerlitz 28, 259
Gare de l'Est 25, 28, 42, 259
Gare de Lyon 28, 43, 258
Gare du Nord 17, 25–6, 28, 259
Gare St-Lazare 34, 49, 276
Gault-Millau guide 254
gendarmes 273
gift shops 230–8
Giotto 182
Givenchy 177
Giverny 209
glasses 235, 287
Gobelins 47
Godefroi Cavagnac, rue 50
Goethe-Institut 200
Gothic architecture 53
Grand Hôtel des Balcons 58, 60
Grande Hall de la Villette 201
Grands Boulevards 33
Grands Surfaces supermarkets, Les 231
The Guardian 270
Guérard, Michel 176
guide books: *Blue Guide to Paris* 207–8, 210, 254
  Gault-Millau 254
  Guide des Hôtels 56, 57, 253
  Le Guide Paris-Bus 35
  Michelin Green Guide 254
  Musées, Expositions, Monuments de Paris et de l'Île de France 194
  Paris Pas Cher 255
  Voyager Quand Même 253
Guillaume, Paul 184
Guimard, Hector 44, 54, 55

hairdressers 255–7
  tipping 280
Hameau, Versailles 208
Haussmann, Baron 33, 42, 172
health care 24–5
health insurance 24, 289–91
Hédiard 176
herbs 235
Hermès 49, 177
Hertford, Marquis of 174
Hippodrome, St-Cloud 204
HIV positive counselling 289
holidays, public 257–8
horse racing 203–4
Horses of Marly 55
Hortense, Queen 210
hospitals 284, 289
hostels 95, 249
Hôtel Crillon 49, 55

Hôtel de Bourgogne 54
Hôtel de Clisson 54
Hôtel de Lamoignon 54
Hôtel de Sens 54
Hôtel de Ville 54
Hôtel des Monnaies 41
Hôtel Le Peletier de St-Fargeau 185–6
hotels 56–62
    booking in advance 13–14
    booking through Hôtesses de Paris 27–8
    classification 57
    credit cards 12
    eating in rooms 60
    finding 62
    getting to 29
    leaving luggage in 62
    noise regulations 270
    phrases used in 61
    prices 9, 22, 57–8
    public telephones 278
    tipping in 59–60, 280
    wheelchair access 253
    when to go 5–6
    women-only 147
hotels, recommended: Auberge de
        Jeunesse Jules Ferry 83
    Cosmos Hôtel 84–5
    Delhy's Hôtel 73–4
    Grand Hôtel des Arts-et-Métiers 65
    Grand Hôtel d'Harcourt 72
    Grand Hôtel Jeanne d'Arc 67
    Grand Hôtel Leveque 76
    Grand Hôtel Malher 68
    Hôtel André Gill 92
    Hôtel Andrea 66–7
    Hôtel Bonne Nouvelle 80–1
    Hôtel Castex 68–9
    Hôtel Central Montmartre 93
    Hôtel Confort 79
    Hôtel de la Loire 90–1
    Hôtel de Lille 79–80
    Hôtel de Marigny 78–9
    Hôtel de Marseille 88
    Hôtel de Nice 69
    Hôtel des Arts 83–4
    Hôtel des Bains 89–90
    Hôtel des Grandes écoles 72–3
    Hôtel du Bouquet de Montmartre 92–3
    Hôtel du Centre 81
    Hôtel du Champs de Mars 75–6
    Hôtel du Chancelier-Boucherat 66
    Hôtel du Jura 82
    Hôtel du Lion d'Or 63
    Hôtel du Palais 63–4
    Hôtel du Parc 90
    Hôtel Jarry 81–2
    Hôtel le Central 71–2
    Hôtel Malar 76–7

Hôtel Nesle 74
Hôtel Notre-Dame 85
Hôtel Pacific 88–9
Hôtel Plessis 85–6
Hôtel Pratic 69–70
Hôtel Prince 77–8
Hôtel Printania 86
Hôtel Rhetia 86–7
Hôtel Richelieu-Nazarin 64
Hôtel Rubens 89
Hôtel Sans-Souci 87–8
Hôtel Sévigne 70
Hôtel Stella (4e *arrondissement*) 71
Hôtel Stella (16e *arrondissement*) 91–2
Little Hôtel 82–3
Regent's Hôtel 74–5
Résidence Vauvilliers 64–5
Le Royal Phare 78
Hôtesses de Paris 27–8
Hoverspeed 16–18
Hugo, Victor 174, 194

identity cards, students 248–9
Île de la Cité 33, 178
Impressionism 180, 192–3
The Independent 270, 279
information sources 258–9
    train information 276
Ingres, Jean Auguste Dominique 41, 189
insects 270
Institut de France 41
Institut du Monde Arabe 188, 253
Institut Néerlandais 199
insurance: medical 24, 289–91
    travel 19, 291
international dialling codes 279
International Herald Tribune 270
international phone calls 278–9
International Reply Coupons 14
International Student Identity Cards 248–9
INTERVAC 97
Invalides 34, 44, 48, 188–9
Irvine, Ian 271
Islam 188

Jardin d'Acclimatation 173
Jardin des Plantes 171–2
Jardin du Luxembourg 44
Jean the Fearless, tower of 54
Jean-Pierre Timbaud, rue 50–1
Jeanne d'Arc 46
jetons (telephone tokens) 278
Jeu de Paume 49, 183, 189, 253
jewellery 234, 235, 237–8, 293
Jewish quarter 51–2
Jongkind, Johan Barthold 194
Josephine, Empress 210

language 2
　days of the week 279
　entrances and exits 252
　in hotels 61
　language courses 255, 259–60
　numbers 271–2
　opening hours 272
　slang 276
Lanvin 49
Latin Quarter 43, 44, 58
La Tour, Georges de 263
laundry, in hotel rooms 60–1
lavatories: in hotels 58
　public 260
　in restaurants 100
　tipping 280
Lavirotte, Jules 54
Left Bank 33, 177, 194–5
left luggage offices 62, 280
Leonardo da Vinci 182
letters 275
　booking hotels in advance 13
Libération 270
libraries 260–1
lice 270
Lido Cabaret 22
lights, in hotel bedrooms 59
Ligue Française des Auberges de Jeunesse
　(LFAJ) 249
long distance phone calls 278
Longchamp 203
lost property 261, 293
Louis XIV, King 173, 182, 189
Louis XVI, King 186
Louis-Napoleon *see* Napoleon III
Louvre 33, 39, 179, 180, 181–3, 189, 252
Le Louvre des Antiquaires 177
luggage 14
　leaving in hotels 62
　left-luggage offices 29
　lost or stolen 293
　what to take 6–8
Luxembourg 46
Luxembourg Gardens 44, 253
Luxembourg Palace 182

Madeleine 34
magazines 272–3
mail 14, 274–5
Maintenon, Château de 209
Maison de la Radio 201
Malmaison 46, 210–11
Manet, Edouard 189, 191
manners 2, 274
　in restaurants 101–2
　in shops 212–13
maps 32–3, 261
　bus routes 35, 36

Métro 34
Marais 33, 41, 54, 177
Marie Antoinette, Queen 187, 208
markets 46, 47
　animals 179
　flea markets 238–42
　flower 178–9
　Foire du Brocante St-Paul 242
　food 175–6
　Marché aux Puces de la Porte Didot
　　241–2
　Place d'Aligre 240–1
　Porte de Vanves 241
　St-Ouen 238–40
Mastercard 11, 213
Maxim's 49
measurements: clothes sizes 247–8
　metric system 262
medical care 24–5
medical emergencies 283–91
medical insurance 24, 289–91
Mégisserie, quai de le 179
Melchites 53
Melia Travel Agency 266
mental health 261
menus 98–9
metric system 262
Métro: Art Nouveau entrances 54, 55
　lavatories 260
　leaving Paris 31
　music in 201
　tickets 12, 38
　travelling on 34–5, 37
Michelin Green Guide 254
mineral water 99, 101
Mint 41
Miró, Joan 194
Modern Museum of Paris 44
Mona Lisa 182
Monde, Le 270
Monet, Claude 184, 189, 192–3, 253
　gardens at Giverny 209
money: *bureaux de change* 27, 263–7
　cash 11, 262–3
　cheques 11, 268
　credit cards 11–13, 213, 268–9, 291
　Eurocheques 267–8
　how much to take 8–10
　lost 292
　money belts 293–4
　traveller's cheques 11, 267
Monoprix department store 230–1
Mont-St-Michel 46, 210
months 279
Montmartre 38, 45, 46, 193
Montmartrobus 38, 45
Moreau, Gustave 189
Morisot, Berthe 191

Morrison, Jim 51, 174
mosques 47
mosquitoes 270
Mouffetard, rue 47
Moulin Rouge 22
museums 179–81
  African museum 50
  Art Moderne de la Ville de Paris 193
  Beaubourg 187
  Carte Inter-Musées 180–1
  cloakrooms 180
  The Conciergerie 186–7
  entrance fees 179
  guide books 194
  Hunting Museum 194
  Institut du Monde Arabe 188, 253
  Invalides 188–9
  Jeu de Paume 183, 253
  Louvre 179, 180, 181–3, 252
  Modern Museum of Paris 44
  Musée Bricard 194
  Musée Carnavalet 185–6
  Musée de Cluny 187–8
  Musée de la Publicité 184–5
  Musée de la Vie Romantique 194
  Musée de Montmartre 193
  Musée des Arts Africains et Océaniens
    191
  Musée des Arts et Traditions Populaires
    173
  Musée des Voitures (Versailles) 208
  Musée d'Orsay 180, 189, 252–3
  Musée du Petit Palais 191
  Musée en l'Herbe 207
  Musée Grevin 194
  Musée Guimet 192
  Musée Marmottan 192–3, 253
  Musée Moderne 42, 253
  Musée National d'Art Moderne 187
  Musée Nissim de Camondo 179, 190
  Musée Picasso 186
  Musée Rodin 190
  Museum of Decorative Arts 184
  Museum of Modern Art, New York 54
  opening hours 179–80
  The Orangerie 183–4
  Petit Palais 179
  queues 180
  Rock 'n' Roll Hall of Fame 194
  Victor-Hugo Museum 194
  wheelchair access 252–3
  see also galleries
music 200–2

Napoleon I, Emperor 44, 48, 182, 186, 189,
    210–11, 279
Napoleon III, Emperor (Louis-Napoleon)
    173, 182

National Express 15–16
National Giro 268
NatWest 11–12, 267, 268
New Zealand Embassy and Consulate 297
newspapers 270
night buses 36–7
Noctambus 36–7
noise 270
Normandie (liner) 185
North Africa 52
Notre-Dame 41, 53
Le Nouveau Guide 254
nuisances 270–1
numbers 271–2

Office de Tourisme 13, 27–8, 56, 258–9
L'Officiel des Spectacles de Paris 195, 202, 204,
    272
olive oil 234
opening hours 272
Opéra de la Bastille 50
opticians 287
The Orangerie 183–4
organ music 200
Orly airport 25, 26, 30–1
ORTF 201

package tours 21–2
Palais de Justice 187
Palais de la Femme 50
Palais de Tokyo 189
Palais Omnisport 41
Panthéon 47
Parc de Monceau 172
Parc des Buttes-Chaumont 172–3
Paris Conservatoire 46
Paris-Match 270
Paris Pas Cher 255
Parisbus 40
Pariscope 272
parks and gardens: Bois de Boulogne
    173–4
  Giverny (Monet gardens) 209
  Jardin des Plantes 171–2
  Jardin du Luxembourg 44, 253
  Parc de Monceau 172
  Parc des Buttes-Chaumont 172–3
  square des Batignolles 46, 172
  Tuileries 253
Pascal, Blaise 263
passports 23, 24, 273
  lost 292
  senior citizens' discounts with 250–1
  temporary 295
Passy district 42
pâtisseries 119–20, 162, 176, 217
pay phones 277
pedestrians 280–1

Père Lachaise cemetery 51, 174–5
perfumes 232–3
periodicals 272–3
Permis de Séjour 23–4
petit déjeuner 57
Petit Palais 179
pharmacists 284–6
phone cards 277, 278
Piaf, Edith 51, 174
Picasso, Pablo 43, 53, 184, 186, 194
pickpockets 239, 242
Pigalle 54
Pilon, Germain 55
PIN numbers 12, 269
Pissarro, Camille 194
Plan de Paris 32–3, 34, 35, 261
plants, markets 178–9
Poison Centre 287
Poitiers, Château de 46
police 273, 281, 292
politesse, la see manners
porters 26
    tipping 280
post 14, 274–5
Post Cheques 268
post codes 275
Post-Impressionists 180
post offices 274–5
postage stamps 274, 275
postboxes 274–5
postcards 275
posters, Musée de la Publicité 184–5
Poussin, Nicholas 182
Prisunic department store 230–1
Private Patients Plan (PPP) 290
Proust, Marcel 174
Provence, rue de 202
public baths 61–2, 244–5
public holidays 257–8
public lavatories 260
puppets 205–6
Pyramid, Louvre 181–2
Pyrénées 51

'Quartier d'Europe' 42
Quartier Latin (Latin Quarter) 43, 44, 58

rabies 294–5
racing 203–4
Radio France 201
Rail-Europ 251
Railcards, British Senior Citizen 251
railways: departures 30
    from airport to city 25–6
    information services 276
    stations 26–7
    student discounts 248
    travelling on 17–18

    see also Métro
Rambouillet, Château de 209
rape 292
RATP 39–40, 45–6, 210, 211
Redon Odilon 189, 194
Rembrandt 182
Renoir, Pierre August 184, 189
renting flats 96
RER 38
reservations, hotels 13–14
restaurants: credit cards 12
    drinks in 99
    lavatories 260
    manners 101–2
    menus 98–9
    open in August 168–70
    open on Sundays 166–8
    opening hours 100
    prices 98–9
    sanitation 100
    for students 249–50
    tipping 100, 280
    women on their own 281
restaurants, recommended:
    Anadolu 108–9
    L'Assiette Lyonnaise 137–8
    Au Gigot Fin 143–4
    Au Petit Ramoneur 103
    Au Pied de Fouet 135
    Au Rendez-vous de la Marine 160–1
    Au Trou Normand 144
    Au Vin des Rues 151–2
    Auberge du Palais Royal 102
    L'Auberge-Hongroise 109
    Aux Savoyards 118–19
    Bangkok-Thailand 149–50
    Le Baptiste 119
    Bistro de la Grille 125–6
    Bistrot Bourdelle 155–6
    Le Blé d'Or 119–20
    Bois et Charbons 144–5
    La Bolée 126–7
    La Bonne Cuisine 157
    Le Bouche Trou 120–1
    La Brouette 121
    Les Byzantins 127
    La Cabane d'Auvergne 127–8
    Cam Mach 135–6
    La Canaille 111–12
    Chartier 140
    Le Châteaubriand 112
    Les Chauffeurs 158
    Le Chaumont-Laumière 161
    Chez Fernand 103–4
    Chez Germaine 136
    Le Choron 140
    Les Cinqs Points Cardinaux 145–6
    Claude Valentino 128

La Comete 112–13
Crêperie de Saint-Malo 152
Crêperie La Rozelle 162–3
Le Cristal 113
Les Degrés de Notre-Dame 121–2
Le Drouot 109–10
Druthil 162
Duhau 141
L'écaille de PCB 129
L'Espérance 150
Le Fait Tout 159
La Fauvette 104
Formula Uno 156
Les Frères de la Côte 129–30
Galerie Point Show 138
Le Galtouse 104–5
La Godasse 130
Hawaii 150–1
L'Homme Tranquille 160
Hyotan 138–9
L'Incroyable 105
Le Jéroboam 152–3
Kenavo 153
Le Limonaire 149
Le Luma 154
La Maison de Verlaine 122
Marco Polo 130–1
Midi-Trente 154–5
Le Moka 139
Nini Peau d'un Chien 146
Orestias 131
Osteria del Passe Partout 132
Palais de la Femme 146–7
Le Palet 106
Pasadena 106–7
Pavarotti 110–11
Le Pavé aux Herbes 122–3
Le Petit Gavroche 114–15
Picpain 141–2
Les Piétons 115
Pizza Tavola 147
Le Plomb de Cantal 155
Le Polidor 132–3
Le P'tit Comic 114
Pupillin 142
Le Quidam 115–16
La Ravigotte 147–8
Relais de L'Île 116–17
Relais du Massif Central 148–9
Le Relais du Sud-Ouest 107
Le Relais Savoyard 142–3
Restaurant B.E.P. of the Ecole Ferrandi 125
Restaurant des Arts 133
Restaurant des Beaux Arts 134
Restaurant Ephese 158–9
Restaurant Kurde Dîlan 110
Restaurant Lÿ 123

Le Roupeyrac 136–7
Le Stado 108
Le Sybarite 134–5
Tanger 157–8
Taverne Descartes 123–4
Les Temps de Cerises 117
La Trattoria 124–5
Vancouver 117–18
Xavier Gourmet 143
restaurants, self-service 100, 163
Le Balthazar 164–5
M. Benvisti 165–6
La Petite Bouchée 164
on rue de la Huchette/rue de la Harpe 165
Samaritaine 164
Reuil-Malmaison 210
Right Bank 33
robbery 291
Rodin, Auguste 190
Rond-Point 44
rooms to let 94
Rousseau, Douanier 184

safety: animal bites 294–5
Bois de Boulogne 34, 174
pickpockets 239, 242
robbery, attack and rape 291
women on their own 281–2
Sainte-Chapelle 53–4
St-Cloud 204
St-Dominique, rue 48
St-Germain-des-Prés 43, 58, 177
St-Germain-des-Prés church 53
St-Germain-l'Auxerrois church 41, 55
St Jean-St François church 55
St-Julien-le-Pauvre church 53
St Laurent, Yves 177
St-Merri church 53
St Michael's Church of England 94
St-Séverin church 53
Sand, Georges 194
sandwich tunisien 52, 165–6
scheduling, Paris-watching 55
Seacats 17–18
Sealink 18
seasons, when to go 5–6
Seated Lion (Barye) 55
second-hand shops 223–30
Seine, river 174
self-service restaurants *see* restaurants, self-service
senior citizens, discounts 202, 250–1
Seurat, Georges 189, 194
Sévigné, Madame de 185
'Shakespeare Garden', Bois de Boulogne 173
shoes 7

shops 215, 217, 220
shops: for bargains 213–23
  bookshops 245–7
  credit cards 12
  gift shops 230–8
  manners 212–13
  second-hand 223–30
  window-shopping 176–8
  see also markets
showers 61–2
sightseeing 171, 211
  bus tours 39–46
  costs 10
silver 178, 234
sizes, clothes 247–8
slang 276
smells 270
smoking 271
SNCF 28, 39
SOS Amitié 261
SOS Dentists 283
SOS Médecins 284
South-East Asians 52
Soutine, Chaim 184
spectacles 235, 287
spectator sports 203–4
spices 235
squirrels 294–5
Stade Roland-Garros 204
stamps, postage 274, 275
statues 55
Stein, Gertrude 51, 174
Stendhal 175
stranded travellers 294–7
street scenes 53–5
street theft 293–4
streets, arrondissement system 33–4
students: babysitters 244
  cheap travel 18
  discounts 202, 248–50
  housing 94–6
'Le Style 1900' 54
Sunday, restaurants open on 166–8
surcharges, rail travel 18
swans 179

take-away food 141, 165
taxis 29, 276–7
  tipping 280
tea 101
Télécarte 277, 278
telegrams 275
telephone directories 259
telephones 59, 260, 277–9
television 207
telex 275
tennis 204
theatre, children's 206–7

theatre ushers, tipping 280
theft 293–4
tickets: bus 37–9
  Carte Inter-Musées 180–1
  Carte Orange 37–8
  Métro 12, 37–9
time 279
Time Out 16, 18, 19
The Times 96, 270
timing, Paris-watching 55
tipping 59–60, 100, 280
tobacco advertising 271
toilet paper 14
Toulouse-Lautrec, Henri de 189, 191, 193
Tour Eiffel 34, 39, 44, 48
tourist offices 27–8
traffic 280–1
traffic lights 281
trains see Métro; railways
travel agents 18, 19–21
travel insurance 291
traveller's cheques 11, 267
  lost 292
travelling: alone v. in company 4–5
  buses 35–7, 39–46
  cheap flights 19–21
  costs 8–9
  Euroline coaches 15–16, 22
  from airport to city 25–6
  Hoverspeed 16–18
  insurance 19
  leaving Paris 30–1
  Métro 34–5, 37
  package tours 21–2
  Seacat 17–18
  Sealink 18
  for students 18, 248
  tickets 37–9
  trains 17–18
  walking 46–55, 280–1
  when to go 5–6
Trianons, Versailles 207, 208
Trocadéro 42
Tuileries 55, 253

UCRIF 94
Uniprix department store 230–1
Universal Exposition (1900) 54
Utrillo, Maurice 55

Vallotton, Felix 185, 189
Van Cleef and Arpels 177
VD clinics 288–9
Venus de Milo 182
Verlaine, Paul 47, 122
Veronese 182
Versailles 46, 182, 207–9
Victoria Coach Station 15, 16

Village St-Paul 177
Village Suisse 177–8
Villette, La 253
Vilmorin 178
Vincennes 50, 203–4
Visa cards 11–12, 213, 268, 269, 290
visas 23–4
Voyager Quand Même 253
Voyages Vacances 181
Vuillard, Edouard 189, 191

Wagner, Richard 41
waiters, tipping 280
walking in Paris 46–55, 280–1
Wallace, Sir Richard 174, 245
Walsh, Alison 253
Walter, Jean 184
washing clothes 60–1
Wasteels 19
water, drinking 99, 101

waxworks 194
weather 6
wheelchairs 252–4
Wilde, Oscar 174
window-shopping 176–8
wine 98, 99
Winged Victory of Samothrace 182
women: hotels for women only 147
    rape 291
    in restaurants 102
    women on their own 281–2

X-Changer 263

Yellow Pages 259
youth hostels 83, 95, 249

zebra crossings 281
zoos, Jardin d'Acclimatation 173